SHELTER
ROCK

Mark M.

SHELTER ROCK

M P MILES

Matador
9 Priory Business Park,
Wistow Road, Kibworth Beauchamp,
Leicestershire. LE8 0RX
Tel: 0116 279 2299
Email: books@troubador.co.uk
Web: www.troubador.co.uk/matador
Twitter: @matadorbooks

ISBN 978 1789016 390
EBOOK ISBN 978 1789019 421
AUDIOBOOK ISBN 978 1789019 438

British Library Cataloguing in Publication Data.
A catalogue record for this book is available from the British Library.

Printed and bound by CPI Group (UK) Ltd, Croydon, CR0 4YY
Typeset in 12pt Adobe Garamond Pro by Troubador Publishing Ltd, Leicester, UK

Matador is an imprint of Troubador Publishing Ltd

For my father,
Mervyn Philip Ralph Miles (1930–2016)

And Joshua the son of Nun sent out two men to spy secretly, saying, 'Go view the land'

SOUTH AFRICA

6TH DECEMBER, 1981 TO

4TH MARCH, 1982

ONE

Angel travelled on the train every morning from his home near fields and a stream to the Comitia building, a grey inhospitable office block with an obscure unmarked entrance beside a small travel agency.

His braided hair, unfashionably long and tied in a ponytail to keep it manageable during the day, the butt of endless jokes, fell in his eyes as he stepped down to the platform. He shook his head to clear it and saw that the carriage had a needless sign on it; they all did. Suddenly and unexpectedly angry, he scowled and looked crossly for someone to blame for his irritation. It incensed him. Most of the signs had been taken down; everyone knew the rules. People knew who the carriage was for without it requiring a pointless notice declaring 'non-whites'.

Angel noticed a scuffle on the sidewalk outside of the station – two policemen trying to lift a man from the pavement, batons drawn. A police vehicle drifted around the corner like a shark circling a kill. A woman screamed, her hands pulling at her own hair. Loud shouting policemen asked the man for something. He cowered on his knees, arms up to protect his face in case the batons should fall.

Angel stepped into the road to walk past them, muttering, giving himself instructions. The woman, distraught, started shrieking at the policeman. He walked quicker to get past them but then slowed, listening to the woman, intrigued by her accent. Angel made a guess that she was speaking Setswana, officially the language of Botswana, but most Africans in Pretoria spoke a Tswana-based creole. He listened to the stress sounds and the tones, more high than low, different to the Setswana he was used to.

"Hey, what are you looking at?"

The policeman who shouted at him had long socks, and shorts held by a wide black belt that glistened as brightly as his truncheon.

Angel spoke Afrikaans, but his pronunciation made it obvious it wasn't his first language.

"I can help."

"What?"

"She's trying to explain," Angel said, pointing to the man shaking in fear on his knees. "He had an accident in the mine and can't work. She was taking him to a doctor."

The policeman put his face very close to Angel's.

"You had better shut up. I don't need any help from you understanding the Population Registration Act. He's Black like you and needs a pass to be here. Move on or I'll put you in the van with him."

Angel stroked the braids on the back of his head. His father, a white Afrikaner civil engineer based in Mbabane, Swaziland, had worked on the Pretoria to Maputo,

Mozambique railway in the late 1940s, a time when engineering projects were completed as much with hard fists as theodolites. Angel had never met him.

Angel's mother was Black Swazi with pretensions to royalty. She came from the House of Dlamini, her father the virile King Sobhuza II of Swaziland. She took the first name of the King's mother, Lomawa, one of Sobhuza's 210 children from one of his seventy wives. When Lomawa started feeling ill, the *inyanga*, the most important of the three types of traditional healers, threw his collection of bones on the ground and puzzled over the pattern they took. The diagnosis seemed uncertain. He prescribed a *kuhlanta*, a vomiting treatment using water and an extract of herbs. She didn't need it. She vomited regularly, every morning. In desperation, and because of her royal status, he recommended a *luhhemane* in the presence of the King. In a mental state influenced by mind-changing drugs Lomawa talked freely about the sickness and could name the *umtsakatsi*, the witch that caused it. She named a wizard not a witch – a white wizard working on the railway. King Sobhuza had the final word. She had a choice: back to the *inyanga* for stronger herb extract to expel her evil and then banishment overseas, or just banishment overseas. Already feeling ill and fearful of the *inyanga's* medicine she chose the latter, left Angel's father in Mbabane with his railway and never returned. She spent her life in the damp small rooms of London's SW1 hinterland and refused to give her baby a name.

Angel smiled at the policeman.

"Well, interestingly, and I have thought about this, the admixture appears to be gender-biased."

"What?"

"You would probably expect my maternal genetic material to be predominately Khoisan," Angel waved a finger at him, "but in fact it is autochthonous Bantu, which may explain your original observation."

The policeman put his hand around his baton, his pink fingers turning white.

"What the *fok* are you talking about?"

"I'm Coloured," said Angel, "not Black." Angel laughed and shook his head. "But I do sometimes wonder. You know…"

"Shut up!" the policeman shouted, spittle dribbling on his chin.

His partner turned, his hand on the shoulder of the kneeling man.

"He looks more Black than Coloured to me," he said. "Only nine per cent are Coloureds. Ask him to show you his fingernails."

Angel knew the drill. Under South Africa's arbitrary and confusing rules of racial differentiation, if the moons of the fingernails showed a mauve tinge then he would be Black not Coloured, a distinction that would affect every aspect of his life.

"Oh please," pleaded Angel, still smiling, "you'll be putting a pencil in my curly hair next and seeing if it stays there when I shake my head."

The woman, still shrieking, scratched at the policeman's face. *Don't hit her. Please don't hit her*, Angel mumbled to himself.

Angel could picture in his head how it would unfold before it happened. He knew with certainty who would move where, how they would smell, what vehicle would pass when it had ended.

The policeman clenched his left hand into a fist to punch the woman in the centre of her trunk, swinging up quickly from low down. He delivered a strong blow under the sternum with a lot of momentum, an unwarranted and excessive martial arts move to the solar plexus to knock the air out of an opponent and cause them to lose balance. The blow compressed the nerves that radiate outward from the coeliac underneath the heart, her diaphragm contracting into spasm. She fell to the pavement, winded, struggling for breath. He lifted his baton to strike the woman he had just punched to the ground.

Angel's hand came from behind the policeman, grabbed his raised forearm and pulled it up, over and down behind the policeman's back, using the acceleration of the arm coming down and its own mass to force the dislocation of the shoulder. Angel turned. The other policeman reached down his leg, looking for his sidearm. Angel stepped backwards, lined himself up and kicked him hard on the side of the knee, like a long punt deep into the opposition's twenty-two at a rugby match. The policeman's leg buckled instantly and he fell, screaming.

Angel lifted the woman into a crouching position, with her upper body brought forward and down over her knees. There wasn't time for the spasm to settle and the breathing to return to normal. They had to move quickly. The man who now stood beside her had a thin fine face with a hooked nose and looked out of place in urban Pretoria. Angel, currently working on a project with the Egyptian General Intelligence Directorate, wondered if he might be Arab. Employees of GID, an incredibly secretive and powerful body with agents throughout the Middle East and North Africa, had immunity from prosecution for all crimes committed while at work. Some in the intelligence world, and in Angel's own organisation, thought this enviable.

"Get away from here," Angel said. Neither the woman nor the man moved. Angel spoke quietly to them. "Batswana?"

The man nodded. *He's San*, thought Angel, *from the Kalahari. He probably came through Gaborone to dig gold on the Witwatersrand. South Africa hasn't been good to him. He was nearly killed by an accident underground, nearly killed today by a policeman on the surface.*

"Go home."

Angel picked the woman up and helped her to the side of the road, waving at an approaching bus. He thought of a Swazi saying: 'long hair', have a long life.

The two policemen from the circling vehicle appeared, one with a shotgun raised and pointing at Angel, barking instructions to his partner. Angel stood very still. He held his arms out straight, palms forward, in the shape of a man tied to a cross, a crucifixion.

"Top pocket! Top pocket!" Angel shouted as well. He needed to make himself heard, to get the policeman's attention.

Covered by the policeman with the shotgun, the other one stepped cautiously towards Angel, nervous and sweating hard. He reached for Angel's pocket and pulled out a wallet.

The detested passbook that Angel abhorred but was made to carry had a thirteen-figure number, the last figure just a control digit.

The first six numbers told his date of birth. Angel was born in 1951 in London, not far from the Swazi Embassy at 20 Buckingham Gate where his mother spent her imprisoned life. St Thomas' Hospital on Lambeth Palace Road was across the City from Cheapside but on a very quiet night, and with a gentle wind from the east, Lomawa from Swaziland might have heard St Mary-le-Bow, and her African son have been born a distinctive Bow-bell Cockney. Isabel, a Spanish-speaking Puerto Rican nanny who brought him up, named him Ángel. He used his father's South African surname, Rots. He often asked Isabel but no one, including his mother, could tell him his father's first name. He was thirty years old.

The next four numbers showed his sex. Over five thousand: male.

And then two numbers, the most important. Two numbers to control people's lives. Two numbers to tell them where to live, what to do for work, what cinema to go in, where to sit, what carriage on the train, what they could be arrested for. Two numbers: citizenship and racial group.

The policeman looked at it and found the important part of the long number, reading it out loud to himself.

"Zero seven?" He looked baffled. "This must be wrong. A zero seven code is for a South African citizen, Coloured."

Angel held out his arms.

"That's me," he said.

Angel didn't sound like any Coloured South African citizen he'd ever met. He tensed and apprehensively thumbed the identity book in his hand.

"How can you be South African?"

"The Army," said Angel.

"The Army? Which bit of the Army?" he asked.

"The busy bit."

In 1969, age eighteen and keen to see the land of his father, Angel had travelled by ship to Swaziland and South Africa by way of Malta, Suez, Mombasa and Maputo, relieved after the sea time to travel the last leg of his journey to Johannesburg on his father's railway over the high country along the south bank of the Komati and Crocodile Rivers.

For want of somewhere to stay he had walked into a recruiting office and joined the South African Defence

Force, which was never that fussy about the nationality of volunteers or their absurd English accents. He initially served with the South African Cape Corps, a non-combatant Coloured service corps, the sixteen weeks of basic training identical to young white national servicemen who had been called up. His English boarding school had been entirely relevant preparation. Volunteering again in 1970 for training with 1 Parachute Battalion, the Parabats, he had to repeat basic: another forty-two weeks' training. He became a soldier without politics, a foreigner in the South African Defence Force. A wretched ten months on the Angolan border of South West Africa followed hunting SWAPO terrorists, making good use of the Spanish from his Puerto Rican nanny with captured Cuban advisors. He left after two years, even though national service had at that time only lasted nine months, his South African citizenship confirmed.

"The other side," said Angel calmly, non-threatening. "Sir, please."

The policeman turned it over and puzzled over the South African governmental identification card.

"BOSS?"

Angel spoke low and slow, melodic, to reassure.

"It's okay. It's okay. It's not called the Bureau for State Security anymore. It's NIS, National Intelligence Service. It's okay."

The policeman relaxed a little. He could hear an ambulance.

"You work for National Intelligence?"

Angel smiled at him.

"Knowledge protects. Sir."

The policeman took another look at the name on the identification document, talking to himself again.

"Angel Rots."

"And there's this," said Angel.

He slowly removed a small thin hard-backed book from his back pocket, creased and stained. It was blue with a crest that was once embossed in gold but had faded and worn. Angel made it a matter of principle to take it out as infrequently as possible.

"It's a British passport," he said in English, with as much Cockney as he could lace into his accent.

The policeman knew what that meant: a 'get out of jail' card.

"That's right," Angel said. "I was Coloured, or possibly Black, but now I'm an honorary White." Angel laughed at the ludicrous inanity, but the policeman didn't smile.

*

Director General Lombard and his deputy Nick Roux stood alone in a vault at The Circle. It had surprised them that despite it being a Friday afternoon two weeks before Christmas, the holiday season starting and the roads busy, it had taken only fifteen minutes to drive from the office in central Pretoria. They had then spent four hours being passed through successive layers of dogs and wire and grim unsmiling faces, delighted to witness such thoroughness, aware that few people were ever allowed to get so far.

"Is that it?"

"You don't need to whisper, Nick."

"It doesn't look like a bomb."

"It's the guts of a bomb, without the bomb casing."

Roux examined the two wheeled tables, separated to opposite ends of the room. Each held a metre-long yellow

9

tube, similar to wide drainage pipe. One tube was fatter, the steel wall of the pipe six centimetres thick, while the other tube had something attached to it that resembled the copper windings of a coil in an electric motor. It looked dull and poorly made, like a prop at his daughters' school nativity play.

"They haven't even joined it together."

"The two uranium sections, the bullet and the target, are always kept separate. They don't ever work on both sections at the same time. It wouldn't be joined together until deployment."

Roux looked around, the building lit bright white by fluorescent tubes. They had entered a giant safe, to be met by a wall of smaller safes. Each heavy safe door had a numeric keypad and a four-handled wheel above a big shiny combination dial. The walls had wine bottle-shaped vents at the top and were lined from floor to ceiling with a mesh like fine chicken wire.

"It's not very big for fifty million dollars."

Roux was aware that budget estimates had recently escalated. The processing plant alone had cost sixty million and a further fourteen million a year to operate. Projections indicated that the total expenditure to produce six weapons would be over three hundred million dollars.

"What did you expect, Nick? We don't have big heavy B-52s like the Americans. This has to be delivered with our small light bombers." Lombard, repulsed by the weapon, was fascinated by the technical details. "This bomb might not look much but with fifty-five kilograms of uranium enriched to eighty per cent it should make a bang equivalent to over twelve thousand tons of TNT, a 12.65 kiloton yield to be exact."

"I expected a big, well… bomb."

"You can make a lot of energy by losing only a little mass if it is multiplied by the speed of light squared. It doesn't need to be big."

"$E=mc^2$?"

"The most famous formula in physics, Nick."

Nick Roux had a morbid curiosity. So much effort had been spent on this over years of independent research – a model of South African perseverance, patience and technical competence.

"How does it work?"

Lombard stepped across the vault and pointed to the end with the copper-coloured coil around it.

"The bullet will sit in here and weigh about forty kilograms. It is a sub-critical mass because of its hollow shape, like a doughnut." He waved his finger at the coil. "This is a cordite charge that shoots the bullet down the barrel of the gun, this yellow pipe, to the fat end."

Roux wanted to touch it but pulled his hand away nervously.

"In there will be the target, a uranium spike about half the weight of the bullet, that slots into the hole of the doughnut."

Roux was sweating slightly in the airless space.

"Sounds easy."

"It is, in theory," agreed Lombard. "Join the two lumps of uranium together to form a critical mass and, hey presto, fission."

"It's a marvel to be proud of."

Lombard wasn't sure. He didn't like to disillusion Roux but the weapon was almost identical to the one dropped on Hiroshima. That put South African technology about forty years behind the Americans. But South Africa had done it alone, on a relatively low budget and with a weak knowledge base. He was proud of that.

"We've developed all the internal ballistics and neutronic programmes," Lombard acknowledged. "There's a bit more to it of course. Fusing to make it go off when you want, protection devices so that it doesn't by accident."

"Doesn't what?"

"Go off."

"When will it be ready?"

"Three or four months; perhaps April."

"Will we test it?"

They had dug test holes in preparation for a completed device, shafts hundreds of metres deep under the Kalahari Desert.

"We could do a cold test at the Vastrap range, if required. A systems test using a depleted core. But not with this one. This will be our first deliverable weapon."

Lombard knew that it was taking a year to produce enough uranium for one bomb, the processing facility at Pelindaba currently enriching just one kilogram of weapons-grade material a week. He was fond of peevishly reminding colleagues at review meetings that even North Korea could make it quicker. In the circumstances, a hot test seemed a little wasteful. Anyway, he thought, an underground explosion, recognisable as a nuclear bomb to seismic observers around the world, was unnecessary. That would be a demonstration of intent, a warning. He hoped it would never get to that stage.

"Our jets can deliver this to the target?"

"Hopefully. If the poor old things can take off and not get shot down on the way."

A viable delivery system was on everybody's mind.

"We could always push it out the back of a cargo plane," joked Roux.

"Don't laugh, Nick. It's been discussed."

"Is it safe in here? Nobody can get their hands on it?"

The weapon had only recently been moved from its place of conception at the Pelindaba enrichment plant, just fifteen kilometres away. The Circle, a new facility for its gestation, was in the middle of hilly vehicle-testing grounds, hidden and closed to the public. Everybody referred to the bomb as a living thing, developing in the womb of The Circle and waiting to be born.

Lombard pointed to the main door.

"It would take four people in agreement to get it out of this vault. Three ministers and the PM need to insert a separate section of the code."

Roux nodded. "And the Director General of the National Intelligence Service is one of them. You have part of the code," he said.

Roux thought Lombard looked tired. His academic background hadn't prepared him for this. He should be lecturing, debating abstract ideas with tutor groups, drinking sherry in the senior common room.

"They've given it a name," Professor Lombard said sadly.

"Will it work?"

"Do you mean will it work, or is it convincing?"

Both Lombard and Roux knew that what they were looking at, a glorified cannon, was the easy part. It was nothing without the unstable isotope U235, and a means to convey the weapon to the intended recipient.

"It wouldn't be fifty million well spent or much use as a deterrent if people didn't believe it would work, Nick."

Lombard hoped they'd never find out if it worked. His personal belief was that using nuclear weapons would be akin to committing suicide.

"Will it work?" Lombard asked himself, scratching his forehead. "It's down to me and you, Nick, to keep the answer to that question a secret."

Securocrat Lombard and his deputy Roux dealt in secrets daily, like market traders. Secrets were the product they bought and sold, hopefully at a profit. But there was one secret not for sale, a secret that only a dozen people or less knew in its entirety.

"Don't forget what the Prime Minister said to us about the British and the Americans," said Lombard. "Make them think we have the damn bomb. It's the only way they'll help us end apartheid on *our* terms."

TWO

Angel Rots met the man on a Sunday. From a farm near Hekpoort they wordlessly walked through grassland along cattle trails, the white blazes on the heads of blesbok flashing in the warm morning sun as they skipped away. They followed a dry riverbed, cooler under the trees, before rising past cairns of Boer fort ruins towards a crest of hills and an isolated slab of red sandstone rock, the wide highveld stretching away below.

"Lovely," the man with Angel said.

He looked taller than Angel had expected, and wide, almost square, with a mass of hair and an untamed beard.

The man leant against a giant boulder, ejected by the same violent geological event that had created the hills. Conveniently spaced hand and foot holds had been eroded into the rock face.

"Let's climb it."

At the top they stood side by side like nervous new lovers. Behind them the Magaliesberg mountain range formed a ridge, sharp as a creased sheet of paper, stretching north-west into Bophuthatswana and east past the dam at Hartbeespoort towards Pretoria.

Angel looked around, grateful for the quiet emptiness.

"No one to see us together here," the man said. "All alone."

"Unless someone followed you," Angel said.

The man turned to Angel.

"They are more likely to be following you. How long have you worked for NIS?"

Angel couldn't believe the time had passed so quickly.

"Nearly two years."

The man touched his toes then stretched backwards, arms high.

"What's the name of this place?"

"Shelter Rock. I like it. I feel the name is appropriate."

"Shelter from who?" the man asked.

"You. The English."

"Surely you mean us," the man said. "Our Mr Cameron talks of you fondly from school."

Angel's surname had been anglicised for schooling, and he was sent to Sherborne, the tuition kindly paid for by the Swazis. They weren't being kind. Angel had been an experiment before King Sobhuza's heir Prince Makhosetive Dlamini travelled to Dorset in splendour to learn from the English how to become King Mswati III. At Sherborne, Angel excelled at languages and rugby, only the latter earning the respect of his peers.

Angel kneeled and looked over the edge.

"Boer women and children hid here to avoid your concentration camps." He looked up at the man standing beside him. "You invented them."

The man sniffed and scratched at his face like a dog.

"You're right. We're bastards."

"Only eighty years ago," Angel replied. "There are a few of them still alive, of the few that survived. The people in control of South Africa today grew up sitting on their parents' knees being lectured about the twenty-eight thousand civilians the English starved and left to die from disease."

"If you hate us, Angel, why do you want to help us?"

"Lots of reasons."

Angel stood back from the edge of the rock.

"Because I love South Africa despite the apartheid nonsense and I don't believe it will always be as it is now. Because you've told me that we are close to having a deliverable nuclear weapon and I'm seriously afraid South Africa would use it if pushed into a corner. Because I believe the British can help to make sure it doesn't happen, that you can apply pressure in the right places and we can avoid this country ending up covered in radioactive dust."

The man looked around.

"So, where is it?" he asked briskly.

"Pelindaba is over there, south of the dam," Angel pointed east towards Harties, the green water of the reservoir shimmering thirty kilometres away, "and The Circle is ten kilometres the other side, closer to Pretoria."

Angel suspected that the man had driven past the entrance on a reconnaissance but would have been unable to see any buildings, The Circle hidden behind a large berm of earth and invisible from the road.

"Let's tick things off," he said, like an efficient manager addressing a staff meeting. "You have the uranium, tons of it. Tick." He pointed to the dam. "You have at Pelindaba, compliments of the 'inventive' English University of Birmingham, a new way to highly enrich it. Tick." He looked

17

the other way, as though he could see into the empty wastes of the Kalahari. "You have a device at The Circle, otherwise why would you dig deep test holes in the desert. Tick."

He stopped, head on one side.

"Hang on, there's something missing." He put his hands in the air as in a eureka moment. "I've got it. How the hell are you going to get your nuclear weapon to the target?" He looked at Angel.

"What you need, my old mate, is a viable delivery system." He shook his head. "And don't try and tell me you can just hang the bomb underneath some crappy old aeroplane."

Angel wanted to go home. The hike in the mountains that he'd been looking forward to all week had suddenly lost its appeal.

"That's why we are here," said Angel. "I need to tell you about some developments in the Cape."

*

The English boy walked out of Jan Smuts Airport, fresh off the flight from London, and stretched his young body in the African night. Immigration had been his first hurdle and he had been unprepared. Firstly, at the most inopportune moment, his onward air ticket out of the country had hidden itself within a book, a large Russian classic. He discovered the ticket only seconds away from having to provide a bond of six hundred dollars, aware he could have found only half of the amount requested. Then, embarrassingly, he hadn't the full address of the cousin he would be staying with, and he'd dithered under questioning. The boy's flight had been delayed during its fuel stop in Nairobi after an unapologetic Captain Carnegie had blown a wheel with a heavy landing. It had taken over four hours to find and fit a replacement, a setback that had made him unreasonable, jaded and stale. He had known that his cousin lived in a town in the Western Cape, but where? Somewhere called Worcester? Or perhaps Wellington?

The Immigration Officer had looked at the boy and thought him too stupid to be a terrorist but had hesitated while considering the book. Dostoyevsky. Possibly Communist. He had contemplated him uncertainly, then with a blow like slamming a door closed slapped a large visa on a blank page of his passport.

Outside the air terminal, Johannesburg seemed much like London, only warmer. He was dressed inappropriately for the South African climate in December, with a tie tight around his neck. Other passengers, met and greeted, looked guiltily at the lonely boy. He had left England full of trusting innocence and it hadn't seemed necessary to make any plans other than to arrive, to get away from home, to travel. Now early evening, alone in a foreign land, he didn't know what to do.

The lights of an airport hotel glimmered enticingly across a busy motorway. Towing his suitcase, the boy climbed a barrier, slipped down an embankment, ran across the road in between cars and walked sweating into an expensive and expansive hotel lobby. The reception staff stared, a little surprised. They hadn't expected anyone else to arrive that night. Guests from the Heathrow flight had caught the shuttle bus provided by the hotel and had already found the bar. The boy could hear them, talking too loud, and they made him more nervous than the thought of having nowhere to sleep on his first night in Africa.

The receptionist watched him condescendingly and stroked his tie.

"Yes, sir?"

The boy shyly handed over his passport, to him a treasured possession. He'd memorised the words written on the inside front cover in a decorative italic script, the document important for what it authorised him to do: to leave the dull restrictions of a cold teenage life.

The man rubbed the smooth flat cleft under his nose with one finger. He read the boy's name as though he was being charged with an offence.

"Mr Ralph Phillips."

The photo, taken on issue of the passport, showed Ralph aged thirteen. Other boys had grown, grown into men, but he felt he hadn't changed that much in the last five years; his complexion, disappointingly, was still described as 'fresh'.

"And you've come from the airport? On foot? Prefer not to take the shuttle?"

Ralph felt a fool. People at the bar started to look at him but he considered it too late to back out now. He felt trapped, and coloured from more than just the exertion of his hike from 'Arrivals' with a heavy case.

"And how are you paying, sir?"

The receptionist relieved him of a fifth of his carefully hoarded and frequently counted cash and smiled below his well-tended moustache.

*

The following day, still weary from the flight, Ralph had for a short while studied cut diamonds for sale in Johannesburg shop windows but then walked through a botanical garden and lay exhausted on a park bench. Ralph opened one eye and read a sign screwed to the wood. He had expected something of the sort, had prepared himself not to be shocked by the injustice. It seemed a little superfluous as, disappointingly, he had seen no black African people in central Johannesburg at all. He wanted to talk to someone about it but a pretty blonde girl with an ice cream scowled and quickly left when he talked to her in English, leaving him with a vague and inexpressible teenage feeling that it wasn't fair.

Confused and tired, he looked around for the poorest looking hotel he could find, anxious to recover his unbudgeted extravagance at the airport. At the drab and gloomy Station Inn an old unctuous overcast man in a greyed shirt took his money from behind leaden bars. His head tapered from a point at the neck to the widest part around his eyes and with a flat crown on top, like a diamond below and above the girdle, all facets grey.

"Where are you from?"

"England," said Ralph.

He smiled at him.

"You don't say. One night?"

"Yes, please. I'm on a train tomorrow."

"Room Ten. If any girls come around and you don't want them just kick 'em out."

"Oh. Okay."

"Where are you heading?"

Ralph had checked and confirmed his destination to be Worcester in the Western Cape, north-east of Cape Town, his cousin's house. Earlier at a central railway station, and still wearing a necktie, he had been mistaken for having money and directed to an air-conditioned reception for the Blue Train, a luxury option selling at a price the grandeur and service of bygone days. Luckily, journeys in the middle of December booked a year ahead. Ralph, relieved but puzzled, slowly realised the size and complexity of navigating the continent. Surprisingly, the train to Worcester, 1,300 kilometres away, took forty-eight hours. On the Blue Train that would have meant two days and nights of what? Ralph shuddered to think. Red-faced men and their prim wives talking about 'The Old Country' he imagined. An altogether more exciting and cheaper option, the Trans Karoo, left the following day. Ralph took the cheapest ticket available, a third-class non-sleeper, curious to find out what other third-class non-sleeping passengers would be like.

At his dirty city lodgings, the room a plain box, the bed appeared too small for any complimentary girls. Ralph preferred it to the airport hotel. Drowsy at three o'clock in the afternoon he slept contentedly.

*

A man drinking rum from a bottle in a brown paper bag, and a soldier going on leave, had already settled on the Trans Karoo when Ralph boarded, taking up most of the cabin. Ralph squeezed nervously into a seat. He would have liked to have sat against the window. Too timid and reluctant to ask, he consoled himself that, at the very least, he might learn a new language. He didn't fancy a *dop* from the brown paper bag but smiled when he found out that he had a *rooinek* and probably a *poepol*. Ralph concentrated on the words as he'd learnt that only ten per cent of the population spoke English as a first language, while fifteen per cent spoke Afrikaans. The soldier told him that it would make little difference. It would be unlikely that he'd have any need to talk to the other seventy-five per cent, so English speakers would make up forty per cent of those that he'd meet, probably more in the Cape. He'd seemed pleased with the success of his calculation.

Ralph wondered about the seventy-five per cent. He'd seen no real Africans at all.

"Where do they all live?" he asked.

The soldier looked at his shiny boots.

"Who?" he asked.

Ralph, embarrassed and uncomfortable, looked at the soldier's boots as well.

The other man unscrewed the top of his rum bottle and spoke quietly into his paper bag.

"They have their own places," the soldier said. "We live apart from each other, that's all, separate."

Ralph wanted to believe in the soldier's utopia of happy African peoples but suspected it wasn't as beautiful as he'd described. He had the suspicion the soldier was reciting a memorised propaganda leaflet given to him in week one of training, with a title like 'What to Say to Foreigners Asking Awkward Questions'.

"Some homelands are really good," said the man with the bottle. "They even have titty bars."

Ralph smiled self-consciously, wondering how he could change the conversation. He thought he'd talk about something less provocative, like sport, rugby or cricket maybe, but the soldier saved him by sharing with them his thoughts on *biltong*. It wasn't a short conversation.

The train crossed a brown river with muddy islands in the middle that looked as if they flooded. Rows of scrubby trees had been planted in straight lines to prevent it all washing away downstream.

"The Orange River," the soldier said with reverence.

Ralph imagined it had a symbolic significance or a history that he should know about. He tried to find the Orange River in his old *School Atlas of the World*, Africa covering two whole pages. Interesting detail on temperature, rainfall and mineral resources filled the margins. Although already hot in the cabin, Ralph assumed it would soon be getting hotter. His atlas showed the Karoo as a brown desert.

The train rumbled over the vast interior plateau of South Africa until a rim of rugged hills appeared through the haze and a narrow coastal plain ran to the blue South Atlantic.

*

The single loud call of a roosting ibis, or a gunshot, woke Elanza Swart from a dream. It was the usual dream, the dream about the day her father sold the farm and everything changed. She lay still, listening to the calming suburban night sounds of Johannesburg's Hyde Park, Africa's richest square mile, and then moved across the bed, her mouth sticky and dry. A man sprawled beside her and grunted as she leant over him to look for something to drink. She would have apologised but she couldn't remember his name. She swore as she knocked over a glass of water and took a handful of pills from a plastic bag, swallowing them with harsh green Chardonnay.

THREE

Ralph had spent two weeks in Worcester being mothered by his cousin before he tired of drinking, *braais* and Christmas pool parties in the English Cape community. He had been well cared for and grateful for it but he wanted to see Africa.

He didn't get very far, just three and a half hours away on a three-stop train that meandered around the Boland of Western Cape Province and ended by the sea at Cape Town. Ralph rented a smelly room in a city apartment from two drama students, Frieda and Lettie, who casually smoked joints as others might have a cocktail, while their high, gay, male friends tried to pick him up. A slang had developed in Cape Town to allow gay men to converse in public without drawing attention, usually based on girls' names. The girls had unwittingly contributed, Ralph imagined appropriately. To be 'frieda' and a 'lettie' had come to mean, to the veiled, furtive, South African gay community, 'sexually frustrated' and 'lesbian'. Ralph had walked away from Frieda and Lettie's house in the quiet dawn of New Year's Day, walked away from Cape Town, wondering why he hadn't fitted in with anybody he'd met and craving the open dramatic vistas of Africa.

He'd taken a month then, hiking the coast from Cape Town towards East London before loneliness finally made him accept a ride from an Austrian printer called Franz travelling to Durban and Johannesburg.

"I got fed up with Cape Town," Franz told him.

"Me too," Ralph said.

*

At Port Shepstone, where the road to Durban rejoined the Indian Ocean, Franz allowed an enigmatic hairy hitch-hiker to join them. He had leonine hair with a dark mane, bearded, with a huge flat skull and broad nostrils. He introduced himself as Zac.

In a bar one evening a bulky staggering drunk started shadow-boxing. Zac, generally inactive during the day but social with bursts of activity at dusk, became brave and unconcerned, mimicking him, until Ralph wondered if they would get out alive.

Determined to find out where Zac came from, Ralph sat with him on the beach munching through his inexhaustible supply of little chocolate cakes. Ralph only established that Zac, mysterious and nomadic, intended on travelling with them all the way to Johannesburg. A company called Gasol needed pipefitters. They provided three weeks' training at three hundred rand a month and then paid six hundred, food and accommodation provided. Zac chatted enthusiastically. Six hundred rand a month beer money. Ralph should join him.

Feeling the need for more than cake, Zac persuaded them to stop at a hotel for a fixed price buffet breakfast. Not content with eating as much as he could, Zac scavenged stealthily, filling his pockets with bacon and cold fried eggs. Ralph hadn't enjoyed his time in South Africa. The airport hotel had unnerved him, as had the confusing sights and unfamiliar people he'd met in Johannesburg. The two men on the train to Cape Town had puzzled and frightened him. His sheltered West Country upbringing hadn't prepared him for Cape Town's predatory gay men and stoned lesbians. Ralph watched Zac deftly slip a plate of sausages into his day pack with experienced hands and laughed for the first time since he'd arrived.

From a palm tree fringed beach at Durban, the road to Johannesburg climbed towards the dry and cool upland savannah around Pietermaritzburg. As they shivered on park benches in the town, a pack of a dozen enormous Rhodesian ridgebacks towed a small woman down the main street towards them, the dogs stopping to snuffle curiously at Zac's pockets.

They rested again at Winterton, a farm town fifty kilometres south-west of Ladysmith. Wide irrigation booms rotated in an uncoordinated dance, making circular green fields at the base of the Drakensberg Mountains. The highest peak in South Africa, Mafadi, towered just south of the town on the border with Lesotho. Ralph couldn't remember who made the decision to spend four days climbing it. They had no tent and no food except for the furry contents of Zac's pockets and a bag full of cakes.

On the first day, striding cheerily from a campsite, the route initially followed the Njesuthi River, giving plenty of opportunities for water stops to wash down the chocolate cake. Ralph felt lightheaded. It must have been the altitude. After six kilometres they left the river and followed a steep path over open grassland directly to a hut. Ralph and Franz stopped and watched elands while Zac stalked them like a great whiskery feline. They couldn't see the hut until the last hundred metres. At one time there had been mattresses on wooden bunks, and fresh water had been piped in but now they found it basic, bare and vandalised. They had covered ten kilometres and climbed only seven hundred metres. It had taken all day and they could look forward to dry cake for dinner. Bush fires lit the night sky and blazed all around, seemingly at times inside the hut.

The next day they had to climb from the hut to a cave, a path following a contour clearly seen but steep-going. It eased, and after two kilometres and several bends in the trail they reached Corner Pass, an ideal opportunity for lunch. It became the start of a rocky climb. Ralph attempted scampering up grassy slopes but repeatedly slipped back down, eventually realising that the easiest way appeared to be straight up through a rocky gully, stepping carefully from one flat rock to another. In sections the gully narrowed and the walls rose vertically. Only by pushing and pulling each other could they make it up without a rope, the rock falling precipitously away below them. They arrived at the next camp at sunset, a cave cut into the rock, with paintings by Bushmen on the walls. They stood staring at the pictures from the light of a burning branch, open-mouthed, and eating cake.

"Jumbo Cameron would love this," said Zac.

"Jumbo?"

"My boss. Where's your camera?" Zac asked. "Take some pictures."

Ralph tried to remember.

"It's in the car with all my film."

Zac nodded.

"The film is in pots?"

"Yeah. Everything marked up on the lids saying where they were taken."

The third day the sun rose above a blanket of cloud below them and lit the entrance to the cave. They summited Mafadi Peak at 3,450 metres, the top of South Africa, and stood precariously on the lip of Leslie's Pass. A clear path led down to rock boulders in a river, the Marble Baths, and under stars they bathed naked in river pools and finished the last of the cakes.

In the morning Ralph felt ill during the short walk down the Njesuthi valley to their base camp, baboons following them as if they would make interesting and unusual prey. Zac bolted for the bottom, a hunted look on his face. When Ralph and Franz got there, Zac had been into the car already and retrieved his green bergen. They waited but never saw him again. Ralph hoped he would soon be welding pipes, making money and baking. They'd been high on his hash cakes for four days.

At Ladysmith they discovered a note from Zac tucked into an old money belt under the seat where Franz's Austrian passport and five hundred dollars should have been. Franz said that Zac, probably ex-Rhodesian and of a breed Ralph would see more of, typified many youths displaced by independence: from Zimbabwe, English-speaking third-generation Rhodesians with insufficient ties to the United Kingdom to get a British passport; from Mozambique, descendants of Portuguese settlers unable to get to Lisbon; in Kenya, Italians dreaming of living in Milan. All of them young and homeless, roaming Africa, voluntarily stateless. Zac's note hoped that Franz wouldn't need to report his passport stolen until he'd had a chance to use it to get to Europe. Both agreed that Zac would need a shave and a haircut first. Ralph's camera bag had been searched, the blue passport he had hidden inside still there, entreating all those whom it may concern to allow the bearer to pass freely without let or hindrance but apparently, and fortunately for Ralph, with a little more hindrance than the bearer of an Austrian passport.

They walked deep in thought around the town. In late 1899 and early 1900, two years after Ralph's grandfather was born, Boer forces surrounded Ladysmith, and three thousand British soldiers died after a siege lasting some 118 days. It seemed relatively recent.

*

In the transport aircraft they were at action stations, skimming the tops of the trees at two hundred feet, the younger men vomiting from the evasive manoeuvres and the tension and fear, until just a minute and a half from the jump the aeroplane pitched up violently and climbed to the drop height. Mushroom-like clouds of dust billowed towards them.

Angel looked around at nervous schoolboy faces, the red strap of the static jump line draped over their shoulders like a hangman's noose, and watched an old corporal carefully stroke a waxy black finger in wide zebra stripes across his white face before examining himself in a small mirror, like a secretary on her way to the office. The man noticed Angel and with a grin offered him a small tin of boot polish.

"Black is beautiful."

Angel smiled and shook his head.

The green-to-go light came late. Their commander had wanted the pilots to determine the release point visually from a bend in the river as they made the final run in. The chief of the Army had overruled him. He'd insisted they take their cue from a side marker. Dust and smoke from the bombing run had obscured the side marker, and the pilot, never under fire before, became mesmerised by the scene unfolding on the ground. It was only a few seconds, but it was late.

The drop zone, despite all the planning, now appeared too small, as if the air-photo interpreters had provided the wrong scale to the planners. Parachutes were landing everywhere, some of them two or three kilometres from the target, some on the other side of the river or in tall trees and maize crops, some in the water.

Angel noticed the wind. A strong wind had taken him south-west of where had been intended and he had come under fire as he descended. They were supposed to be a few hundred metres north of the new tented camp, to regroup, and then attack it. In fact, he had landed right in the camp on top of the tents, a lot of them flattened and ripped by a Mirage's cannon. Angel lifted the flap of a still standing tent and looked inside. It was full of children, on display as if in a butcher's shop window.

Angel moved away quickly and took up a position with others on high ground along the riverbank, a constant stream of people attempting to cross the river and escape from Cassinga, men and women in green combat uniform, civilians, teenagers, children. Angel found it impossible to differentiate targets, and he and his platoon brought fire to bear on all of them.

From their vantage point they could see that the town buildings were now being attacked. Ammunition stores exploded violently. Angel noticed a company of men had come down at least five hundred metres too far south among tall trees and brush. One paratrooper had hit a tree and with a severe concussion wandered as if drunk. They were coming under RPG fire as they sought to unravel the confusion.

C Company had come upon a two-hundred-metre-long escape trench. They were shooting at people moving inside. Angel couldn't see who they were shooting at.

Two companies and a mortar platoon were spread out along both banks of the river, some in the water, others trying to carry equipment up a steep bank. A platoon seemed to be attacking a building that Angel remembered from the plan housed Cuban officers. One of their own jets released rockets at the building just as they entered. Angel yawned. He felt tired and checked his watch: 10.10. He'd been on the ground two hours but it felt like a week.

The town was only just starting to come under attack as his own people recovered their positions from the inaccurate drop. There was so much confusion among the enemy from the shock of the air strikes that Angel's men weren't encountering significant resistance. There were some snipers in the trees but the houses appeared to be cleared without much opposition. People would run from the buildings towards the river and Angel shot at them as they ran away. He could see a toddler, maybe eighteen months old, wandering among the corpses of the earlier bombing, searching for its mother. Three little girls cowered under an old bed, calling to it.

The situation changed as some organisation came back into the enemy. They had anti-aircraft weapons and started using them in a ground role. It stopped Angel's platoon dead. Their commander ordered them to move and attack a line of trenches to the west of Cassinga town and work up towards the anti-aircraft guns. A large group of civilians were clustered together and they fled into the bushes as the soldiers approached.

There were about twenty in Angel's platoon. Two entered the trenches with rifles and grenades, while Angel and the rest stayed on either side looking in. There were a lot of civilians in the trench and there was no question of being selective with their fire. Someone lobbed a grenade into the next leg of the zig-zag trench. A woman's body, clad in green fatigues, blew right out of the trench onto the parapet, the front of her bloodied uniform tattered and in shreds from the explosion. She hadn't been running away. She'd been protecting four children, now dead in the bottom of the trench.

It was a savage noisy close-quarters struggle, complete disarray. Women and children who had taken shelter were screaming among the fiercely resisting guerrillas. The howl of gunfire coming from the bush, mortar bombs dropping around the anti-aircraft guns, smoke, dust, cordite fumes, shouting and screaming interspersed with hand grenade explosions, and the stutter of the anti-aircraft guns battered the quiet African town. When it was over, Angel counted ninety-five dead in the trench. They were the ones in uniform. He didn't count the others.

The battalion second-in-command established a headquarters and aid post in the hospital building. Snipers were shooting at them so he forced the civilian women and children sheltering there to go outside and form a human shield. Cassinga had not yet been secured and numerous firefights were erupting all over the town but since the fall of the anti-aircraft guns the worst seemed to be over.

Angel was sent to collect documents and prisoners for extraction and herded bleary men like shadows into a house. The first wave of helicopters started landing, two hours overdue. The plan had been for the prisoners to be extracted first but at the last minute the plan was changed and critically injured paratroopers replaced them on the first helicopters to leave.

Through the shattered window of the house, Angel saw paratroopers burning every hut and tent that still stood. An ammunition dump and underground bunker exploded. A young girl with her friends pleaded to be taken away in the helicopter as it loaded. She was roughly pushed aside.

A grisly pile of debris had formed by the door to the house, tiny legs protruding. Angel went over to it. He pulled some of the bodies aside with his hands and found a baby girl underneath, alive, unhurt.

A stocky square man from Military Intelligence came from one of the helicopters and entered the house. He had no insignia, no rank badges.

He grabbed a prisoner and screamed at him.

"Where's Dimo? Where's Greenwell?"

He slapped him and pulled out another, a Cuban.

"Where's Dimo?"

The Cuban stared at him.

"Spanish. Anyone speak Spanish?" he asked.

Angel stepped forward.

"We need to know where Dimo is," Angel said to the man.

The Cuban's Spanish was slow and lazy.

"I don't know. I haven't seen him."

Angel shook his head at the Intelligence officer who pulled an African prisoner up and made him stand with his arms outstretched.

"There's only one thing they'll understand," he said.

He brought a machete that had been leaning against the wall. The man started shaking.

Angel pleaded with the Cuban, "Please. Please tell me. Where is Dimo?"

The Cuban said nothing. The Intelligence officer moved quickly and the machete severed the African's right arm at the elbow. The man stood still then looked around and sat down carefully, as if looking for a park bench. He picked up his severed arm from the floor as if it was something he didn't want to leave behind, like a jacket or a bag of shopping.

"Ask him again," the Intelligence officer said to Angel.

Outside, Cassinga had been razed. Ammunition continued to explode. Bodies were everywhere, mostly African, scorched by flames. Charred papers scattered in all directions, some still in the air. The downdraughts from the helicopters fanned the fires, and documents, maps and scraps of paper floated around like leaves.

Angel saw a box on the ground. He wondered if it was a booby trap and went to have a closer look. It was a wooden box: 'Romeo y Julieta' Cuban cigars.

The first wave of helicopters had left, the sound of them leaving soon replaced by the rumbling of heavy vehicles approaching from the south. The radio jamming had worked for a while but they were over two hours behind schedule due to the haphazard drop. The Cubans fifteen kilometres to the south had heard the news and were now responding. There were still two hundred men waiting for extraction by helicopter, tired and shocked now that it felt like it was over. A Buccaneer fired into the approaching Cuban reinforcements. They were only armoured personnel carriers and World War Two vintage Soviet tanks but they had far more firepower than the paratroopers were carrying. The Buccaneer jet left, its rockets expended. Twenty-two paratroopers with ten rocket-propelled grenades stood between the armour and the landing zone where dispirited paratroopers prepared to make a last stand, their spirit now broken, like a team fifty points down with just ten minutes to the whistle.

The loading of the second wave of helicopters took place in chaos, all discipline eroded by the threat of the advancing Cuban column. Angel saw the chief of the Army remove his insignia of rank and cap badge and hide them under a rock in case of capture. He probably should never have been there. He looked guilty, as though he'd committed a shameful act. Other men saw him do it and looked away.

South African jets attacked the Cuban column. A ragged exhausted cheer came from the paratroopers. The Cuban reinforcements had about thirty vehicles and four hundred troops. Some had been destroyed but still they came, ever closer. When they were only two hundred metres from the helicopters, scrubby trees being pushed over in front of them, a Buccaneer without ammunition repeatedly dived at them, skimming the treetops to disorientate the drivers and give the paratroopers more time.

At the landing zone there seemed too many men for the helicopters and Angel was sure they'd never all fit. Men were running crazed from helicopter to helicopter trying to find space. Overloaded helicopters attempted to take off, engines screaming, only to sink back down heavily on their landing gear. Equipment was being thrown away. The prisoners were offloaded and released. The Intelligence officer kept hold of the Cuban, Angel with them, the last ones to leave. The helicopter staggered under the load. It climbed first to treetop height and then accelerated before climbing again. Angel couldn't tell what height they were at. It may have been at five or six hundred feet when the Cuban tumbled out of the door.

The Intelligence officer who pushed him had a tattoo on the inside of his forearm. It was Angel's cap badge, but upside down.

*

Angel, his collar damp, walked quickly away from Waltloo station. His commute home on the train took just twenty-five minutes but it always felt longer. He continued past his house at the end of Loutus Avenue into bare parkland crisscrossed with brown trails, striding towards the river. He knew a jacaranda tree there he could stand against, feel the bark through his wet shirt and in October look up at its purple flowers. He could remind himself, as he had every day for nearly four years, that there had been nothing as beautiful at Cassinga.

*

The director general's office in Pretoria was in darkness, Lombard and Roux illuminated only by the flickering of the television as a video tape abruptly ended.

Lombard stood and stretched and half opened a blind, his back and neck aching with the curse of all very tall men. Roux blinked and then sneezed, his body arcing forward, both hands to his face.

"Excuse me."

Lombard sat uncomfortably in a straight-backed chair staring at the blank screen. Roux waved a handkerchief in the direction of the television.

"Where did this come from?" he asked.

"Marcel at the DST."

"The French?"

Lombard shrugged.

"Trade," he said, twisting his head from side to side, stretching an unidentifiable fault in his neck or spine.

Roux knew what that meant. France was the centre of South Africa's weapons trading activities across Europe, senior French politicians and intelligence officials approving the flow of weapons technology to Pretoria despite a UN arms embargo.

Roux had visited the South African Embassy in Paris, the secret home to dozens of their own officials controlling the illegal arms procurement, and was stunned by the scale of money laundering it required: over a hundred front companies in Liberia and Panama depositing money in nearly five hundred South African owned accounts in Belgium and Luxembourg.

"So, the French want to sell a power station or a frigate and this video is a little sweetener to encourage us to sign the deal."

"Something like that."

"The obvious question is how did the French get it?"

"They recruited a Soviet KGB officer, Vlad someone, code name 'Farewell'. He's a miner."

Roux knew that Lombard didn't mean that Vladimir worked in a mine. Instead, the French had struck gold, a rich seam being dug by their agent 'Farewell' and passed back to the DST.

"The ship, is it ours?"

"Yes, that's been confirmed. The location was twelve miles south-west of Cape Point. You can almost make out Table Mountain."

Lombard rewound the tape. A naval ship rolled in a big sea, it's engines stopped. The cameraman had rolled with it, the start of the video a blurred image of deck and funnel.

"That number, there," Lombard pointed to white on the grey superstructure, "is P1566. It's the *Oswald Pirow*, our newest Minister class strike craft."

The cameraman had panned out, the coastline visible across whitecaps, then zoomed in on an aircraft approaching fast and close to the wave tops. It gained height as it got closer until, directly over the ship, it dropped a grey cigar shape like a torpedo. Lombard paused the video.

"It's a Buccaneer bomber from 24 Squadron. The test is for a new stand-off weapon called, unimaginatively, the S-O1."

"What does it do?"

"It's a glide bomb to deliver a nuke. You can release it sixty kilometres from the target, little wings pop out the side and it steers itself with optical control and inertial navigation, like in a submarine when underwater. Accurate to within three metres."

Roux could see a round glass nose cone reflecting the sun and sparkling in the morning light. It didn't look as if it was designed to fly. The cylindrical shape and the domed front end made it look more like a fish than a bird. As the weapon fell from the aircraft, thin rectangular wings sprang out, swept backwards like a fast jet. It stabilised, heading away from the ship, then pitched up like a horse taking a fence. It seemed to stutter, jerking forward in jumps rather than flying, then fell tail first into the choppy South Atlantic Ocean.

"What went wrong?" asked Roux.

"It had a dummy load that resembled the shape and weight of the actual device. It was too heavy."

"Really? And they couldn't have worked that out beforehand?"

"Apparently not. The weapon weighs more than the glider can carry. It's that simple."

The video came to an end. Lombard paced to the window and opened the blinds. They rattled to the top of the window frame as if angry with him.

"I thought we were just going to drop the bomb from a jet."

"It's not that simple, Nick."

Lombard took a chalk to the blackboard behind his desk.

It always made Roux smile. Lombard had brought it himself from Tukkies, as the procurement division refused to put anything as simple in the office of the head of the National Intelligence Service.

"They can fly high over the target to escape the blast."

Lombard was at university again, lecturing to a class, Tukkies' favourite professor.

"But then they'd most likely get shot down by Cuban-manned Soviet-built air defence systems."

He waved the chalk at Roux.

"Or they come in low, unseen by air defence radar, pull up quickly, and toss the bomb up and forward like in an underhand throw."

Lombard drew wavy lines showing the trajectory of the released weapon and the turn of the hastily departing aircraft.

"It isn't easy. The Americans have onboard computers telling the pilot at what range to pitch up, at what speed, what angle, the precise moment to release. Our guys have to do it all by the seat of their pants. The cockpit workload is incredibly high. They can't do it, not routinely, accurately and with any guarantee of survivability. It's a suicide mission. Hence the S-O1."

"Will they fix it?"

"Unlikely. They'd have to make the glide bomb bigger or the device smaller. Both technically beyond them."

Lombard pushed the Sunday papers off his desk. Headlines all weekend had been of the funeral of a physician in Black hospitals in Soweto, a part-time unpaid union leader. The police had kept him for seventy days in solitary without trial before he hanged himself. Outrage had cut across racial lines, politicians and lawyers, academics and churchmen, all demanding an end to detention. Dr Neil Aggett was white.

"I met him."

"Who?"

Lombard waved the newspapers at Roux.

"They blindfolded him, electric shocks, the works."

He threw the chalk in the bin.

"I thought him quite logical."

Lombard shook himself.

"So here we are, more problems."

Roux could see two immediate problems, both chilling, both out of his control. Lombard must have known what he was thinking.

"Firstly, Nick, for the French to get hold of this video from their miner in Moscow, there must be a Soviet agent here, probably near the top of the South African Navy, sending our secrets back to Russia."

It wasn't Roux and Lombard's responsibility. The Directorate of Military Intelligence would have to find him.

"The DMI will be crawling all over Simon's Town," said Roux.

"The second is that the French, and therefore the whole world, now knows that we do not have a viable delivery system."

Roux understood it was a prerequisite of a deterrent. You had to be able to deliver the weapon or there was no point in having a weapon.

"No delivery, no deterrent, Nick."

Roux could see where Lombard was heading. There was only one possible solution: Overberg, the secret new testing range in the Cape.

"Until we can convince the world that we have a credible missile, we have nothing to work with. Overberg must deliver."

FOUR

Koos Snyman's lavish office in Sandton had been paid for by Blackie Swart. Snyman had represented Blackie at the sale of Wensvolle Farm and since his death had been the executor of his will and trustee of the estate, as well as guardian to Blackie's daughter Elanza, all of it lucrative.

Snyman's grandparents had come to South Africa from Lithuania at the turn of the nineteenth century, attracted by the gold rush of 1886. They settled near the goldfields but outside Johannesburg, so populated by their own kind that people called the town Jewburg. Although faintly Orthodox they became *Boerejode*, unlike many *uitlanders* who had been excluded from mainstream South African life. His grandfather, briefly conscripted along with other citizens on to the Afrikaner side in the Second Boer War, fought under their four-coloured flag at Gun Hill. The young Koos Snyman and his parents rode out a period of Afrikaner pro-Nazi persecution from the Greyshirts in the 1930s, only able to relax when the Afrikaner-dominated National Party came to power in 1948 and, against their previous claims, chose not to adopt an anti-Jewish policy. Snyman went to Stellenbosch to study law the following year aged twenty. He finished his LLB in '54, qualified after articles in '57 and worked for Pretorius Venter Kruger.

After Blackie's death he didn't need to stay with PVK and left to work for himself in his own office, close to Elanza's house in Hyde Park. He made a deliberate, and he now thought inspired, decision to have Elanza's estate buy a property for her close to his own office and, understandably, he had a key. It had been useful on more than one occasion to have somewhere to meet people when he thought that Elanza may be playing away out of town and the house would be vacant – usually girls from the office and other women that he didn't want his wife Danelle to know about.

Snyman thought about Elanza, sadly off the rails from the age of twenty. Since her father had died in Johannesburg six years previously he had seen Elanza spend her inheritance on unsavoury men and less than sweet drugs, and now she needed bailing out again.

Nels had called while on weekend babysitting duty.

"She's in a club. It's appropriately called 'Tramps'."

"Wait for me," Snyman said.

He had stayed late in the office with his young assistant Lizette. She had kicked off her shoes and made them both a cocktail, rubbing her foot against his leg as he spoke on the phone. Snyman scowled with irritation that Elanza was taking him from his work, and Lizette.

*

Koos Snyman occasionally had need to employ Nels of Research Associates for his irregular and more aggressive assignments, but he did so reluctantly. Cornelius Nels had joined the South African Army in 1965, two years before the introduction of national service, and considered himself fortunate to have had a gratifyingly violent career. He had tracked and fought insurgents in South West Africa, had sadistically instructed paratroopers, and had joined ambitious Special Forces units called Battle Group or Task Force. He had been happy but not complete, and not until he joined Military Intelligence and specialised in interrogation did he find his true vocation. Good at the job, his reward, after a particularly challenging operation in which his innovative technique impressed a general, had been to set up a Military Intelligence cover company for deniable special projects. He called it Research Associates, although he became the only associate and did little research, and gratefully pocketed the proceeds of genuine contracts, like his work for Koos Snyman.

They met outside Tramps in the basement of The Diplomat, a central Johannesburg hotel. Nels, occasionally useful, threatened the doorman when he refused access. Elanza had been in there, drunk and drugged. They heard her having sex with a man in a bathroom cubicle and afterwards an acrid smell crept under the door. When Nels burst in she had one foot on the toilet seat and was facing the wall, injecting into a vein on her hand with a shared needle. Nels lifted his elbow into the man's face. Elanza, confused, screamed at him until he knocked her out with a punch to the side of her head and carried her from the club. Snyman, feeling sick, picked up a part-used packet of pink tablets and followed him.

*

The doctor came out of a bedroom in Snyman's Westcliff house and walked past Nels leaning against the wall, gazing at Snyman's wife Danelle. Thirteen years younger than Snyman, only just over forty, she still looked good. Nels decided that her only job, to look good for Snyman, got a little harder each year but she could still do it. It was early evening but she had been drinking wine all afternoon and flicked her hair flirtatiously as she noticed Nels looking at her, flattered that she could still be appreciated by someone.

The doctor glanced at Snyman.

"What's Elanza's age?"

"Born 1956. She's twenty-six."

"She's sleeping now. The drug abuse is pretty long-standing."

"What is it?" Snyman asked.

"It's a prescription drug called Wellconal, a synthetic analgesic as strong as morphine. It's for oral use and not intended for injection but they crush the tablets, mix it with water in a metal spoon and heat it up with a cigarette lighter to help it dissolve. It gives an intense rush for thirty seconds then a state of euphoria for about an hour. On the street it's called Pinks."

"Nice. Sweet girl," joked Nels.

Snyman scowled at him.

"There's miosis from the intoxication but I'm worried in general about her vision."

"Hey, I didn't hit her hard," said Nels.

The doctor and the lawyer stared at the soldier, and the drunk woman laughed into her wine glass.

Nels looked at Danelle and speculated what it might take to get her into bed. His conclusion encouraged him.

"I've got some bloods," said the doctor. "I'll do some tests."

*

Ralph had spent a day walking aimlessly around Johannesburg faintly worried about money before realising that he needed to find a job. His room in a dormitory at the YMCA was the cheapest accommodation he could find but the cost would be unsustainable.

The Diplomat hotel stood impassively on the corner of Klein and Bree Streets. It was washed in a welcoming light that disguised the dark dejection of those obliged to sleep away from home and the oily mock concern of those on the evening shift that attended them. Ralph looked through glass doors at the reception area and at a man standing behind a marble and glass counter talking on the phone. He looked Indian and stern, with a big iron bracelet, a dagger tucked into his belt and an impressive turban. On an impulse Ralph thought he'd see if they would take him on. He walked straight in and nervously asked to see the manager but was told to talk to the owner, sitting commandingly like a Sicilian don at a corner table in the restaurant.

Ralph thought he'd come straight to the point.

"Excuse me. I'm looking for a job."

The man was very white, as though he'd lived his whole life inside the hotel or underground. He had been eating a mound of spaghetti with two forks, one in each hand, shovelling bolognaise into his mouth rapidly with a left then right double action. He held both forks motionless in the air as Ralph spoke, his jowls quivering like a St Bernard. Ralph expected him to talk Italian and was surprised at West Country English, more like a pirate than a Mafioso.

"Where you from, then?" he asked.

"England."

"Where in England?"

"Dorset."

"Where in Dorset?"

"A small town called Gillingham."

"Where did you go to school?"

"Shaftesbury Grammar, sir."

"So did I. You'd better call me Fred. You've got the job."

Ralph stood staring at him, unable to speak. It had been the first enquiry for work he'd made, and at a randomly selected hotel thousands of miles from home. Fred attacked his dinner. It was like a pheasant shoot, thought Ralph. Left, right, load both barrels.

"But you may not want it," he said.

Ralph went to speak but Fred put down the forks and held up his hands for silence.

"Listen to an Old Shastonian for a moment. I need to explain some things to you."

He nodded his head towards the hotel reception.

"You see the Indian gentleman at the front desk, the shift manager?"

Ralph nodded.

"He is a Punjabi Sikh. You won't find another Indian person doing that job at any other hotel in South Africa."

"Why?"

"Shush," said the owner, "just listen. Listen to an old grammar school boy."

Ralph wondered if Fred was drunk but couldn't see the empty squat wine bottle in a straw basket that might have accompanied dinner.

"I brought him with me from the mine when I bought the hotel. He's brilliant."

He held up two fingers.

"He has two engineering degrees from the Open University. He used to bring his assignments to work and I'd post them to England. He'll never be able to go to an awards ceremony to collect the certificates: no passport."

He removed a napkin from his lap.

"He lives in Lenasia with his wife and mother-in-law and five kids. He has no choice. It is an Indian area for the exclusive occupation of his racial group. It's thirty-five kilometres away. Most of his salary goes on a 'goodwill' payment just to be able to rent a house. Six families live in one long structure divided into six units of two rooms. The toilets are shared in the backyard. Three for about fifty people. I have never seen him anything other than immaculately presentable with *kirpan* and *dastaar*."

Ralph didn't know what those things were. He was unsure whether he had been offered a job or if the man was playing a game with him.

"My restaurant manager over there is amaXhosa."

He pointed to a tall, very black man in a suit.

"He's breaking the law doing that job, and I am for giving it to him. It isn't an approved occupation for native South Africans. I have to put in his passbook that he is a waiter. He lives in a matchbox in Emdeni Soweto, a Black area. It's further out than Indian Lenasia: takes him two hours to travel to work, two hours to travel home. He has never once been late for his shift."

He waved at the restaurant manager, who nodded his head.

"He doesn't mind the commute. It gives him the opportunity to look for his son."

"Why? Where is his son?" Ralph asked.

"His son has paler skin. No reason for it, just the way it is, but they classified him as Coloured not Black. His Coloured son can't live in a Black area with his father so he had to give the boy up to a stranger. That was ten years ago. The boy was ten years old at the time. His father hasn't seen him since. He watches every face on the train twice a day, looking for his son. He consoles himself that he'll have had better schooling as a Coloured boy."

He pushed the plate away and a waitress removed it with a smile.

"Mabel here is Coloured as well. She thinks her grandfather was Danish. She stays at Riverlea, which sounds bucolic but isn't. It's a Coloured area, so closer to town, but there's no electricity at her house. Still, she went to school and can read and is quicker at adding up a bill than I am. She asked me the other day what Keats meant by 'beauty is truth, truth beauty' as she didn't know anything that was both true and beautiful. She reads poetry at night by candlelight."

He held Ralph's arm.

"Do you understand what I'm saying?" he asked.

Ralph wasn't sure but he nodded.

"You are talking about apartheid, right?"

"I'm going to tell you two more things about apartheid. Take this information back to Shaftesbury and shout it from the tower of the grammar school chapel."

Fred thanked Mabel as she brought him coffee.

"Firstly, no one teaches white kids how to be racist. They imbibe it, unconsciously."

"And the second?" asked Ralph.

"The second is more worrying."

He drank some coffee.

"There's nothing different about white South African kids. Given the same circumstances all kids would be racist, anywhere. Kids in India, or Iran, or Indonesia. Apartheid is a rotten system, but the white people in South Africa aren't more rotten than any other people in the world. That is the worry."

He raised himself heavily from the table.

"Do you still want the job?"

Ralph started, there and then, his first illegal employment in South Africa, working the cash register in the restaurant of The Diplomat hotel alongside Indian, Black and Coloured South Africans.

*

Ralph quickly learnt that The Diplomat was unusual and probably unique, catering for foreign businessmen, 'Honorary' white citizens like the Japanese, and visiting dignitaries from the neighbouring African countries that the South African government felt obliged to be cordial to. All of them stayed at The Diplomat. As the despondent liberal owner miserably commented with near tear-filled eyes, the authorities tolerated it only because it kept all the rotten eggs in one basket.

"What do you mean?" Ralph asked him.

"A Nigerian selling oil, or a Kenyan buying electrical transformers, needs to stay somewhere. The government allows them to stay here with us; that way it keeps all the foreigners who are likely to be critical of apartheid in one place."

Some unsuspecting white South African visitors, often sent as a joke by their more informed friends, found it too much. Most, although often scathing in criticism when it came to paying the bill, found themselves secretly enthralled by the novelty of Indians in managerial positions and African heads of state in ceremonial dress.

Tramps, the basement club of The Diplomat, took all of them by surprise, even those from outside the restricted confines of South Africa. Fred laughed as he proudly explained it to Ralph.

"Sex between men is a crime in South Africa, Ralph, and I have the only gay bar in the country."

He smiled delightedly, pleased at the endless frustration it caused the authorities.

"They always try and shut us down but they can't because we know the rules. It's not a crime until sodomy occurs, so no doing it on the property."

"Doing what?" asked Ralph.

Fred smiled and patted his shoulder.

"You are a long way from Shaftesbury, Ralph," he said.

At weekends a succession of effeminate white South Africans in drag would fill the hotel foyer day and night, waving and blowing kisses as they lounged in reception to the serious plainclothes policemen outside photographing them through the glass doors. Ralph was young and lean, pretty with boyish good looks like a young thin male model for expensive Italian shirts in a fashion magazine. He fought a running battle to get to the restaurant without proposition, not helped by the night manager letting them all know in unnecessarily loud Afrikaans that Ralph stayed at the Young Men's Christian Association hostel. The YMCA filled the corner of Rissik and Smit Streets, an easy walk for Ralph to and from work, and he never felt at any risk walking home late at night as police patrols scoured the whole of the Central Business District. The YMCA was cheap and convenient, but he hadn't considered the gay angle.

A guest at The Diplomat from Hong Kong, Chinese but travelling on an Irish passport thanks to a costly education in Dublin, and a little older than Ralph, had made a suggestion.

He had befriended Ralph out of loneliness while visiting South Africa to sell barbecue tongs. *Braais* were big in South Africa. They must need lots of tongs, or so the thinking went as he explained to Ralph the logic behind his grand scheme. He would clean up in the South African tong market. He helpfully told Ralph that dressing for work in a borrowed suit and his old school tie only made him look like a schoolboy and that might be making things worse, an explanation to Ralph's problem that he had never considered.

*

Snyman stood in the waiting room of a private clinic in Sandton, relieved when Elanza came out of a treatment room and walked down a corridor, her hand on the wall. He went to follow her but a doctor held his arm and stopped him.

"Leave her. A counsellor will go with her. Can we talk?"

The doctor and Snyman sat underneath a poster for antenatal classes.

"Are you family?"

"She has no family. I'm her trustee."

"I see."

The doctor hesitated.

"I'll talk freely, just as I talked to her. I think she has a new disease. We've only just given it a name. In the States it's been called lymphadenopathy because it's often associated with swollen glands. More recently it's been known as KSOI because of an associated incidence of a skin cancer called Kaposi's sarcoma. We called it GRID and then AID, Acquired Immune Deficiency. We now refer to it as AIDS. It's important to recognise that it's acquired rather than inherited. We added the S because it is a syndrome with several manifestations, rather than a single disease. I think Elanza has probably had it for some time."

He stopped for a moment and looked at the poster.

"I'm afraid there is no cure. And her vision loss is quite advanced."

"Vision loss?"

"Yes. For some time Elanza has been experiencing flashing lights, blurriness, photophobia. She is losing her sight rapidly. It's called cytomegalovirus retinitis, CMV for short. It's an inflammation of the retina caused by infection with a herpes virus. About forty per cent of the worldwide population has it. A healthy body can fight it off but if the immune system is compromised then it's a problem. I would expect rapidly progressive deterioration until near blindness. You must understand, we are only at the beginning of our understanding about the disease. Useful work is being done in France at the Pasteur Institute. There are high hopes for new therapies."

Koos Snyman realised he knew nothing about Elanza, other than the balances of her bank accounts.

"When did she get it?"

"It's hard to say. The progression isn't well understood. It may have been three or four years ago; that's when she started having problems with her eyes. Say 1979, not before '78."

"How?"

"Up until recently we only saw it in homosexual men."

"The gay plague?"

"We don't call it that. We are seeing it in other groups now: haemophiliacs who receive blood, intravenous drug users."

He hesitated.

"Prostitutes."

Koos Snyman thought about Elanza.

"Three or four years ago?"

The doctor nodded.

"She would have been twenty-two or twenty-three, a difficult time for her. Her father died in '76 when she was twenty."

He had to know now.

"How long?"

The doctor remained silent.

"How long has she got?"

"I'll tell you what I told her. The simple answer is I don't know. I would expect her to lose her sight nearly completely. Thereafter we'll provide the best care."

"Can you answer my question?"

"I apologise. I can't be accurate. There may be a range of environmental factors influencing the outcome. Some reports predict an average of nine to eleven years from infection. It's just guesswork. I told her between five and eight years. Not much more than that unless some new drugs are developed and approved."

*

Elanza drank and bartered pills in Tramps, the basement club of The Diplomat. The man whom Nels elbowed, his nose splinted and his face bruised, avoided her. Her vision seemed tunnelled and she wasn't sure if she should blame the Pinks or something the doctor had told her about her failing eyesight. A man in a flowing neon blue ballgown danced with an impossibly slim youth of Asiatic appearance. Both started to zoom away and then come close, except that when they did she could only see the middle of them, the rest in black shadow. It scared her. She fought to see their faces and their feet at the same time. Brushing aside a man with drooping gold earrings like long snakes, she stumbled upstairs to the restaurant, feeling her way along a countertop.

Ralph liked to talk to the restaurant manager, proud and thin in his suit, encouraging him to teach him useful isiXhosa words, or so Ralph believed. They could have been anything. Mabel the waitress would relax and laugh listening to them, an improbable scene unlikely to have been played out in public at any other place in Johannesburg at that time. Elanza barged past them and fell into a booth against the wall. The waitress looked at Ralph and shook her head. She'd been reading a torn and yellowed *King Lear* secretly at night and her lunchtime discussions with Ralph, whom she naturally assumed to be knowledgeable on all things Shakespearian, had allowed her to feel comfortable enough to warn him about a drugged-up white hooker.

Ralph asked the woman if she wanted something. She didn't speak at all but stared at him as though blind. Ralph suddenly laughed, thinking about his earlier literary discussion with Mabel the waitress. He wondered about her real name. Mabel didn't sound very Xhosa.

Elanza slumped and mumbled.

"I know; I bet you'd like a cup of tea," he said. "Mabel."

For Elanza, who couldn't remember when she had last eaten, the sugar in the tea hit as fast as a mainline. Through a dark fog she saw Ralph holding the restaurant manager's arm and all of them smiling and laughing. Ralph went over to her, pleased to see that she sat straighter in the chair.

"You aren't from around here," she slurred. "Where are you from?"

"Far away. Bet you can guess."

She muttered something in Afrikaans that he couldn't catch, a frequent problem for him. Often Afrikaans speakers would call down for room service and he'd apologise, saying as politely as he could that he didn't understand them. Many put the phone down. Why Fred the owner never said anything to him remained a constant curiosity. He imagined any negative comments might be balanced by positive ones from the very English-speaking guests who would bark at him in a Churchillian tone, calling for more gin and wondering if he knew the best form of defence. Attack, he'd tell them, and they'd all laugh.

Elanza tried to focus on him.

"What's your name?"

"Ralph."

"Is that Ralph with an f or ph?"

"With an R."

Later, after Ralph had bargained a taxi to take her home, and with the familiarity of known obstacles she had guided herself to bed, she couldn't remember when she had heard something so funny.

*

At The Diplomat the next evening Ralph beamed with pleasure at the girl he'd given tea, surprised when he saw her sitting in the restaurant. He looked closely at her. She may have been seven or eight years older than him. She looked hunted, exhausted and drowsy, as though a pack had been chasing her. Something struck him about her eyes, the pupils as small as pinpricks. They looked beautiful, yet empty, cold and lifeless. A tall drink stood beside her and Ralph guessed it wasn't the first. The menu had been pushed determinedly almost off the table.

"Where is Ralph with an R?" she shouted across the restaurant.

Ralph went over to her.

"Nice to see you again. Can I get you some more tea?" He looked at her drink. "Or something stronger?"

"Stronger."

Through the evening she sat, scratching, looking around abstractly.

"Ralph with an R, you can get me a cab now."

As she left she stopped and listened to Ralph chatting with the staff by the cash register.

"What are you talking about?"

"I'm telling them I'm going to be a movie star."

Ralph hadn't yet seen Africa, a nagging concern to him. He had a non-transferable flight home in just under three months' time and until then felt trapped by poverty in The Diplomat. His fortune changed with an advertisement on a noticeboard at the YMCA asking for people to appear in a commercial. At an audition the director had asked him to describe a situation where he could do something that he'd always dreamed of doing. He then had to build it up, finally exclaiming the words 'I did it'.

For Ralph it had been easy to talk about learning to fly. Alone in a dark room he had talked up his story, shouting out, "I did it!" The agent had seemed delighted. Ralph hadn't realised that along with looking for actors they had been looking for inspiration. The client, a national savings bank, claimed the subsequent shoot as entirely down to him.

The agent promised him US dollars in cash, just ten per cent of what she would charge the production company but both knew Ralph hoped to work illegally. He had little room to negotiate and he didn't care.

"Oh right. A movie star."

"Tomorrow. Filming at Kyalami. Want to watch?"

She's sad, he thought. *Lonely, like me.*

"Do you earn a lot being a movie star?"

"Yep, four hundred dollars. In notes."

"Do you know me?" she said.

It wouldn't be the first time that someone had been nice to her just to get their hands on her money, after their hands had been everywhere else. Then she hesitated, thinking of what tomorrow had in store for her. A day mostly in bed, frightened to move for fear of hitting something, until the need to drink compelled her.

"I'll come if you bring rum. But I won't watch."

Ralph laughed.

"Okay. Where shall I meet you?"

"You'll have to come to me. Take a cab. Fifty Hyde Park, Sandton. We'll take my car from there. But you'll have to drive. You can drive, Ralph with an R?"

"Sleep well. It's an early start." Ralph shouted after her, "But what's your name?"

She didn't reply and the cab door shut with a slam.

FIVE

R alph drove nervously to the motor racing circuit near Midrand, shuffling tomato juice coloured vodka and cigarettes for Elanza. They arrived late but filming at Kyalami had been delayed. The star of the show, an aeroplane, had gone tech, as had a lot of the production crew. They sat close together on the grass, Elanza holding his arm and asking questions about the set that he wasn't qualified to answer, until he left her to go to work.

"How did it go?" she asked him.

"*Befok.*"

Elanza laughed, the sun warm on her back.

"*Befok?*"

"Yes. It's Afrikaans."

"I know what it is, *bokkie*. Have you said your line?"

"Said it. Don't know if they'll use it. They've got some pros here. That guy over there. The one with perfect hair that looks like he lives in a home furnishings commercial."

Elanza looked up through dark glasses but in the wrong direction.

"And him too," said Ralph, following her stare. "Toothpaste. He's used for teeth apparently. Bent as a nine-bob note. They call him the tooth fairy."

She laughed.

"I've got to do it in Afrikaans now. *Ek het dit.*"

"Well, they definitely won't use that, you *domkop.*"

"*Domkop?*"

"Yeah, it's Afrikaans."

Elanza, surprised at how much she enjoyed his company, thought she should get out more during the day.

She touched his arm. "You want a drink or something after this?"

"I want to eat."

"Eat?"

"Steak."

He repeated his new word as a runner called him to stand pointing at the sky and: "For God's sake, don't look at the camera this time."

"*Domkop.*"

*

Ralph fed Elanza from his plate, like a child, small squares cut from a slab of meat crowned with an asparagus tip. She wanted more wine but when she lifted her glass she seemed unable to find her mouth and a bead would escape and run down her chin.

"What are you doing here?" she asked.

"I stayed with a relation near Cape Town and then I thought I should see a bit of the country before I went home."

Ralph held more meat on a fork in front of her. She opened her mouth obediently and let it melt on her tongue.

"When did you leave Cape Town?"

"05.54. Train number 3205 from Platform Ten. Got me to the beach at Strand about an hour and a half later."

"At 05.54. That's very funny."

"And then I walked to East London."

Elanza swallowed and choked.

"You walked from Cape Town to East London?"

"Yep. I tried to keep as close to the coast as I could."

"How far is that?"

Ralph thought as he ate.

"It's hard to say exactly. I mean, I know what it is by road but a lot of it turned out to be beach walking. I think I walked just over 1,100 kilometres."

"How long did that take?"

"Thirty-five days."

"You walked for over a month?"

Ralph pushed the plate away. Elanza had eaten well but the steak had been huge and it had beaten him.

"Walking is really interesting. You think it's just putting one foot in front of the other. Walking is a science. People have got doctorates and spent their careers studying it. There's something called the preferred walking speed."

"And what is that?"

"A Scottish mountaineer calculated it as five kilometres per hour plus an hour for every six hundred metres of ascent. Naismith's Rule."

"No, *domkop*, I mean what is it?"

"Oh, well it's the speed that humans choose to walk if there are no other outside influences. People with poor vision walk slower."

Elanza looked at the floor.

"Really?"

"Yes. You need to be able to see to know what speed to walk at."

Without realising it people put a value on their time and therefore have a need to get where they are going as quickly as possible. They want to do that efficiently, using the minimum of muscle force and the least stress on their joints. To achieve that goal people look around as they walk and subconsciously monitor the rate that things go past, regulating their pace by speeding up or slowing down. Ralph wanted to explain it to her but something made him stop.

"Five kilometres per hour?" she asked.

"Yep, five kilometres per hour."

"You have a very practical way of looking at things," she said.

"Is there a better way?"

Elanza didn't know. She usually tried not to think about anything. Life improved when she spent it asleep.

"So, how far did you walk in a day?"

"I averaged just over thirty kilometres."

He would walk from six in the morning for four hours as hard as he could and then take a short break. Before lunch he would continue at a more leisurely pace for two hours and then rest most of the afternoon. Around four he would start again, just ambling along, and look for a place to spend the night well before six.

"I did about seven or eight hours a day but only at four kilometres per hour."

Elanza laughed.

"Only four?"

"Naismith didn't allow for temperature and walking on sand."

She smiled. He looked very young, so serious and matter-of-fact.

"What route did you take?" she asked encouragingly.

"I took the commuter train for about fifty kilometres from Cape Town Central, just to get out of town, and then from Strand I walked down the beach."

The town of Strand continued urban and developed as far as Gordon's Bay. From there the road hugged the coast in between the sea at False Bay and a ridge of hills, and it became quieter. There had been a beautiful beach at Kogel Bay with mountains behind, and all the way along the coast to Rooi-Els whales swam close inshore.

"I took loads of pictures."

A track led to a beach at Pringle Bay and then to the lighthouse on the point at Cape Hangklip and onward to Betty's Bay until it merged with the road to Kleinmond. He remembered a long beach past a lagoon to Hawston and then the road again to Hermanus before he rejoined the beach to Gansbaai. He crossed the Uilenkraal River mouth and ran down a pearly beach layered in shells.

"I found a magnificent shell. I've no idea what lived in it."

Ralph pulled a napkin towards him and looked for a pen.

"I'll draw it."

"Just tell me about it."

"Circular, about the size of a big dinner plate, with a wide opening, and it spiralled into the middle."

"Probably a nautilus."

"Hmm. A nautilus."

He followed the coast then as closely as he could down sand and rocky paths to the Quoin Point Peninsula, with waves crashing on the Cape of Good Hope and the surf booming all the way to Die Dam. From there the beach and coastal path continued to Suiderstrand, with shipwrecks washed ashore at L'Agulhas, then on to Struisbaai and more beach to Arniston. Still on the beach he went through some sort of military range with lots of construction work on the other side of the dunes.

"There were some really unusual structures at this place on the beach – Overberg. I wish I hadn't lost my camera."

"Don't worry."

"I think someone stole it and the camera bag from my room at the YMCA after I'd gone to work. It had all my film rolls in it as well. I thought about selling it. Some American guy said he'd give me a 150 dollars US. Olympus: a great camera. Dad gave it to me for my eighteenth."

Elanza tried to drink more wine.

"Shame. Where then?"

"Then I took a shore path to Cape Infanta and then the Breede River, where I nearly got eaten by a shark."

She spluttered Merlot.

"A shark!" she exclaimed.

Ralph nodded. From there it became wild past Jongensfontein and Still Bay.

"I went in some caves at Blombos. They'd found the earliest evidence of fishing there. Apparently a hundred and forty thousand years ago man fished."

After Mossel Bay it became harder to follow the coast, especially from Glentana to Wilderness and then again beyond Knysna, as more farmed and private land ran right down to the sea. From St Francis Bay he could follow the coast again to Port Elizabeth and then more beach all the way through Port Alfred to East London. He'd had enough by then, not of walking but of loneliness.

"I got a ride with two hippies. We stopped off and climbed some mountains in the Drakensberg. I can't remember much about it. We were all high on hash cakes."

"Where did you sleep?"

"On the beach mostly. One night before Plettenberg Bay I slept in a forest under a giant California redwood tree."

She moved closer to him, their thighs touching, and pointed in the direction of the wine bottle. Ralph filled her glass.

"Tell me about the shark."

He had walked over some heathland at Cape Infanta and could see an estuary at the mouth of the Breede River, with the town of Witsand on the other side and the beach beyond leading east. He sat and studied the river for a long time. It looked wide and fast flowing, although when the wind blew out to sea and the tide was coming in, small choppy waves bounced about but wooden branches on the surface didn't seem to be moving. The wind and current had cancelled each other out. He walked a little way upstream to where the river narrowed at a boat park. He found an old wooden pallet lying about and dragged it to the water's edge.

"I planned to swim across the Breede River, pushing my rucksack on a pallet in front of me."

Just as he entered the water two men sweeping a yard had run towards him shouting, waving tired brooms.

"It turns out there is some sort of shark that can live in fresh water called a bull shark."

"A Zambezi shark?"

"Yeah. That's right. Bull shark or Zambezi shark. A huge one had been caught at that very spot about two days previously – massive thing about four metres long."

The men had probably saved his life.

"How did you cross the river?"

"I had to walk up to a village called Malgas."

He found the closest place he could cross, about thirty kilometres upriver.

"It took me all day to get there. They had a strange floating bridge and you pulled yourself across."

He then walked thirty kilometres down the other side to get back to where he'd started but on the opposite bank. It had been a two-day, sixty-kilometre walk instead of a ten-minute, two hundred and fifty metre swim.

"I should have swum across. It would have been worth the risk."

She didn't know the Cape. Her life had been spent on the farm and then lost in town, just about as far from the sea as you could possibly get in South Africa. She would have liked to have walked a beach, to search for shells with Ralph.

"You are crazy."

"Not crazy, just stupid. I must have someone looking over me. An angel or something."

*

Elanza lay across a chair, her head on Ralph's shoulder. A day in the sun, the fresh air, the food, had tired her. She'd drunk very little.

"What made you think of the learning to fly trick anyway? For the TV commercial I mean."

"It's something I grew up wanting to do. I guess because of my dad."

Elanza listened to him.

"Dad loved aeroplanes."

Ralph put his arm around her shoulder. He thought of his father and those times while growing up when, without meaning to, he had been selfish and rude, arrogant and ungrateful.

"I think that if I learnt to fly, if I could take him flying just once, in some small way I could pay him back."

She thought of her own father and the emptiness since his death. She didn't have a sufficient level of clarity to realise that she had been filling the emptiness with something, anything, drugs, sex with men she didn't know, stronger drugs.

She felt the tears well up inside as she pulled him to her and hung on him, feeling him, hoping that with him she would be strong enough to face another night of sadness in the dark.

"So, is there a girlfriend at home?" she asked breezily.

"Oh yes. She's still at school. Getting the grades to go and study medicine."

"She's clever, then."

"Very. In all sorts of ways. Good at science but reads poetry. Plays the cello. Great gymnast."

"Been seeing her a while?"

"Since the summer, our summer back home. Last summer."

"Is she pretty?"

"Lovely. Do you want to see her picture?"

"No."

She kissed him. He felt tense all over, as if someone might punch him.

"Do you love her?"

Ralph thought for a moment.

"It's not easy. I have competition: Jupiter."

"Unusual name."

"Not for a retriever."

Elanza laughed and looked at him.

"Have you made love to her?"

67

"No. Of course not."

She stroked his leg through his jeans. Like a puppy, she thought, out of the round cuddly stage but unsure how to control his limbs.

"Have you made love to anyone?"

He looked away.

"Okay. This will be interesting," she said.

She reached inside a drawer on a little round table.

"Here. Use this. I'll show you."

*

Elanza met Snyman at his office in Sandton the following day, just as he'd returned from lunch. Although sober she had been sick in the night, quietly without waking Ralph. Now she felt weak.

Nels sat there too, calmly picking his teeth.

"What's he doing here?" she asked Snyman.

He didn't answer and Nels smiled a dirty grin.

"Elanza, I want to reassure you that you'll have the best treatment."

Snyman surprised Elanza. He seemed genuinely concerned for her.

"Since your father died, the trust has been prudently managed. There are no money worries. Whatever you need—"

She didn't let him finish.

"I need to make a will."

Awake in the night, hearing the boy sleep beside her, the reality of what the doctor had told her would happen to her had suddenly made her scared. Elanza had worried about it all night. She lived alone, had no living relatives.

"I don't think we need worry about that, Elanza."

She ignored him.

"We'll need a witness," she nodded towards Nels.

"Really, Elanza."

"I'm not a *bakvissie*. I want the sole beneficiary to be Mr Ralph Phillips of Gillingham, Dorset, England. That's Ralph with an R. Two copies. Draw it up. Excuse me."

She took herself to the bathroom, feeling more nausea.

Lizette had typed up a document before she returned, sweating and weak.

"Stamp," she said to Lizette.

Elanza took a cab and asked it to stop at a post office. The driver put the envelope addressed to her doctor in the box. She couldn't think of anyone else, she had no one else, no family and no one she could trust. She definitely didn't trust Koos Snyman.

*

Nels started looking at Tramps, in the basement of The Diplomat. Snyman wanted him to find out about Ralph Phillips so Nels looked where he knew Elanza had been. As he entered from the street bleary customers stared at him and the bar went quiet but, disappointingly, he hadn't needed to beat the barman. In the upstairs restaurant the staff had been nervous but loyal, the waitress contemptuous and angry with the manager for talking to him. He called Snyman after walking to the YMCA.

"He's gone."

"Already? She probably slept with him only last night."

Snyman looked at the phone on his office desk, next to the picture of Danelle in a bikini on a beach in Mauritius.

"We need to find him."

"Find him alive?" asked Nels.

"It doesn't matter. If he had an unfortunate accident it might make things easier."

Nels grinned into the phone.

"Get some help if you need it," said Snyman.

He did some calculations on a large desktop machine, the numbers blinking at him rapidly.

"Blackie was very cautious with the money. He didn't do much with it."

Snyman remembered the arguments he'd had with Blackie about how it should be invested, the schemes he could have participated in, the sure-fire stocks bound to win. Blackie had ignored him.

"Elanza inherited just under seventy-seven million dollars when Blackie died. It's kept pace with inflation at least. I'd say Ralph Phillips of England is wandering around sitting on about a hundred and thirty million."

"Dollars?"

"Of course dollars."

Nels said he knew someone.

*

Nick Roux enjoyed Sunday mornings at the Dutch Reform Church in Waterkloof Pretoria, a quiet time after the strain of a week travelling around the country, firefighting one mess after another and playing catch-up in the office on a Saturday. Sunday was a time for God and family.

His home on Albert Street, almost exactly halfway between the church on Dey Street and the Pretoria Country Club, made it easy for his wife: close to good schools for the kids and in a comfortable safe neighbourhood. He had an easy commute to work at the Bureau for State Security, as it had been known but was now the National Intelligence Service, reporting to Gabriël Lombard, doing important work as Deputy Director of the South African spy agency, work which he tried hard to forget at weekends.

He recognised the square man waiting outside the church and sighed. He turned to his wife.

"You carry on and I'll meet you at home."

Roux's wife looked with distaste at the man ruining her husband's weekend.

"There's tennis for the girls this afternoon at the club. Don't forget."

Roux watched them go.

"Mr Nels, one-time Military Intelligence liaison with the Bureau for State Security. Good morning. What are you doing here?"

Nels had driven early on a Wednesday morning from Johannesburg to Pretoria only to find that Roux was away on business and not expected back until the end of the week. He'd kicked his heels sullenly in Snyman's office for three days, leering at Lizette, knowing he'd be sure to find Roux at the Sunday service.

"Good morning to you, sir. I'm doing private work now. Hopefully useful. And rewarding." He smiled and gave Roux a business card: "Research Associates."

"Yes, I've heard about that."

Roux wasn't impressed. Nels had been on the rough side of Military Intelligence, and Roux remembered him from one particularly brutal operation, aware there had probably been many in Nels' career.

Military Intelligence had always been a problem and continued with unauthorised renegade activities; it was suspected of a recent bombing against the African National Congress at their headquarters in London. Lombard had been furious, and the National Intelligence Service had been forced to deny any knowledge, which had been easy as they'd known nothing about it. Roux assumed that Military Intelligence had done it in retaliation for an attack on a military base outside Pretoria in which two British citizens may have been involved – exactly the type of unapproved vigilante operation that Lombard and Roux had been tasked by the Prime Minister to prevent.

"How can I help you on this fine Sunday morning?"

Roux hoped Nels would take the hint.

Nels smiled.

"We need help following a boy. We need to keep tabs on him. There's a girl who's dying."

"That's very sad, Nels, but National Intelligence is not a detective agency for girls who have lost their boyfriends."

Nels looked around at the affluent, ordered community.

"There's a catch. The girl's father was a very good friend of PW Botha. They went right back to the *Ossewabrandwag*. Doing that sort of favour for the Prime Minister might help any man's career at NIS."

*

Nels walked to his car. He hated the way things seemed to be developing in South Africa. For a long time there had been a jockeying for influence among the three security agencies. The Bureau for State Security, the South African Police Security Branch and the South African Defence Force Directorate of Military Intelligence had been fighting each other for influence, budget and control of their own agenda.

All three had been operating covertly in South Africa, on the African continent and overseas, with very little cooperation. It became well known to everyone from the Prime Minister down that duplication and intra-service rivalries could destroy South Africa's security apparatus. The recent overhaul of BOSS to NIS would hopefully bring some control to these three internally warring factions. Nels became aware that of the three agencies NIS would soon become the most favoured, the first among equals. Its remit, to supply analysis, interpretation and intelligence, made it more appropriate for a 'negotiating' President. To Nels, negotiation resembled a word for treason. He believed in destabilisation using force so that if negotiation became inevitable it could be from a position of strength. It wasn't an opinion held only by Nels.

Nels opened the car door and sat in the seat watching the church empty. Cheerful families, privileged, confident and safe, smiled and held hands. Nels looked away. He didn't feel part of their contented world full of light and hope. The South Africa Nels inhabited was one of darkness and despair.

He decided he wouldn't enjoy working with Roux again, but NIS had foreign assets he couldn't otherwise access. An agreement between the three security agencies at the naval headquarters in Simon's Town had made NIS responsible for intelligence gathering outside South Africa's borders. He could have asked colleagues at his employer Military Intelligence to help but he now had his own reasons for distancing them from his out-of-office hours' activities at his second job with Research Associates, especially in relation to this case of a missing English boy. He didn't want any of his colleagues at Military Intelligence to know about the millions of dollars at stake and to muscle in on this, the golden opportunity he'd been waiting for. He'd let NIS find him using their resources but make his own enquiries domestically within South Africa, in case the boy hadn't yet left the country. He knew just where he'd start as well: with Elanza. It was the one thought that cheered him.

*

The road from Pretoria led north-east after the town of Naboomspruit, towards Messina and Zimbabwe. Little traffic ran on a highway built deliberately straight and wide with no central barrier so that any part of it could be used by fighter jets as an emergency runway – an impressive example of cooperation as civil government projects considered military implications. Ralph remained uncertain if that made it impressive or xenophobic.

Either way, it made for easy walking and Ralph smiled, enjoying himself. He had left the city behind and seen giraffe in the wild. The sun shone warmly on the side of his face and he had four hundred and fifty dollars in his pocket, four hundred of it from a single day's work. He wasn't a virgin.

He stepped cheerfully towards the border.

SIX

Director General Gabriël Lombard, an academic, had an accurate moniker. At age twenty-seven he had been the youngest Doctor of Economics and Political Science ever appointed at the University of Pretoria, and in the National Intelligence Service he'd become known as The Professor.

It had been an unlikely appointment by the new Prime Minister, PW Botha, when he poached Lombard in 1979 to lead the Service, newly born from the mire that the old one had created for itself. Botha realised that South Africa needed a more analytical intelligence gathering security service, and the new National Intelligence Service delivered a fundamental shift in emphasis from the old Bureau of State Security's core belief of 'state' security to one of 'national' security. State implied the apartheid state. National meant everyone, of whatever colour, in the nation.

It may have been exactly because he didn't have any experience in that field that Botha recruited Lombard for the job. Lombard's deputy director, Nick Roux, had come from BOSS but had always been moderate, religious and experienced in national security. Lombard and Roux were a combination that worked well. Lombard, by nature a hawk favouring entry into war, had been convinced when he'd joined NIS that the might of the powerful South African military machine would prevail over security threats foreign and domestic. Roux, more dove-like than Lombard and opposed to military pressure, had educated him with products from the research department, and now Lombard couldn't be so sure of his conviction. There didn't seem to be a military solution. He'd quietly realised, as had Botha, that the only way to find lasting security in South Africa required them to develop a nation. At some point that would mean renegotiating the South African constitution to include all South Africans in the nation, irrespective of race.

Lombard, accustomed to taking Roux's advice, quietly closed his office door so that no one could hear them.

"Let me get it straight, as I'm going to have to take this to the Union Buildings, to the Prime Minister."

Lombard closed his eyes as he talked. He hated Monday mornings.

"The Prime Minister's oldest friend sold his farm for a fortune to a prestigious state-owned company who paid in valuable US dollars to an offshore bank. I'll leave out the bit about the Prime Minister being responsible when Minister of Defence for agreeing the purchase price. We can't stop the money being sent out of the country as it's already gone, but until now we had hoped to have some influence on what it might be spent on as all the beneficiaries are here in South Africa. Am I right so far?"

Roux nodded.

"His old friend died and left the entire fortune to his only relation, a drug addict daughter who is now dying of some sort of plague. She has made a new will with a slimy lawyer who is trustee to her father's estate and has left it all to an English boy she met, just once, and who has since disappeared. We guess that the Prime Minister's dead friend, being *Ossewabrandwag*, would not have been happy with this and we want the Prime Minister to be aware that the sum of money is now huge. If things remain unchanged it will eventually be leaving South Africa for good and be outside of our control. We are going to put our best man on finding and following the boy."

He stopped.

"Why, Nick? Why do we need to follow him? No one has done anything wrong. This girl can leave her money to whomever she likes."

"Our view is that it is South Africa's money. We are concerned because we believe Mr Botha might prefer that the money benefits South African taxpayers, the same South African taxpayers who paid for his friend's farm. We need to find the boy in case the Prime Minister decides he wants to have some influence over the outcome."

"What do you mean?"

"In case Mr Botha wants us to encourage the boy to use his inheritance for the good of South Africa."

Lombard, unconvinced, looked puzzled.

"How would we do that?"

"I'm not sure. That's why we are sending our best man."

"Hmm… Do you have anyone in mind?"

Roux tossed Lombard a file.

"He's the best I've got."

Lombard looked at the front and read the name questioningly.

"Angel Rots?"

Both knew Angel's file. In 1971, aged twenty, and partly thanks to the Open Universities Statement of 1957 but mostly because of his British passport and money from his mother, he had attended the University of Witwatersrand in Johannesburg, an undergraduate studying African Languages in the Faculty of Humanities. In 1974 he did a masters and in '76 a doctorate and, despite a commitment to spend nineteen days a year with part-time soldiers in Citizen Force, a life in academia and teaching lay in front of him.

He became a formidable linguist. Of the family of 535 Bantu languages in Africa, 250 were mutually intelligible. Angel spoke ten of them with fluency and together they covered much of central and southern Africa: Xhosa and Zulu in South Africa; Swati in Swaziland of course; Shona and Ndebele in Zimbabwe; Bemba and Tonga in Zambia, where there were seventy languages alone; Kirundi, similar to Zulu, in Burundi; a Bantu vernacular in Rwanda; Ganda in Uganda; and Swahili in Kenya. With Arabic he covered the continent from Cape to Cairo, and with English from Sherborne School, Afrikaans from the Parabats, and Spanish from his Puerto Rican nanny, much of the world.

In 1977 his Citizen Force commitment increased to thirty days a year, and in 1978 aged twenty-seven his teaching was unexpectedly disrupted by a call-up for the Cassinga Raid, a South African airborne attack on SWAPO deep inside Angola, arguably a 'jewel of military craftsmanship' if there hadn't been six hundred defenceless refugees slaughtered. Certainly, what Angel witnessed changed him. He didn't easily settle back into teaching and academia. The sheltered University of Witwatersrand never felt the same again.

Aged twenty-nine his PhD thesis came to the attention of Nick Roux, who poached him in February 1980. Angel was pleased to go. He had no obligation to Citizen Force while with the National Intelligence Service. At the new NIS, the old Bureau of State Security's aggressive offensive operational and policing role had changed to one of analysis and evaluation. Many of the BOSS personnel left but Angel thrived in the newly named Central Evaluation Unit.

Angel had never been used in an operational capacity by NIS and Roux often thought that was a waste, believing he could have been very useful to them in the field as a protector of apartheid South Africa. He'd had a near Special Forces background, had become an expert linguist, and he had a genuine alternative identity thanks to his place of birth. More importantly, he looked black.

"Send Rots up," Lombard asked a secretary.

*

In an office below, an overweight senior officer from the South African police talked to the wall.

"I don't understand. All along they've been chattering about next year."

Angel sat on a desk then stood up abruptly. As usual, when in a meeting with colleagues, all deferred to him when he spoke.

"He's not saying that," said Angel. "Play it again."

An operator rewound a tape and played a man talking above background traffic noise.

"He's in Lusaka. We're lucky. They're talking Bemba. From time to time they slip into some local dialect we can't catch."

They looked at Angel as he gave a wide hand gesture, a professorial wave as though giving a lecture.

"He could be using one of fifty or more other Zambian Bantu derivatives. We don't have them all."

The tape played the sounds of someone singing far away, a lorry changing gear, faint voices.

"But here. Stop. Again."

The operator stopped and rewound. On the tape the man said "*kusasa*".

"That's not Bemba. He's getting excited and slips up. That's his own language. He's talking Zulu. He didn't mean to but it slipped out."

A junior police officer scratched his head, mystified.

"*Kusasa?*"

His chief answered.

"*Kusasa*. Tomorrow. *Kak*."

The phone rang and the tape operator picked it up. He looked at Angel.

"It's the Director General's office. He wants to see you."

"Christ," said Angel. "Excuse me."

The police officer laughed.

"Tell him you thought the police were beating up your dad."

Angel smiled but said nothing, aware that his dad had probably been whiter than the pink faced policeman.

*

Angel entered Lombard's office, surprised to see Roux there.

"Sir, if it's about that morning on the way to work…"

Lombard stared at him, his fists balling, his eyebrows raised and twitching through stress and fatigue.

80

"What morning? Is that the morning you put two policemen in hospital?"

Roux tried to cut Lombard off but failed.

"When was that, Nick?" Lombard asked.

"Nearly three months ago. Before Christmas. I've already talked to him about that, Professor."

Roux looked at Angel.

"We have a job for you."

Angel tried to be polite.

"I'm working on the Lusaka thing right now. It's…"

Roux held up his hands.

"It's a field job. We need you to find someone."

Angel shrugged.

"I'm an analyst. I'm with Central Evaluation, not Operations."

Lombard, already thinking of bigger problems, looked around the room like a don interrupted from contemplating an intangible problem by a dim student, as if he'd just realised he wasn't in the senior common room at Tukkies anymore, surprised to find himself sitting in a government office.

"That's all we're asking you to do. Evaluate where someone might be."

Lombard looked at Roux.

"I've got some questions, Nick."

He turned back to Angel.

"You did two years' national service at a time when you could have done only nine months. Why? Nowhere to go?"

"Something like that, sir."

Lombard looked at the file.

"Lots of training."

He looked at Angel.

"It must have been especially tough for you."

"They made it tough for everybody, sir."

"And then Cassinga."

Angel said nothing.

"Why?"

"I'm sorry?"

"Why? Why do any of it? Why here? Why South Africa?"

The question had been asked before, often in basic training, every day during the rigours of parachute selection, constantly since Cassinga; a question asked by comrades, demonic instructors, probing personnel officers, students. He'd often asked himself the same question and it troubled him that he didn't know the answer. It became an untranslatable problem, like Finnish or Hungarian, a language not related to any other. The Army had been school but with slightly stricter masters; had been friendships forged in the dust and heat. The Army had been all he'd known.

"I don't know, sir."

At one point during selection they'd been given a twenty-four-hour ration pack to last for three days of extreme physical tasks, the strongest of 'wannabes' giving up from pain and hunger and exhaustion.

"It must have been the quality of the food."

Lombard looked at him. Angel held his stare.

"Who is the 'someone', sir?"

Lombard sighed.

"A *soutie* kid."

Angel laughed to himself. Lombard hated the English. He had used a derogatory term for someone with one foot in England, one foot in South Africa and their salty penis dangling in the Atlantic Ocean.

"Of course. A kid."

Lombard put on his glasses and started to read a blue file.

"Why?" Angel asked.

"Does it matter why? It's a job. Find him. Follow him. Tell us."

"So, that's the job, sir?"

"That's the job."

Angel looked at Lombard.

"With respect, there are better people at this. I'm doing important work."

Lombard looked out of the window. He was tired and spoke softly, as if to a tutor group rather than a lecture theatre.

"The kid is going to inherit money. A lot of money. South African money."

He looked at Angel and spoke more firmly.

"I need a linguist and I need someone who can..." he hesitated, "blend in. You blend in."

Roux smiled. Angel looked at him, puzzled.

"Blend in where?"

Roux made a wide gesture with his arms high.

"Africa," he said.

*

Lombard knew that he and Rots were academics, neither of them politicians. He understood that was a naive analysis as everyone played political games at work, pursuing promotion and influence and power. Everyone except Rots, and that troubled him.

"Can you give us a moment, Rots?"

"Professor," said Angel, respectfully.

"Doctor," said Lombard.

Lombard threw Angel's file on the desk.

"Did you know that our Prime Minister, The Big Crocodile, once joined a group sympathetic to the Nazis?"

Roux snorted.

"Yes. I hear he gave it up quickly when they started losing."

A demonstration had started in the street outside, police vehicles growling like dogs. Lombard looked at Roux. They had become friends while colleagues and trusted each other's judgement.

"Is he really the best you've got?"

"Rots is a fine analyst and an exceptional linguist. I wish I had more like him. We can listen in on the ANC and others in Lusaka and elsewhere, but the enemies of the state rarely do us the courtesy of plotting and scheming in Afrikaans."

It was a true but insensitive point to make with Lombard, who hardly even spoke English. Unfamiliar with it he found himself nervous and worried about looking like a fool. As a boy he'd been taught not to speak the language of the conqueror.

Lombard picked up the file again. Outside, police reinforcements began arriving in smoky black trucks.

"Is Rots safe? Is counter-intelligence happy with him? I mean, he's technically a dual national; he must have friends over there. Didn't he even go to school with the buffoon Cameron, that British Security Service guy responsible for non-proliferation? The *vet fokker* we met in New York."

To Lombard, their opposite numbers in British Intelligence were as much the enemy as the ANC.

"What do they call him?" Lombard asked.

"Jumbo."

"Jumbo the clown," Lombard snorted. "Well, the British would love to have Rots working for them on the inside at NIS. He would be priceless."

"His service record is exemplary. There's nothing to prove he's had contact with anyone in London, and the work I've had him doing is totally Africa-based and ANC-focused to make use of his language skills. Nothing overly sensitive."

Both Lombard and Roux knew that Britain's real interest was the state of South Africa's nuclear capabilities and ambitions.

"If he's the best you've got, you're going to need him. But that won't happen if he beats up police officers on the street."

"I have talked to him about that. I'll remind him."

"I don't think I'll bother the PM with this now," said Lombard. "There are more important things going on. Keep an eye on it and we'll see what develops. It seems rather a waste of Angel's time."

Roux wasn't so sure. He'd be sorry to lose Angel, his most useful member of staff, but somehow he didn't consider this to be a waste of anyone's time.

"It'll be good for him to know we can put him on more routine assignments. Let him cool his heels for a bit. Stop him fighting with policemen."

"When did all this come to light?" asked Lombard.

"Yesterday."

"A Sunday? You've moved quickly."

"I know. My wife's furious."

Roux had called the office from the club. He'd given them a name, Ralph Phillips, British, from Gillingham in Dorset, and gone to watch his daughters play tennis. Within an hour they'd called him back with a police surveillance report and talk of a bunch of photographs. He'd given up on his Sunday afternoon with the family and driven to work. Then it had become a bit busy. The duty staff had been expecting a quiet day but instead found themselves disturbing colleagues across the country and overseas. The Cape Town crew had to drive to Worcester to talk to Ralph's cousin, while Joburg found the hotel where the boy had been working and his digs easily enough but hadn't got to an Austrian printer called Franz until late at night. Pretoria had sat on top of grumpy police officers, and the London office suffered a three-hour drive down the A303 on a miserably cold and wet Sunday afternoon. The nightshift had pestered them for information every hour until daybreak.

"This English kid," Lombard said. "He's been wandering around the country. Is he working for anyone?"

"We wondered that. He fits the profile. He had an IQ test aged eleven and subsequently went to a grammar school, a selective system for the top ten per cent, intellectually speaking. Very quiet at school. Didn't stand out. Just a few close friends. A bit of a loner really; not a big team player. More squash than rugby. Content as a boy to wander on his own through fields with an air gun. Did some time in the Army Cadet Force in his early teens but gave it up when he found motorbikes and cars. He has an unfulfilled ambition to fly aeroplanes."

Lombard smiled.

"He sounds just like me."

"The Security Branch of the South African Police have shown some interest in him. There's a gay bar they monitor in the basement of the hotel he's been working at, illegally they have reminded me. They lifted his camera bag with film rolls from his room at the YMCA looking for pornography. I've seen the pictures. There's nothing much other than normal holiday shots."

"I expect the South African Police enjoyed the gay bar."

Roux smiled.

"I think he's just a lost kid, doesn't know exactly what to do with his life, wandering around hoping to find inspiration. And there's no record of the British using untrained youngsters. That's not to say that he isn't talking to a handler, maybe without even knowing."

"But talking to a handler about what?"

Roux had asked himself the same question. Ralph Phillips had been in the country for two and a half months. He'd stayed with a cousin in the Cape, walked most of the way to Johannesburg and worked in a hotel. He'd had no access to anything of interest.

"Exactly my thoughts," agreed Roux. "Without them being aware of it we've spoken to people he's been in contact with: the cousin, her employer, an Austrian national with whom he travelled from East London, the owner of the hotel in Johannesburg, the manager of the YMCA. The Austrian also told us they'd travelled with a homeless drug dealer and petty thief called Zac, possibly Zimbabwean. Neither us nor the police could trace him."

"You said 'nothing much' other than holiday shots."

Roux looked at Lombard intently.

"Ralph walked the coast from Cape Town to East London," Roux said and hesitated. "There were a disproportionate number of photographs of just two places. Over half the pictures were taken at Rooi-Els and Overberg."

Lombard remained silent for a long time, his hand on his forehead.

"So, this is the real reason you want to send Rots," he asked, finally.

"One of them," Roux agreed.

"The police say anything?"

"No. They wouldn't know the significance of what they were looking at."

"He walked through Overberg?"

"Right along the beach by the looks of it."

"Christ. You need to get on him."

Lombard looked out of the window, deep in thought. Policemen with batons and dogs stood resolute, four deep across the road, preparing to advance.

"What happened to the Zimbabwean? Zac?"

"He stole the Austrian's passport, Franz something, and got on a flight to Frankfurt two weeks ago. We asked the German BND to check. No one entered Germany under that name. They think he may have travelled on to Tel Aviv. I've just spoken to Lev at The Institute."

"Holy Christ."

Lombard never swore.

"The boy is just a tourist, travelling around," said Roux.

"You hope."

Lombard and Roux were aware how high the stakes had now become for South Africa, and Lombard frowned as he contemplated their position. For ultimate defence South Africa needed the ultimate deterrent, and their nuclear ambitions had started in 1948. South Africa's first uranium plant had opened by 1952 and uranium enrichment research continued through the 1960s, aided from clandestine studies by South African and Pakistani engineers at the University of Birmingham, England. By 1977 they had produced a scale model of a 'gun-type' device using non-nuclear material, followed by construction of bore holes in the Kalahari Desert in preparation for a full test. The problem of how to deliver such a weapon hadn't been resolved and became exacerbated by all fifteen members of the Security Council voting for Resolution 418, the 1977 United

Nations arms embargo. Lombard knew that it had always been planned to drop the weapon from an Air Force bomber, but the UN embargo meant South Africa's ageing Canberras and Buccaneers had become unreliable through a lack of spare parts and had become vulnerable to anti-aircraft defences. Missiles would eventually replace the tired aircraft. The small coastal town of Rooi-Els, across False Bay from Cape Town, had a secret rocket engine testing facility hidden in hills behind the beach and, when completed, the restricted Overberg Test Range on the beach east of Arniston would be a new weapons testing and missile launch facility.

Lombard shook his head and scratched through papers on his desk while he pondered the current state of affairs. Overberg planned to continue the testing of Jericho One, a single-stage five-hundred-kilometre-range Israeli ballistic missile designed in conjunction with the French aerospace giant Dassault back in the early 1970s. More importantly, plans were underway for trials of a new three-stage long-range ballistic missile based on the Israeli Shavit, development of which, as the Jericho Two missile, had started in 1977. South Africa had codenamed it RSA Three. The first stage alone would make a missile called RSA One, which would have a range of 1,100 kilometres and be able to reach Angola from mobile launchers inside South Africa. Adding the second stage to make the RSA Two would extend the range to 1,900 kilometres. It could strike the ANC headquarters in Lusaka. The full rocket should, on paper, be intercontinental after a low earth orbit and deliver a payload to New York or Moscow.

Lombard worried more about the ANC than imagining South Africa would ever send a rocket to the US or Russia. From Lusaka the ANC had organised a bombing the previous year against a power station in Durban that had paralysed industry in the area, followed by three separate sabotage attacks around the country. Not six months ago they had planned and executed an attack using Soviet rockets against a military base near Pretoria, not seven kilometres from Lombard's desk.

But Lombard knew that South Africa couldn't threaten to destroy the ANC in their Zambian headquarters until the missiles became operational. For now, the payloads, although originally designed to be transported by aircraft, were to be delivered not by bombers but fired like an artillery shell by a howitzer cannon capable of firing 'special' rounds to a target just fifty kilometres away. They hadn't yet acquired the technology to do this and it was becoming increasingly difficult. The previous year the founder and president of Space Research Corporation, a Canadian company that straddled the Canadian and US border in Vermont, had been arrested for illegally exporting arms to South Africa in violation of United Nations' embargoes. They had been caught with falsified documents while shipping two howitzer cannons and a radar tracking system on board the motor vessel *Tugelaland* to South Africa via an island in the Caribbean. Lombard remembered the PM had been furious about it and they doubted that the necessary equipment would ever be smuggled into the country.

Unlike the Air Force bombers, both the Canadian cannon and the Israeli missiles were 'viable' nuclear weapons delivery platforms. It was Monday, 1st March, 1982, Armscor just a month away from producing South Africa's first deliverable atomic bomb. They called it Hobo.

Roux, aware of what he had been thinking, tried to reassure him.

"He's just travelling."

"Well, he's found something while travelling around," Lombard said. "And I'm not talking about the money. You most definitely need to get on him."

Lombard thought for a moment. Outside, the police appeared to have the rioters under control.

"Do you think he knows about the money?"

An unanswerable silence filled the room.

"And if something should happen to him, who gets the money? The estate managed by the lawyer?"

Still silence.

"I should give Rots some of the details," said Roux. "The boy has got days on him but he's on foot. Rots has just got to find him and keep us informed. Anyway, we'll have a chance to talk to the boy when he comes back to Johannesburg to fly home."

"Say nothing about the photographs," said Lombard seriously. "To anyone."

He then smiled.

"And tell Rots—"

Roux interrupted him.

"I know. I'll tell him to blend in. I hope this kid blends in too because without knowing it he's just become a big fat target for some very unpleasant people."

Roux opened the door but hesitated and turned around.

"There's something else, Professor."

"Yes."

"There's another reason why I think it would be best to use Rots for this."

Roux passed a black and white photograph to Lombard.

"More of the boy's holiday snaps?"

"No, these are different. They came from the *Heining*. A routine counter-intel investigation."

Lombard looked at the picture. It had been taken in the countryside, somewhere by farm buildings with rocky hills behind – a black man talking and a white man listening intently.

"Where did they take this?" he asked.

"Shelter Rock, out near Harties Dam. Apparently he likes to go hillwalking at weekends. Usually alone."

"Pelindaba?"

"Near there."

Lombard studied the photograph. The black man had long hair, the white man as well, but full and wild, like a mane that matched his unkempt beard.

Roux gave him another photograph, an enlargement showing only the white man.

Lombard looked at it and waved it at him.

"We obviously know one of them, but the white guy? Who is he?"

Roux sighed.

"I looked hard at the picture and something about him rang a bell. We don't have a definite ID but we think he's British, and the Austrian we've been talking about confirmed that it's the man who called himself Zac."

Lombard stood at the window. The demonstration had been broken up. White smoke, a gas full of tears, drifted down the street.

SEVEN

ngel found the Pretoria Country Club in Waterkloof and through the main entrance saw Roux with some cheerful friends. Sullen girls dressed as French maids and a thin tired barman gloomily polished glasses.

A security guard with black peaked cap, black uniform and glossy black boots, but everything else about him very white, put his hand on Angel's chest as he walked towards the bar.

"Where do you think you're going? Side entrance for deliveries."

Angel swore at himself for his thoughtlessness. He expected that Roux's summons to the club was really to discuss his future in the Service after the unfortunate incident with the policemen. He didn't need any more trouble.

"I'm sorry, sir. I'd forgotten."

The guard stood at attention, flexing his height by rocking forward onto his toes in an effort not to be looked down on.

"Forgotten?" he said. "You've forgotten The Reservation of Separate Amenities Act?"

Angel knew it only too well. Municipal areas, including beaches, and all public transport, and public services like hospitals and schools, were all reserved for a particular race, with a pecking order of efficiency of service and quality of amenities dependent on skin colour.

"White, Coloured, Indian, Black, we all have our own places," the man explained helpfully. "This isn't Johannesburg Zoo."

The zoo and its lake had been established by a special deed that didn't permit racial segregation. It was one of the very few public spaces in South Africa open to all races.

Angel stared at him, annoyed at the man's stupidity, trying to control his anger which was expanding like a heated gas.

"I'm sorry, sir," Angel repeated. "I thought the law only applied to public places, not private facilities that one had been invited to."

The man leant forward, bent stiffly at the waist like an RSM on a parade ground, his head tilted up at a fat neck.

"Are you one of those clever ones we hear about? Are you Coloured? Educated?"

He spat it out like an offence had already been committed.

Roux noticed Angel and came from the bar.

"It's okay," he said to the guard.

The guard glared at Angel.

"I'm sorry, Angel," Roux said. "We'll talk over here."

Roux led Angel into a beautiful garden. Orange, yellow and deep red *clivia* took shade under the trees among white *grandiflora* with yellow and mauve markings planted en masse. Elegantly tall *arum* lilies with long broad dark green leaves towered over them, while Pincushion *protea* gave a proudly South African touch.

"What shall I do? Pretend to be picking weeds?" asked Angel.

"Very funny."

Angel looked around. An old white lady loudly admonished a black waitress for forgetting something.

"Old Mrs Jeppe," said Roux. "Some relation of the founder."

"Okay," said Angel, keen to leave, "brief me."

"What do you know about Safoil?"

Angel looked at him.

"Go on," he said.

"The Saudi oil crisis in 1973 started it all. Egypt and Syria attacked Israel."

Angel nodded.

"Yom Kippur."

"Right. The US then supplied arms to Israel, and the Organization of Petroleum Exporting Countries countered initially with a seventy per cent price increase and then an oil embargo. In the end, the price of oil went up four times. We have no oil reserves at all and South Africa finally realised its vulnerability due to its reliance on imported oil. The Minister of Defence saw it as a strategic catastrophe. No oil means no jet fuel for fighters and no diesel for tanks."

"And the African hordes with communist help rolling over the veld," said Angel.

Roux nodded.

"Did our nuclear weapons programme really kick off at that time?"

Angel, like everybody, had heard rumours. He'd heard that they were now close to building the first deliverable bomb, that one had already been tested in the South Atlantic, that they were working on weapons safety and delivery systems, possibly missiles.

Roux looked away, considering a lifetime of secrets. He thought about his own mantra, 'Intelligence is the truth well and timely told'. He didn't consider now to be the intelligent time to tell a truthful answer to that question.

"I know nothing about that."

He continued slowly, tapping nervously at the bridge of his glasses.

"Encouraged by the government in the 1920s and '30s, a pioneer in the Transvaal Coal Owners Association did a doctorate at Imperial College London about the carbonisation of South African coal. It's possible to turn coal to liquid, producing high-grade fuel, through gasification using the Fischer-Tropsch process. Although developed in 1923, and used in World War Two by Nazi Germany, the patent remained the property of a British company. We bought the rights to the process after the war, and a new South African company, Safoil, formed in 1950 to make synthetic fuel. South Africa has no oil but it does have huge deposits of coal and water, the two raw materials required. Safoil has invested 2.3 billion rand, equivalent to 3.4 billion US dollars, in production facilities called Safoil Two and Safoil Three, and a township, a new town called Treilea. Safoil estimated that it needed 37.3 million tons of coal a year, and plenty of water, so the new production site needed to be close to both resources."

Roux paused and picked at a flower. Little *vygies* covered the dry areas and rock gardens with large clumps of upright flame-coloured red-hot pokers beside the pond they stood next to. He pushed his glasses up his nose and inspected the flower, turning it around in his fingers and tilting his head to examine it.

"In comes 'Blackie' Swart, an Afrikaner farmer born in 1916 who owned Wensvolle Farm, 150 kilometres east of Joburg. The farmhouse, Roodhuis, stood in the middle of a square block roughly eight kilometres by eight kilometres, or 6,400 hectares. I've seen the paperwork – 7,472 morgen, the old South African measurement of land area. Whatever that is. Probably something to do with how much land a man could plough in a day with a horse... or something. Water came from the Groot Draai Dam. The farm conveniently sat on top of the most extensive coal deposits in South Africa. Luckily for Blackie, he and PW Botha, at that time the Minister of Defence in BJ Vorster's government, had been friends for a long time. Both their fathers fought together against the British in the Second Boer War. Both of their mothers had been interned in British concentration camps. Before World War Two both joined the *Ossewabrandwag*, a very right-wing Afrikaner nationalist group sympathetic to the German Nazi party. When Allied victory in Europe looked certain, Botha gave it up and found God and politics, and Blackie went to farm Wensvolle. He had a daughter, Elanza, who became his sole relative when he was widowed."

The flower Roux had picked lay crushed in his palm, his fingers stained. Roux rubbed his hand down his trouser leg and kicked a small stone off the grass. Angel watched him with curiosity. They were colleagues at work, but he'd never been to his boss's home. Angel wondered about Roux's own often-talked-of garden, his wife, the children photographed jumping ponies, winning tennis trophies, and proudly displayed on Roux's desk. Angel imagined, sadly, that he'd never meet them, never admire the potted *agapanthus* collection he'd overheard so much about.

"Safoil Treilea Townships Limited bought Wensvolle from Blackie in 1974 for ten thousand US dollars a hectare: sixty-four million dollars," Roux continued. "A lot of money at that time certainly, but the land cost less than two per cent of Safoil's total investment in Treilea town and Safoil Two & Three. Blackie died in Joburg in 1976 on the day the first resident of Treilea moved into his old farmhouse Roodhuis."

"Making Elanza a very rich little girl," said Angel.

"Exactly. I'm told her estate is now worth a hundred and thirty million dollars. Blackie's lawyer Koos Snyman became her guardian and trustee to her estate. He didn't do a very good job. Elanza drank, drugged and whored her way through the end of the '70s. She's recently been diagnosed with some new terminal disease and is now all but blind. They're calling it AIDS. She's been given a maximum of eight years to live."

Roux took a breath.

"So, she then gets this lawyer Snyman to make a will."

"And leaves it to who?" asked Angel.

"An English boy she met in a hotel in Joburg. She hardly knew him."

"Why?"

"Why not? She had to leave it to someone. She has no family."

"And where is this *soutie*?"

"The kid? We don't know. He's gone walkabout."

Angel finished it for him.

"In Africa."

*

"And how did we become involved exactly?" asked Angel after a pause while he thought of Africa, the dangers a lone white boy might encounter.

"The lawyer Koos Snyman uses the services of a company called Research Associates. We think it's a front company for deniable Military Intelligence operations. To be more convincing the company advertises for business as private investigators, tracing debtors, finding missing persons, that sort of thing. The company gets to keep the proceeds from any genuine work they pick up even though it's staffed by Military Intelligence personnel and funded by the Directorate of Military Intelligence. I've known the guy who runs it for a few years. He worked for DMI, probably still does. He was their liaison at BOSS when I worked there. His name is Cornelius Nels. He came to me for help."

Angel looked away, stunned. There could be two men with that name.

"Do you know him?" asked Roux.

"No. You keep me locked up at work. I don't get out much. Nick, can I ask a question?"

Roux nodded and looked at him keenly.

"What is the security issue here?" Angel asked.

Angel Rots had always been his protégé. Roux had maintained a firm conviction that in the future Angel would make an important contribution to the country. Roux thought it a valid question but remained quiet.

"So what if she left her money to the kid? That was her choice, right?"

"The issue is that the money had never been intended for an English boy. It was South African money."

"Is that it?"

"Look, Angel, you know how the game is played. The National Intelligence Service, our employer, needs to make sure that the Prime Minister uses us as his first choice for security information and that he comes to The Professor and me when things get tough. In this way NIS can control what information he is given, factual information based on quality research which will be of long-term benefit to the nation and not reactionary inflammatory self-serving claptrap from the hawks at Military Intelligence or the thugs from the Security Branch of the South African Police."

"We are trying to gain favour with the Prime Minister?"

"Yes, if you like to put it that way. We're proposing to look after the best interests of the dying daughter of his old friend, and recover a ton of taxpayers' money, to gain favour with Mr Botha. It's one small thing among many that we're doing to convince him that we are the pre-eminent supplier of security information."

"Are we helping this Nels character as well?"

"No, we're keeping Cornelius Nels completely out of the loop. He's working for the lawyer and he came to me for help to find the boy, but I have no problem whatsoever in taking information from Nels and paying him nothing in return."

Angel put his hands in his pockets.

"Is this punishment for being a bad boy?"

"What?" said Roux.

"The policemen. Am I being sent out of the way before you sack me or something?"

Roux sighed.

"No, Angel."

"I couldn't help myself, Nick. They had no need to beat that guy in the street. It was so unnecessary. Something should be done about these people."

"You are the best I have and I need your help, Angel," Roux said. "But what you did to those policemen I would term uncontrolled and unprofessional. You know the rules. We see this sort of thing all the time. You should have just walked on by."

Angel looked away around the garden. There was a vibrant orange and blue flower like a crane's head with a crown of feathers. He pointed at it.

"*Strelizia*," said Roux. "This isn't punishment, Angel. This is an important mission which will be of benefit to the Service. Take it seriously and do it well."

Roux looked at him earnestly.

"And be the grey man, Angel, the one no one notices."

Angel held out his arms and looked down his body.

"The grey man. Me?"

They both laughed.

"Okay. What do you want me to do?" Angel asked.

"Until you hear otherwise, find him, keep us informed and look after him."

"Look after him?"

"Protect him, so that we know where to find him, and if the Prime Minister wants us to we can try and influence the outcome."

"Does he need protection?"

"He's a naive kid, wandering around on his own. It's a cruel world."

"Wouldn't it be better if he just had an accident out there in this cruel world and disappeared?"

"If that happened we might have even less influence over what happens with the money. The lawyer is ambitious. He'd probably just do a bunk. It would be easy for him: the money's already out of the country. And Nels would sell his grandmother for a slice of the pie."

"Who is the boyfriend?" Angel asked.

"The English kid? I don't know a lot. You'll have to dig about for more background than this."

Roux gave Angel a file, the slim total of the information

that Roux had acquired from the police and his own research, without, as Lombard had insisted, Ralph's photographs, or reference to them.

"Elanza might be a good place to start. She's the key. Get to know her. Make friends with her but do not disclose our involvement to anyone, neither Elanza nor the boy when you find him, or anyone in your department at work. I'll find somewhere for you to use as a base."

"Will she even talk to me?"

Angel thought about the daughter of an Afrikaner farmer born in 1916, a one-time member of a very right-wing nationalist group and with a name like Blackie Swart.

"Will the colour thing be a problem?"

"I doubt it. She's very nearly blind. She'll never know."

*

Nels, excited at the thought of going to Elanza's exclusive house in Hyde Park, Sandton, had found her at home in a white open-plan living room, lots of pale leather and chrome and glass, the floors a washed wood. All the furniture had been pushed against the walls. She coughed and staggered across the room to the kitchen as though nearly blind.

"Hello, my pretty," said Nels.

Elanza couldn't see him but recognised his voice.

"Piss off."

"I only want to have a little chit-chat."

He walked across the room towards her.

"Your new pretty boy Ralph. Where is he?"

"Ralph? I've no idea. He left heading north, but where, how and why he didn't say."

Nels believed her.

*

Angel walked from the train station through the wealthy Hyde Park neighbourhood looking for Elanza's house. Although only sixty-two kilometres from Pretoria, and the train supposed to take an hour, it had taken ninety minutes and had been a longer walk from Sandton Station than he'd thought. Late and lost, he looked around for numbered sign boards. He saw a few happy smiling faces in costly European cars and many tired sad African faces waiting at bus stops.

Angel whistled. Number Fifty looked a very impressive property. He'd seen such places in magazines – flat roofs on square pillars, all white, the walls green glass, the pool black not blue. He noticed two vehicles standing in the drive as he walked up to the house.

*

"Do you just like pretty boys," Nels asked her, "or would you like a real man?"

Elanza had always been proud and was now angry.

"I can't see one."

Nels laughed and crept over to her quietly. She couldn't see him but she knew he must be there. It made her nervous. He moved closer, staring at her with their faces nearly touching. Elanza looked around wildly.

Suddenly he clamped his hand around her neck. Her hands tried to pull his away and he bent forward and kissed her hard on the mouth. He stopped and let her go. She swung a fist at him but he'd been expecting it. He swatted her arm aside and pulled her over face down on to the couch and held her with one hand on her back. He pulled off her shorts with his free hand, and behind her got himself ready. She started screaming.

"You can't. I'm sick. You know."

"What can I say?" he said. "I'm a risk-taker. That's where the fun is."

She struggled until he put one hand between her legs, and then she stopped, lay still and lifted her bottom up.

Nels, excited now, whispered to her.

"You little whore."

The door opened and Nels looked up to see a large man standing in the entrance to the room. Angel dropped his hand to a fire extinguisher on a wall bracket just beside him. He pulled it off the wall and held it, filling the doorway.

EIGHT

Angel thought Nels hadn't changed at all: a filled-out version of the Army training instructor he well remembered, a man cruel and sadistic like a cancer, something malign. Angel despised him and the girl, their privilege to live in such a place and yet behave as farm animals.

Nels stopped and let Elanza go, pulling up his trousers hurriedly. She wasn't the first woman he'd tried to rape but he didn't need spectators, or witnesses. He shoulder-barged Angel as he walked out.

"You have a go," he said.

Angel felt relieved he hadn't been recognised, that he'd been just one of the forgettable legion of recruits, white and black, that Nels had abused in his ignoble career. Angel went to Elanza and sat beside her on the couch. She looked around vacantly.

"I'm sorry to have disturbed you."

"I'm not," she said.

"Are you okay?"

She nodded and coughed at the same time.

"Friend of yours?" he asked.

"He works for my lawyer. His name's Nels. Who are you?"

"My name is Angel Rots."

"Did my lawyer send you too?" She spat out his name: "Snyman."

"No. He doesn't employ me."

"He employs that pig Nels."

"I work for an old friend of your father's. Snyman contacted us and we wondered if there was something we could do to help," he lied.

She didn't believe him.

"Which old friend?"

"An old friend from before the war. Your father probably never mentioned him."

She sorted herself out while listening to him.

"You sound odd. Your Afrikaans is terrible. You sound like a fucking baby."

Angel thought all Afrikaans speakers sounded like babies but he didn't like to tell her. It sounded like a baby's language, baby Dutch, certainly compared to Arabic. Now that was a real language.

"My mother is in England. I grew up in London."

"And your father?"

"He's from here."

Angel looked around the room.

"This is a beautiful house," he said.

Elanza moved away from him.

"Is it?"

"Have you lived here long?"

Elanza had lived there since soon after her father had died, since Snyman had thought it better for her to be in town, to make it easier for him to keep in control.

"A while."

"Can you tell me about Ralph?" Angel asked.

"Why? Did Snyman tell you about him?"

"I want to help him. Your father's old friend wants to help him."

Elanza banged her fist on the arm of the chair in frustration.

"That bastard. Snyman has no right to tell people about my private affairs."

Angel said nothing, waiting for her to compose herself.

Elanza tried to light a cigarette with shaking hands, moving her head around to catch the flame. Angel took her hand and guided it to the right place.

"Thank you."

She smoked quickly, her head bobbing slightly up and down.

"Are you still here?" she asked him.

"Yes. Take your time. I've nothing to do."

Elanza was curious. His accent was weird and untraceable, notable for its contrast to Nels'. Unlike him this man Rots sounded compassionate and kind-hearted.

"Tell me about yourself," she asked.

"Same as everybody. I joined the Army. I went to varsity. Now I'm a teacher."

"Teaching what?"

"Languages. But not Afrikaans."

She laughed.

"And what did you do in the Army?"

"I was an interpreter. Spanish."

"What bit of the Army?"

"Parabats."

"Oh, tough man. You should have gone with that other bastard. Talk about old times."

"About Ralph," said Angel patiently.

She remained silent, pensive.

"Tell me about the Parabats," she asked. "Was it tough like they say?"

"It's like they say."

He needed to build a relationship with her, to get to know her and for her to trust him.

"We were beaten down and then built up. It's the same in any army. Just more beating."

"How?"

Angel remembered doing eight hours' physical training every day, hard PT. They did fifteen-kilometre runs just to end the day after training. They would carry telegraph poles twenty kilometres. They'd drag tractor tyres around for hours then play rugby, except that they would have to use the tyre as a ball. He looked around the room and thought it cold, not cool.

"We each had a concrete block weighing twenty-five kilograms. They called it a marble. We had to carry it everywhere. And run, never walk, even from the latrine to the cookhouse."

Angel thought of his time in training.

"We had one instructor, renowned for being a complete psycho, who had a crazy tattoo on the inside of his forearm. He went to someplace in Simon's Town, drunk, gave the tattooist a picture of the Parachute Battalion cap badge, pointed to his arm and passed out. The tattooist did it upside down. It should have been an eagle in the strings of a parachute with the number one on it. Instead it looked like a jellyfish."

Elanza smiled.

"One recruit he hated more than the others: me. Maybe I looked different. He made me carry two marbles. Kept asking me: 'Why are you here?'"

Angel paused.

"Another recruit he made lie on his back and hold his marble above his face with straight arms. He left him there an hour. The recruit was a strong guy. He got impatient then so he kicked his arm. The marble fell on the guy's face. Fractured his skull. If he wanted you to quit he'd always find a way. Nearly always."

He stopped.

"It's rumoured he killed the tattooist. Went back the next night. Waited until closing time and then snapped his neck."

Elanza said nothing.

"So, why Ralph?" he asked.

"He was nice to me. Made me tea."

"Tea?"

"And he made me laugh. I asked if he spelt his name with an f or ph. He said an R."

She laughed again remembering.

"The only person who's been nice to me since…"

She stopped.

"Where was he going?" Angel asked.

"He wanted to travel. Africa. Foolish boy. He talked about seeing Victoria Falls."

"Vic Falls?"

"Yes."

Angel got up to go.

"Okay. Thanks. Anything I can do for you?"

"No. Yes. Come and tell me what you find out. Where he is. Don't bring him to me. I don't want to see him. I can't see him."

He made ready to leave but turned.

"I'm sorry I was late. The train," he held up his hands in exasperation. "I could have prevented it. I would have been here."

"Not your fault," she said. "You know you should have let him."

"What?" said Angel.

"Nels. You should have let him finish. I'd have killed him."

*

Nels, angry and frustrated, drove north. Lunchtime traffic around Pretoria slowed him but thereafter he drove dangerously fast, an inner rage at the thought of losing the boy, of being beaten, making him blind to the risk.

He calculated his chance of finding Ralph to be very low. The boy had left Elanza on 23rd February, eight days previously. Nels had no idea of Ralph's route or how he planned to travel. Ralph could be anywhere, most probably already out of the country. He hoped that the boy had stayed on foot. In that case it might take him ten or twelve days to walk to the border. Ralph could still be in South Africa, but not for long.

Clear of Pretoria he made Pietersburg in three hours on empty roads through fields of tobacco, cotton, maize and citrus, too early in the year to see the jacaranda in flower. For another hundred kilometres the endless N1 ran over a red landscape to the line of the Tropic, the Soutpansberg Mountains a hazy blur on the horizon beyond Louis Trichardt. Nels climbed slower now around hairpin bends and through tunnels, the empty Far North stretching towards the border with Zimbabwe. In the desolate countryside around him shy remote farmsteads, widely spaced, were quietly raising beef.

Nels had driven nearly five hundred kilometres in five hours and stopped the car at a sign that said 'Game Lodge'. He stretched, knowing he had only sixty kilometres to drive to the border, maybe two days on foot. A dirt track led to the Bakstaan Boerdery, a cluster of low blue roofs 1,500 metres from the road, a farm producing little except wall trophies for hunters.

A man shuffled slowly down the track kicking red dust, tired eyes never leaving his feet, and walked past Nels without looking at him.

"Hey, you."

The man didn't stop or look but carefully held a bucket brim full of milk with two hands to avoid spilling it and continued walking.

"Hey, I'm talking to you!" Nels shouted.

He had grey stubble and thick black arms and a shirt buttoned to the neck. Nels stood in front of him, blocking his way. The man looked in his bucket.

"I know you understand me," Nels said slowly. "What do you speak up here? Venda or some crap?"

The man said nothing, his eyes on the milk.

"And look at me when I'm talking to you."

Nels lifted his foot and kicked the bucket of milk. Half of it slopped over the pail so that the man stood with his bare black feet in a white puddle. He set what remained in the bucket down and straightened. His shoulders went back and he lifted his head, looking at Nels with his head on one side, his brow furrowed and black eyes staring.

"Don't you fucking look at me like that!" Nels shouted at him. "I'll kick your black arse!"

The man relaxed and took a step backwards out of the milk.

"You work around here?"

He nodded and looked back up the track.

"Have you seen a boy? A white boy on the road."

The man picked up the bucket as if making to leave.

"I know you understand Afrikaans. You'd better say something soon or the rest of that milk is going over your fucking head."

"Milking time," he said and looked down the road.

"What?"

"I came to do the milking and saw a white boy with a blue bag."

Nels smiled. Fourteen kilometres behind him, south of a track to Mudimeli, he had passed a farm by the side of the road. His map showed another farm the same distance ahead near a place called Mopane. There was absolutely nothing in between the two. They were in the middle of nowhere. A white boy alone on the road would be very unusual. It had to be Ralph.

"That's better. Now, what time is milking?"

"I come to work at midday."

"Which way?" Nels asked quickly.

"That way," he pointed to Zimbabwe. "Walking."

Nels thought quickly and looked at his watch. Five in the afternoon. Ralph must be close, maybe twenty or twenty-five kilometres up the road. He would have to be quick. There was only an hour and a half of daylight.

The man watched Nels drive away until the car blurred and disappeared. He picked up the bucket and stood in the middle of the freeway facing north, the direction the vehicle had gone. With a wide swing and a roar he threw the bucket, a white stain spreading over the African road.

He drove carefully, eyes scanning both sides of the road but found little to see. Straight tracks led to dusty red settlements set back from the freeway. Nels slowed and looked up each one. The whole country seemed deserted, no movement, no people, no cars.

At a pull-in, a halt for tourists by a giant baobab close to the road, nothing caught his eye: still no sign of life. Nels drove on. The road ran up over a small hill then wound down towards a dry river. Set down from the road stood farm buildings with stock-handling yards made of wooden posts and galvanised sheets, an occasionally used facility for cattle but now completely empty.

Nels stopped and checked the trip meter he'd re-set at the game lodge. It read twenty-four kilometres – about a five-hour walk. He checked his watch, the sun now low – less than an hour until it set over the wastes of the Northern Transvaal and Botswana.

He looked at the buildings and corral below him. The stockyards were uncovered but beyond them the setting sun hit the green roofs of open-sided cattle sheds. With no one around it appeared to Nels a perfect place to spend the night, quiet and sheltered. There would be water somewhere, cut off pieces of timber to make a fire, maybe facilities for staff when sorting or drenching cows. With a little searching and only slight pressure on weak bolts a boy might find a canteen, possibly tins of food left for the next muster, all unoccupied in the middle of nowhere.

Nels walked to the back of the car, watching the corral a hundred and fifty metres away and the buildings a hundred metres beyond. Nothing moved. He scanned the yards in the foreground left to right, and the buildings further away right to left. Down left right, up right left. Down left right, up right. He stopped and stared at a post holding the roof of the shed. The sun had nearly gone, the whole corral bathed red, but something a different colour leant against the roof support. Something blue: a blue rucksack. Nels, twenty kilometres south of Messina, South Africa's northernmost town, and just thirty-five kilometres from the Zimbabwe border at Beitbridge, had found Ralph.

*

Nels realised cheerfully that Snyman hadn't insisted that Ralph needed to be found alive. It gave him a pleasurable feeling he hadn't had for a long time. Nels knew a way to stop Ralph for good.

He raised the boot of the car and lifted out a large flat wooden box painted matt green, placing it carefully on the roof. It had two sturdy fabric carrying handles and three strong flip-over catches on the cover. Stencilled letters in white said 'L42A1'.

Nels opened the lid. The weapon inside was a long rifle and looked to be entirely made of wood. The wooden stock joined a wooden fore end with a hand guard of the same wood both below and above the barrel. The only gun metal visible was the trigger guard and at the very end of the barrel around the fore sight. It glistened like a polished branch in the last of the sunlight, treasured and well cared for, a favourite. It had started life back in '44 as a BSA No4, an old 'three-oh-three'. Nels liked to imagine its history from that time, the conflicts it might have seen, Malaya or Korea or Suez. It had definitely come to Africa for the Mau Mau Rebellion, which

Nels thought appropriate. In 1971 the most accurate of the old No4s had been sent back to Enfield in North London for conversion to the new standard 7.62mm ammunition. A wooden cheek piece had been added and a Rose Brothers mount to take the L1A1 telescopic sight. It had become a sniper's rifle.

Nels rested it on the roof of the car and spat on his hands, working the bolt backwards. He considered himself a purist but used .308 Winchester ammunition rather than 7.62mm simply because he found it easier to acquire soft-nosed bullets in that calibre. He fed a stripper clip of five into the streamlined ten-round magazine in front of the trigger guard and slapped the bolt forward. The rifle had never been designed to be a marksman's tool but a battlefield weapon. Nels wasn't concerned. He estimated the distance to the shed to be two hundred and fifty yards, half of the rifle's effective range.

Nels focused on the rucksack, then moved in an anti-clockwise circle in the deepening gloom inside the cattle building. A shape moved and then rested. Nels fired two rounds in six seconds, as quickly as he could work the bolt. He had become out of practice. He should be able to do two shots in four seconds, to fire thirty rounds in a 'mad minute'. He admonished himself, not for the slow time but because he knew straight away that he had been well off aim. Both rounds had fallen short by a long way. They sounded as if they had gone through the tin sheets on the side of the handling race, the corral structure rattling, a section hanging limply now at one corner.

"*Kak*," said Nels.

He knew what the problem had been and swore at himself for being impatient and careless. The scale rings on the telescopic sight were held in position by friction only. They often slipped in transit and needed re-setting. Nels held the top of a small adjustment drum to prevent it rotating and at the same time inserted the nose of a round into a recess on the scale ring, slipping it back with a sideways pressure to what he knew to be the zeroed setting.

He re-sighted quickly into the building. The shape he had aimed at had gone. He fired three more into the space where he imagined the target had been and fumbled a new clip of five into the magazine.

"*Fok.*"

That had been his second mistake. He knew now that he should have loaded a full ten rounds to start with. He took his eye away from the sight and looked around the farmyard.

"*Fok fok fok.*"

The blue rucksack had gone.

Nels raced down the slope through scrub, past the corral and into the cattle shed. There was no one there. The sun had gone, the inside of the building now almost dark. He walked to the back wall. Water ran from three tightly grouped holes in a cattle drinking trough and ran over an improvised bed of straw.

*

In the high-priced investment in Westcliff that he sometimes called home, Snyman thought about his life and about Danelle, unsure what they meant to each other. They'd been married when he made junior partner at Pretorius Venter Kruger in 1969. She'd been twenty-seven, he forty. They'd bought the big house in Westcliff six years previously, just after Blackie had died and Snyman had started business on his own. Everything seemed if not quite perfect at least comfortable, but over time his evenings working late in the office had become more frequent and the bags of empty booze bottles had become heavier.

Danelle had drunk a lot of wine and Snyman could tell it wouldn't be long before they started arguing. There seemed little he could do to prevent it. He had learnt a new Yiddish word from an elderly vituperative Jewish client, a derogatory label for an overly groomed materialistic woman. Looking at Danelle he thought she had to be *kugel*.

"Why are you so smartly dressed?" he asked her. "Every evening is a fashion parade."

"I've nothing else to do. I've no kids."

She wanted to fight now. She'd never wanted children but at times like this it became too tempting not to remind him that it was down to him – his inadequacy not hers. Snyman, familiar with the process, knew his Jewish ancestry would be next. This would be a repeat of a play they'd been to many times.

"You spend more time thinking about Elanza than me," she told him.

"Well, Elanza is paying for all this."

He pulled at her dress and ripped it off one shoulder.

"She's sick," Danelle said spitefully. "She's a dirty whore. I know about it. The dentist told me. I went for a polish. Dr van der Merwe said you can get it from blood. The Four H Club he called it… Haitians – well, that's no surprise, is it?"

Snyman imagined that made perfect sense to Danelle. It would be no surprise to her that a new disease should originate there. Where else would you expect it to come from? Snyman differed to her in his attitude to apartheid. He had been brought up with mild hints to an orthodox religion.

He knew of Jews who had become prominent in the anti-apartheid movement but he remained merely indifferent, his indifference entirely different to Danelle's fear.

"And then there's homos, hookers and heroin addicts," she continued. "At least she was only two of the four. You brought her here. What if we all get it? What would your rabbi say about that?"

"Don't be stupid."

At times like this it came as no surprise to Snyman to hear that South African males had the highest incidence of stress-induced heart disease in the world, and the world's highest per capita suicide rate. He wondered if they also had the greatest number of female psychiatric hospitals. He knew where another patient needed treatment – right there in his kitchen.

The doorbell rang and Danelle, staggering slightly and grateful of the opportunity to be acerbic and tarty, smiled at Nels and let him in.

"In here," said Snyman.

Snyman showed Nels into his office. Danelle looked after them but Snyman forcefully shut the door.

"Does Elanza know anything?" he asked.

"Not much. He went north. I looked."

"Did you find him?"

Nels had boxed his rifle and left the corral in the dark, driving slowly into town, but hadn't seen him. From dawn until midday he'd driven the fifteen kilometres between Messina and Beitbridge six times, slowly at first, becoming quicker as he became angrier. Ralph had gone.

"No."

"So, we'll leave it to your contacts, then."

"And when I find him? What do you want me to do?" asked Nels.

Snyman said nothing.

"I want twenty per cent of what you will have when Elanza dies."

Nels took Snyman's silence to mean he agreed and let Danelle show him out. She opened the door for him and let her ripped dress fall off her shoulder. Nels smiled at her and put his mouth close to her ear.

"I don't want you when you're drunk, sweetheart. I want you when you'll remember," he whispered.

Nels walked out of the door. He'd have her, but later. He thought of his share. Twenty-six million dollars. Yes, Danelle could wait.

SOUTHERN AFRICA

5TH MARCH TO 12TH APRIL, 1982

NINE

Ralph arrived at the border with Zimbabwe, tired after ten days' walking through the Far North, the Limpopo River and the crossing at Beitbridge in front of him.

He had been spooked two nights previously at a deserted corral, tin sheets banging and rattling around him. With the last of the twilight he'd crossed the main road and spent the night hidden below a riverbank, his bed the sandy bottom of a seasonally dry tributary. In the morning he'd looked around and seen the land bare and clear, as easy to walk on as the road. A direct route across country guided by a railway line would lead him to the border without having to go through the town of Messina, an ugly sprawling shanty already visible twenty kilometres away. It would save an hour. Heading due north around an escarpment he skirted the town by the edge of a hard-baked airport runway and re-joined the railway to Beitbridge, the sleepers echoing under his feet. His last night in South Africa had been spent miserably wet in another dry riverbed just three kilometres short of the border, which at four in the morning had filled with water after a shower and flooded him out, his belongings soaked inside his rucksack.

Over the bridge the road forked and Ralph had a decision to make. The road to the right led north and east to the Great Zimbabwe, a ruined city of five-metre-high stone structures standing without mortar and built by the Shona in the eleventh century. Ralph had picked up a tourist pamphlet at the border and read that it had taken three hundred years to complete. In the 1950s and '60s Ian Smith's Rhodesian government put political pressure on visiting archaeologists to deny that the Great Zimbabwe could have been built by African peoples. Ralph had read that, such was the prejudice of the time, Rhodesians needed to be reassured that black Africans couldn't possibly have had an advanced flourishing community in the 1100s, trading gold and ivory with China and raising cattle on a commercial scale, or build unaided the largest ancient stone structures south of the Sahara. The road from the ruins then led onward through Umtali to Mount Inyangani, the tallest peak in Zimbabwe, before continuing through Harare, the only recently renamed capital, and finally into Zambia north of Kariba. Ralph's guidebook said that from the top of Mount Inyangani one could look over beautiful red-leaved msasa trees and rocky hills full of wildlife and waterfalls far into Mozambique. Looking the other way, it had always been known for fantastic sunsets and called the 'World's View'.

To the left the road also ran north, but west through Bulawayo and into Zambia at Victoria Falls, over seven hundred and fifty kilometres away. Walking there would take nearly a month.

It had been a question hard to resolve. After bagging the highest peak in South Africa with the bearded Zac, the temptation to climb Mount Inyangani proved difficult to ignore, if he forgot about the very real risk of stepping on a land mine while walking anywhere near the Mozambique border.

Ralph turned left, unable to give up the once-in-a-lifetime opportunity of seeing the Zambezi River fall over a hundred metres at the world's largest sheet of falling water, Victoria Falls.

*

Angel had been given an office of his own in the basement of the Comitia building. Roux said that no one would see him and if they did they would think he worked as a cleaner. He didn't care. Roux had installed a phone, and Angel had lined the walls with maps stolen during night-time forays to other departments. The *Heining*, named after the Afrikaans word for a fence or hedge, wouldn't come down to the basement. They were a counter-intelligence division known for raiding other government departments looking for classified files left lying about, or even NIS's own offices after hours checking to see if desks had been properly cleared of secret documents.

Ralph's route from Johannesburg to Victoria Falls on the Zimbabwe–Zambian border hung on the wall in different scales and detail. A sleeping bag sprawled on the floor. Despite his South African citizenship, and NIS being his employer, Angel had been racially classified as 'Coloured', the only non-white person working in the National Intelligence Service. He lived in a unique and complex legal situation. He was a South African citizen by virtue of two years' national service in the South African Defence Force, a black man who had volunteered to join a white man's army. He was also a British citizen thanks to his place of birth, his British education and language skills the assets that had attracted his employer. This dual nationality made him an 'honorary' white person, but a foreigner would never have been employed by the state in such a sensitive position. Angel had to forego the significant privileges that his tatty blue British passport would provide him, not the least being that, thanks to The Group Areas Act, a Coloured person had to live in an area separated from white people. Angel had come to accept it. He liked his home fifteen kilometres east of where he worked, not that he saw much of it. The other Coloured people were friendly, hospitable. His NIS identification gave him authority to travel wherever he liked around the country, but where he lived remained controlled, making it easier to stay at the office. His white colleagues at work sympathised.

He hesitated before picking up the phone.

"Hey, Zelda. Angel."

"Hey, honey. Thought you'd been arrested."

Zelda worked full-time for South African Airways, administering overfly rights in their head office. It wasn't difficult work. To put additional pressure on apartheid South Africa, black African countries denied SAA overfly rights, forcing their special extra-long range but low passenger capacity Boeing 747s to fly uneconomic routes over the Atlantic Ocean and clear of African airspace. The routing at sea 'around the bulge' of Africa with a fuel stop at Ilha do Sal in Cape Verde added nearly a thousand nautical miles to the route. Although bad for business it made Zelda's day job easy. It remained only for Zelda to negotiate European airspace, a considerably easier proposition. It gave her plenty of time for her other job, working for NIS, an idea Roux had copied directly from Israel's Mossad. Working for El Al had for years provided excellent cover for agents of 'The Institute'. A note on Zelda's file at NIS read 'notably promiscuous' and Angel was always tempted to tell her.

"Angel, honey, I'm sorry. No hard feelings, right?"

They had been recent and spirited lovers. Angel vividly remembered how he'd felt at the time Zelda had left him – brief feelings of anger and hate that led quickly to a long lonely emptiness.

"You'll be okay. I mean, you're a good-looking man."

He'd never thought about it. Tough military training had sculpted his body into a hard angularness that hadn't worn off over time, like a creased origami figure. His face, finer than it should have been and stretched so that his big chin and forehead seemed too far apart, looked like a cartoon of a cowboy or a boxer.

"And so adventurous. You'll soon find a nice girl."

"A nice Coloured girl?" he asked.

"Angel, it could never have worked. You know that. We had some fun. A lot of fun. You are a strikingly powerful man."

"Enough, Zelda, please."

Angel knew she was right but that only made it more painful. It could never have worked – as well as being illegal. The Immorality Act banned sexual relations between white people and non-whites. Both of them could have gone to jail for seven years. He needed to put it behind him and concentrate on work.

"Do you have contacts at other airlines?" he asked.

"Maybe. What have you got?"

"I've got a name. And a route. Sometime in the next two or three months."

"That's a lot of tickets to look through."

Angel thought that if Ralph had planned on seeing Africa before he flew home, it was probably safe to assume he didn't imagine he could do that in less than two months. His flight back had to be sometime after two months and in time for the short British summer. That would tie up with a six-month visitor visa being issued to him on his arrival in December.

"Phillips R. Joburg to London. Start looking in May. Won't be after the end of June."

"You want the date of travel?"

"Yes. And Zelda… cover your tracks on this one."

"And what do I get?" she asked suggestively.

"More work."

Angel put the phone down. It rang immediately.

Roux sounded tired. Angel had no idea what he spent his time working on but it wasn't doing him any good. Zelda, who had a documented record of having sex with anyone she felt needed cheering up, would probably find a way to help him relax, he thought bitterly.

*

Angel went to Elanza's house and found her in the kitchen.

"Can you manage like this?" he asked.

"I have some help in the day. I need to try when I can."

She stood making a sandwich. She had a bowl of honey but while searching for a knife she knocked it over. She put both hands on the table and Angel worried she would cry. She looked very thin.

"I have some news," said Angel. "Ralph crossed at Beitbridge."

Roux had passed on the message. A flag that Angel had asked to be put on Ralph's name had surprisingly been acted upon by an observant immigration officer, but stupidly they had let him leave before consulting with NIS.

"I've asked them to let me know when he comes back through."

NIS requests were often ignored. He held out little hope that he'd be lucky twice.

"And I have his return flight details. I'll follow him to the airport."

Without doubt Nels would be there as well, he thought.

"He has a budget ticket. No changes allowed to the date of travel. No refunds. Elanza?"

She started crying. He went to her and she put her head on his chest. He'd had little physical contact with white women, just fleetingly with Zelda, and he wondered if simply holding her was breaking the law. He'd ask someone at work. They'd probably laugh. Nervously he held her until she stopped.

"Hope does not kill," said Angel.

She listened to him curiously.

"You smell odd too. You talk like a fucking baby and smell like one."

Angel had heard students at university and secretaries in the office saying, while considering him to be an exception, that black people smelt differently to white people. He wondered why.

*

On the road to Bulawayo there were few cars. A man wearing a creased tanned face and a business suit had stopped his vintage Jaguar to give Ralph a lift, but he had declined, enjoying the freedom of walking. He didn't want to hear the man's opinions on anything; he had some idea of how the conversation would go.

Zimbabwe had been an independent country for just two years, since April 1980. Ian Smith had gone and Robert Mugabe replaced him. It wasn't yet peaceful, even though the war between them had been declared over, and tension still existed between the two rival former guerrilla armies of the Shona and the Ndebele. A Methodist minister, Canaan Banana, became President. It was a ceremonial role. The real power resided with the Prime Minister, Robert Gabriel Mugabe. Mugabe had quickly established a one-party state and used a North Korean trained security force, The Fifth Brigade, to crush his political rival J Nkomo. Rumours of ethnic cleansing and mass graves of Nkomo's followers from the Ndebele tribe in Matabeleland abounded. Ralph thought an ex-Rhodesian sports car owner, probably on his way back from a meeting with his stockbroker in Johannesburg, wouldn't have an impartial view of the situation.

He walked on alone towards Gwanda, the capital of Matabeleland, a sprawling rural town of about five thousand people along a railway line. It was cattle country, an agricultural trading town. A factory made clay bricks from the heavy red soil. In size, shape and economic activity it resembled Ralph's hometown. The Mtshabezi River could have been the River Stour as it wound through Gillingham in Dorset, twelve thousand kilometres away.

An hour and a half walk out of the town, where the railway ran parallel to the Bulawayo road, a sandy track led west towards the river two or three kilometres in the distance. It looked like a good place for the night. The straight road led to a dusty crossroads with a simple square farm building, then onward to the river and beyond to the Matubo Hills and the Matubo National Park.

Ralph stopped at the farm building and looked around. It appeared deserted. A rough wooden door, swinging on one hinge, flapped against its frame. A sound like a muffled saw, or a cloud of flies, came from inside.

A man came from around the building and looked at Ralph, the whites of his eyes yellow in his black face. He carried a thick stick, knurled into a heavy knob at one end.

Ralph thought a cheerful honest approach might be the best.

"Hi. I wonder if you can help me please. I was looking for a place to camp tonight."

The man looked at him blankly, unspeaking, the club lying motionless against his leg. Another man, bare to the waist, came and stood by the man with the club, his white hands and forearms blooded red. He wiped them clean on a grey towel that said 'Sun City'.

"Did you look inside?" the white man asked.

Ralph realised he'd made a mistake. He shouldn't have stopped at the farm building but continued on to the river. He'd need to be more cautious in future. He deliberated running but the building stood at a crossroads of straight tracks with nowhere obvious to hide. A shiny new Toyota Land Cruiser parked by the side of the building had its engine running to keep the cab cool.

"Did you walk from Gwanda?"

"From Naboomspruit."

The man stopped cleaning blood from his arms and glared at him. It wasn't a look of friendly curiosity.

"It's a town 215 kilometres north of Joburg. I walked from there," Ralph explained.

"Are you alone?" he asked.

Ralph said nothing.

"Did you look inside the building?" he repeated.

The man walked towards him, still wiping his white hands.

"You know the conservationists want to protect them, to protect the 'environment'. But hey, we're part of the environment too, right?"

He glanced back at the black man with the club.

"We've hunted these animals for generations, for food and to protect our crops. Now we should save them? For who? For the recreation of a few privileged tourists?"

He looked at Ralph, his faded rucksack, his dusty boots and frayed shorts.

"Present company excepted."

He stood in front of Ralph now.

"You know the only way to conserve Africa's wildlife is to link it all together. The needs of the wildlife, the environment," he hesitated, "and the people."

He put his hand on Ralph's rucksack.

"Do you have a camera? Did you take any pictures?"

Ralph pulled the rucksack away.

"Of course not."

He needed a way out now; a camp somewhere down the road, anywhere but here, was suddenly very appealing.

The man looked at him curiously.

"Did the sight of blood upset you?"

"I didn't see anything. I needed somewhere to camp the night and this guy came out."

Ralph pointed to the black man, Mr Club Man, the Backpacker Killer of Gwanda.

The white man warmed to his theme.

"You know we aren't the problem. Some people want to shoot poachers on sight or to ban small farmers from 'slashing and burning' wildlife habitats. But you should look to yourselves first."

He poked Ralph with a red and white finger in the chest.

"Think of the demands you make on the developing world just so you can have a teak deck outside in the garden for your little drinks parties."

He pulled Ralph's rucksack away from him and threw it to the other man. He talked to him in Shona or Ndebele, or something. The man put down the club, pulled open the top and tipped the few contents onto the ground. He kicked them around with his foot and silently shook his head.

The white man nodded towards the black man with the club.

"If they found these local guys something better to do, something that would feed them, buy medicine for their wives and schoolbooks for their kids, then they wouldn't have to sell me rhino horn," he said.

He walked over and pushed everything back into Ralph's rucksack, picked it up and gave it to him.

"But it'll have to be something good. A kilogram of horn in Vietnam or China has twice the value of a kilogram of gold."

The two men got into the Toyota. The white man who had done all the talking smiled at Ralph.

"You're lucky. We don't need to kill you. If we were selling cocaine it would be different. We earn more money selling horn than drug dealing and without any of the risk. No one goes to jail for poaching rhino."

They left the way Ralph had walked, back to the Bulawayo road.

Ralph sat on his rucksack, watching them leave, now too late in the day to go anywhere else. He could walk down to the river and find cover there to hide in but he didn't think they would be back. He looked in the door of the building. He had been right about the noise, on both counts. Flies covered the corpses of six rhinoceros and sat in the blood that had come from their horns, cut off by an electric saw.

Ralph walked for four days from Gwanda to a camping ground in Bulawayo. He didn't have a tent and slept fitfully through thunderstorms until, dispirited, he sheltered in the laundry room and sat on top of the spin dryers to keep off the floor and away from snakes. He still had two weeks' walking to Victoria Falls.

*

Lombard and Roux met in a church neither had ever visited late morning in the middle of the week. They had arrived separately, with different alibis for their staff at the office. An elderly lady arranged flowers and smiled at them. They smiled back and waited patiently until she left clucking like an old hen.

"How's Rots getting on?"

Roux leafed through a prayer book, his head down.

"With some difficulty to be honest, Professor. He's playing a waiting game, expecting the boy to return here for his flight home."

"What's the problem?"

"Well, it's one boy and Africa is a big place."

Lombard straightened in the pew. He felt cold. Unlike Roux he went to church infrequently and when he did they always made him shiver.

"There's something you aren't telling me," he said. "Come on, Nick. Talk to me."

Roux looked at him.

"It's more a problem of motivation."

"The boy's?"

"Angel's."

Roux had finished with the prayer book.

"I need to give Rots more background, explain the importance of the mission. The money thing, the inheritance, is a little…" he hesitated, "a little weak."

Lombard stared at him.

"Absolutely no way."

"But Rots has clearance."

"Not for this. He wasn't born here and he has dual nationality. His clearance is not Top Secret."

Both were aware that South Africa's nuclear deterrent, the ace in its hand, had always been an elaborate sham, a beautifully complicated fiction. The research and collaboration with Pakistani scientists, the novel enrichment process at Pelindaba, the infrastructure and test holes dug deep in the Kalahari Desert, the made-up trade with Israel in hydrogen isotopes to initiate and boost a reaction, none of it completely true. The atomic bomb casings left on show at The Circle to be conveniently photographed but which would always be just empty shells, the smuggled long-range Canadian mortars or technically complex French and Israeli missiles to deliver a weapon that had never been completed, all existed for show. Even a fortuitous and unplanned image on a US satellite over the Southern Ocean near the South

African Prince Edward Islands that experts claimed to be a double flash associated with a nuclear test. All of it an imaginary deception, a pretence, an invented stick, not to beat domestic insurgents but to bribe foreign governments for the support that white South Africa would need to survive the change that all knew would inevitably come.

"I needn't tell Rots everything," said Roux. "Just give him something."

"We can't trust him with any of it, Nick. He's too smart."

"Can I talk to Angel about the Zac character?"

"No. What reason could you give for a suspected British agent to be involved?"

Roux looked around gloomily.

"Do you have any more information on Zac?" Lombard asked.

Roux sighed.

"No. Nothing. He vanished."

Lombard spoke in a whisper.

"If the British find out from grainy enlargements that the new facilities at Rooi-Els and Overberg are fake…"

Lombard, unable to finish, became lost in thought. It didn't matter. Roux already knew that if anyone found out about their charade then South Africa's bargaining power would evaporate, and the consequences could be devastating.

"A few rolls of film taken by a kid walking along the beach may well be all that stands between an orderly transition to majority rule with a new black government restrained by powerful foreign influence or the final bloody confrontation between black and white that many South Africans are secretly hoping for."

Lombard got up to leave. Roux would stay alone and pretend to pray for thirty minutes. He wouldn't have to pretend.

Angel sat miserably in his temporary office on Skinner Street, thinking, looking at his maps.

"Where are you, Ralphy boy?" he asked himself.

Gloomily he looked at the phone. He didn't relish the idea of calling Zelda again. Her hasty termination of their short-lived love affair still left a sour taste. He'd be abrupt, solely business. He dejectedly dialled her number.

"Angel. Honey," she purred.

"The flights to London. Tell me about their route."

"Well, they're all quicker than SAA. As you know we can't overfly Africa. The others are quicker because they're shorter. They go a great circle route."

"What's that?"

"A great circle route is the shortest distance between two points on a curved surface. The earth is a sphere, an oblate sphere squashed at both ends, but maps must depict the earth as flat. You need something called a gnomonic projection to show a great circle route as a straight line on a map, but that distorts the shape of the land so it all looks weird. On an ordinary small-scale map that covers all of Africa and Europe, a straight line is not the shortest distance between two points. The actual shortest distance would appear on a normal map as a curved line. Between Joburg and London it would bend out a little in the middle, either west towards the Congo or east towards East Africa, somewhere around The Horn, and then curve back in. A great circle route. There's not much in the Congo, or anywhere in central Africa other than Kenya, which is why all the flights from Johannesburg to Europe, except SAA, stop both ways at Nairobi to fuel."

A chill went over Angel.

"And there's something else about his ticket you should know, Angel."

He wasn't interested. Her voice, as always, was irritatingly seductive. He couldn't listen to her.

"The airline won't…"

Angel interrupted her angrily, still resentful and brooding on her behaviour.

"Forget it. Just say that last bit about Nairobi again."

Angel suddenly worried about Ralph's flight home. He'd assumed he would leave for London from Johannesburg, the departure point stated on his ticket, guessing he wouldn't have enough money to buy a new one. He now wondered if Ralph's plan had changed, if he had decided to join the same flight but at its refuelling stop in Nairobi. Angel shook his head and put the phone down abruptly on Zelda. Ralph was heading for Kenya.

*

At Victoria Falls, the 'Smoke that Thunders', the hotel of the same name still had an air of colonialism, Ralph guessed because of its distance from Harare. He had expected it to be pockmarked from machine-gun bullets, scarred from revolutionary war. Instead, English-speaking girls in bikinis lounged by the pool and drank South African Lion and Castle beer. Africans dressed in white served tea. No African kids splashed cheerfully in the water. A war for independence might never have happened.

Ralph sat on a sunbed near the pool and unlaced his boots. He stretched out on his back and sighed, the first time he had lain flat but off the floor since leaving Elanza. He smiled to himself as he remembered her. Ralph had walked over a thousand kilometres from Naboomspruit to Victoria Falls in just over a month but Elanza hadn't appeared in his adolescent thoughts until now. He had left her feeling guilty, afraid he'd used her. He wondered now if it had been the other way around. Either way he was grateful to her. She had been interested in his walk along the coast from Cape Town and he had enjoyed telling her about it. He would have liked to have told her of Zimbabwe, to discuss his plans and consider her opinion. He was hungry for more adventure. Apart from his aching feet his young body was toughening rather than wearing out, and he hoped she would have encouraged him to continue.

A pink-faced man shouted at him across the hotel garden.

"Scenes so lovely must have been gazed upon by angels in their flight."

"I'm sorry?" said Ralph.

"Dr Livingstone said it about the Falls."

He introduced himself chirpily.

"Roger Graham. The water spray has corroded the bridge. They won't do anything about it."

"It's not safe," said his wife.

"Need a lift?" asked Mr Graham. "Come with us if you like – plenty of room."

His wife smiled and held a small handbag in front of her as if in church.

Ralph looked at his feet. His boots had hard plastic soles with lumps chipped out of them, one starting to peel away at the front. Ralph had found a thick black rubber band by the roadside and slipped it over the toe to prevent it separating completely. The fabric of the boot was a nylon material, light but hot and unbreathable. At the ankle the nylon had stretched into a mesh, patterning Ralph's skin underneath with a tattoo of dark brown spots.

Inside, his feet were pale and crinkly as though they had been sitting in water for too long. Blisters covered the insides of his toes where they rubbed against each other, and the nail of a big toe was completely loose, blood seeping around the tape he had used to hold it on. A rot had started between the smaller toes, deeply cracking the skin, the flesh tender and red underneath. They itched, and when he rubbed between them a clear slime would coat his finger and his hand would smell like an autumn garden rubbish heap with some poor summer hedgerow animal curled up dead inside.

"Thank you," said Ralph gratefully.

Wreathed in mist, the iron bridge trembled but held as Ralph crossed. The pink-faced man and his prim wife in a proud purple Range Rover led him deeper into Africa, heading away from Johannesburg, away from his flight home.

*

Angel visited Elanza in a private hospital in Sandton. She had become very thin and struggled daily with a medication that made her feel sick.

"You look good."

"I look like shit. The doctor says I'm officially wasting. I've lost six per cent of my BMI in six months."

"You should listen to the doctor. He is *inkomati*."

"What?"

"It's an African saying. Siswati. It means a cow. It's used for anything that's constantly producing something, like a cow always giving milk. Or a river that never dries up. In your case, a doctor that always gives good advice."

"That's crazy. You're making that up. How can a word for a farm animal mean so much?"

"I know. Who said Africans were simple, hey?"

He puzzled her with his silly Afrikaans accent, how he knew stupid African expressions.

"Where's Ralph?" she asked.

"He's not coming back. He's going on to Nairobi. He's going to join his flight home there."

"How?" said Elanza. "He's no money."

"Walking on foot I guess. Or hitch-hiking."

"Find him, Angel. Guard over him and keep him safe."

TEN

The Grahams had a Range Rover that steamed and grumbled its way through the Zambian miombo towards Lusaka.

Around the Zambezi at Victoria Falls the country had been sparse thin grasses and occasional scrub with tall cathedral mopane trees. Mrs Graham told Ralph that the shape of the mopane tree's leaves meant they were often called the Butterfly Tree. They would turn brilliant shades of red and yellow as they dried like flames in a brown garden bonfire.

Further north into Zambia the mopane had been replaced by the miombo, a mosaic of clumps of mostly *Brachystegia* trees with much more ground cover, prone to grass fires in the dry season. In the miombo, the natural vegetation of most of Zambia, the baobab trees protected themselves from the frequent bush fires with an almost cork-like fire-resistant bark.

The Range Rover ran on strip roads like a freight train. Strip roads were common in Zambia and Zimbabwe, a unique solution in the 1930s for opening the countries of Northern and Southern Rhodesia. Two tarmac strips, one for each wheel with bare earth in the middle, reduced the cost of road building by nearly forty per cent. It required cooperation when meeting vehicles coming the other way as both had to move off the road and use only one strip. The slow speed of the manoeuvre enabled first-hand traffic information to be relayed through the driver's window, a very sociable way to drive.

"A lot of warthog in the road a few kilometres up," said a passing motorist in an old van.

He wasn't comparing nature notes. Warthog were a serious motoring hazard. Reluctant to move and believing they could take on an approaching vehicle, they would stand immobile. They never won but it often resulted in a damaged and leaking radiator a hundred kilometres from anywhere. Warthog had very hard heads.

"They've no fuel at the Shell," said Mr Graham.

Navigation was by petrol station in Zambia.

"Hope you're okay. Watch out for a monster pothole about two k before the BP."

"See you Wednesday at the bazaar, Mary," said Mrs Graham to the lady in the van, a pale headscarf keeping the dust out of her hair.

The Grahams were old colonial Brits still living a privileged life in the leafy suburbs of Lusaka, with house staff inside and gardeners for the gladioli collection under the acacia trees. In the war, Flight Sergeant Graham had flown a Lancaster bomber from poorly lit fields in East Anglia through the dark to Germany. Against the odds he always came back, his face as grey as the dawn. He now lived in the bright sharp light of Africa and ran a business supplying and servicing fire extinguishers to the mines and businesses of the Copperbelt.

On the crumbling Great North Road, Ralph learnt, mostly from Mrs Graham, of an Africa that few would recognise – of tea parties and polo, of the problems with staff, of the bad or simple (or both) second sons of lords and earls who had been no good for the Church or the Army and were sent to Africa out of the way.

"Oh, you must go to Shiwa. Such a beautiful house," she told him as the Range Rover stumbled off the edge of the broken tarmac strip.

"A mansion, my dear," said her husband. "Built by one of the Gore-Brownes. Sir Stewart."

He looked at Ralph as though he could clarify things completely.

"His father used to be governor of New Zealand. But I expect Ralph knows them."

"Of course. Your family probably knows them."

Mrs Graham looked at Ralph as if she'd committed an embarrassing faux pas, like calling the Queen 'Ma'am' so that it rhymed with 'ham'.

"They were Surrey people, I believe. From Weybridge."

Ralph nodded. He didn't know anyone in Weybridge. He didn't like to say that he or, as far as he knew, anyone in his family had ever met any sort of knight, or any governor of the dominions or anywhere else. His family were small-town shopkeepers, treasurers of the carnival committee, on the board of commissioners for small local charities. They had always been busy, respected and indispensable; strong, reliable and enduring pillars of their little community. His mother when first married, and without a hint of unnecessary pride, had worked part-time at a small local factory, gossiping and stitching the hides of the dead, wet Dorset cows into ladies' gloves. Ralph's father, unlike Sir Stewart, had never been to Harrow School or taken up car racing at Brooklands for want of something to do. He had finished his education aged fourteen and cheerfully filled accumulator cells with acid at a motor garage and later enthusiastically sold electrical goods and children's toys.

If Ralph's father had ever met the Gore-Brownes, or people like them, it would only have been when summoned at eight in the evening to visit, immediately please, in a three-wheeled car with a fabric roof that never properly sealed out rain or cold draughts, to change a battery in their radio set. Or when trying to get money from them for a television that they'd bought from him nine months previously but had 'quite forgotten' to send a cheque for.

"It's easy to get to Shiwa. If you get off the Tanzam at Mpika and head up the road to Tunduma on the Tanzanian border, but just after Chitembo turn on to the dirt road that leads west to the escarpment. They'll send a carriage, don't you think?"

"Sorry, my dear, but wouldn't Ralph do rather better to stay on the Tanzam until Kasongo and go north up the M1 and then east on the dirt road over the escarpment to Shiwa?"

Ralph suddenly realised he had no compass. And the names meant nothing to him. Of the two options, he preferred the one through Kasongo. It sounded so African.

"What's the Tanzam?" he asked. The confusing geography had finally got the better of him and consulting his old *School Atlas of the World* provided little help.

"You aren't the first man to feel lost in Zambia," Graham explained as he expertly dodged potholes. "The strange shape of the country came about after Cecil Rhodes tried to encircle the Boer republics of the Transvaal and Orange Free State and make them more…" he hesitated, "amenable to British influence. Rhodes just seized anything left of central southern Africa from land that hadn't been claimed by Belgian, German and Portuguese settlers, you see. Its borders, Ralph, are a legacy to colonialism and don't correspond to any single tribal area or to any kingdom that existed before we Europeans arrived."

He glanced at Ralph in the mirror.

"Under these conditions it was predictably difficult after independence for Zambia's new leaders to generate any sense of national identity. Something like seventy languages are spoken by different tribal groups within Zambia's borders."

He looked at his wife, who nodded obediently as he spoke.

"Fortune smiled on the country and gave Zambia a leader up to the task. Kenneth Kaunda, a charismatic farmer and teacher, was passionate in his desire to see Zambia develop into a just and equitable society. He alone seemed able to unite the dissimilar but relatively small population and take advantage of its natural resources. Copper was the key, Ralph. His big problem was that landlocked Zambia, reliant on this single export commodity, was dependent on trade routes to the sea through, what were at that time, the colonial administrations of Southern Rhodesia, Mozambique and South Africa."

He slapped his thigh.

"The Tanzam became the solution. Not a river as you probably thought, Ralph, but a railway. A Chinese railway across uninhabited wilderness, rugged mountains, deep valleys and diseased swamps from the Copperbelt in Zambia to the Indian Ocean at Dar es Salaam on the Tanzanian coast nearly two thousand kilometres away."

Graham stoked the Range Rover's boiler and accelerated past a grey-footed baboon watching them approach over its dog-like muzzle as if at a racecourse.

"Of course, good old Cecil Rhodes, as well as defining the borders of Zambia and designing the strip roads that we are driving on, had the idea of a railway to carry copper ore to Tanganyika way back in the late nineteenth century. A 1949 map showing his route turned out to be almost identical to the one finally taken by the Chinese surveyors who built the Tanzam."

Mrs Graham murmured something in praise – at the foresight of Mr Rhodes or the eloquence of her husband, Ralph wasn't sure.

"The World Bank looked at the project and concluded it would be uneconomic to build, but when Tanganyika and Zambia became independent their Presidents Nyerere and Kaunda, who were both socialist and supported liberation movements, decided that a rail link would protect their countries' political and economic independence. Copper ore could be exported without restriction. Remote agricultural regions along the railway could be opened up to the markets of the big capital cities."

"How clever," Mrs Graham cried. Her husband held her hand while she leant over and tenderly brushed her lips against his neck. Ralph felt an intruder, as though he might be eavesdropping on something marital.

"Nyerere invited Chinese surveyors to produce a plan but Kaunda, nervous of communist involvement that would annoy the UK, actively sought Western backers. Thanks to The World Bank report, none were interested. Rhodesia then declared a Unilateral Declaration of Independence from the United Kingdom after Britain demanded power sharing with the African population, and Rhodesia threatened to sever Zambia's trade links to the sea. Kaunda finally changed his mind. The railway would be Chinese built and financed."

Graham took a breath; he'd been talking quickly, rising to a crescendo.

"Over an eleven-year period, China sent fifty thousand technical and construction workers, and invested five hundred million dollars, on the longest railway in Africa and the largest single foreign aid project ever undertaken."

Mrs Graham licked her lips, staring at him with admiration and pride.

"The US then funded the Tanzam Highway in competition to the railway. They feared a loss of influence in the region, you see, Ralph, but the American road was nothing like as ambitious or dramatic a project. For the railway the Chinese had to place over three hundred thousand tons of steel rail across some of Africa's wildest and most rugged landscapes, and had to build three hundred bridges, twenty-two tunnels and thousands of culverts. Along the way, ninety-three stations were built, all in the architectural style of Mao Zedong's revolutionary red China. And they died for their comrades in Africa: I think sixty-four Chinese and 160 Africans in construction accidents. But wait for this, Ralph – they finished the bloody thing two years ahead of schedule!"

Graham summed it up, his wife waiting intently for the climax.

"More than anything, Ralph, the Tanzam is an enduring symbol of Chinese solidarity for the developing world and Chinese support for African independence. And, just as importantly, China would always have a copper supply."

Mr Graham slumped in his seat, exhausted. Mrs Graham smiled shyly at Ralph and lit a cigarette, blowing a long cloud through the window.

They had covered just over 260 kilometres from Victoria Falls and had been driving for five hours – fifty kilometres per hour on poor roads through the miombo, then past small dusty settlements with large markets on either side of the road, then miombo again. Beyond the little town of Choma there were clear views through the trees towards the Nkanga River. Ralph could see sable, eland, puku, and occasionally hartebeest, wildebeest and kudu – timeless views of Africa.

"I think I'll get out here and look around for a bit," Ralph said.

Mrs Graham seemed nervous.

"Are you sure? It's still 210 kilometres to Lusaka."

"Good idea," said Graham. "Scout out the lay of the land."

Mr Graham, an old pioneer at heart, loved being deep in pioneer country.

"The Tanzam starts in a town called Kapiri Mposhi," he said. "It's two hundred kilometres north of Lusaka, through Kabwe. Please get in touch if you need a ride. I have vehicles from work going to the Copperbelt every day."

He gave Ralph a business card: RG Fire Systems Limited.

At a dot on the map called Pemba the Range Rover hissed to a stop.

"Will you be all right?" asked Mrs Graham.

"Of course he will. The Baldwins are just up the road. Ralph will probably stay with them."

He looked ahead out of the window down the track, as if on the footplate checking a signal.

"Lovely people the Baldwins. Poultry farmers. They have family on the Isle of Wight. I believe Sir Nigel is to be Lord Lieutenant."

"Oh, silly me. Of course he'll know the Baldwins," said Mrs Graham.

Ralph watched them go, the rumble of the Range Rover replaced by that of thunder.

*

The town of Pemba stretched for barely a hundred metres on either side of the Lusaka road. Ralph bought bananas and little bags of peanuts for dinner from as many different stands as he could: a conscious effort to spread his meagre wealth around to many hands. He filled his water bottles at a tap on the wall of what looked like a barber's shop, or an abattoir, or both. An incongruous roadside stand, the last on the outskirts of the town, displayed an odd table of items. Ralph immediately felt sorry for the smiling local entrepreneur. He couldn't imagine the last time anyone had stopped, on the spur of the moment, to buy a mixed set of plastic measuring jugs or a soft fluffy yellow toy duck. He bargained hard for a box of Christmas crackers. The vendor seemed pleased but they had been cheaper than the amount Ralph had just paid for his dinner. The boy was either a lousy Christmas cracker salesman or Ralph had been ripped off on the peanuts. He imagined the latter. Ralph left the town with rain on the road someway in front. It kept pace with him, steaming and retreating before him as he walked towards Lusaka. It was early afternoon, time to clear the town and find somewhere for the night.

Ralph wasn't worried about having nowhere to stay. He had walked 760 kilometres through Zimbabwe from

Beitbridge on the South African border to Victoria Falls and had spent every night somewhere off the road. It had taken him over three weeks of walking six or seven hours a day, usually from early dawn until before midday. Nervous of built-up areas he had spent a night in the secure compound of Bulawayo's camping site when he'd been unable to get through the town's suburbs in one day, but the rest of the time he had slept alone in the bush. He'd learnt a few things along the way.

His rucksack, once a vivid electric blue but now dirty and scruffy, was deliberately unlikely to appeal to many thieves. Inside he had no tent, just a lightweight sleeping bag and a length of foam mattress cut to save space so that when he lay down it covered from his shoulders to his hips. His rucksack became a pillow at night. He had a head torch, two army-issue kidney-shaped black plastic water bottles, an aluminium mess tin with a fold-over handle, and a small collapsible entrenching tool. From a chemist in Pretoria he'd bought a bottle of two per cent iodine solution and an eye dropper. It made up his entire first aid kit. Four drops in a litre to make sterilised water, and rub some neat on cuts, scratches and bites to prevent infection.

If passing through a village in the late afternoon he would ask for the headman and enquire where he could camp. People were generally fascinated by him. Later in the evening he could be guaranteed to have company drift towards his campfire. More often, he would find himself nowhere near habitation so he would look out for a big tree and camp under it. It reduced the amount of dew that would be on him in the morning. He would pitch away from anything that looked like a well-worn path, as it always proved to be a game trail. He found that riverbeds, often inviting and comfortably flat, could turn into a raging torrent with no notice. When clearing stones from the campsite he checked carefully underneath for large, African-sized creepy-crawlies.

He built a fire sparingly, as the locals did, most often with small bags of charcoal bought from street vendors by the side of the road. If picking up dead wood he'd kick it over first to check for scorpions or snakes. He'd learnt that the best fires were when he dug a narrow shallow trench, never more than half a metre long, and lined the sides with flat stones. The stones kept the heat when the fire went out and it was easy to pull out the stones in the morning and kick the soil over the ashes, filling in the trench and leaving no trace that he'd been there. The fire would never keep wild animals away. That seemed to work in the movies but not in the bush. Hyena, and one night south of Bulawayo near the Matobo National Park a troop of baboons and then a leopard, seemed completely unfazed by it. It didn't seem to matter how bright he let it burn.

Bigger animals were a danger as he wasn't in a tent, mainly because of the risk of being stepped on. One night in the Hwange National Park, in between Bulawayo and Victoria Falls, a matriarch elephant and three cows, remarkably agile for their size, stepped over him. It was important, but difficult, not to wake up and startle them.

He never carried foodstuffs that weren't sealed and never cooked or opened tins at his camp in the evening. He would make a hot meal from the embers of his fire in the early morning for breakfast and rigorously clean all sweet-smelling food residues from his mess tin by rubbing them with sand. He would always pee before he got into his sleeping bag so that he didn't have to get up in the night.

In the morning he'd carefully check his rucksack for unwanted hitch-hikers. Even a small spider could give a nasty bite. His boots always spent the night with him at the bottom of his sleeping bag so nothing could crawl inside. In general, snakes, spiders and scorpions needed to be antagonised before they bit. It wasn't uncommon to find a snake on top of his sleeping bag in the morning, attracted by his body warmth during the night. He'd gently roll away from it. Walking through a town by a dry meandering riverbed called Esigodini he'd watched an African treated for a snake bite. Nobody cut open the wound and sucked out the poison. Instead, women boiled bandages and wrapped them while scolding hot over the site. The idea wasn't to draw out the toxin but to coagulate it. The poison was a protein, like egg white. If heated enough it would form into a solid and then couldn't be transported in the bloodstream. They had effectively stopped it spreading.

He was concerned about malaria. At a concentration strong enough to control African mosquitoes the pesticide DEET could dissolve some plastics. Ralph covered up with loose clothing in the evening and slept with a piece of netting over his face. It seemed an altogether healthier option.

He never worried about his personal safety if he could get as far out of town as he could possibly get before dark. Human animals troubled him more than wild animals, and he needed to get at least two hours' walk out of a built-up area to feel safe. Even then he would check that no one was watching and then quickly walk some distance out of sight of the road. At times he would camouflage his camp with a screen of scrubby bushes. On occasion, when he had asked at a bigger village for somewhere to camp, and for no rational reason other than a feeling deep in his gut, he would head off in the direction indicated by the headman but skirt around when out of sight and go completely the opposite way. He was never scared. It was just a game, like being back at school or in the Army Cadet Force, a giant 'Escape and Evasion' exercise through Africa.

It was a game and he was still a boy, with a boy's inexpressible longing to become a man. He felt that wouldn't happen quickly enough at home with an attentive loving family around him. He needed to be uncomfortable, to challenge himself physically, to be tested. If he could do that in Africa he would return triumphant, mature, respected as well as loved.

When he dreamed of home he imagined schoolfriends listening to his adventures in awe with open mouths, of a girlfriend impressed and tender, a mother fussing at his glorious homecoming and a father quietly proud. To achieve that dream it was nothing to him to feel hunger, to be numbed by fatigue with bleeding blistered feet. These were the trials that would change him and bring him to manhood.

He reassured himself by recalling that, other than the poachers in Zimbabwe who had frightened him with their callous harshness, his journey had been trouble-free – not effortless but easy. It was easy unless it rained, then it was miserable without a tent.

*

Ralph had walked nearly ten kilometres out of town when he caught up with the rain. It didn't start slowly as gentle drops, building as he walked, getting progressively heavier. Instead, one moment he had been dry and the next soaking wet, the water running in streams from his bush hat, turning into small rivers as it ran down his chest.

Ahead, about two hundred metres off the road, stood a huge baobab tree. He had been walking towards it for some time but now he ran, red mud splashing up his legs like at a point-to-point in March, the going soft. Underneath the tree there would be some shelter. Night was coming quickly and nobody moved on the road. Ralph resigned himself. Tonight had to be spent standing, wet and chilled, in the dark, getting what shelter he could from the branches of the baobab. He found some peanuts loose in his pocket and ate them individually, picking wet pieces of paper bag from each.

Ralph looked at his lodgings. The baobab, the most easily recognised tree in the savannahs of Africa, had become the defining icon of the African bushlands. Ralph had heard it called the 'upside-down' tree, its branches resembling roots as though it had been pulled out and replanted the wrong way up. Big baobabs could have a diameter of ten metres and grow thirty metres tall, some of them thousands of years old.

Someone touched his arm and startled him, a girl in her late teens, who Ralph hadn't seen approaching. She stood tightly wrapped in a *chitenje*, a brightly coloured cotton cloth about two metres long. Local women used them as towels, or sarongs, or picnic mats, or simply swathed them over their normal clothes to keep them clean. They were practical and cheap and made a bright splash of African colour on the tall, very beautiful and completely dry girl.

She took his hand.

"Please. Come."

She led Ralph around to the other side of the tree. A fertiliser sack covered the trunk at ground level, faded but with part of the formula of its contents still visible: '30% P2O5' and 'Made in China'. She stopped and looked at Ralph, pulled the sack to one side and stepped inside the tree.

It was a huge hollow trunk, seven or eight metres across and towering fifteen metres into the dark above Ralph's head. The earth inside had packed dry and hard like concrete. A small fireplace built precisely in the middle of the circular space had been lined at the bottom and sides with grey stones. A thin column of tangy smoke drifted into the blackness and brown husks glowed red in the fireplace with no flame. Outside the night stayed hot and wet, but inside it felt cool and dry.

"You are welcome to join us," the girl said.

Ralph looked around. As he became accustomed to the dim light he could make out little groups of people, all looking at him curiously. Old women with few teeth smiled at him. A man drinking from a bucket wiped a foamy scum, like a high-water mark, from his top lip before passing it to an older man next to him. Six children played a game with some sticks, while three more played with a yellow bird, holding it in cupped hands and talking to it in soft voices. There were twenty people within the tree and room for another dozen.

Ralph set his rucksack down against the inside of the tree and touched the trunk. It felt soft, spongy to the touch.

"My name is Ralph. Thank you for having me," he announced.

The girl brought a mat made of some woven fabric.

"You should use this to keep warm."

A man shouted across the tree to her. The only word Ralph understood sounded like 'Peters'. The girl answered him in a local language.

She looked at Ralph.

"He wants to know if you have any Peter Stuyvesant. Cigarettes. Anything to smoke."

"I'm sorry."

The girl shook her head at the man. He didn't look disappointed. He smiled at Ralph and shook a long pipe at him.

"He wants to know where you are from," the girl said.

"England."

The old man, and some others, understood the word.

"Manchester United!" he shouted.

"United," some chorused.

"Not really," said Ralph. "Further south."

A man brought the bucket from the other side of the tree and mimed Ralph to drink.

"What is it?"

"*Chibuku,*" she said. "Shake-shake."

She took the bucket and drank.

Ralph looked in the bucket and saw an opaque thick brown liquid, foaming on the surface.

He lifted it up.

"United," he said.

"United!" they all shouted.

He took a deep pull from the bucket. It tasted thick and sour, freshly fermented, and fizzed on his tongue. It seemed to amuse the others that he had tried it.

"What is this place?"

"This is The Tree of Life."

"A baobab?"

"Practically all parts of the baobab can be used for something. It can provide food and water for people and livestock, shelter, clothing, medicine, tools for hunting, nets for fishing. Everything you need in life."

A lady brought food. In South Africa the staple was called *mieliepap* or just *pap*, often eaten with soured milk for breakfast or with grilled meat from a *braai*. The same thing in Zimbabwe was a maize meal porridge. They called it *sadza*.

Here it looked like a stiff cooked porridge of ground maize but the Zambians called it *nshima*. It had the heavy consistency of mashed potatoes and they ate it with a tasty relish made from vegetables, fish or chicken. On the savannah, meat was often absent in the diet of cattle-keeping people. They would consume the milk and the blood but their animals were a hard currency, too valuable to kill and eat.

"Is the trunk usually hollow?"

"These trees are very old. Over time they naturally have open spaces in the trunk. Sometimes it is hollowed out in parts by men with a small axe. It doesn't affect the tree. Many baobabs are used as village meeting places. One is a prison. Another is a bus shelter that can accommodate thirty or forty people. Usually they provide protection for animals or storage. There is a famous tree that an administrator, a Major Trollope, used as a bathroom complete with a flushing toilet."

She lowered her voice.

"In some the dead are stored inside, suspended between earth and sky."

Ralph took another drink from the bucket. It wasn't so bad. She offered Ralph some *nshima*.

Ralph looked at her. She had shake-shake bubbles around her mouth.

"What's your name?"

"Mutinta. It means… umm… 'different' in the Citonga language."

"How is it that your English is so good, Mutinta?"

"My father is a doctor. He is in Lusaka, but we live here, in Pemba. Or wherever the cattle are feeding. I had an exchange with a church to study in America. I spent three years in Philadelphia at the International Baptist High School. I didn't like it."

Ralph tried to picture Mutinta in Pennsylvania, sitting in a garden chair instead of on the floor in the dust; drinking milkshake instead of home-brewed shake-shake; eating a burger made from a valuable cow instead of maize porridge. It wasn't easy.

Ralph leant back and relaxed. He looked at Mutinta, wanted to hear her talk.

"The Tree of Life. So, what else can it do?"

"It makes medicine. A powder of the roots is good for malaria and the bark reduces fever. The leaves are good in a poultice for inflammations and insect bites. In Zambia we make an infusion and bathe babies with it to keep their skin soft."

Two of the children, tired, came and sat beside her. Mutinta covered them with her *chitenje*, one on each side.

"And you can make things with it. Like string for fishing nets, or sacks from the soft root bark. You can completely strip the bark from the trunk without hurting the tree and make anything from the fibres: rope, baskets, mats, cloth, fishing line. You can't do much with the wood. It's spongy and won't burn. It's good for making canoes or fishing floats." She poked the embers of the fire with a stick. "It's better to burn these dry husks that surround the fruit. The smoke keeps away mosquitoes. Or you can put it in your pipe if you run out of tobacco."

"As good as Peters?"

She laughed.

"I don't know." She pointed to the old United supporter. "Ask him."

The children under Mutinta's wings looked at Ralph. They wore a mismatched selection of oversized cardigans and hand-me-down shorts and little rubber boots. Their hair had been closely cropped so that he couldn't tell if they were boys or girls. They had beautiful large eyes and smiled easily.

He suddenly remembered his earlier shopping trip, the smiling street vendor in Pemba. From the top of his rucksack he pulled a dry box of Christmas crackers. He had the attention of the whole tree now, inquisitive eyes in the gloom watching him with curiosity. He took out two crackers and gave one to each of the children with Mutinta. They rolled them in their hands, the shiny gold and red foil glinting in the firelight. Ralph positioned their hands, one on each end of the cracker, and helped them pull. A crack like a thick stick snapping echoed inside the tree. The children screeched with excitement. A yellow paper hat and a small plastic aeroplane fell to the floor. The bucket of shake-shake hung motionless between two men. Mutinta picked up the toy and the paper hat, unfolded it and took it to the old man with the pipe. He took the hat from her, studied it, and with some ceremony put it on his head, his wide face beaming in the half light. They had a long discussion about the model jet. In the end Mutinta found a flat rock and put it on the ground in front of the old man. He placed the toy on the rock, turning it for a view from every angle. The other children gathered around Mutinta. There were twelve crackers in the box. Mutinta made sure that different children experienced the excitement and shock of pulling a cracker, then she would take the hat and the toy to the old man.

Seven serious proud men, drunk on shake-shake, and three old ladies with no teeth, sat at the other side of the tree, crowned kings and queens in a round court. A treasure trove of small gifts sat on the flat rock. The aeroplane, a whistle, a thing that made a whooping noise when you pulled one end, a small spinning top, a square with sliding naughts and crosses, a compass the size of an old penny.

*

In the quiet darkness Ralph felt Mutinta come and lie next to him. The children had fallen asleep in a heap, like puppies. The men snored and twitched the other side of the tree, the shake-shake bucket on its side, empty.

She whispered to him.

"Tell me about England. Is it like Philadelphia?"

"Parts of it are probably a little like that. Where I live in the south it is cattle country. But not like here. The land is always green and the cattle always fat. Some of the people too."

Mutinta thought of her trip to America, the way she had to sit close to people she didn't know, the nauseous smells from food like the kind you would give to old people.

"Will you fly from Lusaka with Kenya Airways?"

"I am travelling on foot to Kenya."

"Do you know the way?"

"I have a rough idea."

She thought for a while.

"Will your father be worried about you?"

That, thought Ralph, is a very good question. He hadn't been in contact with his father since leaving Johannesburg. He wasn't sure that he could remember much about their last conversation. He thought he'd told him that he would tour around, check out the sights. Now he realised that his father would be very worried about him. It upset Ralph to think that he might be anxious, and he made a mental note to contact him from Lusaka, even if only with an airmail bluey telling him of his plans. Ralph felt a little homesick. He put it down to the *Chibuku* beer.

He turned and looked at the dying fire. Mutinta put her arm over him. He looked into the fire thinking of home, and it took a long time before he could sleep.

When he woke in the morning he noticed that the fertiliser sack door to the tree had been hitched open. Harsh sunlight made a bright yellow column over the floor. He lay in the shade alone, not a sign of Mutinta, the old man or the children. Suddenly he didn't want to be in the tree. The tree felt unwelcoming, dark and cold. Outside he could see the sunshine and a beautiful bright morning after the rain. He got up quickly, desperate to leave.

As he reached for his rucksack something on the top sparkled in the light through the door: a compass, the size of an old penny, a present from Mutinta to help him find the way.

ELEVEN

Nels drove through the Zambian town of Monze on the road towards Lusaka with the sun setting in his rear-view mirror. By necessity he'd been creative with his travel plans, his options limited due to his South African passport not being welcomed, or even accepted, in most African countries.

He'd driven at dawn not through Zimbabwe but to Gaborone in Botswana, just four and a half hours from Johannesburg. Botswana was reliant on South Africa for trade and communication with the rest of the Continent, and a fifth of all the males in the country travelled to the goldfields of the Witwatersrand to work in South Africa's mines. It made the President of Botswana slightly more pragmatic than his neighbouring leaders. Other than a few San bushmen in the Kalahari, it was a land of a single tribe, the Tswana. It made his country poor but peaceful, and he wanted it to stay that way. Visas were not required for South African citizens.

A new all-weather road linked the capital Gaborone to Zambia via a ferry over the Zambezi River near Kasane, at a point where four African countries touched borders. It was a rugged, lonely, twelve-hour drive. Botswana was bigger in area than France but with a population only slightly greater than Marseille. Nels was impatient, and leaving his car at Gaborone airport he flew to Kasane, via a pit stop at the bar of Riley's Hotel in Maun, with an ex-Army colleague who transported cash by air for Barclays Bank.

Nels had known the pilot Albert Smith for years. Together they had drunk and fought in hot and dusty barrooms across southern Africa. Smith's chequered professional flying career had come to an end when Wenela Airways, who regularly crammed African labourers onto canvas seats and flew them to work on The Rand, crashed a Skymaster soon after take-off. Smith hadn't been flying that day but Wenela ceased operations overnight and he'd taken what work he could find.

Together, in a faded Andover loaded with paper and coin for the bank, they'd flown over a broad empty tableland, seeing only cattle-raising and meat-packing stations dotted over the desert and salt flats. At Kasane, Nels had rented a car and driven fifteen kilometres to the new ferry, the old one bombed and sunk by the Rhodesian Air Force in the Bush War.

In the queue for Zambian customs on the other side of the river he'd paid a fixer twenty-five dollars to do the paperwork, and another twenty-five to compensate for his stupidity in leaving his US passport in the hotel in Gaborone. The fixer had taken his money and smiled. He knew the difference between an American and an Afrikaans accent.

He'd then had a slow four-hour drive through Livingstone, scanning both sides of the road. It had been a long day, his eyes now gritty and tired. Nels was only three hours from Lusaka.

Ralph had walked thirty-two kilometres that day on an empty stomach and felt faint from hunger and lightheaded with thirst. There seemed little chance he'd find anything to eat or drink. He should have looked for something in Monze, the last place he'd walked through, but he'd been reluctant to stop, fearing he wouldn't get going again. The road had forked about two kilometres out of town and then run straight as a gun barrel towards Lusaka. Wiggly dusty goat and cattle trails meandered away from the road on both sides between round mud-walled cottages with thatched roofs. He'd covered a further five or six kilometres in a daze before realising that the sun was setting quickly behind him, his long shadow walking ahead. Ralph checked his map. He wouldn't make the next town before nightfall: Magoye, still twenty-seven kilometres away. He should camp.

A large baobab stood alone, its branches in leaf. Ralph remembered Mutinta and her advice to him the previous evening. A baobab, The Tree of Life, provided both food and water.

"You can eat the roots in time of famine," she'd said, "but the leaves are better, like spinach. They make a great soup."

Ralph looked at the tree. Spinach-like soup from baobab leaf might be his only option. He'd need water.

"How do they provide water?" he'd asked her. He recalled her answer as she had fed him maize meal *nshima* washed down with a bucket of shake-shake.

"The hollow trunks can be carved out by hand in three or four days and used to store water. A hole is drilled through the trunk to get the water out and a bung put in. A medium-sized tree holds about 1,500 litres but a large baobab could hold five times that. The water will stay sweet for several years if the hollow is kept closed. You can channel water in to it to keep it topped up by making an opening just above the axil of a branch. Some people dig away the soil around the tree and line it with rocks to make a shallow pool for rainwater to collect in and then take it up to the top with a bucket and rope and tip it in an opening at the top. In the dry northern provinces of Kenya it became the only way to cross otherwise waterless country, and an organised chain of water trees stretched across the Kalahari for Bushmen. If anyone left the bung out they would be killed. These trees have a long history of helping travellers."

Ralph, encouraged, walked towards the tree. With luck there would be a pool of collected water at the base, leaves to pick and boil, and shelter inside a hollow trunk. The headlights of an approaching car conveniently illuminated the way in the quickly fading twilight.

*

Nels' eyes blurred as he stared ahead down the straight road. It was nearly dark, his headlights creating fuzzy yellow shafts of light in front and on the sides of the narrow two-lane highway. A railway paralleled the road, a constant fifty-metre-wide strip of bare scrub separating the two for the last five or six kilometres and continuing into the distance.

Nels decided he'd done enough. The chance of anyone walking around alone at night was very slim. He looked at the railway line and realised he'd made a mistake. It was most likely that the boy had taken a train. Ralph could be miles away, possibly already out of the country.

Nels swore, slowed, and steered the car carefully over the scrubland between the road and the railway in a wide careful U-turn. His headlights showed the railway tracks hidden under long brown grass and a trail through the scrub to a big old baobab standing at a crossroads of dry dirt paths just twenty-five metres the other side of the railway.

Something moved against the tree, something white in the car's lights. Nels stared and blinked his eyes, forcing them to focus.

Nothing stirred.

He stopped the car short of the railway tracks and turned off the engine. The night was still and quiet. He stood in front of the car, leaning against the hot bonnet, hearing the engine ticking beneath him as it cooled.

Nels walked slowly towards the tree down the beams of the headlights, fine dust floating around his feet. The baobab was wide, too wide to see around unless he circled the trunk.

He stood very close to the tree and sniffed the night air. There was a tangy smoky smell. He looked around for village cooking fires but saw nothing, no sign of flickering light. It was as if the smoke was inside the tree.

Nels shook his head. That was impossible. He was tired.

He ducked under a heavy branch nearly touching the ground and walked to the trunk, stumbling into a shallow ditch lined with flat stones that wound around the perimeter. It was half full of water.

There was nothing to see. Just a heap of white fertiliser sacks piled against the dark side of the trunk.

Cursing, Nels strode to the car and slammed the door behind him, the rear tyres kicking clouds of red dust into the taillights as he accelerated back onto the highway.

Gordon and Ann Baldwin were known throughout the region as religious and industrious poultry farmers. Their farm at Calvary Hill stood beside a straight road out of Lusaka that ran to the satellite station over the high plateau, an area of flat land made into small fields cleared from scrubby bushes. Twenty-five kilometres from the bustling capital it was quiet and peaceful, almost contemplative, an avian retreat.

It hadn't always been that way. During the Rhodesian Bush War, the guerrilla leader Nkomo had been in exile in Zambia with his Zimbabwean African People's Union. In September 1978, Nkomo laughingly took responsibility for shooting down a civilian Rhodesian airliner near Kariba with a Soviet ground-to-air heat-seeking missile. The Rhodesians retaliated the following month, their air force attacking ZAPU camps within Zambia and effectively taking control of Zambian air space for the duration of the raid. Rhodesia maintained that it hadn't been an act of war against Zambia.

At Calvary Hill Farm, a Rhodesian Air Force thirty-millimetre cannon shell casing had fallen from the sky, struck a chicken on the head and killed it. Much worse was to come. In November 1978, just four years before Ralph's visit, forces loyal to Nkomo raided the farm. They kidnapped and badly beat three foreign visitors staying at Calvary Hill with the Baldwins.

The situation at Calvary Hill Farm had stabilised since elections in Zimbabwe and independence. Nkomo had left Zambia to continue the fight, not against Rhodesians but against his fellow countryman Mugabe, with whom he had been unable to reconcile his ideological and, mostly, tribal differences.

As Gordon showed him around and explained the history, Ralph couldn't help wondering if the Baldwins had ever heard of the Grahams, or even bought fire extinguishers from RG Fire Systems Ltd. They were chalk and cheese. The Grahams would eventually return to a bungalow near Elstree or Maidstone and become 'whenwes': "When we were in Africa…" The Baldwins, however, were serious Africans and this would always be their home.

Gordon and Ann had two sons, both at school in Lusaka. Ralph was a similar age, a great distance from home, and the Baldwins were Good Samaritans. They made him a deal. He could stay at Calvary Hill in return for help on the farm. There would be a compulsory church parade. Ralph didn't think twice. Praying with a few chickens seemed a small price to pay for the chance to eat, sleep in a bed and plan his next moves.

The pervasive feeling of peace at Calvary Hill, which Ralph assumed must be due to something spiritual, meant that eating and sleeping were easy. Planning, however, wasn't straightforward, and he was cartographically challenged.

He discussed his problem with the Baldwins.

"I need to re-evaluate my position," he told them at dinner. "I'm not too sure which way to go."

"God will guide you," said Mr Baldwin and attacked his roast. They ate a lot of chicken.

"Yes, of course he will, but how would you get to Nairobi?"

"I would put my trust in the Lord."

"Excellent, excellent. But could you trust him to know if I need to get a Tanzanian visa before I leave Lusaka, or are they available at the border?"

Mrs Baldwin stopped eating and stood up.

"For I know the plans I have for you, declares the Lord, plans to prosper you and not to harm you, plans to give you hope and a future."

"Hmm…" said her husband. "Isaiah?"

"Jeremiah. 29:11."

Domestic conversations at mealtimes with the Baldwins were always spoken through biblical quotes and proverbs. Ralph tried to bring them back to his current dilemma.

"What I really need is a good map of Africa. My atlas is so small. And old. It doesn't even have the Tanzam on it."

Mrs Baldwin, a mother and attuned to small hidden clues, for once talked to him in English rather than Bible speak.

"Ralph, you need to take care. It's not the route that you need to worry about. There aren't that many options. It's some of the people you are likely to meet along the way that you need to be careful of."

"In journeyings often, in perils of waters, in perils of robbers, in perils by mine own countrymen, in perils by the heathen, in perils in the city, in perils in the wilderness, in perils in the sea, in perils among false brethren. Corinthians," said Baldwin.

"Only let me take care of all your needs; however, do not spend the night in the open square."

"Well said, darling. Kings?"

"Judges."

"Bugger," said Baldwin.

At times they would throw verses at each other, like stones.

When he went to his room a heap of maps littered the bed. Ralph scanned through the pile. With them he would be able to travel with confidence at different scales, knowing elevation and the names of key bridges over important waterways along his whole route. Ralph set about measuring distances.

*

Gordon Baldwin broke open a flat woody pod from a vine plant climbing the outside wall of a chicken shed and pulled out two large round beans. Away from the dining table and around the chickens, and especially when considering anything botanical, Mr Baldwin would talk the language of a farmer and not something written at the time of King James.

"You know you can eat these. Morama beans. They're a staple food in Botswana and Namibia. They boil or roast them. Very high protein content. I wondered if we could mill it into the pullets' feed."

Ralph and Mr Baldwin had been walking through rearing sheds, checking automatic feeders and drinkers, looking for dead birds, monitoring ventilation. Inside the sheds, a mat of yellow chicks scurried over a litter of dried guano and wood shavings. They would eat constantly from open red troughs and drink from plastic bell-shaped red buckets, positioned so that the birds would never be more than two metres from food and water. Somebody must have worked out that red would be an attractive colour to a chicken, blood red. Tubes with a corkscrew-shaped auger inside were suspended off the floor, the clattering noise of them switching on to refill the troughs bringing chicks scurrying to feed. They probably didn't need to eat, thought Ralph, they just had nothing else to do, the noise of the feed tubes the most exciting part of their short sixty-day life in the dim, calming light.

Even with huge fans in the roof, the smell of ammonia soon became overpowering. Outside, Ralph breathed in the fresh air.

"*Tylosema fassoglensis*," said Baldwin, holding the bean pod for Ralph to look at.

"I looked at those maps you put on my bed. I've covered 4,180 kilometres from Cape Town."

Baldwin looked at the weeds growing around the base of the shed.

"Hmmm. How much of that did you have to walk?"

Ralph had measured off the distances. He'd taken a local train from the centre of Cape Town on an hour and a half long ride to the beach at Strand. He'd done 1,233 kilometres with Franz and Zac in a beat-up Peugeot travelling from East London to Johannesburg. He'd had a very quiet two and a half hour ride out of Johannesburg and around Pretoria with an Afrikaans-speaking bar owner who eventually got fed up with him and turned him out at a town called Naboomspruit. And he'd ridden in regal splendour in the Grahams' Range Rover from Victoria Falls to Pemba. He'd been in a vehicle for 1,763 kilometres.

"I've walked over half of it," Ralph said proudly. "Two thousand four hundred and seventeen kilometres on foot."

"How many days' walking is that?"

"Seventy-six days."

Baldwin had found something interesting. He pulled brown scrub out of the way of a green plant.

"What are you going to do now?" Baldwin asked.

"Well, I could turn around and go back. It's 1,789 kilometres to Johannesburg."

Ralph could do that. He could retrace his steps. He would have seen Victoria Falls at least. He could watch the rest of

Africa out of a small window from thirty-nine thousand feet with sternly smiling cabin crew.

"Or I could carry on to Nairobi and join the plane there."

Baldwin had found a twisty herb with a clump of succulent green roots. It had a flower on a tube with a swollen base. The end looked like a cage, dark purple and hairy on the inside with yellow spots near the base.

"From here to Nairobi via Dar es Salaam must be three thousand kilometres," said Baldwin.

Ralph corrected him.

"Three thousand and forty-seven if you go on the railway to Dar es Salaam then by road to Nairobi through Mombasa."

"So, it's one and a half times further to go on to Nairobi than it is to go back to Johannesburg."

"It's roughly seventy per cent further."

Ralph had been pedantic with the numbers but he'd spent half the night working it out. A corporal instructor in the cadets had once told him that with time and distance problems: 'Remember, son, if in doubt, tabulate.' Ralph had produced an impressive table on the back of his vaccination certificate. He knew all the numbers but the question of which way to go still wasn't clear to him.

"You would take the Tanzam train from Kapiri Mposhi to Dar es Salaam?"

Ralph thought about his finances before replying. He had spent about a hundred US dollars since leaving Johannesburg. For six weeks he'd spent just over two dollars a day. He still had three-quarters of his earnings from the film shoot at Kyalami, Elanza watching him work and laughing at his Afrikaans. Some enquiries he'd made in town before coming out to Calvary Hill suggested that a third-class ticket for the whole route to Dar on the Indian Ocean would be ten dollars, maybe half that if he changed money on the black market and not in a bank. It seemed very cheap. Ralph didn't imagine the Chinese who'd paid for the railway would be seeing a return on their investment anytime soon.

"So, of the three thousand," Baldwin continued.

Ralph helped him out.

"And forty-seven."

"Of the 3,047 kilometres to Nairobi, how much of that is on the Tanzam?"

"One thousand eight hundred and sixty-three kilometres."

"Over half of it?"

"Roughly sixty per cent of it."

Baldwin studied the plant.

"You don't know how you would get from Dar es Salaam to Nairobi through Mombasa, but for the rest of it you have a lift organised to Kapiri Mposhi with these people…" he hesitated, "the Grahams? I don't know them, although they may have heard of us. Someone in town probably told them I have a brother with a knighthood. I can't stand all that snobby English nonsense. I thank God I'm just a chicken farmer. Anyway, from Kapiri you will be on the train. That part will be easy at least. There won't be any problems with the Tanzam."

Ralph nodded.

"This is *Ceropegia nilotica*," he held up the plant. "See these umbels of tubular flowers? We are at 1,170 metres at Calvary Hill. Unusual to see them at this altitude. 'I am prepared to go anywhere, provided it be forward.' Do you know who said that?"

Ralph guessed at something biblical.

"Caleb?"

Baldwin stopped talking and lifted the plant to Ralph, to wave him off.

"Livingstone," he said. "Keep going. Go all the way to Nairobi."

Ralph had hoped to hear just that. It would be a long way through a darker Africa than he had travelled up until now but his health remained good, he had some money and he had a workable plan.

"Just don't go to Uganda. We have missions there and I don't hear anything good. Idi Amin has gone but thanks to him it is still a bitter and suspicious place."

He examined the *nilotica* seriously.

"God will be with you."

*

Angel leant against his desk and looked at a map on the wall. Zambia looked like a dumpy capital letter L but turned on its side, its borders a mixture of wiggly lines that followed rivers and made straight connections across desert and swamp. He walked to the wall with his head tilted on one side and put his finger somewhere near the middle: the capital city of Lusaka.

Angel held out little hope of any help in Zambia from official channels. The country was an authoritarian one-party state. People voted yes or no for a single presidential candidate on the ballot paper, Kenneth Kaunda, the founder of a peculiar African socialism and friend to other communist Eastern European benevolent dictators. This legal dictatorship allowed the ANC to use Zambia as a base for their offensive operations. KK was South Africa's *bête noir*.

Angel's one chance was with a contact he'd made while at the University of Witwatersrand and had carefully nurtured since then. David Mwansa was from Kasama in the Northern Province of Zambia, a nephew of the *Chitimukulu*, the paramount Chieftain of the Bemba people. As an economic strategist he had been a guest lecturer at Wits during the period that Angel had taught languages while working on his doctorate. David now shared his time between being head of the Mwansa clan, a director of Grindlays Bank and an untitled position at ZSIS, the Zambian Security Intelligence Service.

Angel used the formal iciBemba greeting when he called. "*Mulishani?*"

"Angel, what a surprise. The devil himself."

"That's very funny, David."

"How are things?" he asked. "Still oppressing your brothers? Been busy cattle-prodding a few natives?"

Angel had heard the rumours as well. An electric cattle prod gave a stronger shock than a stun gun but from the end of a long stick, a torture device said to be employed by the South African Police.

"Not lately, David. How are your ANC friends? Tell Mr Tambo we enjoyed his little speech."

Angel checked the calendar on his desk. It was 8th April. Three months earlier to the day, President Oliver Tambo had celebrated the 70th anniversary of the ANC's founding at a gathering in Tanzania. He had declared 1982 to be the year of massive action against apartheid.

"I'll pass that on, Angel," he replied. "And how are things in Cape Town? I hear your record-keeping isn't as good as it once was."

On 20th March a powerful bomb had exploded behind a court in Cape Town that housed the personal files of thousands of Africans. It was part of an ANC campaign to create confusion by destroying the administrative records of black people. No one had been injured.

"We are still picking passbooks out of the trees, David."

David Mwansa laughed.

"To what do I owe the pleasure of this call, Angel?"

"I'm looking for someone in Zambia," Angel said.

"Angel, you know I can't help—"

Angel cut him off.

"It's okay. It's nothing political. He's not an ANC member. It's an Englishman; well, an English boy actually. He's lost."

"He's lost or you've lost him?" asked David.

"Both," said Angel.

David was suddenly interested.

"A white English boy?"

"Most of them are," said Angel.

"What's so important about him that NIS is involved?"

Angel would have liked an answer to that same question.

"Nothing important," he lied. "We're doing a favour for someone, a political someone."

"You just said it was nothing political."

"You know how it is, David. We serve and don't ask the reason why."

"Hmm."

Angel thought he'd change the subject.

"He crossed into Zimbabwe at Beitbridge on foot just over a month ago – 5th March."

"He's walking?"

"I believe so."

"Extraordinary. Is he still alive?" asked David.

"I believe so."

Angel thought about it. Perhaps David was right. The boy had been alone in Zimbabwe for thirty days, at a time when the country was recovering from a violently tribal civil war. He may well be dead in a ditch. He shook his head to clear the thought and his braids rattled.

"My question is, David, how would he travel north through Zambia?"

"North?"

"To Kenya."

"Do you have a map?"

Angel jumped up from the desk and stood in front of the wall.

"Go on."

"Well, it wouldn't make any difference if he crossed into Zambia at Victoria Falls or north of Kariba."

Angel traced it on the wall map.

"The dam?" he asked.

"Yes. Either way he'd come through Lusaka."

"And then?"

"Going north there's only one way."

"Tanzania," said Angel.

"Correct."

"And how would he do that?"

"I'll ask around if you like. See if I can find something out. But only because it's you, my brother."

"*Natotela*, David."

"My pleasure, Angel."

Angel went to put the phone down.

"David!" he shouted.

"Yes, Angel, I'm still here."

"How would he travel to Tanzania?"

"There's only one way, Angel. On the railway."

Angel could see the black line on the map. It started north of Lusaka heading north and east into Tanzania then onward to Dar es Salaam on the Indian Ocean, close to the Kenyan border.

"He'd take the Tanzam," said David Mwansa.

TWELVE

Ralph looked out of the carriage door at the ground, the train moving fast even though it was going around a long gentle curve. Local men began jumping off and rolling in the dust.

A train guard put his head out of the door and looked ahead.

"End of the curve. We'll speed up soon."

A man a little older than Ralph stood beside him, speaking English.

"You've got to jump, mate."

Ralph looked out of the door, the speed already increasing.

*

Ralph had spent a night on the floor of the Sikh temple in Lusaka waiting for a ride north in a van delivering fire extinguishers to Kapiri Mposhi, the driver a silent moody drunk.

The train station at Kapiri had been huge, silent, a temple to Chinese engineering or a great hall for Chairman Mao's people, and completely empty of rail passengers. A Zambian Police Force band, resplendent in white, played to an empty ballroom.

Ralph found a ticket office. There were two trains: an express left at 10.00 that night and took thirty-six hours to reach Dar es Salaam; or a stopping train left the following morning at 10.35 and took forty-eight hours. Ralph calculated that the slow train would have to average 38.8 kilometres per hour. It seemed sufficiently fast when he'd been walking less than that distance in a day. The slow train also went through the Selous game park during the day, providing a free safari. Ralph took a third-class ticket for the following day and rented bedding for the trip. The ticket officer took his money with a bewildered smile. There were no beds in third class.

*

On the train progress had been slow. In six hours they'd covered thirty kilometres. Ralph could have walked quicker.

A guard came to inspect tickets.

"You have no visa for Tanzania?"

"No. Someone told me I could arrange it at the border."

"The embassy for visas is in Lusaka."

He looked through Ralph's passport carefully, but selected pages at random and examined each as though he couldn't read.

"I've come from Johannesburg," explained Ralph. "And I'm just travelling through Dar and Mombasa to get to Nairobi."

The guard gave him back his passport wordlessly.

The young man lying on the upright wooden bench lifted a hat off his face and sat up. He pulled a blue passport from his back pocket and gave it to the guard.

He winked at Ralph.

"Morris," he said and held out his hand.

It looked fat and puffy, like a glove that had been blown up. It was scarred on both sides, a mess of small deep cuts where the flesh had been cut out and longer deeper rips on the palm. It resembled a road map of an inner city in relief.

"Hi, I'm Ralph."

"Smoko," Morris said. "Coming for a cuppa?"

Ralph followed him to a carriage where a lady sold black sweet tea in glasses.

"Where are you from?" Ralph asked him.

Morris mumbled with a mouth stuffed full of chapati.

"You're Dutch?"

"New Zealand, mate. Not old Zeeland."

Morris was travelling up from South Africa, on a strict timetable in between jobs. He'd 'taken a shufti' around Johannesburg and done a safari in Kruger National Park. Neither had impressed him.

"I'm here to go up Kili really."

Ralph liked him immediately.

"Have you got a map?" Morris asked.

He put his empty glass on the countertop and pointed to Ralph's.

"Skull it. We need to take a squiz at your passport as well."

*

Morris stretched himself and threw the Baldwins' map of central Africa on the floor between the benches.

"Mate, you've got two problems."

Ralph had already prepared himself for bad news. A private conversation with the guard outside the toilet had not given him much encouragement of his entry into Tanzania without a visa. There had been much shrugging of shoulders and sucking through stained teeth.

"The bloke is wrong about the visa. I guess the United Kingdom is in the Commonwealth, right?"

"Well, yes. Of course."

"Yeah. I thought so."

He thumbed through the pages of Ralph's passport.

"You don't need a visa, then. Commonwealth countries and some neutral European ones like Ireland, and Scandinavian countries for some reason, none of them need a visa. They issue you with a 'Visitor Pass' at the border."

"That's great."

"But your problem is these."

He pointed to a page with something stuck on it: a visitor permit for The Republic of South Africa, 'No Remuneration Allowed', with a stamp – 'Immigration. Jan Smuts Airport'.

"The Tanzanians hate the South Africans. They'll kick you out if they see these, just because you've been there."

He searched through a side pocket on his small backpack. With swollen fingers he peeled off a white adhesive label and pressed it on the page in Ralph's passport that showed his offensive visit to the bottom of the continent. The South African stamps were hidden. On the label were eight lines of Chinese characters.

"What does it say?"

"I've no idea, mate. Look. It's in Chinese."

"Will that work?"

"Hope so."

He held up his own passport.

"You've got bigger problems anyway."

Ralph stared at him.

"You are going through to Nairobi? Yeah, I thought the same. Kilimanjaro is in Tanzania but just over the Kenyan border. It would have been much easier to fly to Nairobi and just cross over. Instead I've had to come up from Joburg."

"Kili?"

Morris nodded.

"The problem you've got, mate, is that the Kenyan border with Tanzania is officially closed."

Tension between Kenya and Tanzania had been high since 1977 when the East African Community collapsed, mostly due to differences in the Tanzanian socialist economic model and the Kenyan capitalist system. The EAC had been an economic union between Kenya, Tanzania and Uganda. The jointly held assets included the railways, the ships on Lake Victoria, the airlines and the Post Office. One day, Kenya had unilaterally seized all the assets. And then when Tanzania invaded Uganda to oust Idi Amin, an action almost universally applauded, they had been criticised by Kenya. It had taken several weeks for Tanzania to rout the remnants of Amin's army as it retreated further and further north. At the end, over ten thousand Tanzanian troops remained in Uganda, trying to maintain law and order. Nyerere, President of Tanzania, maintained that his intention had been to see a civilian government elected and to withdraw his troops as soon as possible, but Kenya felt threatened and closed the border between the two.

"It's harder crossing from Kenya to Tanzania. The other way is possible but who knows. It's a gamble. First you must go to the Ministry of Home Affairs in Dar es Salaam. They may give you special permission. Or they may not. If they like you they'll give you a document that you should present to the Chief of Police in Arusha, who may then issue you with another form which allows you to cross the border at Namanga, and only at Namanga. Here."

Morris pointed it out on the map. It was nowhere near Mombasa.

*

Progress on the Tanzam had been steady during the day but as night fell the train slowed and occasionally stopped for no reason on dark straight stretches, a long way from anywhere.

Morris talked of Kilimanjaro, at 5,896 metres even higher than New Zealand's Mount Cook. He'd never done anything that high, even though he liked tramping. When off work he'd often go over to the Southern Alps and do the Kipler. The Routeburn Track was better, with great views of the Humboldt Mountains and up the Valley of the Trolls toward Lake Wilson. It was a lot lower than Kili of course. If he went up Conical Hill from the Harris shelter he would only get to just over 1,500 metres.

"How long does that take?" Ralph asked.

"Takes me about three days. I like to take it easy, look around. There are good shelters along the way. Somebody did the whole thing in three hours."

"You wouldn't do Kili in three hours."

"Mate, I tell you, I'm worried about the altitude sickness.

I'm going to take the long route, maybe take nine days, do it slow, get acclimatised. The best routes let you walk high but sleep low. More climbing, as you're up and down a wee bit, but better for you."

Ralph wondered what Morris did for a living that gave him time off to go to Africa just to climb a mountain.

"I'm a deckhand on a deep-water freezer trawler out of Timaru," he explained.

In January the cockies sold livestock before the grass started drying off for the summer and the beasts ran out of food. They got busy at the meatpackers at that time, knife work cutting beef and sheep and venison, so Morris worked there as well if he wasn't at sea.

Ralph Laughed, "Cockies?"

"Farmers. They're all a bit cocky. They can't help it. Must be living out in the wop-wops on your own. You're the king of your own patch of land; makes you act like you're king of everywhere. Cocky."

"You get a lot of time off then?"

"We work a trip of fifty or sixty days and then have two months off."

"Sounds easy."

"Easy? You bust a gut, mate."

Morris worked six hours on six off for seven or eight weeks, numbingly hard work. He got wet, smelt like a fish, and needed to have his wits about him. He lived with his head on a swivel and slept, along with three other men, in a space the size of most people's bathrooms. He'd witnessed accidents too, people falling right across the deck in bad seas. There was a crane for lifting the metal doors that spread the net out, each door weighing five tons, and he'd seen people fall out of the crane when the ship pitched about. Luckily, he'd never seen anyone go overboard. He had help treat bad burns from the steam of the fishmeal cooker.

"So, what do you do on the boat?"

"You know, shoot and haul the nets, work winches, mend nets," Morris replied modestly. "It helps if you've a mechanical aptitude."

The nets were shot and trawling for three hours, and while they were out there was always something to fix. Wire splicing was the worst. The wire was on a drum and led to the warps that were attached to the nets, 2,500 metres on a drum so they could fish to 1,200 metres deep.

"It's twenty-eight millimetres thick, six-strand. Twice a trip we splice a new loop into the wire. It's a tough physical job working a huge marlin spike. And you better get it right. If you lose a net that's a hundred and fifty thousand down the pan."

Ralph was curious about Morris' life, looking for guidance to help him decide what he should do with his own. He asked, thoughtfully, "What sort of boat is it?"

"Depends where you are and what fish you're going for. Some are trawlers or long liners in the Cook Strait going for hoki. Some go down into Antarctic waters for toothfish in the summer. There are skipjack tuna boats with purse seine nets and a helicopter on board for spotting the fish; they go out in the western or central Pacific. My boat is a big boat – a factory ship. The *Endeavour*. We've got a crew of forty. She's almost seventy metres long, nearly 2,500 tons. She's a stern trawler with twin nets. We go out in the Southern Ocean."

"Do you make good money?"

"Are you kidding? That's what we do it for. First thing I do when I start a trip, I put a hundred-dollar bill on the inside of my locker and write on it in a fat pen: 'This is why I'm here'. I left school at fifteen, wanted to be outside doing something and not stuck in a classroom. They all thought I might be a piker. I bought my own house when I was twenty-one. In cash. For working half the year."

Looking at his own scarred hands Morris explained that the Endeavour was a factory ship and that the factory worked shifts for twenty-four hours a day, so Morris had to fish day and night as well.

"But we don't just fish and say, 'Hey, you tinbums down there in the factory, pull your finger out your arse and pack this stuff.' The factory sets the pace."

They fished to keep the factory supplied at the rate it could work. If Morris and his team got ahead of the factory then the fish would go bad before they could pack it. Fresher fish meant that more of the higher-value skinless steaks and fillets could be packed. The rest of it, the heads and the bones and the junk, were cooked up and powdered into fishmeal as they went along. The only thing they left behind them was a trail of dirty warm water in the clean cold Southern Ocean. Everything had been used.

"I tell you, mate, it stinks. The whole boat and everyone on it. We smell so bad," Morris laughed, "but we don't care. it's the stink of money."

Ralph was thinking in unexpected moments that took him by surprise of his future. "Will you do it forever, then?" he asked, wondering what was in store for him back in Dorset, back home.

"I started as a factory hand, cutting and packing fish. It's better on deck. It's tough, like playing a rough rugby match for six hours. The skipper, he got his deep-sea captain's licence when he was twenty-three. Bought his own boat eventually and went after toothfish in the Ross Sea. He left school at fifteen too. Blondie – he's the first mate on *Endeavour* – he said I should think about getting some tickets."

Ralph envied Morris his active life and not for the first time thought what a great country New Zealand must be. Wild countryside with mountains for 'tramping' in, space to breathe, a country where you could work hard and be rewarded well for doing a physically demanding job in clean air. A country that bred men like Morris. Men that could earn their way and with quiet confidence travel about the world, taking a little bit of everything they saw back to their own quiet beautiful place.

*

In the early dawn the train stopped and didn't move. Morris woke Ralph from a fitful sleep.

"What's up?" said Ralph.

"We're at a bridge in the boonies."

"Where are we?"

"Chuck us the map, mate."

The scale looked small but useable.

"Here. Somewhere after this station," he looked hard at the name, "Keyaya and before the next one, this place Makasa."

After a town called Chamdamkulu, the Tanzam crossed a river that meandered south-east before turning south-west and joining the swamps that fed Lake Bangweulu. They were about 750 kilometres from where they had got on the train at Kapiri Mposhi, not halfway to Dar es Salaam, and over 1,100 kilometres still to go. They had been on the train for twenty hours.

"What's the problem?"

"It's puckeroo. Munted."

Neither sounded good. Morris translated.

"The bridge looks too dodgy to cross. We've stopped to look at it and shake our heads. Thankfully some local built a fire on the track to warn the driver. Want a shufti?"

The train had stopped some way short of the bridge on flat wetland and swamp, with the rail track raised on an embankment of stone and shingle. The train hissed at them like a big cat as they stepped down and joined a knowledgeable crowd inspecting the bridge. Flash floodwater had washed the riverbed away around the concrete base of a steel support and the middle of the bridge tilted drunkenly like a poorly ballasted ship.

The ticket inspector with the stained teeth provided little encouragement.

"How long?" Morris asked.

"A week. Maybe two."

"We'll stay here a week?" asked Ralph.

The ticket inspector looked at him as though he might be simple.

"No. We'll go back."

"Can I get off here?"

"If you like. But no buses on the road in Tanzania. No fuel. Better to get off at Nseluka."

Ralph and Morris got out the maps.

"Here. Nseluka," said Ralph.

Morris studied the map.

"Oh. I got it. You could go up to this place on the bottom of Lake Tanganyika, Mpulungu, and then around the top."

"How far is that?"

Morris measured it off.

"Through Nendo, Senga Hill, Mbala – 170 kilometres."

Ralph did a rough calculation and guessed it to be a four- or five-day walk.

"And then how do I go up the lake?" he asked.

"Must be loads of boats," Morris assured him.

Morris measured again.

"It's the same distance as from Invercargill to Nelson. This lake is as long as the South Island."

It was the longest freshwater lake in the world and the second deepest.

"Get a boat to the top here in Bujumbura Burundi, then around Tanzania so you avoid the border problem. It's a bit of a tiki tour but you'll be giving your ferret a run in Nairobi before you know it."

"What will you do?" Ralph asked him.

"I'll go back to Lusaka and go to the airport. Get a plane if I can. Or I might give up on it and try and get to South America. Have a root around Buenos Aires. Or try to. I could go home that way around. Come back and do Kili another time."

*

From the doorway of the train heading back the wrong way Ralph saw the ground speeding past.

Ralph looked at the ticket collector.

"I thought you said it stopped at Nseluka?"

"I said you could get off at Nseluka. I never said it stopped."

"That's true, mate," said Morris unhelpfully.

"You have to jump now," said the guard.

"But it's going too fast."

"Stop whinging. Come on, rattle your dags. Hurry up."

Morris gave him a friendly push through the doorway.

Ralph flew with rucksack in hand, then tumbled forward, rolling painfully on his shoulder before ending face down looking at gravel and dust. He stood up, brushed himself down and watched the train disappear. In the door of the carriage Morris laughed.

He looked around and found he'd landed just outside the village. A few other men who'd jumped had already started walking north. From Cape Town to the Zambian Copperbelt, Ralph had been following a path well-trodden by explorers, missionaries and empire builders. His truncated trip on the Tanzam had brought him beyond the Benguela Swamp which, until the Chinese, had been an impenetrable natural barrier to the route north. Cecil Rhodes had never surveyed this far, his dream of a red line from Cape to Cairo curtailed by marshland, bog and disease. In the morning light it looked untamed, unexploited, virgin Africa. He heard a subtle faint noise from the village, answered even fainter from beyond. It was the sound of drums, African drums of villages along Ralph's path communicating at the dawn of the day. Ralph, 5,060 kilometres from Cape Town, had finally found Africa.

*

Angel had gone to see Elanza on a Sunday, expecting her to be fractious. Instead he found her in high spirits, a cocktail of prescription medicines momentarily in the correct combination to alleviate her pain and depression.

"I want to go out," she'd said.

"Out? To a bar or someplace?" Angel had asked, already anxious about what she had in mind. He'd wondered where a rich farmer's daughter might go for a Sunday lunchtime drink and in his mind had settled on the Main Bar at the Rand Club, a vast colonial affair with lots of mahogany and the walls filled with the severed heads of herds of African animals. It would have been a little difficult for him to go with her.

"I want to feel people, to hear kids having fun," she'd said.

"Johannesburg Zoo," Angel had quickly suggested.

For an hour he'd led her along Tiger Track, around Baboon Bend and Elephant Walk, Elanza listening to children chattering about eland, rhino and lemur. She had soon tired, and Angel had taken her to an outside restaurant in the park but immediately regretted his decision, feeling uncomfortable among tables of white families. Johannesburg Zoo and the park around Zoo Lake were a unique public space, open to all races, but only white people sat at the restaurant under the trees with a cool Chenin blanc and *gambas a la plancha*. A young girl with a drinking straw in her mouth stared at him with her head on one side. Her mother noticed him and they left, the woman dragging the girl by the strap of a satchel.

Angel watched the early autumn sunshine, still warm in April, flicker through the old oak trees around Zoo Lake on to Elanza's face and hair. She closed her eyes and tilted her head back to catch the sun, her neck thin and sinewy, fragile but beautiful.

"Could you see anything of the animals, Elanza?"

Elanza shook her head.

"Not a thing."

Angel felt pity for her, imagining a life of black nothingness.

"I'm sorry."

"Why are you sorry?" she asked him.

"Well, just darkness must be…"

Elanza held his arm.

"Oh, it's not dark, Angel. It's beautiful and light. Ever-changing colours I couldn't describe. It's distracting though. You can't turn it off. Closing your eyes doesn't help. It's all still there, still bright and light. It's like being deaf but with a constant ringing in your ears."

Angel felt her hand on his arm. For the first time in his life he was with a woman whom he could care for and who might care for him, tenderly and in public.

"What can you see right now?" he asked through a lump in his throat.

"I can't see a waiter bringing me a Bloody Mary."

"What else?"

Elanza sat upright and stared ahead as if concentrating.

"Right now, it's a warm brown colour like a dark wood but with something glowing blue in the front. Now it's bright blue with yellow flecks but I think quite soon it'll all be orange. There are squashed shapes like pyramids and clouds, but in a moment it'll all be different. It's like fireworks, bright and noisy, but all the time. I sit and stare at it, longing for quiet darkness."

A waiter approached them and crossed his bare arms. Angel looked at them, pink and freckled, and propped his British passport against a big peppermill on the table where the waiter could see it.

"At last," said Elanza.

The waiter took her order and turned to Angel.

"And you? What do you want?"

"He was a little rude," she said as the waiter walked stiffly away, and then, "You spoke English."

"Did I?"

"Your English sounds odd too. Very Michael Caine."

"My mother's fault."

Elanza relaxed into the wooden chair. As she leant backwards Angel could see over the empty table vacated by the woman and the young girl to the other people in the restaurant. A man sat alone at a table among the families. He had a camera with a long lens.

"I would have liked to have seen London," Elanza said.

Angel looked at the man. There was something about the way he was dressed. He looked like a tourist but one that had thought too hard about what to wear. He was a caricature of a tourist, unsuccessfully hiding his identity in the same way that Angel could always spot an off-duty junior soldier – his trainers too clean, his jeans pressed, his polo shirt collars starched.

"Hmm?"

"Your mother in London – how is she?"

"I'm not sure."

Elanza sat upright.

"What?"

"I haven't talked to her lately," explained Angel lamely.

Elanza had been ten years old when her mother had died unexpectedly at home. Her father had held her wordlessly, then together they had moved sheep to water. She had heard him crying that night, then he'd never spoken of her. Elanza hadn't cried at all.

"You probably see more of your father," she said.

"He moves around a lot. In fact, I don't know where he's living now."

Elanza felt she was pushing him to talk against his will.

"We should find him," she said and held his hand. "I'd like to meet him."

Angel had been trying to find him for years, had quietly utilised resources at work to help in his search. He had little to go on. A man named Rots, first name unknown, age unknown, an engineer who had worked on the railway over thirty years ago.

"I'm sorry, Elanza, I should be getting back."

"Sure… Angel, have I said something wrong?"

Angel had watched the man leave. He hadn't stopped to photograph the picturesque flamingos on the lake.

"No, nothing wrong. There's a guy over there I recognise from work."

Elanza, curious, asked, "Oh really? Shall we go and say hi?"

"Too late. He's gone."

"Shame," she said, disappointed. "What's his name?"

"Heining."

A cloud had drifted across the sun, now lower in the trees. It felt cool, winter just around the corner. Angel shivered.

"Heining?" she asked. "That's an unusual name."

"He's an unusual guy."

Angel took her arm.

"Come on. Let's go. You'll get cold."

The waiter watched them leave, walking close together and holding hands, and shook his ginger head.

*

Nels met Roux at Burgers Park, four hectares in the centre of Pretoria named after the second President of the Transvaal. It had originally been set aside for a park in 1874 but it had taken until 1892 for it to be finished. A young government botanist with the very English name of James Hunter had eventually completed a Victorian-style English park, complete with curved paths and a cast-iron bandstand for tea concerts, deep in the heart of the Afrikaner homeland.

At lunchtime Roux liked to relax in the park and enjoy a brief respite from the office. It had been a difficult morning. A South African government procurement minister had been on a business trip to France, talking with the giant arms supplier Dassault, vainly trying to find ways to circumvent restrictions on arms exports to South Africa. Roux had received a call from his opposite number in Paris to say that the minister had slept in a swanky hotel with a woman they knew as Paula, known to them as being KGB. He thoughtfully suggested that if the minister needed such diversions, the French External Documentation and Counter-Espionage Service in Paris could find him prettier and safer women. It remained only for Roux to point out to the minister that such behaviour would likely be a security risk. He felt a moment of contemplation in Burgers Park to be most definitely in order.

Nels found Roux on a bench by a World War One monument honouring the South African Scottish Regiment. He had become frustrated with the National Intelligence Service for not finding the boy. NIS seemed anything but intelligent.

"You know Treurnicht might be right," said Nels. "Botha may not be around for much longer. It could be a long trek. You might want to make sure your horse is following the right wagon."

Andries Treurnicht, an MP, minister and Dutch Reformed churchman, had quit PW Botha's ruling National Party in opposition to Botha's limited reforms to apartheid and his talk of power sharing. Treurnicht had taken twenty-two right-wing MPs with him and formed the Conservative

Party. They'd immediately held a vote of no confidence in the Prime Minister.

And the ANC bombings continued to scare and disrupt: bombs on the Administration Board in Soweto twice; guerrillas attacking the Koeberg nuclear power plant near Cape Town; bombs against the Department of Internal Affairs near Durban; against railways and depots and bridges; limpet mines against power transformers, under cars and along oil pipelines.

Roux worried that he might be wrong about South Africa's future. What if he and Lombard persuaded Botha that the only way forward would be to make a deal with the ANC for a transition to majority rule, and then they were all murdered in their beds in revenge for what they had done wrong for so many years?

If Botha became replaced by a more right-wing government, Roux couldn't imagine what might happen. Maybe they would have to fight to the last man standing. In that situation a new government would need a respected National Intelligence Service more than ever, if only to keep the likes of Cornelius Nels under control.

Roux thought about the hills behind the seaside town of Rooi-Els and the long beach with the Overberg test facility just the other side of the dunes. He had a few unsettling doubts about Angel's abilities. He worked after all as an analyst and not a field agent. Perhaps it would be useful to have two people looking for Ralph, in case Lombard's concern about the suspected British spy they referred to as Zac was correct. Roux didn't like Nels but considered he should be prepared to use him to safeguard South African nuclear secrets. He felt like he might be making a deal with the devil.

"I'll tell you on the condition that if I ask you for a favour one day you'll do something for me."

Nels nodded.

"Such as?"

"If I have an employee that's gone bad, for example."

"You want me to kill him?"

"I'm not sure yet. I'll let you know about that."

Nels smiled.

"An employee who works for you?" he asked.

"Yes."

Nels scratched the side of his head. Ridges of flesh moved on his scalp underneath stubbly hair.

"What sort of employee?"

Roux looked sadly at the ground in front of him.

"A Coloured employee."

"Oh yes," said Nels cheerily, "that wouldn't be a problem."

Roux wondered if he was doing the right thing. Nels scared him. He was something malevolent and menacing, like a shark.

"Ralph's going to Nairobi and flying home from there," he said.

CENTRAL AFRICA

13TH APRIL TO 5TH MAY, 1982

THIRTEEN

The small fishing town of Mpulungu, Zambia's only port, crouched in the lee of a small island on Lake Tanganyika. Water, the life blood of the town, made it different to any place Ralph had been through. At its heart, in the marketplace and fish-drying area, boys from small wooden boats threw buckets of wet fish onto tarpaulin sheets, or scooped them dry into old sacks. Brightly painted fishing boats moored stern to the beach and spread red nets to dry, while women washed clothes and hung them over bushes. Around the market stood clusters of mud huts with reed roofs, left with untrimmed shaggy fringes like cheeky boys. Dusty paths went straight to the water where women carried baskets on their heads and children lay like fish in the shallows of the calm lake.

From jumping off the train Ralph had walked through Ngolo and camped the first night twelve kilometres south of the town of Nendo, the sound of village drums following him all the way. The next night he made Senga Hill and looked for the mission, but the missionaries had not been as accommodating to a dirty English boy as the Baldwin family near Lusaka had been, their God working only for locally lost souls. He slept that night out of town under a bridge. Halfway to the next town of Mbala, where the road bent and went over a river, curious children walked with him in a long cheerful line.

An old German ship, the *Liemba*, usually steamed up the lake to Bujumbura but had been delayed. At its berth a rusty cement freighter loaded cargo, the bow grounded in green reeds by the water's edge.

A very dark man in a clean white vest directed operations by shouting at scurrying deckhands through the stub of a blunt cigar.

Ralph shouted up at him.

"I'm looking for the captain. Mr Georgolidis?"

The crew stood motionless, looking at him then looking at the man in the white vest on the bridge. He said something to them in an African language and they laughed.

"I was told Captain Georgolidis might take me up to the top of the lake."

Ralph wondered if they were familiar with it.

"To Bujumbura," he explained.

The man in the white vest slowly removed his cigar and examined him with one eye closed through dirty brown smoke.

"Are you English?" he said.

"Yes I am. Sorry."

Ralph often felt as if he needed to apologise for his nationality. He felt he carried around the guilt of a small wet island that had taken foreign lands at will, plundered them, and at best had treated the locals with a benevolent paternalism.

The man in the white vest seemed to understand. He smiled down on him from his commanding lookout.

"Please don't apologise."

His English reminded Ralph of the vicar at home, announcing in church a birth, marriage or death. He spoke slowly and deeply, cautiously annunciating his thoughtful words with deliberate care.

He studied Ralph curiously.

"My name is Winston. Like the Great Man."

He laughed loudly and the deckhands looked at him and laughed as well.

Winston stared at them.

"I am the captain."

"I took the train. The Tanzam. It had to go back as a bridge had been washed away."

Ralph felt he needed to explain.

"I had thought of getting a ride on the road to Dar es Salaam with a truck."

Ralph expected him to say something but he continued smoking his beat-up cigar for a long while. He spat into the water.

"There are petrol shortages in Tanzania. There is very little road traffic."

"Exactly," Ralph felt relieved. "That's what someone said."

"Julius Nyerere is a fool. Socialism based upon a collective of agricultural villages. Ha. Simply medieval. He calls them *ujamaa* farms. Everyone should be a farmer. Ha. Even government ministers. I told him it wouldn't work. Egalitarianism. Ha."

Winston inspected his cigar, seemed offended by it, and shouted some more at the deckhands.

Ralph tried again.

"I'm really trying to get to Nairobi. I have a flight from there. To England."

Winston, finally beaten by the remains of his cigar, threw it into the lake. It bobbed with other flotsam along a faded mark, well underwater, that at one time might have been a Plimsoll line.

Winston looked at Ralph.

"My dear fellow. You are welcome to come with us. It's a three-day trip…" he hesitated, scanning the sky, "if we have no headwind."

He looked at Ralph's rucksack.

"But I'm afraid you'll have to bring your own food."

"I don't have much money. To pay for the passage."

Winston didn't answer. He jumped in a single bound from the bridge, disappearing into the hold. A huge hand appeared at dock level through a scupper, Winston's face following it as he peered over the gunwale.

"Do you play chess?" he asked.

From the bow of the ship Winston's booming voice vibrated the length of the hull. He had stopped the men from loading more bags of cement.

The *Independence* was ready for sea.

*

The *Independence* had barely cleared the point, wet lines still being coiled on deck, and in the engine room gear oil pressure on a big brass gauge made in Glasgow not yet steady, when Winston set the chessboard.

Busy deckhands peered through the windows from the fly bridge, and a boy in a cut-down boiler suit, stained from grease and thick oil, stood ready to relay moves through an old speaking tube to the chief still sweating in the noisy engine room below. Chess looked to be a serious business on board the *Independence*.

Ralph made a bold move at the start of their first game, peeling a pawn off the board from a sticky pad and pressing it down hard to fix it determinedly onto e4.

"Stop!" shouted Winston.

A boy at the helm, too small to see over the panel, reached for the engine room telegraph. Winston glared and shouted at him, and his hand jerked back to the wheel as if shocked. Winston took out his cigar and looked at Ralph.

"Sir. Before we go any further I want to applaud you."

The crew joined Winston and clapped.

"I don't know if you have a Danish or a Cochrane in mind but I must tell you that I admire aggressive openings."

He looked at Ralph through his smoke.

"As in life, gambits that put pieces into play are so much more interesting."

The clapping stopped.

"I knew you wouldn't disappoint."

Ralph, his chess a relic from an indulgent schoolmaster looking to occupy restless minds, had been surprised at his unexpected ability. Ralph's opening never varied since he'd watched his teacher cruelly checkmate a small boy in four devastating moves, but he had no idea how to progress a Kings, a Danish or a Cochrane.

There was something more surprising and unexpected about Winston. His chess expertise and his eloquence appeared at odds with his scaly bare feet, voluble management style and filthy chewed-upon cigar stuck in an unshaven scarred face. And there was the curious idea of the captain of a rusty cement freighter discussing economic theory with the president of a neighbouring country – too delicious a concept to leave unresolved.

"So, about Nyerere's farms," suggested Ralph.

"Shhhh."

The whole crew in and on the bridge repeated their captain's command.

"Shhhhh."

Ralph waited quietly for his turn and then recklessly moved a bishop into battle a long way forward from his own foot soldiers, a move to harass and unnerve with no clear view of what he might achieve.

Winston grunted. The boy steering had turned away from the wheel, leaning against the binnacle and concentrating on the board with his head in both hands. Winston countered with a challenging knight that took first blood, an innocent sacrificial pawn, and the boy relaxed and glanced forward through the spokes at the lake ahead. Chess, still like draughts to the boy, meant that the more white pieces the captain cleared from the board the better. The crew collectively exhaled. Ralph realised he wasn't playing Winston, but the *Independence*, the ship and her crew.

Ralph thought he'd try a different tack.

"Have you always been captain of this ship?"

Winston thought for a moment before answering, a pawn hovering in the air.

"As a great man, not my namesake, once said, 'What matters is that the individual feels more complete, with much more internal richness and much more responsibility'."

Winston considered what he'd just said.

"I don't think I've paraphrased him."

*

After the initial excitement of the dynamic opening moves, the game settled into one of attrition, Winston and Ralph exchanging pieces in rapid-fire exchanges that delighted the crew, both looking to exploit a weakness.

Ralph thought of a less contentious question.

"This is a curious chess set. Do you need to have the pieces secured to the board on such a heavy ship?"

Winston looked up from the game. They were approaching Kasanga, a village on the Tanzanian side, wooden dugouts launching from the beach like partridge from cover.

"Anchor!" Winston shouted.

The bridge cleared in a scurry of bodies fore and aft.

"I'm sorry," he explained. "Duty calls. Please stay here if you like."

A wind had picked up from the north. Small waves widely spaced coursed down the lake in neat parallel lines. Winston headed into the wind and rang the telegraph to stop. As way fell off the ship he looked sideways at the shore through a bridge window rather than ahead. At the instant a pole on the beach became stationary against a bare tree on the hill behind, he lowered his raised hand. The anchor chain clattered through the hawse pipe, paying out in noisy bursts as the ship started to drift backwards and the chain pulled free from the pile deep in the hold. Winston raised his hand again to the foredeck crew. A rusty dog thrown over the chain seized a link like a bone in its tired jaws, and with a groan the *Independence* took up the slack and came to rest.

Cheerful boatmen immediately surrounded her, hanging on to the hull and squinting as they looked up into the sun which sparkled on the water around them. The crew bartered for fruit and yams with the boys in the canoes, although many seemed to have nothing to sell.

Women dressed in black embarked and camped in a circle around the windlass on the foredeck, like a coven of witches around a cauldron.

"Ahmadis," explained Winston.

It was the first Arab influence Ralph had seen in Africa. Winston peered through a smoky circular Perspex panel in the bridge window. At one time it would have spun around furiously, throwing rain and enabling a clear view.

"They'll get off at Ujiji."

"Where is that?"

"Ujiji was the start of one of the main Muslim slave trade routes to Zanzibar. It's at the top of the lake just south of the Burundi border. Near Kigoma. About two and a half days. Depending on the wind."

Winston watched the women settling down in their own space at the bow, protected by a high bulwark with an overhanging lip.

"They have an interesting interpretation of Islam. They wish to revive the forgotten Islamic values of peace, forgiveness and sympathy for all mankind. They have one of the most active missionary programmes in the world, especially here in Africa."

"So, you are just giving them a lift up the lake? Like me?"

"They could go on the *Liemba* but they feel happier travelling with me. Fewer prying eyes. And Ahmadis are sometimes persecuted by other Muslims as heretics. I do a public service where I can. I'm like British Rail but with less industrial action."

"Have you been to Britain?"

Winston ignored him.

"Ahmadis have a fundamental belief in angels. They are messengers from God to human beings, sometimes appearing to man… in one form or another."

He knocked an old, slightly conical, graduated clear plastic tube, cloudy with age. A red disc on a spindle fluctuated wildly halfway up the inside of the tube.

"Wind's getting up. We need to be in a snug berth before dark."

He pulled a chain in the ceiling. A whistle blustered over the choppy Tanganyikan water, short long long short, and a Blue Peter stiffened in the strengthening African wind.

*

By nightfall a fresh gale howled down Tanganyika. Two to three metre waves chased each other into the darkness, heaping up and streaking white foam. The stars danced wildly across the sky, the whole of heaven and earth blown around by an angry wind.

The *Independence* had anchored for the night in fifteen metres of black water behind a fist of land coming off the Tanzanian coast, south of a small fishing village called Kirambo. At sunset a thick snubbing line, fat as a forearm, had been attached to the anchor chain. It creaked painfully in the fairlead as the ship, blown beam to the wind, lifted the chain clear of the water far ahead before swinging back the other way.

The Ahmadi women had retreated from the bow during the three-hour passage from Kasanga, the *Independence* pitching into the sea as it ploughed north. They fluttered like distressed birds under the bridge. Ralph had been outside with the intention of talking to them but had found it hard to walk against the wind on the leaning deck. He'd returned to the smoky chess game inside, the heavy watertight door caught by a gust and slamming shut behind him like a mortar.

Winston stood at the wheel, unconsciously balancing himself with the roll of the ship as he looked down the deck toward the bow, illuminated by a white riding light strung below a black ball that twisted and untwisted recklessly in the gale.

He had been master since old Georgolidis had retired himself, before his drunkenness had forced the issue, but the sea hadn't been Winston's first calling. His career switch had shocked many but not those who knew him well. His tutors at university, and his colleagues at the Ministry of Foreign Affairs on Independence Avenue in Lusaka, were not surprised. They understood the perfect world order a good captain could create with a seaborne command. The ship *Independence* was a self-supporting commune, its members reliant on one another. Winston had discovered, to his great surprise, that no matter how skilled each individual crewman, how dedicated they may be to the cause, a commander was still required to coordinate their action, to conduct the orchestra. Decisions that had to be taken for the efficient running of their little world could not be decided by committee. People liked to be led.

With this realisation his life changed, and his politics. He found that his crew worked best when they had ownership of their own part of the machinery of the ship. They worked better when there was competition from other crewmen who could do their job and take it away from them. When they were productive in this way the ship reached the top of the lake quicker, carried more cement, made more profit. With their profit the crew could own things: clothes or food or decorations for their cabin. Aboard ship these things didn't lead to inequality, or greed, or selfishness.

The ship, his small state, did not need to be directly

controlled by the crew to be happy, efficient or productive. Winston's lifelong belief in revolutionary socialism had been replaced by ship capitalism. It didn't make him particularly happy to have come to that realisation. Some sort of violent overthrow of the captain class would have been so much more exciting.

Ralph walked up to the bridge.

"I went to see the ladies but it's difficult to even stand out there."

Winston glowered at him.

"Why?"

"Well, it's blowing pretty hard."

"Why did you go to see the ladies?"

Ralph looked out of the bridge window, not knowing what to say. Crewmen started lashing down deck cargo with straps and fighting to control wayward tarpaulin sheets.

"Did you want to understand their culture?"

Ralph looked at him.

"Maybe learn something of their struggles in life?"

"I just wondered if they were all right," said Ralph.

"You know nothing about them but you had a concern for their welfare."

Winston relaxed and felt sorry for him. He was being unfair. Ralph was just a boy.

"Are you religious?"

"I don't know. I think I'm trying to find that out."

"Come, let's finish this game. I'll tell you all about our other passengers."

*

"I've been to your country," Winston told him.

"Really? Where?"

"Oxford mostly. Balliol in particular. After Zambia University I was a Rhodes Scholar."

"What did you study?"

"Beer. And Politics, Philosophy and Economics. Rumour has it the three are related. Sorry, the four are related."

"Did you enjoy it?"

"I enjoyed the beer."

Winston reflected on stone quadrangles founded in 1263, the medieval hall, the 'Old' Common Room, and football on Master's Field. There had been a resident tortoise named after a German Marxist, with a student minder known as Comrade Tortoise.

"I enjoyed the competition. It was useful to discover that I wasn't the cleverest person I knew. I enjoyed singing songs over the wall, taunting Trinity. We were radicals; they were bourgeois snobs. I still remember the Gordouli."

"What year was that?"

"1974. How old were you then?"

"Eleven."

"It was the time of the three-day week. Coalminers go on strike so you save electricity by only working in your satanic mills for three days instead of five. Not so good for industrial output. Not what Adam Smith had in mind. A State of Emergency existed in Northern Ireland. The Labour Party tested a nuclear weapon. Oops. Kevin Keegan scored twice for Liverpool in the FA Cup. Monty Python broadcast their last episode on BBC2, and five previously all-male colleges of the University of Oxford admitted women undergraduates for the first time. But sadly, not Balliol. Not until 1979."

Winston had focused Ralph on the left side of the chessboard as he talked.

"You see, I understand your world. Allow me to educate you on mine," he said.

There was a threatening move coming that Ralph couldn't see, and Winston was distracting him.

"Long before you Western Europeans took slaves from Africa to the New World, my continent had been bled of its human resources. For at least a thousand years, starting in the ninth century, enslaved Africans had been sent via the Red Sea, or ports like Zanzibar on the Indian Ocean, or across the Sahara, to be sold in Muslim countries. Maybe seventeen million of us to be slaves for Muslims."

Ralph was countering with no attacking plan, a momentum building.

"The Atlantic slave trade took about the same number, depending on who you listen to, but was much more intense. You've got nothing to be proud of. It may have been the English who banned the slave trade, when you could afford to do so, but up until then you were the biggest shippers of slaves across the Middle Passage to pick cotton or cut sugar on your estates in the West Indies or the American colonies."

Too late, Ralph saw open space on the right of the board. Winston's Queen stretched her fine legs and moved gracefully from one side to the other.

"In the end it was about money. African lives suffered to make profit for Englishmen. Engerman gives the contribution of slavery to the British economy as five per cent of your national income. I think that's low. I believe old Williams had it right. Profits from the slave trade and from your sugar colonies directly financed your industrial revolution. After all, the development of James Watt's steam engine had been funded by Caribbean plantation owners. The ports of Bristol and Liverpool grew on the back of slave trade ships and their merchants. Your fine industrial City of Manchester was based on the manufacture of cloth from slave-picked cotton. Birmingham became the biggest gun-producing town at that time, making muskets to trade for slaves. And all the while London's lucrative coffee houses consumed slave-cut sugar."

Winston looked at the board. Moved a final piece.

"Mate."

*

By morning the wind had blown itself out. The *Independence* hauled its anchor in a flat calm, the only evidence of the previous night's storm a floating trail of plastic sheets from the fishermen camped ashore around the anchorage.

They had been lucky with the weather. At times Winston had been sheltering somewhere along the east or west bank for up to a week waiting for the wind to die down. The length of Tanganyika meant that after a fetch of 673 kilometres waves of six metres could be produced at the southern end of the lake, waves big enough to break the back of a laden ship at anchor in the shallows.

Winston and Ralph looked over the guardrail.

"Looks deep. Is it?"

"Second deepest in the world. Second largest reservoir of fresh water in the world. Nearly twenty per cent of all the world's fresh water."

Winston spat down the side of the ship. He turned back to Ralph but looked through him, gazing at the top of the lake now visible through the haze.

"There's something I want you to remember. I quote, 'Above all, always be capable of feeling deeply any injustice committed against anyone, anywhere in the world. That is the most beautiful quality in a revolutionary'."

"The same great man?"

Winston nodded.

"Che Guevara." He pointed west. "He was over there in the Congo. Teaching Marxist ideology and the theory of guerrilla warfare to troops that didn't really want to fight."

He hesitated.

"There's something else. Something I didn't tell you last night."

The water of the lake looked deep and still.

"Not many Europeans ventured into the interior of Africa to actually capture slaves. The risk of disease was too great for them. Slaves were bought, traded for guns and cloth and alcohol."

A tear filled his eye that wasn't solely from cigar smoke.

"They bought the slaves from Africans. Africans sold Africans into slavery."

Winston held Ralph's arm.

"You need to know that before you travel further."

His grip tightened.

"You need to remember that in Uganda."

Clouds gathered to the north. There would be more wind.

FOURTEEN

Bujumbura's Boulevard du Port led from the dock where the *Independence* had berthed into Burundi's steaming capital.

Tall Tutsi women walked majestically down wide tree-lined avenues and underneath the verandas of French colonial houses, their pace necessarily slow. The rainy season still had two months to go and the heavy wet air remained a physical weight to push against.

Ralph dripped into the centre of town down the *chaussée* of a previous president and the *rue* of an independence hero. The central market area had burst its banks, and vendors of soap, penny sweets and old clothes flooded onto the sidewalks of neighbouring streets.

He threaded his way through the African market smells of charcoal and shrivelled vegetables, old fish, rotten animals, the living and the dead, politely acknowledging the calls of all those who wanted to sell to him and smiling at the maimed beggars, pickpockets and whores.

Unable to find what he was looking for in the town centre, Ralph eased off when he got to the government ministry buildings and ran easily with a tide of people behind him down narrower streets heading west, his wallet hanging comfortably around his neck on an old bootlace, lying against his chest under a faded tee shirt.

He ended up wet with sweat and back where he'd started, slightly south of the commercial port, looking over the lake from a noisy bar that was filling up fast at the hour before sunset with French and Canadian voices. The Cercle Nautique bar and restaurant at that time of the day had a shifting population. Expat aid workers discussed in acronyms real progress being made at the grassroots level. Idealistic young administration staff in a chic tropical mix of worn jeans and African women's clothing demonstrated that they had become fully embedded with the culture by going native with the suave local driver from the agency office. Language teachers with a two-hundred-dollar qualification had a pretty 'private lesson' hanging off their shoulder. Engineers who had spent the first six months of their annual contract assessing, as they'd expected, the high level of inefficiency in local services were scouting around during the last six months for the next field post in Laos, Papua or Tashkent. They came and went, leaving little wake and no discernible mark of their quiet passage, so that even the barmen at the Cercle Nautique wondered if they were in Burundi for any reason other than to buy Heineken or Amstel.

Ralph bought a plate of *mélange*. He ate rice, potatoes and strange coloured vegetables, while watching hippo come out of the lake for the evening, and then wandered to the bar.

*

When Nels walked in to the darkened room from the light of the River Road he noticed a smell, a Nairobi smell, an overpowering bitterness that caught in his throat like acid. Yellow eyes slouching around the walls followed him, while half-naked sickly thin girls with stiff hair rubbed themselves against him and stuck like leeches. Nels scowled into the gloom. It wasn't the sight of the dregs of Kenya deposited like sediment in the bar that upset him, it was the smell, a stench of hopeless worthless lives. It reminded him of what he despised and why his country needed to keep fighting, to stay strong. Nels hated Africa.

A man larger than the rest unstuck himself from the wall. A burn on the side of his face extended from above a closed and weeping eye to one side of his mouth, stretched by scar tissue into a lopsided leering smirk. He stood in the open doorway to the street, blocking more light, filling the room with his dark shadow.

Nels waited, calmly as though fishing, and looked at the burnt man. He didn't think there would be any point in talking to him. The big ones were always stupid. He needed a rat that could think.

"You want a girl?"

The voice came not from the burnt man in the doorway or the wall of staring faces in front of Nels but from a whiskery man with big gaps in his teeth leaning against a red and yellow oil drum used as a small table. He slurped at a glass bottle. Nels smiled at him, the buck rat among his mischief.

"I've got a girl I know you'd like."

He put down the bottle and licked his lips. A large medallion on a thick gold chain, too fat for his thin neck, clattered against the oil drum. Nels moved towards him and the big man in the doorway stepped back into the room.

"You want to check a few over?"

He flicked his fingers and two sad and unsmiling women lifted themselves reluctantly from a low wide couch, while a third sat on its worn armrest, her knees far apart. Nels looked at them coldly.

"Keep the girls," he said. "I'm looking to do some other business."

The man at the oil drum didn't seem disappointed.

"Business is my name. Mr Business."

Mr Business looked up with undersized eyes.

"Let me guess," he said. "You want someone taken out."

Nels said nothing.

"I know. Your wife. It's always the wives. Or the husbands," he chuckled.

"It's a boy," said Nels. "A white boy."

Mr Business looked at him with respect.

"A boy. How interesting. I'll give you a good deal if it's only a boy."

"I don't know when. If I can find out I'll let you know. Otherwise just watch…"

Mr Business nodded to the burnt man and interrupted him.

"How about a little distraction, before we talk business. On the house."

The burnt man came back with a girl in a short tight dress. She leant against Nels' arm and looked at him through faraway eyes.

"How old is she?" asked Nels.

"Does it matter? Sixteen probably."

Nels looked at the girl, her skin stretched smooth and shiny, her lips still thin and tight.

"She's not fourteen," he said.

Mr Business shrugged and looked around.

"Something else?" he said.

"Yes," said Nels. "Something younger."

*

The Protestant Mission at Vigosi had been difficult to find. For a start, Ralph couldn't find the church. He had expected a church, preferably with a large illuminated cross on top of a tower and the sweet song of a gospel choir filling the neighbouring streets, leading him, showing him the way. Instead he stumbled in the fading light down suburban roads full of potholes and across hard bare earthen yards until a faded hand-painted sign pointed to a collection of block and tin bungalows.

Behind a low wall of rough red brick, rusty iron bars sticking through the top, lay a long narrow building. A track led to it, and across the path bed sheets hung like sails put out to dry in a calm.

The door of the building opened like a hatch in a boiler. Light and smoke and noise spilled out into the yard.

A large man, bare to the waist, came out and urinated steamily into a bush.

Ralph waited then walked toward the door. Chickens disturbed from their roost screeched at him.

The man turned at the noise and peered into the gloom. He said something that Ralph didn't understand. It might have been Dutch or German or Russian.

"Hi, sorry to bother you. Is this the Protestant Mission?"

The German looked at him. In the light from the door Ralph looked young, pleading and weak. His only serviceable shorts were an old pair he'd had at school for sports when he was thirteen. Although he'd lost weight they were tight around his brown legs. His blond hair had become wavy as it had grown long. College girls in Muenster would pay a lot of money to have it look so good.

"I'm travelling through and I wondered if you might have somewhere I could stay."

"Fuck off."

A woman came to the door. She had a cigarette in one hand and a glass of red wine in the other. She spoke French to the German. His name was Rainer. What the hell was he doing out there with the door open? The room would be full of bugs. She'd had dengue fever once. If she got bitten again she would probably die.

She saw Ralph standing outside, his rucksack at his feet.

"Oh."

"*Bonsoir*," said Ralph.

Rainer grunted.

"*J'ai demandé en ville. Au bar,*" he explained. "*J'ai besoin dormir.*"

"Stop." The woman held up her hand and looked at him. "This is too painful. English. Please."

"Thanks. Well, as I said to this gentleman, I came up the lake and I'm trying to get through to Nairobi."

The German filled the door. Ralph looked at him.

"Is it Rainer? Well, Rainer was just giving me some advice."

Rainer laughed and went inside.

The woman didn't answer. This sort of thing seemed to be happening more often. The mission wasn't there for the benefit of kids whose parents could well afford to support them while they had their little travelling adventure. The real work needed to be helping the local children. You helped

221

one or two of these teenagers as they passed through, and then without knowing it you were in some guidebook as a free place to stay and they were forever knocking on the door. The mission was being taken advantage of. The mission should be a Good Samaritan, but more selective, helping the truly needy. Wout would have to decide.

"You'd better speak to my husband. Come in."

She turned away.

"And shut the damn door," she shouted at Rainer's back.

Rainer didn't turn. He lifted one arm, his back to both of them, and they followed him into the room.

*

It was a narrow dining room with kitchen facilities at one end, Ralph assumed for church functions where they broke bread and ate little fishes after Bible study. A red and white checked plastic tablecloth covered one end of a long table, set for four.

Rainer sat down at the table next to a dark-haired girl with shiny olive skin. Ralph wasn't looking but he thought it may have been recently oiled. She wore a white top with very short sleeves that slightly pinched the soft paler flesh under her arms when she stretched to tap her cigarette against an ashtray on the table.

The woman who had let him in went and talked in a hushed voice to a thin bald man preparing food, cutting a dusty shrivelled sausage into thin red and white marbled slices. He wiped his hands on an apron and held her by one shoulder, looking into her eyes as he quietly talked.

Ralph looked around the room, then at his feet, then the ceiling – anywhere other than the table and the dark-haired girl. Her beauty made him stumble like a clown and he knew he would be inarticulate should she talk to him.

The thin man came over to him from the kitchen, still wiping his hands.

"Welcome."

He paused and looked at him with his head tilted.

"Phillips. Ralph Phillips."

"Ha ha ha."

Rainer started laughing and the dark-haired girl smiled at him.

"Like Bond," laughed the German.

Ralph flushed.

"Welcome, Ralph. My name is Wout. I believe you've met Rainer."

He nodded toward the table.

"And my wife."

The woman walked over and shook his hand.

"Margaux," she said and looked at the floor as if ashamed.

"And this is Azzurra. Dr Azzurra," said Wout.

Ralph didn't want to glance at the table. He bent to look at something on the top of his rucksack, an irritating loose strap. He'd been meaning to fix it for a while and now seemed the perfect time to attend to it. He realised too late that it must have looked as if he had made a stiff little bow. His scalp started itching. Azzurra smiled at him and sipped her wine.

Wout turned back to the kitchen.

"Eat with us."

Ralph hesitated.

"Oh, um, that's fine. I've eaten."

Wout poured steaming pots onto serving plates.

"Ralph. The best thing about having an Italian friend is that she always knows where to get good food."

He put dishes on the table. The food smelt of flowers and lush grass in warm sunshine.

"Azzurra brought salami and pasta. Eat with us."

Azzurra picked at a thin string of pasta falling off the plate and tilted her head back, stretching her neck. There was a bone just below the triangle of her jaw. Ralph wanted to ask her what it was called, to touch it with his fingertips. It wobbled as she caught the yellow ribbon of food on her tongue.

"They are gifts from my family in Torino," she said.

Azzurra looked at Margaux.

"And I have this."

She held up a long triangular-shaped chocolate wrapped in gold foil, isosceles not equilateral, like an upside-down boat. Margaux screeched.

"*Gianduiotto*. It's the best," said Azzurra. "Much better than Belgian."

Margaux feigned shock.

"That cannot be true. But I am happy to try."

Wout smiled. He came from Bruges, Flemish and Dutch speaking. Margaux was Walloon and very French. In the end they were both Belgian and sorted out problems in a Belgian way, with discussion and compromise. It had been the strength of both their working lives and their relationship. That and their love of the church.

Ralph thought it safer looking at Wout.

"This is good of you. Giving me a free place to stay would have been enough."

Margaux peered up at him.

"It won't be for free," she said.

Rainer waved his knife in Ralph's direction.

"You can paint roofs?"

Rainer put a rough Westphalian hand on Azzurra's fine Torinese wrist.

"How are your little people, Azzurra?"

Ralph wasn't looking. He didn't really notice how she slid her hand from underneath Rainer's to push a coil of hair, like an upside-down question mark, away from her eyes. They were pale blue. Azzurra.

"Azzurra works with the Twa," he explained to Ralph.

Ralph concentrated on a fork full of firm pasta, slippery with butter and with shavings of soft cheese. He had no idea that butter and cheese could taste so good, so delicate.

"Interesting," he said.

Rainer stared at him.

"You know all about the Twa of course."

Azzurra watched Ralph eat.

"You like the pasta?"

Ralph nodded and something caught on the end of his chin. He rubbed at it as inconspicuously as he could.

"It is called *Tajarin*. It's just lots of good egg yolks and the right sort of flour."

"It's delicious."

"The cheese is *fontina*. You should buy it in the summer, when the cows are moved to the mountains. When you cut it you can smell the rich herby pasture the cows were eating and the clean Alpine air."

She looked at Rainer.

"They are called Batwa, not Twa. There are three groups of Batwa, depending if they fish, hunt or make pots. I work with the Impunyu, the forest dwellers. Hunter-gatherer Batwa. I'm worried they will soon completely disappear from the forests of Burundi."

Rainer smiled at her.

"Then no one will know about the Twa, Rainer."

It was only slight, just a twist of her upper body, but she had moved away from Rainer. Ralph ate the *tajarin* with fresh enthusiasm.

"The Pygmies of the central African Great Lakes area were the original peoples of this country. The first people in the world. Now it's easier to get funding and support for panda bears than it is for our own descendants."

Azzurra put down her fork and poured Ralph more Barolo. It was the Cannubi vineyard's Barolo, the light-coloured but rich and powerful wine with complex and exotic aromas from Piedmont. Had Ralph known about wine he would have considered putting Azzurra and Barolo together to be an entirely appropriate pairing. She looked at him, held his eyes with her own. Ralph couldn't breathe.

"They are not considered citizens by most African states. They are kept as slaves from birth by other Bantu. They don't have identity cards, deeds or rights to land, no healthcare other than what my organisation can provide, no schooling. Their home is being cut down or turned into 'national parks' that they are not allowed to access. Soon they won't have a home. They will live exploited by all on the edge of their forest."

Rainer leant across the table, his knuckles white around the wine glass.

"What do you think about that, Ralph?"

Ralph thought of Captain Winston on the bridge of the *Independence* sailing up Lake Tanganyika, of listening to his talk of Marxist political theory while losing at chess.

"I think that above all else we should always be capable of feeling deeply any injustice committed against anyone, anywhere in the world."

He looked at Rainer and thought him brutally ugly, like a dog bred to fight.

"You know all about Che Guevara of course."

Check. But not yet Mate.

Ralph looked at Rainer, not at Azzurra, but he was certain that she smiled.

*

Margaux smoked a cigarette and watched Ralph on the roof. He'd been busy. She could see a tell-tale trail of glowing red paint snaking up the hill, ending where he sat on the top of the furthest bungalow. As usual, Wout had been right. Ralph had turned out to be rather a deep-thinking character. He'd been quiet and respectful. He'd done dishes without being asked. He'd made very acceptable, possibly excellent, omelettes for breakfast from eggs he'd got up early to find. He'd kept the local kids busy playing soccer in the dust while they'd been in conference with the Anglican bishop, making them scream when he'd pick up the ball and run with it rather than kick it to them.

She loved Wout for his faith in people. Wout had always been a good man, one of the rare ones that saw good in others. Ralph hadn't exactly been robbed on the road to Jericho though. She watched Ralph go back to his work, pleased that Wout had agreed that Ralph should pay for his keep. There wasn't much more to do. She'd pick some grapefruit and squeeze him juice for when he finished.

*

Ralph sat on the roof wondering what time it was. He put his fingers together like a salute and held them at arm's-length, trying to measure height above the lake. His mind felt slow and muddled, the day still hot. Five fingers together were fifteen degrees. One hour of arc. He drank some water.

It wouldn't work. He needed to be at sea level looking at the ocean. The ocean was away to the west, over Tanganyika, then over two thousand kilometres of scrub and brush. The surface of Lake Tanganyika must be at nearly eight hundred metres elevation. And he was higher than the lake, looking down on it from the mission. Plus the height of the roof he was sitting on. His height of eye above sea level was... He gave up trying to calculate the geometry.

Azzurra came for him when the sun blazed two hands above the horizon, hanging immobile over the Congo. The arrangements had been vague. Ralph had listened dumbly to her over dinner. She might be able to give him a ride to the Rwandan border when she visited the Pygmies. The roads were atrocious. They'd need to travel in daylight. Perhaps he could help her with something in return? She needed to make arrangements. It would take a few days.

Most importantly, and for four hot and happy days on the mission roofs Ralph had thought of little else, she had left after dinner alone. Rainerless. *Sans* Rainer.

Checkmate.

*

In Pretoria, Angel walked as unobtrusively as possible up Paul Kruger Street towards Church Square. He kept his head down and stayed on the edge of the pavement, ready to jump into the road out of the way of other whiter pedestrians. He turned left before the central post office down the quieter Pretorius Avenue heading toward Princes Park. His colour meant he wasn't allowed in but he knew that if he entered in the south-west corner and went straight to the river no one would see him. It was noiseless in the park, mid-afternoon and too late for the lunchtime crowds. He sat peacefully, his shoes off and feet in the cool river water, pushing gravel around with his toes. He needed to think.

David Mwansa had called from Lusaka with disturbing news.

"What do you mean it's closed?" Angel had asked.

"It is impossible to cross from Tanzania. The border has been closed by the Kenyans. Kenyatta was a foolish Western puppet and Moi is just as bad."

Angel hadn't wanted to discuss the politics.

"What does that mean?"

"It means, Angel, that if your English boy took the Tanzam train all the way to Dar es Salaam he could not then get further north; he would have had to return to Lusaka. Unless…"

"Unless? Unless what?"

"Unless he flew."

"He's no money."

"Or unless he got off the train before the Tanzanian border and went up the lake."

Angel had been standing at the wall map at the time. He had seen the lake stretching long and thin from the very top of Zambia. He had followed it with his finger, knowing that it continued into the heart of Africa.

"Is that possible?" Angel had asked.

"There is a passenger vessel on Lake Tanganyika. It's often broken down."

David had laughed.

"Or there's always Winston."

"Who is Winston?"

"An old university friend. Bit of an oddball. Brilliant mind; could have run the economics of the country a lot better than KK's current bunch but took himself off to captain a ship on the lake. Is this conversation recorded?" he'd asked. "Do not tell anyone I spoke ill of the President's team."

Angel had still had his finger on the map.

"But you know that if he gets to the top of the lake," David had reminded him, "to get to Kenya he has to travel through…"

Angel had already seen the route and where it led.

"Yes. I know, David."

Both had remained quiet, each lost in their thoughts, and the call had ended silently without goodbyes.

Angel wriggled his toes at curious tiny fish in the river. He knew he'd have to go to Kenya. There was nothing he could do from Pretoria. He wouldn't tell Elanza about it. The chances were it would be a wasted mission.

Angel had already worked out Ralph's likely route from the top of the lake to Nairobi. Ralph probably had no idea of the risk he was taking. The thought of where Ralph had to travel through made Angel shiver. He had to go through Uganda.

FIFTEEN

Azzurra's pickup truck was white, United Nations white, with two long Italian words and then *Medica* in red writing on the door. The logo, also red, had three letters, one inside the other, made into concentric circles with a wide annulus and a big fat 'Make way, I'm a doctor' red cross right in the middle.

Azzurra had been driving fast while the road was good. Fast in Burundi seemed to be sixty kilometres an hour, a speed that allowed them to travel over bad patches of road which made the suspension snarl but didn't break anything.

They were heading north and east out of Bujumbura, the late afternoon sun harsh on the side of Azzurra's face so that she wore her wide-brimmed hat tilted, like an Anzac soldier. She wore long trousers and a full-sleeved shirt, olive green but not of any recognisable camouflage pattern. Ralph expected matching black boots. Instead she had brown canvas shoes with ridged rubber soles that gave grip without holding too much mud. Ralph considered that on most people the whole outfit would be practical, possibly vaguely military. On Azzurra it came straight from a Milan fashion house's 'tropical rainforest' spring collection. She wore neither make-up, perfume nor jewellery. Some women had no need. A very few women knew they had no need. Her watch looked as if it had been free with her breakfast cereal but her sunglasses were smoky grey and gold-framed. Ralph pondered how many hours picking flowers in Burundi an accessory like that might be worth.

"What are these flowers?" he asked.

They had been driving under an hour, climbing through cultivated land, now approaching the small town of Bubanza. Rows of yellow and white flowers, like tall daisies, ran away at right angles to the road. Groups of women and children snaked in irregular lines down the fields, cutting the flower heads and throwing them over their shoulders into wicker baskets on their backs.

"They are chrysanthemums, for pyrethrum. It's a natural insecticide, extracted from the flowers after they've been dried in the sun. It's used for mosquito sprays and household insecticides to control cockroaches and ants."

Ralph looked at the fields. They were the size of his father's garden. Every year Mother would nag at him to dig over a small patch for summer vegetables. Eventually, as every year, he relented and spent crisp mornings in April turning the heavy Dorset clay to be planted with stick beans and marrow. They would stand, steaming cups of tea in their hands, planning what to grow, working together every year, their small garden just one of the many little links that happily bound them. Unlike the Burundians, they farmed their small field for fun.

"They are tiny little plots."

Azzurra stopped her glasses from slipping forward as a dew of sweat formed on her nose.

"It's small-scale production here, a cash crop for subsistence farmers with only a thousand square metres of land. Most of the pyrethrum is grown in Kenya, bigger fields, but still planted, tended and harvested by hand."

Ralph watched the children working.

"They receive a fraction of what the extract is worth but for some it's the only money they earn. From their small area they may pick a hundred kilograms of dried flowers. That's equivalent to a hundred dollars, some of which will pay for school or medicine."

Ralph looked at her. She'd pushed her hair behind one ear. He was curious to know how long it took before the tiny hole healed over where her earring usually went. A week? A day?

"A hundred dollars doesn't sound very much. How long does it take them to pick a hundred kilograms?"

She shook her head and waved a beautiful Latin finger.

"To sell a hundred kilograms of dried flowers they have to pick four hundred kilograms of fresh flowers. A good worker can do twenty kilograms of fresh flowers a day."

Ralph did the calculation but didn't say anything. A hundred dollars for twenty days' work. Five dollars a day.

"Production isn't so good down here. The chrysanthemums like cooler temperatures at higher altitudes, two thousand metres or more, and free-draining volcanic soils. When it's hot and dry you get lower yields and less pyrethrum in a flower."

Ralph looked at the children in the fields, noticing something about the way they walked, the size of the baskets on their backs and the way they lifted them.

"They're not children."

She looked at him and sighed.

"No, Ralph. They're not children. They're Pygmies. Pygmy slaves."

*

Ralph turned in his seat.

"Tell me about them."

"In Burundi, and Rwanda, the Tutsi have been the feudal overlords for hundreds of years. The Hutu were the majority and they did all the work. At the bottom of the heap was a small population of Batwa Pygmies."

Azzurra stopped talking while she drove. Once through Bubanza, the road, although surfaced, deteriorated. It wound around on itself in hairpin bends, climbing all the time.

"The Pygmies weren't farmers. They were forest dwellers, hunting for wild animals and birds with nets and poison-tipped arrows. They would trade meat or honey with nearby farmers for cultivated foods. Today only a few still hunt. Most are forced to do manual labour in the villages. The Tutsi and Hutu call it a time-honoured tradition. It is slavery. They are paid with cigarettes, or used clothing, or often nothing at all. They have no choice. They have nowhere left to go. The tropical forests are cut for quick profit from the sale of hardwoods, or cleared for growing tea or pyrethrum. Governments have been funded to make nature reserves from which Pygmies are banned. Or they are evicted to make way for money-spinning big game trophy hunting."

She looked at Ralph.

"Pygmies rely on the forest; as it disappears so do the Pygmies."

Ralph put his arm out of the window to direct air onto his face. He felt nauseous from the winding road, the heat, and from somewhere behind him he smelt petrol fumes.

"So, what happens to them?" he asked.

"They are forced to live with no rights at all, abused by everyone. The social fabric of their small semi-nomadic groups breaks down. Alcoholism, domestic violence, high infant mortality – all are now common."

Azzurra checked their progress on a map which she tried to open with one hand. Ralph held it for her as she traced a route with her fingernail, cut short but clear varnished like a table on an expensive yacht. It was an aviation chart and had very little detail, just a thin red line meandering out of a purple blob, which Ralph took to be a big town, leading to a small circle. Most of the chart was coloured shades of brown, with a slash of green running north to south which may have represented forested land. A large number in blue with a smaller figure beside it dominated each grid square. In the square they were travelling through it was ten with a smaller number four alongside. The road they were on didn't even appear to be shown.

"They were the guardians of the rainforest. They would take what they needed and share it. Now individuals and big corporations are given exclusive rights to extract a resource, be it trees or minerals, and they keep taking it until all is gone. It's in direct contrast to how the Pygmies care for the whole ecosystem. They have no access to traditional natural medicines made from forest plants, or to their sacred sites."

She gave up on the map.

"Today they beg. They've no idea it is wrong. In their minds they are taking what others should be sharing."

The road abruptly ended outside of a town called Ntambe, on the border of the Province of Cibitake. It was further from the capital than Bubanza Province and less visible, with a much smaller budget for roads.

A trail of brown dust now enveloped the pickup. In places, previous flooding had washed a bare hill, stripped of its trees, from one side of the road and put it at the other, the way ahead hidden underneath a moraine of mud and stone. The school at Masango, long and narrow with high windows like a chicken shed, paralleled the road. Free-range children, recently released, scratched in the dirt.

The dust lay on her face like a fine foundation.

"Commercial logging operations have put male labourers in camps close to Pygmy communities."

She made a false laugh.

"Sexual exploitation is the worst."

Azzurra looked at Ralph, and he saw a bead of moisture that wasn't sweat running down her cheek.

"Pygmy women are now forced into prostitution."

Ralph thought he should give her something to wipe her eyes. He had nothing. He spared her discomfort by looking ahead.

"Make it known. Surely then the government would have to do something. Tell people the truth."

She wiped her eyes and smiled.

"There was a man from Torino, a little like Che Guevara. It made me smile when you talked about him at dinner. His name was Antonio Gramsci. He was the founder and first leader of the Italian Communist Party. He came from my city. He went to my university. He said, 'To tell the truth is revolutionary'."

She briefly squeezed Ralph's hand.

"Sometimes telling the truth isn't revolutionary enough."

*

After Masango, still climbing, they travelled east along the top of a wooded ridge into the forest, the sun low and behind them.

Azzurra pulled off onto a rutted track that skirted a bulge of woodland and stopped in a clearing. They had made good time thanks to dry roads – just two hours to drive a hundred kilometres. Ralph stood exactly six thousand kilometres from the ocean at Cape Town, in the very heart of Africa.

"This is primary evergreen forest. Untouched. Just as it existed thousands of years ago."

Ralph heard them before they emerged from the trees. They were singing. A yodelling sound would be answered by a chant as in a rugby club, and from further away a noise like an owl hooting.

Azzurra pointed to a backpack on the seat.

"Can you bring my medical bag? Leave your rucksack in the truck."

She stood quietly by the door of the vehicle.

There were four of them – a hunting party. They arrived in close file with the point man stalking carefully, his bow and arrow at arm's stretch ready to engage. Behind him a boy held an axe and another carried a bundle of net on his back, suspended from a wide strap around his forehead so that his arms remained free. A very old man with a wiry beard came behind carrying a wooden spear nearly two metres long, almost twice his height. He talked with hard clicks and then sang. He pointed at Azzurra and screeched and then sang again.

"Pygmies sing a lot. Not that they have much to be cheerful about."

She touched the old man on his face with the back of her hand and spoke his name.

"San-ge."

"Can you talk to them?" asked Ralph.

"No. They only have a small vocabulary. Most of their words deal with collecting honey."

Azzurra pulled two twenty-litre oil cans from the back of the truck, both about half full, and gave one to each of the boys. The sun set below the treeline.

"We've got to go. There's just thirty or forty minutes before it's dark."

She turned and followed the Pygmies. A game trail led through bamboo and banana plants at ground level, while tall red-barked hardwoods grew a round crown of huge wide-spaced branches, forming a closed canopy towering forty-five metres above their heads. Underneath, in the forest, it was already nearly dark.

The forest opened into a clearing with a huddled group of ten quickly built huts made from springy saplings bent over into the shape of an igloo and covered in dried banana leaves. Grey charcoals smouldered under a tripod of branches supporting some sort of meat wrapped in green leaves, slowly roasting.

Azzurra looked around.

"We're going to stay the night."

She wiped her hands on her trousers and tucked in her shirt.

"I've never done this before. You may have to smoke a pipe. Be polite."

"Is this the whole village?"

"The camps are small. There are rarely more than fifty people in a group. When someone dies they bury them and move. Make a new camp."

"Is San-ge the leader?"

"It depends what they're doing. It's a very egalitarian society. Whoever has the most experience or talent represents the rest. San-ge is a sort of spokesman when I visit. They don't really have a leader."

She took her medical bag from him.

"Western aid agencies hate it. They feel that if they aren't talking to a head man their message won't filter down to the rest of the community."

A group of children with swollen bellies danced, the boys in reed skirts and headdresses.

Azzurra walked towards the children.

"I'm going to take a quick look at the kids."

Ralph watched her work. She smiled and mimed for them to open their mouths. A child hung on to her leg so that she had to shuffle to inspect each set of teeth. While looking in their mouths she dusted ulcers on their arms and legs with cheap zinc and neomycin powder.

A woman opened the leaves over the fire, prodding an animal like a small deer, blackened and un-butchered. Ralph looked at the children's swollen bellies. It wasn't much protein for fifty people.

"I've seen what's for dinner," he told her. "But I'm not sure what they hunt around here."

"They definitely do not hunt gorilla, no matter what people say. The only endangered species they may occasionally take are the great blue turaco bird and black and white colobus monkeys. Normally it's common ground animals like shrews, or mice and rats. There are lots of different types."

"Nice. Could be a large rat cooking, I suppose."

She laughed.

"It'll be an aardvark or a duiker. Try not to eat it. It won't harm you but their need is greater. Kwashiorkor."

Ralph nodded.

"Is that why they're only a metre tall? Is it just poor nutrition?"

"They are less than one and a half metres tall," she corrected him. "It could be that the forest canopy reduces the UV levels. With low sunlight there is low vitamin D production and consequently low levels of calcium, leading to their small skeletal size. It's just a theory."

San-ge led them to sit by the fire where women danced in shuffling steps.

Azzurra stretched her legs out straight on the ground.

"The Egyptians knew about the Pygmies four thousand years ago. They called them 'The Dancers of the Gods'."

Men and women took turns with a bamboo tube pipe, smoking, watching and then dancing.

"What are they smoking?"

"It's only hemp flower heads. It's not narcotic. It may make your head spin but you won't get high."

San-ge brought Azzurra the pipe.

She sat cross-legged and held the pipe in her lap. Her head disappeared in a cloud of pungent sour smoke. When it cleared her eyes were closed.

Ralph took it from her.

"I thought you said it wasn't narcotic."

She lay back and stretched her arms and legs into a star, as if to make a snow angel in the African dust.

"Mmmmm."

*

Ralph awoke in the dark, with rainforest noises very close. It had surprised him how noisy it was. By day there had been times when he'd needed to shout to make himself heard. At night it had changed into whooping sounds and clicks. In the predawn, as he lay on the ground and stirred with some stiffness, eyes still closed and with a heavy head, he listened hard to differentiate the source. There was a chattering high above in the treetops, crickets and frogs were everywhere, and then something hissed in his ear.

"Wake up. Time to go."

Azzurra sat on a log, tying her shoelaces. Ralph watched her. She had a hairpin in her mouth. She twisted her hair into a messy ponytail, coiled it up and pinned it in a bun on the top of her head, crowning it with her bush hat. It was a very intimate, personal moment that he felt privileged to share. He would have been happy to stay forever with the Batwa, eating rat, watching Azzurra do her hair every morning.

San-ge and others were coughing and scratching, shaking life into numb limbs.

"What time is it?" he asked.

His mouth felt dry and sticky, his arms itching and covered with fine cuts from razor-edged leaves.

Azzurra stood up.

"Come on. I need your help. Bring those."

Stumbling, he followed her and the men back into the forest, his arms already aching from the weight of the oil containers she'd asked him to carry. The only illumination came from thousands of fireflies that congregated on the tree trunks and lit them up with a soft glow. In places, luminous mushrooms and lichens cast enough light to see the path and Azzurra's legs. The Pygmies moved soundlessly in front of them but Ralph, unable to see and burdened, crashed and swore. He felt lightheaded and needed water.

They emerged into an area of felled trees. Ralph couldn't see but felt that they'd all stopped in front of him. He put down the oil containers and shook his arms. A stream ran noisily to one side of them. The light in the clearing was dark grey while all around remained black, like dawn at sea. In the greyness greyer shapes stood angularly.

"What are we doing?" he asked.

"It's a new logging camp. They haven't finished it."

Azzurra walked toward the buildings. There was a small collection of six square rooms, roughly built from fresh timber with uncovered plywood sheets making a flat roof, a structure open on all four sides, possibly a kitchen or for machinery storage, and a larger rectangular house with no windows. Azzurra walked toward it with San-ge.

Ralph looked around for the other Pygmies but they'd disappeared back into the forest. He picked up the oil containers.

"What are we doing?" he repeated.

"The loggers are moving in. This is the first camp."

Ralph stood in front of the central house and in the dawn light looked inside. It had been partitioned with eight by four sheets into tiny rooms, hardly big enough for two people to lie down, the size of a single bed.

He looked at Azzurra. She stood back from the door.

"It's one of the first buildings they make. It's for the women. The Pygmy girls they'll take from San-ge."

She picked up one of the oil containers.

"It's a brothel."

Ralph knew now why she'd given him a lift, what help she needed from him. He understood why they'd spent the night with the Pygmies, the smell of petrol in the pickup that had made him feel sick.

"You want to burn it down?"

She looked at him as she had the previous evening when they'd made love on the dirt floor of a bamboo hut, passionately with tense lines around her neck, breathing quickly, eyes wide.

"I understand," he said. "Sometimes telling the truth isn't revolutionary enough."

*

As they left the logging camp San-ge, excited by the flames and smoke from the burning building, made shrieks and hooting noises into the forest.

Azzurra looked at her hands, unable to stop them shaking. It had been the same the time four men had come to the Pygmies. One had been wearing a very faded camouflage jacket with matching cap, the rest a mixture of old tee shirts and cheap shiny sports gear. Everyone had been carrying automatic weapons and had taken up undisciplined postures, leaning cross-armed on the guns slung around their necks, or resting the end of the barrel on their shoe. One had very short hair and round dark sunglasses that even in the dim forest light he had kept on, looking furtively yet blindly at the Pygmies. None of them had been soldiers.

Azzurra had known what they were and her hands had started shaking as she picked up her medical bag. There had been no way of telling if they might be paramilitary vigilantes for Batutsi or Bahutu. They probably hadn't known themselves. They were kids taken from towns, kept high on khat and given an old gun. At a time when both sides in a civil war were under the international spotlight it helped to have cheap, unrecognisable and deniable thugs to do the dirty work.

They had arrived carrying an injured man laid face down on a bamboo stretcher, one side of his trousers soaked with blood. Azzurra had quickly asked them the most important question, in French. "*Quand?*" When? They had been vague. They'd all been drunk. It had been the previous evening. Or in the night.

Azzurra had guessed straight away that the 'golden hour', when prompt treatment may have meant the chance of survival would have been high, had long past. Nervously she'd tried to keep her movements decisive, not crazy or panicked. She'd given reassurance, knowing it was herself she was trying to reassure.

It had been a gunshot injury to the buttock from close range. The exit wound looked clean like the entry, much as if a fat pencil had been pushed straight through. There had been little time for the bullet to become unstable and start to yaw or tumble. Azzurra had been taught that military ordnance was designed to be deliberately unstable by moving its centre of gravity. A high-powered rifle bullet would then deliberately cause massive tissue damage as it cartwheeled and thrashed its way through an enemy's flesh. The injury that Azzurra had been looking at had probably been caused by a handgun, possibly as an accidental discharge. The boy had doubtless thought it cool to put the gun in the back of his trousers, like in the movies.

The bullet had penetrated cleanly and the permanent cavity created had been narrow. There was undoubtedly some stretching of the elastic tissues from the stress wave but the bullet had not fragmented. There would have been secondary fragments, bits of clothing fabric, but as far as she had been able to tell no bone had been shattered.

Azzurra had known that there was no good area of the body to get shot in. Even gunshots to fleshy areas like the shoulder and thigh could kill quite easily. The subclavian artery in the shoulder fed into the brachial artery, a massive vessel supplying the arm. The brachial plexus formed a bundle of nerves controlling arm function and was, like the shoulder joint itself, impossible to repair if shattered by a bullet. It was the same with the thigh. Just a tiny nick in the giant femoral artery would lead to massive blood loss that could be fatal in minutes. She had seen such injuries while training in Turin and Milan. A gunshot to the buttock was probably the one with the most chance of recovery, assuming timely control of blood loss and no infection.

She had applied dressings to both wounds and pushed them hard, then increased the pressure as much as she had been able. They had soon become saturated so she'd put more dressings on top, desperately trying to stop the blood moving, as only then would it clot.

The boy in front of her was lethargic, conscious but breathing rapidly and with an increased heart rate. The bleeding had been a steady dark red ooze, not pulsing, but at one time it must have been gushing out.

She had recognised that he was in advanced shock. He had lost forty per cent or more of his blood. He would soon lose consciousness and have a cardiac arrest. With a large rock putting weight on the wound dressing, she had prepared a nasal pharyngeal airway, coating one end in lubricant gel.

The other men had stood away, curiously watching the boy like interested but remote observers.

More blood had filled the dressings. It had to be venous. He'd been unlucky: the bullet had hit the gluteal vein. Azzurra had applied more dressings, more pressure, his blood coming through her fingers, on her face, in her hair. Then he'd died and she'd wondered why she stayed in Africa and what she could hope to achieve there.

Then, as now, she held shaking hands to her chest and questioned herself. Then she had been unable to save the boy, and now she was unable to save the Batwa. The fire had destroyed the camp brothel. They'd build another and the Batwa would move anyway. Unlike herself they had a healthy avoidance strategy.

She should go home. She could live comfortably in Turin, do a worthwhile job at the hospital or the university, paediatrics maybe. She would go to the Porta Palazzo market and spend her mornings in the cafés, the Fiorio or Al Bicerin. She might walk in Parco Del Valentino, buy art in a galleria and sit in the evenings with friends in the Piazza Castello, San Carlo or Bodini. She could find a nice boy and make her mother happy.

"Ralph. What are your plans?"

"Well, I'm really thirsty and I'd like to eat something."

Men were like children, or dogs. She'd had men that were Labradors, big, devoted, slightly stupid. She'd had men like greyhounds, lean and athletic but sensitive and needy. Ralph, like a happy scruffy mongrel, seemed cheerful, amenable and independent.

She could love a dog like Ralph, or an Italian version of him – Raffaele maybe. She could work in Turin and they would live in a little apartment by the Po. In the summer they could go to Monterosso in the Cinque Terre to sail or swim, and in the winter drive to Bardonecchia to ski. She could have children.

She was dreaming but her hands were calmer now. She remembered the Batwa girl in hospital, younger than herself but with too many children, suffering from an ulceration and infection of the cervix following a uterine prolapse. She'd had to fight for treatment to save her.

She should check. She could drive now to the hospital in Ngozi, twenty kilometres to Kayanza and then just over thirty more, maybe an hour.

"Come on," she said. "I have water in the car."

*

In Kayanza the road forked in the middle of town, left to the border with Rwanda and right to the hospital at Ngozi. Azzurra stopped the car and looked at Ralph. He was very young.

"What are your plans?" she asked again.

He looked ahead to the road that meandered to the border. It led downhill through cultivated land of maize and sorghum, an easy eight-hour walk.

"I have a flight to London from Nairobi. It's a cheap ticket."

He looked at her uneasily.

"I can't change the date."

She smiled.

"There's a truck park on the Rwandan side of the border. It's always busy. Everything has to be brought in by road from Kenya."

Ralph nodded.

"Talk to the drivers. They're Somali. They'll take you along. White men are a talisman that makes the trip easier for them. Usually."

She held his hand.

"You'll be in Nairobi in four or five days."

There seemed no point in delaying, early morning always a good time to talk to people at the hospital. She'd be there in thirty minutes.

She looked at him and the morning sun lit her hair like a beacon so that Ralph expected it to flash a warning letter in Morse.

"In Burundi we say *Amashyo*."

Ralph repeated it.

"It means 'May you have herds'."

"And the response?"

"The reply is *Amashongure*. It means 'May you have herds of females'."

Both laughed.

"Ralph. I have to go."

Ralph hastened to leave, gathering his rucksack.

"But of course. You'll be late."

"I didn't mean that," she said. "I have to go, because this is what I do."

She smiled at him.

"For the moment anyway."

Ralph opened the door. He stood stiffly on the road, looking forward to the walk to loosen up.

"*Amashyo*, Azzurra," he said.

"*Amashongure*, Ralph."

He lifted his rucksack and stretched backwards, arms high, bending at the waist. Ahead some animals hobbled down the road, a man herding them forwards by throwing stones. Ralph thought he'd catch up with him quickly. He'd talk to him about his sheep. Were they sheep or goats? Tails hanging down. Sheep. He stepped out, almost a jog. When he looked back Azzurra had gone, her wheel tracks in the dust already fading as if washed by a tide.

SIXTEEN

Angel had arrived in Kenya hoping to find Ralph waiting at a budget hotel for his onward flight to London. It would be easy. Instead he'd wandered, growing increasingly anxious, as he failed to track Ralph down. A group of Dutchmen he'd talked to in the 'Olde English Pub' at the Intercontinental Hotel had been certain a boy meeting Ralph's description had a bed in a dormitory at the Iqbal Hotel on Tom Mboya Street. Angel had found it popular with travellers. It appeared clean, central, with hot showers, a safe place to leave baggage, and only six Kenyan shillings to sleep on the floor. At the black-market exchange rate of just under eighteen shillings for one US dollar it made it about thirty cents a night. Angel thought this probably even within Ralph's meagre budget. It turned out to be a false trail.

Two Swedish girls, with whom he'd shared an as-much-as-you-can-eat south Indian vegetarian curry at the Super

Hotel on River Road, thought he may have been at the nearby Zahra Hotel. They had recently asked a cute English boy to share a room with them to save cost, but he'd seemed embarrassed and paid the full twenty shillings to be on his own. Angel had checked it out and had then started to worry. The Zahra, and others in the River Road area, seemed especially dangerous at night. Reports of armed robberies and muggings were common. He was relieved to find that Ralph hadn't been there.

In desperation Angel had hovered outside the British Embassy at Bruce House on Standard Street, waited outside the railway station on Moi Avenue, checked that Ralph hadn't tried to cash cheques at American Express or use their Poste Restante, and chatted in Swahili to bored girls at the Airways Terminal in town. Over a bowl of beans and potatoes at a food shack at the bottom of Latema Road he'd concluded that Ralph had not yet arrived in Nairobi. He wasn't sure if this was good or bad.

As a last chance he took a twenty-five-cent bus ride from the city to the Salvation Army Hostel near Kanakore Market and spent an uneasy night in a ten-shilling mixed dorm. In the morning, feeling as if hung over, he boarded a number thirty-four bus from outside the Ambassador Hotel to the airport and watched British Airways counter staff preen and strut around their check-in area. By then he already knew what he had to do.

In the airport gift shop he bought road maps of the Great Lakes area at various scales, and from Haji Motors, off the Mombasa Road on the way back into town from the airport, he bought a ubiquitous Toyota Hilux with a ripped brown vinyl bench seat. It was the two-door second generation model, ten years old and with a tired two-litre engine driving the rear wheels only. The registration was Kenyan, three letters and three numbers, starting KP for Nairobi area vehicles that had been first licensed in 1972. There had been a discount for cash dollars and no questions asked. He drove back into town smiling.

At Rajabz Apparelz, 'Bringing class & finesse without straining our clients' pockets', he bought a white cotton *kanzu*, cheaper than linen. The ankle-length loose tunic had maroon embroidery at the collar. With a green and gold *kofia* cap it became formal wear for both Muslims and Christians, and suitable for a wedding.

The Thorn Tree Café, under the New Stanley Hotel, seemed somewhat touristy but reassuringly busy. Angel wondered if he should leave a note on the travellers' noticeboard. *Looking for Ralph Phillips, eighteen and English, flying from Nairobi to London, in relation to a million-dollar inheritance from a druggie heiress he once slept with. Contact the South African National Intelligence Service on...* It was preposterous. With a sigh, Angel spread his maps and considered his plan. He had little time in hand. He had a seven-hour drive before dark.

*

Ralph stood and looked up at the night sky. Earlier that day he'd crossed the equator, and at a town called Kayabwe on the Masaka to Kampala road Ralph had re-entered the northern hemisphere. Ursa Major must be somewhere above his head. From the two pointer stars Merak and Dubhe, he should be able to visually trace a line to find the direction to Polaris, and if he mentally multiplied by five the distance between the same two stars he would know how far along that line to look for the often-faint Pole Star. It would show him the way north, the way home.

It would be low on the horizon, too low to see. At home, Polaris was nearly four hands above the horizon. In Kampala, so close to the equator, Polaris would always be just out of reach, like so much else in Uganda. Ralph couldn't see the horizon anyway, he could only see the sky. The lorry driven by Somalis had pulled into Kampala at dusk and driven straight into a compound for the night. It was a small rough square, big enough for three trucks, with corrugated iron sheets on a wooden frame about six metres high as a security barrier all the way around. Cheerful men with guns patrolled inside like rats in a cage. A wide door had been pulled open to let the truck enter, then chained and padlocked. Above the iron sheets occasional streams of tracer raced across the Ugandan night, automatic gunfire echoing around them.

Ralph thought how lucky he'd been to find a ride from the Rwandan border to Kenya through dangerous Uganda. The first part had not been easy, mostly due to a difficult customs officer in Burundi. After leaving Azzurra, he'd walked eight hot hours and had arrived at the border post exhausted. He'd been told to wait. The wait lasted all night and half the following day. He'd slept fitfully in a mosquito-ridden customs waiting room and, scratching like a dog, was told to wait some more. He'd quietly left and crossed the bridge into Rwanda without completing the Burundi formalities. He'd walked down the road, didn't stop for the guard and crossed the bridge into Rwanda expecting to be either called back or shot. Halfway across, in no-man's-land, he found himself sweating and shaking and singing a hymn faintly remembered from school. He'd never considered himself religious but at that time he found himself praying that someone should look over him.

The rest, however, had been easy: a truck stop near the border, a cup of sweet tea with a gentlemanly old man, an empty fuel truck returning to Mombasa. He had now been travelling hairpin roads up and down steep Rwandan mountainsides for three days, the Land of a Thousand Hills living up to its name. It had been torturously slow but he'd loved being with the gentle Somalis, strikingly tall people with ebony skin and aquiline features. They'd been calm, quiet and dignified, content not to talk, happy to ignore strangers. With them in their venerable steaming Bedford, eating their plain boiled pasta for dinner, sleeping with them under the lorry, listening to them talk softly in their own language, Ralph was happy too.

In two days he would be in Nairobi, in a week London. Ralph thought of home, now close enough to imagine.

*

Elanza was sitting outside by the pool when Nels came, listening to the birds. Her hearing seemed to have improved as her sight diminished. She'd never noticed before but now she could pick out hundreds of different bird sounds. Loud rose-winged parakeets squawked, announcing someone's presence.

"Who is it?" she asked.

A voice answered her when very close.

"Me."

Without warning Nels slapped her hard across the face with the back of his hand and Elanza, startled, screamed. Tears ran down her cheek from shock and anger.

"You bastard!" she shouted.

Elanza tenderly touched the side of her face and could feel it swelling.

"Is that it?" she sobbed. "No chit-chat first? Is that Nels' foreplay?"

"Shut up."

Nels went to strike her again. She instinctively flinched and he stopped his hand short of her face.

"Where's Ralph?"

"I don't fucking know," she cried, frightened and fearful of what he could do to her.

Nels knew that Ralph was heading to Nairobi but he didn't know how or when. He didn't believe Elanza would know either but he thought he should try.

"What are you going to do?" she screeched. "Rape me?"

She started sobbing again.

"Well, let's just get it over with."

Nels looked at her shaking, her hair a mess, her body very thin, her bones prominent at the shoulder and neck, the skin tight and greasy over a skeletal face. He would go and find Snyman's wife. Danelle's frivolous and vacuous playful teasing was more tempting to him than Elanza's whore-like submission.

"No," he said. "I don't want to rape you. I don't go for blind girls. I like girls to watch as I rape them."

Elanza wept as he left her, sobbing with fury and rage – at him for his foul maliciousness and at herself for the injustice of her pitiful condition.

*

Angel had left Nairobi with a mental map of his route, mumbling the names of the towns he'd pass through: Kikuyu, Naivasha, Gilgil, Nakuru, Kericho, Kisumu. At a viewpoint on the ridge road the Rift Valley spread below him – Africa.

He looked at his hands on the steering wheel and, not for the first time in his life, wondered where he belonged.

He stopped at a roadside market near Kericho, unable to resist the opportunity to talk a Nilotic language. The people there hadn't been Maasai; they lived further south along the Tanzanian border; and the Maasai's close relatives the Samburu, hair dyed red from ochre, were much further north. Both Maasai and Samburu were nomadic Rift Valley plains pastoralists and didn't live this far west. Kericho was still too far from Lake Victoria for the market traders to be Luo, who were predominantly fishermen and easy to identify. The Luo were one of only a few tribes that didn't circumcise. Instead, six front teeth in the lower jaw were removed on reaching manhood. At the Kericho market they had to be Kipsigi, highland pastoral peoples. They would talk Kipsigis, a form of Kalenjuns, a tonal language of the Nandi cluster.

From a Kipsigi herder he'd bought the goat, a brown nanny with short horns, ripped ears and a curly white tufty beard. He'd paid too high a price but considered it had been worth the money.

Angel pulled the red pickup truck, faded with age, to the side of the road outside the Kenyan border town of Busia. It was dusk, as he'd planned, but Angel wanted it to be fully dark. He looked behind him at the goat, now quiet, lying tethered to a bar in the back of the truck. The goat and his new clothes had been two expenditures he didn't anticipate his boss at the National Intelligence Service would agree to reimburse. The clothes had been a rational purchase in Nairobi, the goat an opportunistic addition he'd made en route, an inspired improvement to his cover story.

Angel got out and looked around at the border town of Busia ahead.

"So, goat, do you speak Lugandan?"

"In Lugandan we do not say 'Good morning'. We say, 'How was your night?'"

"*Wasuze otya?*"

"To which you reply '*Gyendi*', 'I am OK'."

"Okay? *Kale?*"

"I am, *nze*, a goat, *embuzi.*"

He stroked its head.

"*Nkwagola*, I love you. Maybe not."

"You are a *kirabo*, a gift."

"Do you understand? *Otegeera?*"

The goat stood and urinated.

"Ah. I'll call you Oku as in *Okufuysia*, which means 'to allow urine to flow from the bladder out of the body'."

"No. Your name should be *Ekibi*, bad. As in a bad smell."

He looked at the truck. Urine ran out of a small drain hole in the bed of the pickup and down the number plate.

He would have to change them from Kenyan. He'd steal some number plates and switch them. With stolen Ugandan plates it wouldn't stand scrutiny – he had neither useable personal identification nor any vehicle documents. If challenged he'd have to rely on his cover story and something to divert people's attention. Ekibi the goat seemed the best he could hope for in Uganda.

The White Nile from Lake Victoria ran through the country and made it one of the best watered areas of Africa. It should have been the Garden of Eden. Instead its recent history was one of violence and anarchy headed, firstly, by Milton Obote and five years of military law. This was followed by more of the same from Idi Amin, his protégé then rival. Amin had gone and Obote was back in power. Not much had changed for Ugandans.

Uganda was complicated – a classic divided kingdom. Obote was of the Bunyoro tribe from the north. The Bunyoro were a Nilotic tribe, pastoral and nomadic because the north was dry. They were poor, and put upon with slow and bad decision-making by elders as was the traditional way.

Amin, however, was Bugandan and from the south. The Bugandans were Bantu, and agricultural rather than pastoral thanks to the Nile waters. It had made them prosperous compared to the north. Colonial development had concentrated on the richer south of the country. Here were the railways, the seat of government, cash crops like cotton and sugar and tea, and missionary education.

The brutal medieval infighting between north and south had ruined the country and terrorised its people, yet it didn't need to be this way. Ugandans were not naturally barbaric, but industrious and innovative. In the fourth century the Bantu people had perfected the art of smelting iron in a preheated force draught furnace to make carbon steel. Siemens didn't do that in Europe until the nineteenth century.

The survivors of Amin's genocidal purges against Obote's Bunyoro people in the north were now armed and in uniform, conducting similar actions against Bantu-speaking Bugandans in the south, for whom they felt no empathy or pity.

Angel crossed from Kenyan Busia to Ugandan Busia in the predawn darkness. The town straddled the border but only the main road from Kampala had a customs post. The border was porous. Just a short way from town one of many dirt roads allowed vehicles to go around the border-crossing inspection point and rejoin the main road outside of Busia town.

It was a gamble. The border crossing from Kenya to Uganda at the town of Malaba further north had a busier road, but the crossing itself was a river bridge and impossible for Angel to circumvent. He could only hope that Ralph hadn't come that way.

Outside the town Angel found what he'd been looking for, and his Hilux soon wore new registration plates. They were still three letters and three numbers but they started with a U not a K.

Angel's plan had been simple. With the Kenya to Tanzania border closed the only route available to Ralph coming from the south was through Uganda, and all routes through Uganda went through the capital Kampala. He would retrace the main arterial road from Nairobi to Kampala and make enquiries along the way. There were unmeasurable risks. Of all the places on the continent of Africa that an employee of the apartheid South African National Intelligence Service would be most in trouble if discovered, Kampala would be near the top of the list. Angel had travelled into Kenya on his British passport, as South African visitors to Kenya needed a visa that entailed a day in the Pretoria High Commission being glared at in disgust. He'd hidden his passport with his Western clothes and dropped it in a left luggage facility at Nairobi's domestic terminal, sanitising himself of all identification before entering Uganda. He'd put his long hair on top of his head, under the *kofia*.

Blend in, he told himself.

It would have been safer to drive on the many unpaved roads. Of all the roads in Uganda only seven per cent were paved, just two thousand kilometres out of twenty-seven thousand. There were very few random roadblocks and security searches on dirt roads and, although slower, the opportunities were limitless in every direction.

Angel saw the police car as he came up to the road junction, seventeen kilometres inside Uganda from the border. It was exactly where he would have put a roadblock. The traffic from Busia slowed as it came through a forest and a lorry parking area by the side of the road gave a wide pull-in area. A rough sign advertised the Garden Pub Hotel and Accommodation. Angel wasn't sure when they might last have had guests.

There were three of them, unarmed. Angel wasn't nervous but curious and interested in what might be the right price. Too big a bribe invited suspicion, too little might show a lack of respect. Both showed no local knowledge, and that might lead to annoyance and aggression. It depended on the time of the day. It was early morning, which Angel thought should help him. They might be hung over but not drunk, and with the whole day ahead they might be lenient as there would be plenty of earning opportunities still to come.

Angel also considered his cover. He wore his *kanzu*, his formal clothes, on the way to his brother's wedding. Slightly too high a bribe might be safer and just reflect his good spirits and wish not to be late. His cover story was that he worked in Kenya. It gave him good reason to have dollars, and at a black-market exchange rate of twelve times the bank rate it would have made it cheap for Angel and attractive to the soldiers. It may also have made them curious. In the end he decided to use local currency and he picked a figure that he estimated to be the price of a three-course meal at an expensive hotel in Kampala, the Apollo or the Speke or the Imperial.

Angel put both hands on the wheel as the Toyota stopped. He pitched his Lugandan with a hint of Kikuyu to show he'd worked away from home, a plausible excuse for any tonal mistakes he might make.

It had been technically quite interesting. Some quick thinking on his part had been required when passing his bribe, as the Lugandan system of cardinal numbers was quite complicated. Twenty to fifty were expressed as multiples of ten, but sixty to a hundred were numerical nouns in their own right. He'd very nearly asked them if ninety shillings would be alright by telling them he had nine tens.

He hadn't needed to explain that he was with the groom's family, that he'd missed the *kwanjula*, the day a bride introduces her future husband and the people who will escort him, because he'd been working away. He hoped that his goat would help with the *mutwalo*, the bride price. He'd do what he could as the girl was already pregnant. He smiled then but the soldiers didn't. They took his money and waved him through.

Angel drove down the road and laughed.

"Ekibi, you stink, but you are the best damn goat I've ever bought."

Angel had noticed two things as he'd driven toward Kampala. In the countryside there was no wildlife, and in the towns there were mostly kids and sick people.

From where he'd been stopped to the town of Iganga, and again through countryside to the Nile crossing at Jinja, he'd seen no animals except dogs. There was nothing left. Amin's soldiers, hungry for hard currency and armed with automatic weapons, had exterminated elephant, rhino and other big game for ivory, horn and skins. In ten years, Uganda's herd of forty thousand elephants had been reduced to 1,500. White rhino didn't exist. In some areas the carcasses and bones of elephants littered the ground where they'd been gunned down in groups of up to a dozen at a time.

In the towns there were different visible reminders to Uganda's chaos. Its people were dying. The government spent just two dollars per person a year on healthcare, and it clearly wasn't enough. Angel saw untreated ulcerated tumours on the face, neck or jaw of children suffering with Burkitt's lymphoma, a malignant cancer of the lymphatic system common in malarial areas.

Other people were anaemic or suffering from whooping cough. Many were severely malnourished or dying from diseases simply unknown to health officials. A new disease was spreading in sixteen to forty-year-old men, and women, by heterosexual contact. They called it Slim. Angel guessed it to be a local name for Elanza's illness.

Angel noticed the children of Jinja, orphaned by war and the death of parents from disease, living on the city streets in unsupervised small groups. There was an estimated one and a half million of them throughout Uganda, ten per cent of the population. Several thousand of them had attached themselves as young boys to the Ugandan Army and become *kadogos*, child soldiers, and were now destined to remain on the periphery of society for the rest of their lives.

After Jinja, Angel drove through square tea plantations and entered the Nabira Forest and the town of Lugazi. He'd been driving for nearly three hours and was becoming increasingly nervous about Ralph's safety. He was only forty-five kilometres east of Kampala.

*

The Somali driver pulled into the petrol station for fuel at the same time as an army Land Rover. It passed slowly alongside the lorry and parked across the forecourt exit to the road, not blocking it but restricting the space, making it difficult for a lorry and trailer to leave suddenly. There were three soldiers inside wearing big red berets, too big for their heads, as though a quartermaster had made fun of them. Folds of woollen material bunched up on the top and then fell over the side, covering one ear. They looked like clowns. Ralph smiled at them, resisting a temptation to laugh.

The lorry driver nervously wound down the window. All three soldiers had guns on slings over their shoulders, the barrels pointing forward and down. They were lean and unsmiling.

Ralph's door opened. A soldier wordlessly motioned for him to get out of the lorry, then pushed him into the middle of the forecourt.

The driver had a discussion in a language that Ralph couldn't understand. The third soldier brought Ralph's rucksack and dropped it at his feet.

"Sit down."

Ralph looked around at the dusty stained concrete and sat on his rucksack. A soldier pulled it from under him and Ralph sat down angrily, cross-legged on the ground.

The soldier talking to the driver stepped down from the truck window and looked at Ralph curiously. With a hiss of brakes the lorry pulled away and slowly wound around the Land Rover onto the road. It headed east, changing gears quickly, east towards Kenya.

"Oh, that's great," said Ralph.

He tried to recall the next big town along the way, the next opportunity to get a ride. Was it called Ginger or something?

"What are you doing here?" the soldier asked.

All three stood around him, their guns now off the shoulder and held with two hands. Before Ralph could answer, he shouted again.

"What is under your shirt?"

"It's my wallet."

"Take it out."

Ralph pulled it out from under his shirt. It hung around his neck.

"Open it."

Ralph hesitated.

"It's just some money," he said.

The soldier stepped forward to see.

"Open it," he commanded.

Ralph did as he was told. A single US dollar bill was the only thing inside. A fifty-dollar bill.

The soldier stepped back. He looked at the others for guidance, reassurance, or in disbelief at their good fortune, Ralph wasn't sure which.

"You are a spy."

"I'm sorry?"

"You are a spy and we arrest you."

"Don't be silly. I'm not a spy. I'm just travelling through to Nairobi to catch a plane. Look, I have a ticket, here."

He reached for his rucksack but a soldier kicked it away.

"You are a spy. If you give me the money I will let you go."

It was a game, thought Ralph. A stupid game with pretend soldiers in silly hats.

"No. I'm not a spy and you can't have my money. It's all I have."

"Take off your shoes," he shouted.

"What?"

"Take off your shoes."

All three lifted their guns. They rattled and clicked as they put them to their shoulders. The foresights on them had a round protective cover, something that flipped up with a green dot on it. The barrels were very close to Ralph's head. He could see them clearly. The outside of the very end of the barrel was threaded for screwing something on, the threads filled with grey mud. Ralph wondered if he should say something.

*

Lugazi town straddled both sides of the Kampala to Jinja highway. On the outskirts Angel saw a dusty beat-up ambulance, donated jointly by a Rotary club in England and a charity in Germany. It seemed the only asset of the Kawolo Hospital, that and a line of homemade incubators for premature babies heated by domestic lightbulbs.

Further towards the centre of town Angel slowed as he approached the bus station and then stopped. A line of people were watching an army vehicle at a Total service station on the opposite side of the road. The green Land Rover had parked at an angle, an attempt to block the exit rather than take fuel, its passenger door left wide open.

Three soldiers stood in a semicircle. Angel guessed they were Acholi from north central Uganda, Obote supporters. Unlike those at the roadblock these looked more disciplined and they were armed. A boy sat cross-legged on the tarmac, his hands on his head.

He looked thin, his hair curling at his shoulders. He had shorts and a faded beige tee shirt with some black writing in large letters on the front. A dusty blue rucksack lay at his feet. A soldier waved a gun at him and the boy started to remove his walking boots. Angel guessed that despite his youthful appearance he was about eighteen years old. He had blond hair.

Angel thought quickly. He had very little time. All three men had weapons pointed at the boy. Their guns had a distinctive shape with a forward curve to the magazine and varnished plywood stocks, pistol grips and hand guards. The weapon was influencing Angel's course of action. They were AK47s.

Production of the AK had been licensed by the Russians to dozens of countries. Some had been perfectly engineered but many were not. Angel imagined these were most probably Egyptian, not the best but not the worst. Accuracy of Egyptian AKs was 'good enough' up to about three hundred metres. Beyond that distance even expert shooters couldn't put consecutive rounds onto a target.

He looked closer at the men. All the weapons had the stock attached; often they had been removed. It was a small point but Angel recognised it to be in favour of the soldiers. The weapon was more accurate with the stock, but more importantly its cleaning kit lived in the butt. Although renowned for its ruggedness and ability to endure large amounts of foreign matter without failing, the AK did appreciate occasional cleaning. But had they been taught how to strip the weapon? Many users, including the Soviets, simply threw them away if they stopped working. Soviet doctrine said that it should be cheap and disposable. Very few operators went to the trouble of replacing the small parts and springs, as required after every few thousand rounds. Perhaps the weapon would not even fire, and conceivably they may not have any rounds. Under Amin only a few trusted units were allowed ammunition.

Angel had to assume they worked. He needed to be at the service station, grab the boy and then be three hundred metres away out of the effective range of an AK before the soldiers reacted. How long would that take? With the Hilux he could cover that distance quite quickly. A quarter mile was about four hundred metres. Could his two-litre Hilux do a quarter mile in twenty seconds? Maybe when new but now, ten hard years later, it would probably be closer to thirty seconds. And he needed time to get the boy into the vehicle. It could be a total of a minute. Would he be able to create a diversion that gave him sixty seconds to get the boy on board and clear of the range of an AK47?

He looked at the Land Rover parked across the fuel pumps. They were tough vehicles but so was the Hilux, which had a pedigree going back to the Toyopet SB, a one-ton light truck, and like the Land Rover also dated from 1947. The Land Rover's bodywork was aluminium. If he hit it laterally in between the wheels, rather than at the front or back, the Land Rover would crumple a little, absorbing some shock.

Angel started the Hilux and pulled into the bus station, his back to the service area. He got out of the pickup, untied the goat and pulled it down to the ground. He stroked its head.

"*Weeraba*. Goodbye, Ekibi."

An old man stood with three young girls. He may have been caring for his granddaughters, their parents long dead. Angel handed him the rope.

"*Ssebo*, take the goat. For the girls."

He sat back in the Hilux and put on his seatbelt. He took the *kofia* from his head and pushed his hair to the back out of his eyes, rolling up the soft hat and wrapping it around the top of the steering wheel.

Across the road a soldier placed Ralph's walking boots on the sidewalk. It had to be now. Angel took a deep breath.

SEVENTEEN

Ralph saw a red pickup truck reversing towards the
service station at speed. It crossed the main road,
the gearbox whining, its momentum building.
With a muffled crunch it struck the Land Rover amidships,
in between the wheels, pushing it sideways across a petrol
pump that snapped backwards and immediately caught fire.
The pickup pulled forward sharply, free of the Land Rover
but trailing its own tailgate and the Land Rover's driver's door.

An explosion rocked the forecourt, the shock wave
pushing the pickup further away and throwing the soldiers
to their feet. Glass shattered in the garage shop, and smoke
and debris covered Ralph on the ground.

Through it all a man appeared. He stood as if on a cloud,
the sun shining through the smoke. It illuminated him
from behind and dazzled Ralph's eyes. The man was dressed
in a white robe, his long hair flowing either side, his arms
outstretched. He appeared to be wearing a strange hat that
glittered like a crown of light, or a halo.

Ralph wondered fleetingly if he might be dead. The man called someone's name. It was his name. He shouted for Ralph.

Ralph stumbled towards him on bare feet and was pushed into the Toyota. The man seemed pleased. He smiled as he accelerated onto the road, heading east.

He started laughing.

"Under a minute," he said.

Ralph stared at him, unable to speak.

Angel drove hard, the feeble Toyota engine screaming as they re-entered the Nabira Forest. He didn't want to talk. Angel used English infrequently, aware that when he did it was with the Cockney accent of a boyhood roaming London's grittier streets, one that stubbornly refused to be polished by an expensive public school in Dorset.

Ralph started to shake. He looked at his feet.

"Where are my shoes? Where are we going?"

Angel said nothing. Ralph watched him concentrating, looking frequently in his mirror. He remembered sitting on the ground and the soldiers ridiculously accusing him of being a spy.

"They asked me to take them off," he said. "They probably thought it would be harder for me to run away."

Angel looked at him. Pairs of shoes left by the side of the road had become a symbol during Idi Amin of a life taken by government troops, a warning. In eight years, Amin's soldiers had murdered an estimated three hundred thousand Ugandans in a Commonwealth country. They had left three hundred thousand pairs of shoes by the roadside. Obote's troops were just continuing the tradition. It shouldn't be hard to find Ralph a new pair of boots.

"You were just minutes away from being shot and killed," Angel said.

"What do you mean?"

Angel needed to cover the thirty-seven kilometres back to Jinja as quickly as possible. A roadblock there at the Nile River bridge would seal them off inside Uganda.

"Be quiet. We'll talk later. We must cross the Nile as soon as we can. If we can do that we have a chance of reaching Kenya."

"What do you mean?" Ralph repeated. "Who are you?"

Angel took no notice of him. He'd been driving fast but slowed through the town of Njeru. They were close to the Nile crossing, the most dangerous time. Angel needed Ralph to be alert but he seemed in shock.

"Listen."

"Hmm."

"You have been in great danger."

Angel let that soak in.

"But now you are safe."

He looked at him consolingly.

"Who were you travelling with?"

"They arrested me for spying. They wanted my money," Ralph said, and pulled a stained leather wallet from under his tee shirt at the end of an old brown bootlace.

"Did they take your money?" Angel asked.

"No, I said I needed it."

Angel, amazed that Ralph was alive, realised that he'd been very lucky.

"Who were you travelling with?" he said.

"I got a ride with a truck. They stopped for fuel."

"From Kampala?"

"No, from the border with Rwanda."

"The Rwanda–Uganda border?"

"The Burundi–Rwanda border," Ralph corrected.

It made sense. Fuel trucks going to landlocked Burundi from Mombasa.

"They left when the soldiers came and pulled me out."

Angel nodded.

"Somalis?"

"Yes."

They'd been wise to leave. Ralph hadn't been such a good talisman after all, more like a target.

"Okay. Now pay attention. If we can get over this bridge we'll be safe. I can take you all the way to Nairobi. But if they've put a roadblock on the crossing we'll be in trouble."

Ralph nodded. It was nine in the morning, a busy time with building traffic. A bad time, or possibly in their favour, Angel couldn't decide.

"Can we just take another bridge?" Ralph asked.

It was a reasonable question, except there wasn't another bridge.

"This is the Nile crossing point where the river leaves Lake Victoria. There are rapids and falls all the way to Lake Kyoga. The next vehicle crossing is an unreliable ferry at Masindi Port about 250 kilometres north. The next bridge across the Nile isn't until Karuma Falls, but that's over three hundred kilometres away. It's about a four-and-a-half-hour drive."

Angel thought of the logistics. Three hundred to the next bridge then nearly four hundred back along the northern side of Lake Kyoga, through Saroti and Mbale to the Kenyan border. A seven-hundred-kilometre round trip through dangerous country. His cover story wasn't designed for that. He had no papers and the now damaged vehicle on false plates had been in an incident with soldiers earlier. He'd entered the country illegally, and he had a conspicuous foreign boy with him.

"It is impossible to drive around," Angel said. "If we have problems our fallback is to go south through the town toward the lake; it's only a few kilometres. We'll dump the vehicle and cross the old railway bridge tonight on foot."

"Who are you? Why are you helping me?"

Angel didn't reply. He hadn't thought this through. He remembered that in training at The Farm, students had been taught that the best and easiest lie was the one as close to the truth as you could get away with. You couldn't pretend to be an airline pilot if you'd never flown a plane.

"I'm Swazi. I've been sent here by my government."

"Your English is very good, like a real English person."

"All Swazis speak good English. We have English-run schools."

Ralph nodded. He'd heard of schools like that in South Africa.

"I haven't been to Swaziland," he said.

He watched the traffic as Angel drove.

"How did you know I was in trouble?"

"You mean other than the guns pointed at your head?"

Ralph stared at him.

"I used to be a policeman but now I work for the UN. I monitor what's happening in this part of Africa from my office in Nairobi and report the situation to my boss."

He spoke softly.

"I know how much trouble you were in, Ralph."

They moved slowly but without stopping towards the river. The Nile road crossing ran initially along the top of the Owen Falls Dam to an island midstream. A short bridge crossed the final part of the river.

"Do you have a hat?"

Ralph shook his head. Angel gave him the *kofia* to cover his blond hair.

"Here, put this on and look at the floor."

They passed a police vehicle. Ralph glanced at it and at a hydroelectric station below.

"Head down," said Angel. "Nearly there."

The Nile looked slow for the longest river in the world, as though it would run out of power and trickle into the sand. From the bridge it still had 6,853 kilometres to flow to the Mediterranean Sea. Ralph didn't think it would make it that far.

A lorry in front slowed on the final bridge but then accelerated and they were across. It was still over 120 kilometres to the Kenyan border but the routes they could take across country were now infinite. Angel relaxed. He felt tired now after action. He'd had a bad night in a cheap hotel, driven for over ten hours and had a night without sleep waiting to cross the border. The contact at the service station had awakened him but the adrenaline had long worn off.

Thirty minutes from Jinja, in a small town called Mulingilile, Angel stopped by the side of the road and looked at his maps. He yawned.

"Are we stopping?" Ralph asked.

"No, we need to keep moving."

Angel thought hard. *Should they swap vehicles? Should they steal another one here in this town?*

"Is it far to the border?" asked Ralph.

"About a hundred kilometres."

Angel felt their luck couldn't last much longer. He didn't know how they would get through a roadblock.

"We are going across country from here. We need to get off the main roads."

He measured the distance with his thumb on a map.

"It's a little further and it'll be slower but the chance of a random police or army stop will be much less."

Ralph knew what he was thinking. Alone he might talk his way through a roadblock. With Ralph along it would be impossible.

"What if I just get out here and find my own way?" he said.

Angel thought about it before replying.

"No, you'll never make it."

"You don't have to look after me, you know."

Angel suddenly became angry with the boy. His fatigue and anxiety rose to the surface in a hot bubble.

"You have no idea where you are. These people will shoot you out of curiosity, just to see if your blood is the same colour as mine."

Ralph reached for the door handle.

Angel held his arm.

"Sit there. If you move, I might shoot you myself."

He threw the maps on the seat and pulled from the road that ran through town onto a hard dirt track. Red dust, redder than the Toyota, trailed them like smoke from a tank on a firing range.

*

The Toyota ran uncomfortably over corrugations in the dirt track for over an hour through rural hamlets shown on the map on Ralph's lap as Lugolole, Mayuge, Buganda and Kyemeire. His finger traced their dusty progress. Ralph estimated they had a little over fifty kilometres to go. He looked at the man driving. No words had been spoken since Mulingilile, and Ralph struggled to understand why he'd been so angry with him. He sounded like a policeman. Perhaps that had made him taciturn. It could be down to hours walking the beat in Swaziland, directing traffic, or rounding up stray goats from the road.

He ventured to find out.

"We're making steady progress."

It was a positive statement. Ralph expected an encouraging response but the man just grunted. Ralph wondered if he might be slightly simple, even potentially dangerous. He thought to engage him in conversation about their route, or the economy of the villages they were passing through, calmly, in the way that he would talk to an aggressive drunk, but the man surprised him by talking first.

"When do you leave Africa?" he asked, his head tilted to the side, his long braids of hair rattling on his shoulder.

"Oh, um… well, I have a flight from Nairobi next week."

Angel knew which day next week. He knew the time, the flight number, the aircraft's call sign and its hours to next overhaul, the name and home address of the rostered captain and the seat already assigned to Ralph. Zelda, the National Intelligence Service's agent at South African Airways, had, as usual, been very accommodating.

"Do you have somewhere to stay in Nairobi?"

For a moment Ralph wondered if the man was gay. He made light of the question.

"Oh, somewhere cheap I expect."

The man thought for a moment.

"Madame Roche's is a nice guesthouse. It's cheap and safe. It's out of town. Ask for the Aga Khan Hospital. You can't miss it."

"I will. Thank you."

"Do you need money?" the man asked.

Ralph laughed to cover his nervousness.

"Well, that's kind of you but I'll be fine. Thank you."

"How much money do you have left?"

Ralph thought it was a curious question, as if the man knew how much money he'd had to start with.

"Oh, enough I think."

"How much?"

Ralph hesitated. He kept most of his cash rolled up tightly in a small plastic bag slipped inside the aluminium tube frame of his rucksack. He thought he had about 250 dollars inside his rucksack, the money in his wallet around his neck just a sacrificial decoy. Ralph hoped it would be a significant enough amount to deter thieves from searching further. It would be a pity to lose it but better than losing the lot.

Ralph lied.

"About fifty I think."

"Dollars?"

Ralph nodded.

Angel said nothing.

"Are you sick?" he asked, and then after a while, "Any fevers? Stomach problems?"

Ralph laughed.

"No, I'm fine thanks."

"Do you drink local water?"

"Well, yes, I do as a matter of fact."

"Hmm," said the man.

He seemed to relax.

"Have you spoken to your father recently?"

Ralph was amazed.

"What? No. Have you?"

Angel looked at him.

"You know you could go to the British Embassy in Nairobi."

"What for?"

"They would give you a phone number that your father could call at an arranged time. You could send a cheap telegram giving him the details and then speak to him."

Ralph thought about it.

"There's no point. We never really speak when I'm at home. I mean, we talk, but not about anything important. You can't debate with my father. Any opinion other than his own isn't considered much."

The man shook his head.

"I expect all fathers are like that. It doesn't matter. Talking about rubbish is enough to make a bond."

"But we'd just argue."

"A father you argue with is better than no father at all."

Ralph thought about it quietly.

"So, what are you going to do when you get home?" the man asked.

It was a question Ralph had been asking himself for some time and he had come no closer to an answer than he had been when he'd left school. Some grammar school boys had always known that they would study engineering, be a bank manager, or run the family haulage firm. Ralph was sure only that whatever he did it should be outside. Anything other than working deskbound in an office.

"I'm not sure. I thought about joining the Army. Or agriculture."

The man's reaction didn't do anything to change Ralph's suspicion that he may be mad or dangerous, or both.

He braked hard, unexpectedly, and the Toyota shook like a dog as it came to a stop in a red cloud as at sunset. He put his face very close and gripped Ralph's knee hard. His eyes were black and a stubble like a burnt field covered his chin and cheeks. Strong muscles quivered in his neck as if in spasm.

"Be a farmer," he said.

*

The track had been leading south-east through Buinja, but at Lumino it headed north into the outskirts of the Ugandan side of Busia. They had made the border.

Angel stopped clear of the town at twelve thirty, lunchtime. They had covered ninety-eight kilometres of dirt road in three hours without being challenged.

"We need to split up now," he said.

Ralph tried not to show his relief.

"I'm going to drop you at a crossroads in town. It's about 1,200 metres from the border. You're going to need a Kenyan entry stamp or you'll have problems at the airport when you leave Kenya. I'm going to tell you what to do."

"Okay," Ralph laughed.

"This is serious. Walk to the border but do not go through customs. Do you understand?"

Ralph nodded.

"Find a café off the road where you can sit out of view of the street but within sight of the border post. Choose somewhere that has a back door, a way out if someone comes for you through the front."

Ralph stared at him, uncertain about what the man would do but convinced now that he was mad.

"Watch the border for new guards coming to work. The shift change may be at four or five o'clock this afternoon.

When you see fresh people arriving for work go through the border, but pick an officer who hasn't been relieved, one who is still waiting to go home. Tell him you've been travelling with the church. Make one up; there are hundreds of them. St Simon and St Jude's Holy Evangelical Truth Mission or something. Three hundred metres through the border on the other side is a bus station. Wait for me. It will be after dark. Maybe eight this evening. I'll collect you and we'll drive to Nairobi. We'll be there for breakfast. I'll pay."

"Okay, what will you do?"

"Sleep until dark and then drive around the border post."

He flicked hair from his eyes.

"Your rucksack is in the back."

Angel looked at Ralph's feet.

"Do you have some shoes?"

Ralph looked in the back of the pickup. His blue rucksack lay covered in red dust as though back from a trip to Mars.

"Yes, I have some spare boots."

"Do you have some long trousers and a collared shirt?"

"Possibly."

"Okay. Put them on before you cross. Be godly."

"Godly?"

"Yeah. You've been here in beautiful Uganda visiting associates from your church back home."

Ralph wasn't convinced.

"St Simon and St Jude's?"

"Yeah. That's right. See you in the bus station after eight."

Angel drove slowly through the town and stopped at the crossroads.

"It's that way. Go quickly."

He felt he was pushing Ralph away when he should have kept him close, to keep him safe, but he had no option.

Angel couldn't leave Uganda through a border post, as he'd entered illegally, and Ralph couldn't leave Kenya without an entry stamp. They would have to split up. He hoped Ralph would take his advice on where to stay in Nairobi.

"What's your name?" Ralph asked.

"My name is Rots."

"Rots," Ralph repeated.

Ralph got out of the truck and closed the door, then stopped and put his head through the window.

"Rots."

Angel looked at him.

"At the service station. How did you know my name? You shouted for Ralph."

Angel didn't answer.

Ralph still held the window.

"I'll speak to my father," Ralph said.

The Toyota pulled quickly forward.

"And you should find yours!" he shouted.

It was too late, the truck soon out of sight.

*

Angel drove two kilometres north on the road to Tororo and stopped. He had some time to kill but everything was going to be okay. He felt certain Elanza would be pleased. He looked forward to telling her all about it.

After dark he drove two kilometres east on a dirt road and crossed the unmarked border. In the light of a dull street lamp he changed back to Kenyan number plates and threw the Ugandan ones in to a ditch. He drove the third side of a two-kilometre square on the Kenyan side to the bus stop. It was a quarter past eight.

At the bus station a woman sold him bananas. He'd suspected all along that Ralph wouldn't be there. A seven o'clock bus had left for Nairobi, arriving at three in the morning. A *mzungu* boy had been on it. She'd sold him bananas too. It was a lousy time to arrive but Angel was certain Ralph would be all right, and he knew where to start looking for him.

*

Number Three, Parklands Avenue, Nairobi, slouched opposite the Aga Khan Hospital. Comfortably north of the centre of Nairobi it was a sprawling run-down bungalow eaten away in places by termites, with a large leafy garden in which Madame Roche, a buxom Polish lady usually full of vodka, kept notorious clothes-eating dogs. The rooms inside had been turned into dormitories of tiered bunkbeds made from shipping pallets that wobbled precariously. Many thought it safer to camp in her garden. Madame Roche's had long been a favourite of budget travellers, providing them with a bed and then breakfast served in a garden full of trees and flowers for only a dollar a night.

Angel had been watching the house and the people of Nairobi from the shade of a flame tree for five days and had concluded that Kenya was still very tribal. Maasai, Nandi, Kipsigis, Luo and Baluyia, some mad on *bangi*, paraded in front of him as he waited and watched out for Ralph. The British had actively maintained tribal conflicts at one stage. Divide and rule. Jomo Kenyatta's dictatorial rule had seemingly continued it. Opposition parties had been outlawed and their leaders imprisoned. Kenyatta's own Kikuyu people became the dominant tribe, running business and government. Angel assumed that that was why Kenyatta and his successor President Daniel Arap Moi were so staunchly against President Nyerere of Tanzania. Tribalism and socialism didn't go together.

Angel ran his hand over his head. With regret he'd shaved his braids, and his hair had been cut short. He'd allowed an itchy beard to colonise his face. He scratched at it relentlessly. His white *kanzu* had gone as well, replaced by jeans and a black tee shirt, soft brown boots and a baseball cap.

He restlessly checked his watch. Sunrise was still forty minutes away but the sky had already changed from black to the colour of dull gunmetal. Angel shivered. Elanza needed to keep warm. The weather would be cooling in Johannesburg as well in May, maybe eight degrees at night. At least it was a dry month, with plenty of sunshine even if the daytime temperatures dropped lower. If she kept warm at night she could sit comfortably outside by day and hopefully not pick up a chill. He wished he could be there now. Soon it would be over and he could go to her. He checked his watch again: 4th May; the day of Ralph's flight home.

In the end, his mind wandering, Angel nearly missed him. Ralph surprised him by crawling from a side window of the guesthouse thirty minutes before sunrise. Angel watched him, amused.

You cheeky little monkey, he thought.

He followed him at a distance. Three locals, one with a *panga*, were also following Ralph but hadn't checked behind them, amateurs high on *khat*. Angel assessed the risks but Ralph made it on to the bus to the airport. It was early; he'd have all day to wait in the terminal. That didn't matter, thought Angel; Ralph was safe.

EIGHTEEN

When Veronica Aspel walked into Jomo Kenyatta International Airport at five o'clock in the morning the terminal still had a sleepy quiet feel. The first flights of the day out of Nairobi to Entebbe and Addis were at six, both repositioning flights and generally unpopular with travellers. The rush came later.

There wasn't any need for her to be at work at that hour. Her airline didn't need her until three hours before the first departure, but she liked to be in ahead of her manager Mr Green. She could get so much more done without him, and she preferred the early shift anyway. It was cooler and she'd be finished for the day by ten and by the pool at the club before lunch.

The evening shift didn't agree with her nearly so much as she didn't start work until nine thirty at night, just as everyone else started getting into the swing of things in the pub. For Veronica and her colleague Sarah, the evening flight was always busier. Mr Green often helped at that time, but only with the First and Club class passengers. If all went well and the northbound flight departed on time she'd be home at two in the morning, feeling hot and tired, her feet aching in the stupid shoes the company made them wear, her head ringing from Nigel Green's nasal whine about the sixty-minute turnaround.

It turned out to be an exotic posting, though, and easy – only two flights a day. The southbound overnight flight from London to Johannesburg arrived in Nairobi at eight in the morning. A lot of people got off the plane but few checked in. The northbound flight from Johannesburg to London didn't arrive until midnight. One of the pilots had explained to her why the flights were only early in the morning and late at night. It had something to do with the height above sea level of the runway at Nairobi and the hot daytime temperature. The 747s could only take off with enough fuel when it was cooler.

Veronica saw the boy sitting on the floor at the desk as she walked in. His legs and arms looked thin and brown, like a girl's. His hair looked thick and wavy and blond. His clothes needed a wash but they were so pale and thin that a good cleaning would probably finish them off. His dusty rucksack wasn't worth checking in. It needed putting in a skip.

"I'll be with you in a moment, sir," she said.

Ralph smiled.

"Thanks. I've got plenty of time."

"Johannesburg?"

"London."

"Oh, I can't check you in for tonight's flight yet, sir."

"That's okay."

Ralph wasn't leaving until after midnight. He'd arrived at the airport over eighteen hours before his flight.

He looked at the girl he was talking to. She looked very English. A nametag said 'Veronica Aspel' and a sign on the counter at the desk, 'Nairobi Station Crew Team Member'.

Veronica took another look at his dusty clothes. She should probably get rid of him before Mr Green turned up. Nigel Green's manner with those customers who weren't fur and pinstripe was brusque to say the least, especially early morning when he knew his appearance wasn't the best, his fleshy face still pink from shaving and his hair flat on his head from the shower. A scruffy economy passenger messing up his check-in area wouldn't make for a good start to his day.

"Shall I just have a quick look at your ticket?"

Veronica tilted her head to one side as she looked at the flight coupon. Ralph could tell something was wrong so he smiled at her again. The ticket had faded a little and become mottled with dust and stains. Perhaps she couldn't read it.

"I'm sorry, Mr Phillips, but there's a problem with this ticket."

Ralph was suddenly worried.

"I've got the right date, haven't I?"

"Yes, sir. It's the right date. The thing is you should be joining the flight in Johannesburg. It's a condition of this type of ticket."

It was clear to her that he hadn't grasped the implication. She felt sorry for him. He looked a nice boy.

"You're changing the place of boarding, you see," she explained. "The ticket states 'No changes allowed'. I'm afraid we can't let you fly."

"What? You must let me on. I've paid for that ticket."

Some other passengers for Johannesburg were arriving. She didn't want a scene.

"I'll see what I can do."

She pointed to some chairs by the wall.

"Why don't you wait over there. I'll talk to the station manager. He'll be in shortly. He's my boss," she confided. "I'll come and find you when I've had a chat with him."

"Station manager? What does he do?"

"He's responsible for all flight and ground operations, for example aircraft handling, passenger services and air cargo."

She lowered her voice.

"To be honest, at one of the smaller stations like this, he also sells tickets, makes public announcements, checks in baggage, moves boarding stairs, prepares manifests and operates the teletype machine."

She could have added, 'All while desperately trying to sleep with Veronica.'

Ralph was unimpressed.

"Important man."

"I can't get him to make a decent cup of tea though."

Veronica, with years of experience managing anxious and confused passengers, smiled at him conspiringly so that Ralph would do as he was told. He moved his rucksack and sat down calmly under a picture of an elephant.

Veronica watched Ralph sitting quietly away from her desk while she dealt with her job. She wondered where he came from. She was a West Sussex girl from Warnham, a little village near Horsham and close to Gatwick, the reason she'd got into the airline. He sounded like a southerner but further west, more like her own father, who had moved to West Sussex from Devon to milk a huge herd of dairy cows down by Steyning.

When she'd closed the check-in, Veronica went to see Nigel Green in his little office. He looked up at her from his desk with a possessive glare. She was a good-looking girl and often looked at. She'd become used to it. It didn't usually mean anything.

"I'm closed up."

"Okay. Any problems?"

"Only a gentleman complaining about sitting too far back."

"Economy?"

She nodded.

"He was just fishing for an upgrade."

Green grunted.

"And could you look at this for me. It's for tonight's London flight. The guy's trying to board here instead of Joburg."

Green looked at the ticket and sighed.

"Well, he's buggered then, isn't he."

He made it a statement, not a question.

"I just wondered if we should help him out. It's a very quiet flight. I checked. I mean, the plane he should be on will arrive later, and his seat on it will be empty as he didn't join the flight in Joburg."

Green had joined the airline in the hope of being sent to CSE Kidlington for flying training and was sometimes still disappointed that it hadn't turned out that way. He'd always wanted to be a pilot. Now he had to keep a smile on his face and watch pilots swaggering about his station, chatting up his girls, taking them dinghy sailing on Lake Naivasha on their layovers. Few of them had any idea that being a station manager was a far more demanding role than being a glorified bus driver. He had to know the operations manual backwards. And he did; it was one of the things that made him good at his job, everyone told him so. More importantly, 'Terms and

Conditions' were his speciality; he was known throughout the business for it. The girls respected him for it. Veronica, for instance, just couldn't take her eyes off him. He'd noticed that she was clearly very impressed with his customer relations skills, his no-nonsense commanding way of dealing with the dirty travelling public. Veronica was a sweet girl, but this sort of thing was obviously way beyond her. He looked again at the ticket she'd given him – Phillips R Mr.

Green stood up, walked out of the office and proudly adjusted his company tie. *Oh my God*, he thought. *The very dirty travelling public by the looks of it.*

"Good morning, sir. I see you've changed your place of boarding?"

"Yes. I wanted to see Victoria Falls, you know, in Zimbabwe."

"Yes, sir, I know where Vic Falls are."

"Well, I just kept coming north. I suppose events overtook me."

"Hmm. Were the events beyond your control? Were they unusual or unforeseeable circumstances the consequences of which you could not avoid?"

"Not really. I just thought I'd get on the plane at Nairobi not Johannesburg."

Green looked at Veronica. It was a look of triumph and wasn't pretty. It was the same ugly look she knew would be on his fat face the moment his hot hairy body pressed her into the mattress.

"It's quite simple, Veronica. It's 3c1."

He looked at the boy over the top of his shiny half-framed glasses.

"I'm sorry, Mr Phillips, but this ticket is valid only for the transportation shown on it from the place of departure."

He thought some more.

"In addition, Veronica, 3c5 says, and I quote, 'If you change your transportation without our agreement, your unused flight coupon'," he waved it at Ralph, "'will not be valid for travel and will have no value and we will not carry you until you have paid the difference'."

He knew he shouldn't lecture Veronica in front of a customer but this was too useful a training exercise. He'd share what knowledge he could now and discuss it in more detail later. Maybe he should invite her to lunch at his villa.

Veronica stared at him.

Ralph was confused.

"Paid what difference?"

"I thought I had made it clear. It is the difference in the price between a ticket from Nairobi to London and this ticket."

"But you just said this ticket has no value."

Nigel looked impressed.

"Yes, that's right."

"I have to buy a new ticket and you won't give me any money for the one that you won't let me use?"

"I'm afraid so."

"But I already have a ticket for the flight that stops here."

"Is it an agreed stopping place?"

Ralph tried to speak Green's language. He wondered where he could find the rule book. Stuck up Green's arse probably.

"It's shown in your timetables as a scheduled stopping place along the route from Johannesburg to London."

Nigel momentarily felt threatened but recovered without showing any weakness in front of Veronica. Women didn't like that.

"Ah, but is it set out on your ticket?"

Green looked.

"No," he said simply.

"Veronica?"

Veronica had been checking.

"The best-price one-way ticket is 679 dollars. Sorry."

Ralph stared at her.

"Plus taxes, fees and carrier charges, Veronica."

"Plus 177 dollars."

"856 dollars. Sir."

Nigel smiled. This was what he was paid to do after all. The airline wasn't a charity.

"But that's more than I paid for the ticket from London to Johannesburg and back."

Ralph looked in his wallet at a fifty-dollar bill. He had about 230 dollars hidden inside the frame of his rucksack. He was 576 short.

"I don't have it."

Veronica looked away.

"How am I going to get home? Am I going to have to go back to Johannesburg?"

Green looked at his watch, large and gold and fake.

"Not unless you can run back there in about eight hours, sir," Nigel quipped. "Changes to the date of travel are not allowed either."

Ralph thought quickly.

"How much is a ticket on the flight you're just checking in to Johannesburg?"

"That's a good idea," Veronica said brightly and tapped at a keyboard.

Green had already skipped halfway back to his office. He wasn't going to be beaten on home turf.

"Check-in for this morning's flight to Johannesburg is now closed, sir. We have a very short turnaround time here in Nairobi. I'm sure you understand."

Veronica Aspel felt ashamed. She'd already decided, but now she knew that she wouldn't ever sleep with Nigel bloody Green, even if her career depended on it.

*

Ralph was still in the airport when she left, looking slightly lost, staring at the departures board. The destinations reeled: Maputo, Frankfurt, Doha, Jeddah, Cairo. Ralph seemed lost in thought. Cairo, Johannesburg, Amsterdam, Lusaka, Khartoum, Abu Dhabi, Paris.

"Mr Phillips."

"Hmmm?"

He watched the board. Khartoum. Cairo.

"I'm sorry I couldn't help you with your ticket. What are you going to do now? Can someone send you the money?"

Ralph had been wondering the same thing. He felt sure that wouldn't be a problem. He'd go back into town and call home. Nothing would be damaged but his pride.

"Yeah, I'll sort something out."

He looked at her and lifted his rucksack.

"I thought I'd keep going overland. It might be an interesting challenge."

It would be a fantastic challenge, he thought. *Cape Town to Cairo. That would be something. Through swamps, across deserts probably, and all through hostile country. It would be like the books I'd read as a boy about prisoners of war escaping enemy territory. Wow.*

She looked at him, a Sussex girl far from Horsham.

"Isn't that a long way?"

"I'm not sure."

He thought of the plan of Africa in his *School Atlas of the World*. Kenya was about halfway up.

"I guess it's about the same as it is from Cape Town to here."

"Do you know the way?"

"Not really. North."

He suddenly felt very excited.

"I'll have to buy a new map."

Veronica smiled. This will be a good story for the bar. Sarah was on the late shift so she'd be able to go into town tonight with the layover crew. She frequently volunteered for the job of showing them around. The boys always wanted to go to the bar in the Hilton Hotel to look at the exquisitely tempting local prostitutes. Nigel Green often went there. It was quite all right going with the flight crew though. With them it was all show, just for a giggle. In her experience, pilots were very homely and conservative and just a little dull, a bit like accountants. Flying, after all, was a very 'procedural' job and she often thought women would make much better pilots than men. It was all about following rules. There were rules to follow about what you did with the aeroplane and when you did things; she'd seen checklists sticking out of pilots' cases. There were rules from the ground about where to go, and how high, and at what speed; she'd been shown the pale blue charts printed on what felt like tissue paper, with thick straight radial lines between circles, like the spokes of a bicycle wheel. In the end, flying was just about doing what you were told. Well, she'd had years of that. And the physical part of flying wasn't physical at all, nothing a woman couldn't do if she had normal hand-to-eye coordination. That wouldn't be a problem for Veronica. With her usual tennis partner she would regularly thrash allcomers in mixed doubles. She'd love to try and fly for the airline, but what were the chances of a cowman's daughter getting to sit at the pointy end? Bollocks to them. It would be fun to have a go anyway. And if she ever came to Nairobi at the front of a 747 she'd give Green hell if they lost the cargo or delayed the refuelling. She would talk to Jim about it.

"Well, good luck."

She went to leave but turned back.

"I don't know if it'll help but I've a friend at the Nairobi Club that I play tennis with. He's a pilot at Wilson," she told him quietly. "He might give you a ride out of Kenya at least. Ask anyone for Jim. Say Veronica sent you."

*

Angel waited in the airport, drinking coffee, watching. He wasn't concerned so long as Ralph stayed inside the terminal. He only had to monitor the exit.

He checked his watch. 10.30am. His own flight back to Johannesburg wasn't until 4.05pm. He had plenty of time.

He looked into his coffee cup and scratched his beard. When he looked up Ralph was outside.

Angel ran through the glass doors in time to see the three men who'd followed Ralph from Madame Roche's walking away. They'd obviously been well paid and were being thorough, unnecessarily waiting in case Ralph left the airport. All four of them were heading to the bus stop to go back into Nairobi. Angel, panting, climbed aboard as it pulled into the traffic on the South Airport Road, relieved that he'd cut his hair and changed to Western clothes from his *kanzu*. He could walk right by Ralph without being recognised as the man who'd given him a ride in Uganda. Angel wondered if it wouldn't be easier to be upfront with Ralph and tell him of Elanza's will and the money, but he couldn't see a way to do that without disclosing his identity and NIS's involvement, mindful that Roux had told him not to reveal either to Elanza or the boy.

They got off after fifteen kilometres by a golf course at Bunyala bus stop, Ralph walking south and west down Aerodrome Road, the men some distance behind him, waiting for an opportunity.

Now, Gents, and Lady, contrary to popular belief fighting three on one is not possible. Full stop. The only thing you can do is to reduce the number of threats before anybody realises, so that you are back to fighting two or preferably one. If you fail at your first strike to disable at least one of the opposition your best option is to run. Do not ever stand facing three men who are ready for you. It will never have a successful outcome.

They were walking through a building site. It looked like one day it would be a stadium, a football field with a running track around the perimeter, but it had been only partly completed. The stands were uncovered, apart from the one on the west side where the emperor would sit.

Remember, there is no easy way to do this. Do not imagine that you can plan it all in advance. This is not a carefully choreographed sequence of moves like some sort of ballet. No amount of training, no clever holds or quick moves to shift your opponent's centre of gravity will help. It is always just brutal and uncoordinated. If you are quick and lucky you might get two and the third might run away. Aggression, speed, surprise. Shake yourself up like a bottle of pop and explode.

There was a moment just before Angel reached level with them when he knew it wouldn't work, that he should walk on, but the warning came too late. The last thing he remembered was thinking it lucky that he'd cut his hair.

Surprise them. Run at one of them from behind. Knock him over. Hard. If any of them have a weapon, target him first. He's the leader you need to neutralise. You must get him down. When he's on the ground jump or stamp repeatedly on his lower back, his groin, his neck, his head, his face. Forget everything you have been taught. Go berserk. Reduce the number of threats.

The *panga* looked dull and well used but nonetheless frightening.

Now it gets difficult, because the two that are left have been alerted. 'Flight or Fight'? It's not that simple. More like 'Freeze, Flight or Fight', in that order. The 'Freeze' part is a natural first reaction from primeval times, when we were hunted. When you are immobile you are difficult to see, and if you are seen any movement is often the cue for a predator to attack. It gives time for the surge of hormones to take effect, mobilising your energy and focusing attention. Move quickly to use those few moments while they 'Freeze'. It may make all the difference. And there's always the chance they may take 'Flight', if you are lucky. If they 'Fight' you will not have a choice about which one to take on first. They will come together. Get close. Don't box. Rip and twist and scratch and roar and spit and bite. It will be down to who is more determined and it will hurt.

It was suddenly dark. They were in the shadow of the west side of the stadium and rolling in a tangled ball of arms and legs.

Angel looked around through a gloom. His shirt had been pulled partly off over his head and mud covered one side of his face and obscured his eye. A warm stickiness covered the other side and stuck in his beard. He pushed himself up onto one knee. One of the three looked conscious but was howling, holding the side of his head where most of an ear used to be. One he wasn't sure of but he lay motionless, face down, with one hand to the back of his head and the other twisted forwards so that the fingers and palm of the hand stretched out flat against the inside of his forearm. One had run. And Angel hurt all over, just as his instructor had told him he would.

*

A maid answered the door, suspicious of white men, and demanded that Roux give his name. She left him, the front door ajar, and Roux could hear her talking in the wide-open space of the living area.

"Miss Elanza, there's a man here to see you."

He could hear Elanza cough.

"The same man as last week? Nels? Piggy looking man?"

Roux didn't hear the maid's reply but Elanza had moved closer to the front door.

"I don't know anyone called Nick. Go and get Horatio from the garden."

Roux wondered why all domestic staff in South Africa had the names of historic figures. In the past he'd met Homer and Caesar, Cromwell, Napoleon and Luther, and now a British admiral.

This wasn't the only thing that troubled Roux about South Africa. He'd talked candidly to his wife, who was shocked and frightened for the kids but trusting and supportive. He'd told her that within ten years their lives would be very different, that the pressures that sanctions imposed on the country would, over time, cripple South Africa and force it to change. She hadn't believed it, and sitting where they were, in the ordered leafy suburbs out of sight of urban violence just the other side of town and rural suffering in the new native homelands, he could understand her difficulty. But Roux knew. He read the reports that others would never see, the evidence of atrocity and barbarity that his white countrymen committed in the name of national security.

He'd told his wife of Angel, of his aspirations for the man's future and Roux's confidence in the healing role people like Angel would have when apartheid ended. She'd recognised his pain, almost like the loss of a loved one, when Angel had disappointed him and left Roux questioning his own judgement.

'Talk to his wife,' she'd helpfully suggested.

'He's single.'

'A girlfriend, then. Someone he sees regularly. Ask a woman.'

Roux could think only of Elanza and had driven from Pretoria after work, exhausted.

Elanza was sitting by open glass doors leading to the pool when the maid showed him in. A big man in a blue boiler suit knelt by the pool pretending to work on the filtration, an unnecessary and very heavy sledgehammer beside him.

"Who are you?"

"Good afternoon. My name is Nick. I know Angel. I'm a work colleague."

Elanza was curious but wary. Angel hadn't talked about his work. She knew so little about him.

"He's not here."

"I know," Roux said cheerfully. "Off on a business trip. Always running around. To be honest I don't think it's doing him any good. I'm a little worried."

Elanza put her hand on a green glass table and the maid put a bottle of water in front of her, guiding her fingers. Elanza nodded and drank.

"What's wrong with him?"

"Nothing. Probably just work stress."

Elanza held the bottle tightly.

"You said you work with him?"

"Yes. Over two years now."

"Is he good at his job? The translating. Is he popular?"

"Oh yes. Very good. Everybody loves him."

Elanza nodded.

"Any girls love him? Secretaries?"

Roux smiled.

"No, nothing of that sort. Angel's like a warrior monk."

They both laughed.

"Does he talk about work?" Roux asked.

"No."

"Does he talk about sport?"

"No. Unusual, isn't it?"

Roux didn't think so. Two weeks earlier a law had endorsed racial separation of residential areas, schools and amenities but for the first time had excluded sport. Roux thought it unlikely that a black athlete would be playing for the Springboks anytime soon. It was a ruse. He was sure that Angel would think the same.

"How about his family?" he asked.

"Not really. His mother is in London and I don't think he sees his dad much."

Elanza drank from the bottle, her eyes at the ceiling.

"I think he should see his father. I feel he wants to talk to him," she said.

"Politics? Does he talk about that?"

"About the situation? The white black apartheid thing?"

Roux watched the maid take the empty bottle from her and the gardener unscrew the same screw he'd been working on for thirty minutes, both listening.

"He knows lots of African words. He's very funny."

Elanza chuckled.

"People in the office talk about changes, everything changing. Does Angel?"

Roux had seen many signs of change. Lombard had been away in Botswana with the Prime Minister, meeting the President of Zambia to discuss the situation in South West Africa. It was the first such meeting in six years. Then, in the middle of April, just three weeks ago, the law had been changed to allow Coloureds and Indians to hold senior government posts. There were seeds of change, looking to be nurtured.

Elanza started coughing. She threw her head between her knees, retching. The maid put her hand on her back tenderly and the gardener brought a bucket.

"I'm sorry," said Roux. "I shouldn't disturb you."

He got up to leave.

"Angel's coming back tonight. He called me," Elanza said. "I told him to come here from the airport but he won't stay the night. I don't know why."

The maid and the gardener looked at Roux, then at the floor.

"I'll see him tomorrow," she said.

"Oh, that's good."

Roux held out his hand automatically. It hung in the air, unseen, untouched.

The maid showed him to the door, her eyes cast down.

"She doesn't know, does she?"

The maid didn't move until Roux was sitting in his car.

NINETEEN

J im Gray straddled the fat main tyre as though riding a horse and watched the rain run off the trailing edge of the wing. It made streams as it followed ridges in the aileron but closer to the undercarriage it fell off the inboard section as a sheet, impossible to see through. *More water than is in the Lagan*, thought Jim. May in Nairobi was always wet. The temperature cooled during the day and warmed up at night but always the rain, like a good summer in Belfast.

Jim leant backwards and looked up into the wheel bay. When the aeroplane had left the Oklahoma City factory in 1945 the aluminium would have been painted a pale green. Now, getting on for forty years later, very little paint remained, just a few flaking patches in the dark corners that hadn't been blasted by sand and grit from unimproved fields in wartime Europe and peacetime Africa. Jim had been flying for as long as the aeroplane, and in similar theatres. He knew that there was very little left of him that was original either, just a few flaking patches in dark corners.

Jim was sixty years old, short and lean with a head disproportionately large to the rest of his body so that he looked like a cartoon of himself. His wiry frame wasn't, as many unfairly suspected, due to a diet entirely of alcohol. Jim knew that those who thought this were wrong because to prove to himself that he wasn't dependent he would stay dry one day every week. On that day he would eat.

It pleased him that he could still pass any medical that his employer Skyways threw at him. He put this down to the tennis. Off court he became mild mannered and softly spoken but, slightly out of character, he played tennis hard, aggressively and always to win. Like flying he'd been playing a long time, since evenings at the Lisburn Racquets Club back in his hometown on the border of the counties of Antrim and Down. Recently, tennis had become gruelling. He'd become slower off the baseline than he used to be and sometimes when he got the ball from his pocket to serve, his hand would shake. He hoped his tennis partner had never noticed.

Jim licked his finger and rubbed a streak through the dust on a stainless steel part of the undercarriage leg above the oleo, near a flange welded forty years previously. It had been beautifully done in perfectly regular overlapping crescents like half-moons. Jim mumbled to himself with satisfaction, unable to see evidence of the hairline cracks he was looking for, but his concerns remained. The undercarriage was robust at absorbing the vertical up and down loads when Jim landed deliberately hard onto short strips, or when Quebec Jean his co-pilot bounced her after flaring too high. It had been well engineered to withstand the fore and aft stresses of rough runways made of hard red Kenyan dirt, corrugated into deep creases. Jim looked for the tell-tale signs of fracture caused by sideways loading as twenty-six thousand pounds of aeroplane skipped across the runway, when landing in a crosswind for example, or when on take-off Jean wasn't assertive enough with his rudder inputs to keep her tracking in a straight line while on the ground.

Jean Dalbec had escaped a life in Canadian asbestos mines by learning to fly and, although young, had accumulated significant experience of bush flying. He scared Jim. Forty years of avoiding risk told him that Jean was one of those pilots, like some he'd briefly known, who were dangerously fearless. To Jim, fear had become a valuable defence mechanism. Pilots like Jim, who had flown in wartime while others tried to kill them, knew about fear. Talented but peacetime pilots like Jean Dalbec had been through a tough day when they'd spilt coffee down their trousers.

Jim turned around and looked forward past the cowl flaps of the port engine, open like the petals of a small flower after a shower, through the rain, over the weeds growing vigorously in the deep cracks of the apron, to the rusty doors of the hangar that hung limp, immobile and mildewed. Jean was nowhere to be seen. Pallets strung with net and a sign of the favourite charitable aid agency of the month sat half in and half out of the hangar, water running off unprotected maize flour and powdered milk, gifts from the people of the USA. ACROSS: Aid Commission for the Rehabilitation of Southern Sudan. Jim, exasperated, sighed as he dismounted the aeroplane's wheel.

"Jean!"

Jim put his hands on his hips and bellowed into the rain.

"Jean!"

A shape, barely visible through the fall of water, appeared at the wing tip.

"Jean?"

"No. My name is Ralph. Veronica sent me."

Afterwards, Jim remembered that it'd been when the boy had mentioned Veronica that he'd known that it would be a good trip, that the gear would hold up to another of Jean's rough landings, that the wet load wouldn't make them too heavy to take off, that Loki would have fuel for their onward flight to Juba and return to Wilson. The delayed departure, the rotten area forecast, the prospect of an uncomfortable night camping in the hold, all became instantly manageable. At the time all he'd been able to say was, 'She's a good girl.' He'd meant it, and it had made him smile.

"What's your name?" he asked.

"Ralph Phillips."

"Any relation to Jack?"

"Who?"

"Jack Phillips."

"I'm not sure."

"Never mind."

He studied the boy standing in the rain. He looked light.

"Do you think you can find a truck in the hangar and pull those pallets inside out of the rain? Could you do that for me?"

"No problem. I love being around aeroplanes."

Jim grunted, suddenly and unexpectedly happy. There'd been a boy a long time ago in Northern Ireland who'd loved fetching and carrying at Long Kesh airfield just to be around aeroplanes.

"I can take you to Juba," he said to the boy. "We'll go as far as Lokichoggio this afternoon and stay there the night."

Jim felt certain that the boy had no idea where it was.

"Lovely. Thanks."

Ralph looked at the nose of the aeroplane.

"What is this? She's beautiful."

Jim looked at him and smiled.

"This… is Betsy."

*

In the cockpit the pilots were arguing. Jim sat with one buttock on the edge of his seat and scratched his head, while Jean Dalbec stood hunched against a panel and looked sullenly at the floor. Jim spoke quietly as if to a frightened horse, while Jean talked and ate at the same time, projecting small pieces of pastry and red meat onto the floor around him.

Ralph made himself comfortable close to the cockpit among sacks of food aid and looked around. The fuselage sloped steadily downhill from where he sat to a wide double door still open on the port side at the tail. It was like sitting in the back of a Land Rover, bare aluminium ridged and riveted, the floor scuffed shiny with use, creased and bent where heavy loads had been dragged and dropped.

Jean, still eating, walked sulkily to the tail to shut the hatch. He kicked the restraining straps that held the pallets securely as he climbed back towards the cockpit. He stopped by Ralph, peered through a yellowed Perspex window, broke off a handful of the pie and offered it to Ralph.

"*Tourtière?*"

Ralph shook his head.

"It's like pork pie."

"No thanks."

Jean nodded. Ralph felt he'd been rude in some way. He asked him about the aeroplane.

"Is this a Dakota?"

Jean shook his head side to side, scattering crumbs.

"Kind of. It's a DC3C. She used to be a C-47 and flew with the US Air Force. She survived the war, so in 1946 Douglas rebuilt her with two 1,200 horsepower Pratt and Witney radial piston engines and sold it on the civilian market. They reinforced the floor so she could carry a load of six thousand pounds and gave her a big cargo door. Problem is that if you have six thousand pounds of cargo on board you can only fill the fuel tanks to about two-thirds full or you'd be over the maximum weight. Still, carrying three tons for over a thousand statute miles is quite something for a forty-year-old aircraft."

He felt very proud of her.

"Half a million rivets!" shouted Jim. "Tough as guts. One of these got rammed by a kamikaze pilot. He crashed, but the C-47 just shrugged and flew home with a Mitsubishi Zero-sized hole in the middle upper fuselage."

Jean swallowed a large mouthful of food.

"This particular plane did a bad bounce in '63 and ripped off most of the left wing tip. She flew around minus half a wing and landed okay," Jim said and peered at them over the back of his seat. "Something we don't want to repeat, hey, Jean."

Jean stared through the window and wiped his mouth with the back of his sleeve. He plugged two jack plugs into a frame and gave Ralph a headset. Ralph took it from him, unsure which way round to put it on.

"How fast does she go?"

"Jim doesn't like to go too fast."

Jim knocked a clockwork gauge with his knuckle. A needle bounced inside the glass as he did it.

"At one time she would have cruised at 180. We were lucky to see 165 a while ago. She's probably gained a few pounds over the years," he said.

Jean spun around angrily towards Jim.

"It was my idea to take the de-ice boots off and empty the de-icing fluid tanks. That gave us an extra fourteen knots to get us back to nearly 180."

Jean walked back into the cockpit and threw himself into the right-hand seat. He started mumbling to himself as if intoning a prayer.

Jim tapped the end of the boom mic attached to his headset. Muffled thumps chased each other through Ralph's head.

"Ralph."

"Yes."

"We are going to Lokichoggio for the night and to take on fuel. Three hundred and sixty-three nautical miles. It's about two and a bit hours."

"Okay. Not Juba?"

"Not enough fuel for Juba direct. Our load is limited to just enough to get to Loki with a reserve, and we've reduced the weight of cargo to only four thousand pounds, otherwise with our performance here in Nairobi at this high altitude we won't even get off the ground. Isn't that right, Jean?"

Jean said nothing.

"We usually take off early morning when it's cooler. That makes a little bit of difference. Doesn't it, Jean?"

Jim knew he was being unfair. The delay hadn't been Jean's fault. Through his headset Ralph heard Jean trying to talk to someone. Five Yankee Bravo Mike Bravo was obviously Betsy's real name but no one wanted to respond to her. Jean talked to Jim instead.

"Reduced power take-off?"

"Are you kidding me?" said Jim.

Among the DC3 community there was intense debate on the use of less than full power when taking off. In Betsy, Jim liked to use full power, forty-eight inches of manifold pressure and fully rich. Jean enjoyed discussing it because he knew how much it irritated Jim, who would always rise and take the bait.

"Jean, if you always use derated power you'll create ridges in the cylinder walls so that when you do need full power, like when an engine fails, you'll break all the piston rings off. United Airlines proved in the 1940s that their engines lasted longer when used at full power."

Jean thought he'd fan the flames.

"But in Quebec we used reduced power on take-off for years and never had a problem."

Jim tried to remain calm.

"The enriching feature on the carb for additional engine cooling only operates at full power," he said.

"But full power is limited to one minute. That's not long in the take-off sequence."

Jim knew that Jean enjoyed being deliberately argumentative.

"Jean, you Canuck. Just work through this for me. Where are we?"

"Nairobi Wilson."

"And that is in?"

"Kenya."

"Good. Hot Kenya. Not cold Canada. And how high are we?"

"It gets hot in Quebec City in the summer."

"How high are we?"

Jean consulted a chart on the glare shield. He enjoyed this game.

"Five thousand five hundred and forty-six feet above sea level."

"Excellent. So, considering the hot Kenyan temperature, and the high altitude, what altitude does the aeroplane think we are at?"

"It's not always hot. It's May. This morning it was only sixteen degrees."

"Okay. This morning, how high did it feel?"

"Our density altitude was 6,944 feet."

"Right. So, the aeroplane would perform as if it had been trying to take off at nearly seven thousand feet when we are only at 5,500. What would that mean?"

"We couldn't carry a full load."

"And? I feel like I'm pulling teeth here."

"We would have a long take-off run."

"How long?"

"The graphs say that at twenty-three thousand pounds we would need a take-off distance to clear a fifty-foot obstacle of 5,400 feet."

"And how long is the longest runway at Wilson?"

Jean looked away and smiled.

"Five thousand and fifty-two feet."

"Thank you. Do you still not want to use full power?"

Jim could have murdered a drink.

"Just take it to the end of the runway. I want to feel the tailwheel in the dirt when we've lined up. And push those throttles to the stops when I say. Sweet Jesus."

*

From a square window on the starboard side Ralph could see Lake Turkana, painfully blue. His eyes burnt as he looked

308

at it, then watered as he focused on the brown of northern Kenya. Unlike Nairobi, it hadn't rained here for a long time. There was nothing alive down there, a landscape of just two colours.

A watery voice talked to him, filtered by the headset but still softly Irish.

"Look roughly at the middle of the lake, on the far shore. There's a sort of dimple."

"Yeah, I've got it."

"That's a place called Koobi Fora on Allia Bay. Leakey's dig, although Kamoya his sidekick is making all the big finds."

"Finding what?"

"Man. It's the birthplace of civilisation. Didn't you know? We're all African."

Ralph strained his eyes for signs of anything but saw no men, no civilisation, no Africans at all.

"Is it far to Loki?"

"Under half an hour to go."

"Have you been in Kenya a long time?"

"Since the end of the war. Well, in Africa anyway."

"What's Lokichoggio like?"

"Dry."

Ralph looked ahead. To the north, a wide meandering sandy brown riverbed and Loki's long runway were already visible. They were thirty kilometres from the Sudanese border and still in Kenya, but the last real Kenyan town was Lodwar, two hundred kilometres behind them. Loki didn't look like a Kenyan town, or like any African settlement that Ralph had been through since leaving Cape Town three months previously. To the west, the sun was setting over the Sudanese state of Sharq al Istiwaiyya, Eastern Equatoria, but Ralph looked east over Turkana County into Ethiopia and it was already dark. Beyond, out of sight, was Arabia.

Ralph, speculating anxiously on the route to Cairo, wondered what he was doing in Africa. He shivered, unsure whether it was from apprehension or a fever.

*

Captain Gray had control and landed on the unlit east–west runway in fading light, a 'wheeler' on the two main wheels only, rarely three-pointed, pinning the aeroplane to the ground with a sharp forward twitch of the control column, and running tail up to keep airflow over the rudder until abeam the hardstanding, softly down at the back controlling it all the way, unlock the tail wheel, differential power to turn while taxiing and save the brakes – forty years of flying distilled into a fluid, effortlessly gentle, sequence.

Jim looked around to see who else was there. Unusual aircraft carrying 'flag of convenience' registrations, and in questionable states of serviceability, littered the apron. Unregulated operators from obscure Soviet states or Far Eastern peoples republics busily made money from aid agencies, grand or unheard of, until the cash or spare parts ran out. Carcasses of aircraft robbed of wheels, engines and avionics rotted where ignobly pushed. They were the lucky ones. Others had blown tyres or gearboxes during take-off, or simply failed to stagger loaded and wheezing into the hot thin air, their charred remains bulldozed from the active runway. Loki was the 'Wild West' of aviation.

Jim noticed a newer aircraft, the engines in nacelles on top of the wing rather than suspended below.

"Hey, Jean, is that a new thirty-two?"

Jean followed his gaze. It was a similar story every time.

"It's Russian. Looks just like an ordinary twenty-six to me."

Jim wasn't to be corrected.

"No. It's the new Ant. I've got to talk to them."

Jean busied himself tidying the cockpit. There was only one thing Jim wanted from the Russians and it wasn't discussing their new aircraft's improved hot and high performance.

*

Ralph swung his legs over the edge of the open cargo door and jumped to the ground. Small campfires glowed in the dark, near and all around.

There was no perimeter fence at Loki. Turkana people still lived among the acacia trees close to the narrow runway as they always had, seeking the blessings of life and occasionally appeasing ancestral spirits in the traditional way as heavy transport aircraft thundered overhead. Colonial administrators had at one time made Turkana a closed district, deliberately segregating them from the rest of Kenya. Little had changed with independence, Kenyans in government disputing their own census that showed Turkana people to be such a large and significant ethnic group, larger than the Maasai.

Ralph walked slowly to the circular turning area beyond the threshold, people's homes little more than a wingspan from the edge of the runway. The houses were a domed wooden framework covered in animal skins, big enough for a family of six. Goat and camel, corralled for the night, slept in brushwood enclosures.

Women made use of the fringe of the hard runway to pound palm nuts, the dry husks blowing away in a light breeze. As he approached they lifted their colourful fabric wraps held like tunics on one shoulder to cover their shyly smiling faces. Their heads were shaved and strings of bead necklaces rattled at their throats. Men sat nearby on small one-legged stools chopping meat with a steel circular disc with a sharp edge, a wrist knife worn like a bracelet. They threw cubes of goat into a tightly woven basket to stew for dinner and eat with maize porridge. Ralph wondered if there might be food on the aeroplane.

*

Quebec Jean stood at the door to the aircraft and studied the night sky.

"He's drunk," he told Ralph. "I won't talk to him."

Ralph looked inside the fuselage. Jim sat in his seat singing to himself, a bottle beside him already half empty.

"Loki is supposed to be dry but he swapped the diazepam in the medical kit for Russian vodka."

"Is he okay?"

"Who cares?"

Together they went inside. Jim heard them approach and put the vodka on the floor, the open top of the neck of the bottle held between his knees.

"Jean was right, the old Canuck, just a knackered old Antonov twenty-six. I tell you, anyone would need Valium to fly that thing."

He thought seriously about the Russians.

"Nice muckers, though. From Kiev."

He started to sing again, quietly, as though not to disturb the Russians parked the other side of the apron.

"What time in the morning, *Captain?*"

Jim, although drunk, noted the inflection.

"Hundred and seventy nautical miles to Juba. Just under an hour."

"What time, sir?"

Jim turned on him angrily.

"You just get the fuel. Seventy-three gallons an hour in the cruise. But she's guzzling over three times that at take-off. And don't you forget." He laughed to himself. "She drinks the stuff at full power."

"I won't forget."

Jean turned to Ralph.

"I'll see you in the morning. I'm going down to the tail."

Ralph watched him lay a bedroll in the aisle at the far end of the aeroplane. With the door wide open Jean could lie down on his back and still see the stars. Ralph felt hot and would have liked to have sat in the door, the breeze around him and stars above.

"Who was Jack?" he asked.

Jim moved in his seat and lifted the bottle.

"Jack Phillips? Phillips & Powis Aircraft, one of the forgotten, great, British wartime aircraft manufacturers."

Ralph thought it best to let him talk.

"Their companies designed and built nearly sixty different types of aircraft. Over seven thousand aeroplanes, trainers, tugs, STOL cargo."

Jim took a mouthful of vodka and made a noise through his teeth after he swallowed.

"Phillips & Powis and a guy called FG even designed a jet to break the speed of sound. They made a model of their supersonic jet, the M52, and it was last seen on radar heading out into the Atlantic at Mach 1.3 something. I think that was way back in '43. The Americans were having a go as well but couldn't control it when transonic. Phillips & Powis cracked it with an all-moving tail."

Jim punched Ralph on the shoulder.

"The little men from Woodley aerodrome found the solution no one else could."

Ralph looked down into the aeroplane. He couldn't tell in the gloom at the far end of the fuselage if Jean was awake.

"Just as they finished the first airframe, the government cancelled the project and Phillips & Powis went bust. You see, after the war the country was bankrupt. We owed America billions of dollars, and the only thing we had of any worth was what you call intellectual property. Phillips was forced to give all the design work to what became NASA. It should have been a technology sharing deal. The US shared nothing. They took the M52, copied the all-moving tail, and the Bell X-1 and Chuck Yeager were able to go through the speed of sound."

He looked at Ralph and lifted the bottle.

"You should be very proud of him."

Ralph had never heard anyone in his family mention Jack but he said nothing. In his experience people in drink talked and others listened.

It was hot; hotter at night than in Nairobi. Ralph listened to Jim with sweat running down his back and beading on his forehead. He felt dizzy. He should have eaten something.

Jim's thoughts started to wander.

"My first solo was in a Phillips & Powis aircraft. A Magister at Long Kesh."

Ralph struggled to concentrate, confused.

"I don't know where that is."

"An RAF airfield in Northern Ireland, south of Belfast."

Jim looked at the bottle.

"You know why I'm still alive? I'm a coward. I scare easily."

Jean sat at the back of the plane listening, his hands loose in his lap. He looked forward. The cockpit was filled with recumbent pilots, Jim through drink in the left seat, the boy in the right with a fever.

"Jean scares me. He hasn't had the fear, you see. No one's tried to kill him as he flew. It's always just been for fun."

Jean went forward and took the empty bottle from him.

"Do you want me to help you lie down?"

"I'll sleep here. Done it before. In the war I did three trips to Stockholm in one night. In my Mossie. Nine and a half hours' flying, forty-five minutes on the ground. It's in my log book if you don't believe me."

"I believe you, Jim."

"So dark at night. So lonely. Eyes blurred looking at instruments, looking for fighters. Asleep in my seat before I set the brakes."

Jean watched him until he slept and returned quietly to the back of the aeroplane.

*

Ralph awoke shivering with cold, shaking chills running up his back. He felt a pain low down in his abdomen and he'd been sweating all night, his clothes still wet and sticking tightly to his body. His mouth was dry but he felt too weak to stand and look outside for water. He held his head to shut out the noise of a truck revving its engine close to the wing. African voices were shouting and Jean was laughing. He was alone in a damp, cold, noisy world.

Jim saw him sitting up.

"How are you feeling?"

Ralph shook his head.

"It feels like a bad flu."

Jean came through the aeroplane and slipped into his seat.

"The fuelling is done, boss. And I did a walk around."

Jim had his head in a bag behind his seat. He pulled out a sachet with writing on it, a clear liquid.

"Chew the corner off this and see if you can drink it. If you can do that without throwing up it's because you need it."

"What is it?"

"Ringer's lactate. Saline, intended for intravenous," said Jim.

He turned to Jean.

"How much fuel?"

"A bit more than we need. I took her to half tanks. That'll see us the 533 miles all the way back to Nairobi with an hour and twenty minutes' reserve."

Jean consulted a flimsy stained notepad.

"I think it was half tanks. I heard Air Canada is going to change from imperial to metric. They're bound to mess up pounds and kilograms and turn a 767 into a glider over Manitoba or somewhere."

Jim smiled and passed Ralph some water. Jean was all right. He was being too hard on him.

"And there's no weather at Juba," said Jean.

"No weather?"

"Well, no reported weather. You know what they're like. Nairobi, however, is going to be CAVOK all day."

"No rain? Amazing."

Jim looked out of the port window. The fuel truck had moved clear.

"You fly this leg, Jean. Start when ready."

"Okay."

"I was thinking. We've got plenty of runway here, right?"

"Over six thousand feet."

"Yeah. And what's the density altitude? Four thousand and something?"

"Four thousand one hundred and seventy-eight."

"That's what I guessed."

Jim watched the refueller get out of his truck and wave. He waved back. With half tanks of fuel, they would be nearly 2,400 pounds under max gross.

"Why don't you try a reduced power take-off? Save Skyways a bit of money."

*

Ralph looked out of the window. He had covered himself in a foil blanket from the emergency grab bag but still felt cold. There was little to see. They were flying to the north of the Didinga range of hills, shrouded in cloud. The bare brown land beneath them gave way to sparse trees and bushes. Ralph could see no tracks or visible roads, no huts, villages or towns. He had no idea how he would have walked overland to Juba.

Through his headset he listened to the coded conversation of the pilots as they checked power, mixture, fuel system and gauges, Jim reading from a list. Ralph, still shivering, saw a river underneath him. The Nile at Juba looked brown and slow. He'd crossed over it at its source in Uganda, hiding his face under a borrowed hat, and now, as the sweating returned, he hid his face again in his hands.

*

From its source in Uganda, the Victoria Nile had quietly left the world's largest tropical lake at Jinja, tripped over the Bujagali Falls and entered Lake Kyoga, bigger than the whole of Greater London but only five metres deep, with shallows full of water lilies and the swampy shoreline covered with papyrus and hyacinth.

At Murchison Falls it squeezed through a gap only seven metres wide and, still young, playfully fell forty-three metres, but entered the swampy delta of Lake Albert as a lazy sluggish stream.

Draining from the north of Lake Albert as the Albert Nile through forested cliffs and ravines, and running east as well as north, it left Uganda, making a ninety-degree bend at the Sudanese border town of Nimule. It had run 645 kilometres from its source.

It flowed north now following the edge of an escarpment, widening as it matured, and as the Bahr al Jabal, the River of the Mountain, arrived at Juba, the most southerly navigable point of the great river. It had covered over eight hundred kilometres from the bridge at Jinja, sometimes unwillingly, sometimes sighing and bubbling, to get just five hundred kilometres north toward the Mediterranean Sea and oblivion.

Sweating with fever Ralph bribed a guard for the issue of a visa he should have bought in Nairobi and walked trembling from the open terminal into the southern Sudanese town of Juba. From crossing the source of the Nile at Jinja he'd travelled 1,600 kilometres in a Toyota Hilux through Uganda and on a bus to Nairobi, and then in a rattling vintage aid plane via northern Kenya.

He was, like the Nile, just five hundred kilometres closer to his destination: Cairo.

TWENTY

Angel and Elanza sat close together at her house in Hyde Park. Angel liked to spend as much time with her as he could, helping in small ways, comforting when he was able. Both were bruised about the face.

"What happened?" he asked. "Did you fall?"

"Nels came back for seconds. He wanted to know where Ralph was. I can't imagine why he thought I would know. I haven't seen Ralph for ages."

Angel thought about the men in Nairobi.

"He found out some other way," he said.

"I had the feeling he already knew but that he had some unfinished business – me."

Angel, too angry to reply, thought of the man who would beat a blind woman.

He put his arm around her. Elanza rested her head on his chest and lay her hand on his thigh. Angel stroked the top of her head.

"Do you want me, Angel?"

Angel stiffened, his arm falling to her side. She sat up abruptly.

"What is it?" she asked.

Angel shook his head.

"Is it the thought that Nels has been through there?" she spat.

"Elanza, please."

"Don't worry. He didn't in the end, thankfully. He prefers fighting to sex. Or maybe I'm the wrong age, or the wrong gender."

She coughed and tried to stand.

"Or the wrong species. I don't know."

Fat blue veins pulsed in her thin pale neck.

"You have sex with women, don't you?"

Angel took her face in his two hands. He knew she wasn't able to see him but he held her empty stare with his own, looked at her with longing for the relationship they both craved, wishing that she wasn't blind and that his skin colour didn't matter.

"Yes, Elanza. I have sex with women. I make love to women. I know that there is a difference."

She slumped, deflated, as though shrinking in size as he held her.

"Angel, I'm sorry."

Elanza thought she might love him, and it scared her. It seemed that since her father had died everyone she met, other men she had briefly thought she'd loved, had tried to take advantage of her. At first she'd worried that Angel would be the same. Her wealth was to blame. She understood that; everyone wanted her money. Eventually it had ceased to matter, but it made her sensitive to those few rare moments of genuine kindness. The boy Ralph had been kind to her and made her a cup of tea. She'd loved him for it, loved him for a simple unselfish kindness. She gave her love easily and instantly on those infrequent occasions. She felt that Angel would be compassionate and kind-hearted and could have her love too, even though she knew little about him.

"Tell me about the women who have loved you, Angel, about your friends."

Angel didn't believe he'd been loved at all. He'd been an outsider his whole life, looking in at a different world: a Swazi at a school in Dorset, a soldier in a foreign army, an oddity at university tolerated for his language skills. No one had loved him there. He had compensated by making his work his whole life but no one had loved him there either. He had few friends and no loves. He was respected at work but the colour made it difficult. He wasn't invited to weekend *braais*, department fishing trips, or stag dos. His mother hadn't even loved him enough to name him. Zelda had dumped him.

"There was a girl at work."

"What happened?" she asked.

"It didn't work out."

"Why?"

Angel wanted to tell her it was because of his colour. Zelda had taken him as she took many others, randomly, like choosing a manicurist. They had conducted an intense and clandestine affair, having sex in obscure locations: her car in a basement car park, the middle of a corn field, an office toilet. He'd never taken her for a drink, never had dinner cooked in her apartment, or been introduced to her friends. At a well-planned rendezvous at a remote fishing lodge by a reservoir they'd spent a weekend making love for the first time rather than having sex, and then she'd dropped him at a station on a quiet Sunday afternoon and told him they wouldn't see each other again. He knew why.

"We didn't have that much in common."

"Did you love her?"

"Who knows?"

But you are different, he thought. *You are blind to my colour. I can love you and you won't end it as Zelda did, leaving me alone in a foreign place. I won't ever be an embarrassment to you in front of your friends because you don't have any friends either.*

She looked very tired and thinner than ever. He sat with her, feeling the bones in her shoulder.

"Talk to me, Angel."

"What about?"

"Anything. Tell me what happened at Cassinga."

Angel stroked her arm. It was a long time before he talked.

"It was 4th May, 1978. Yesterday marked the fourth anniversary. The South African Defence Force carried out an airborne assault on a town in Southern Angola. We claimed that it was a key SWAPO military headquarters, a training camp and a logistics base. SWAPO claimed it was a refugee camp and that the six hundred people who died in the attack were innocent civilians. We said we'd dealt SWAPO a significant military blow. SWAPO said that we'd carried out a brutal massacre of old people, women and children."

Angel wondered if she was asleep. He had no idea if she was listening. He could feel her head on his shoulder and her steady breath on his neck.

"We travelled by train from Johannesburg to Bloemfontein. A Bedford troop lorry took us to the De Brug training area. It felt different. It felt like more than just a training camp exercise. At an old derelict farmhouse, tents had been pitched in neat rows beneath the blue gum trees, and we were issued kit."

Training started at once. There seemed little doubt they were preparing for something big. They had all been civilians until a few days earlier and needed some brushing up. A 'weeding out' process took place and their numbers depleted.

"These younger conscripts were in awe of the swaggering older hard-looking men like us. But they were in the better position – young, at a peak of fitness and hardened by operational deployment. We'd been out of uniform for several years, and softened by civilian life."

Their commander addressed them, turning off the public address system. In two days' time, he said, they would jump more than two hundred kilometres inside Angola and attack SWAPO's main headquarters.

"It was exciting. We'd trained for years just to do an operation like this. A formation of C130s roared overhead and we all cheered."

Angel looked at Elanza. She held his hand and kissed him softly behind the ear.

They trained afterwards with enthusiasm. They were given Soviet rocket-propelled grenades and tank mines. No one had ever seen them. A sergeant cut one open and having worked it out began to train the others on the unknown weapons. He'd even worked out the weapon's weakness and had them practising with it in crosswinds. They retrained as mortar men and took turns house-clearing in the old farm buildings.

Their commander was away when a chaotic rehearsal jump was organised. They blamed the Air Force. It had been the only opportunity to practise and it had been wasted.

"Military Intelligence gave us a list of questions we had to find answers to if the opportunity arose to interrogate prisoners. They told us what documents to seize, who to bring home. Top of the list was a guy called Dimo."

Orders were given and a sand model of the town constructed in an old cowshed. Maps and photos covered the walls. Specific orders were given about children. They were not to shoot children. Security remained tight at the camp after orders. The next day they loaded on to buses for the airfield to be flown to a staging area in South West Africa.

"We joked as we waited, imitating our Captain, 'And don't shoot the children'."

Angel moved his arm from her shoulder. She lay with her head in his lap, her head turned away. Angel stroked her hair and pushed it behind her ear.

"It was a false alarm. A staff car came to a halt in a cloud of dust beside the lead bus. The operation would be postponed for forty-eight hours. It was all too familiar. Hurry up and wait. Same in any army."

For two days, they continued with training but it felt more like an effort just to keep them busy. Their peak had been reached and passed. A platoon commander took them to see the model in the cowshed – 'Political reasons' was his explanation of the delay. At the end of the forty-eight hours they were informed of a further twenty-four-hour delay. A Canberra had overflown the town and seen a new camp being erected, probably to accommodate people for the May Day Parade.

"My platoon had the specific task of clearing this new camp. They suspected that our reconnaissance flights had been observed and up to five hundred new recruits with Cuban instructors brought in for additional defence."

While the politicians agonised over the operation, the soldiers waited in the wind and the dust. A rumour started that the Minister of Defence had been the cause of the delay, asking for a more detailed briefing so that he could field questions afterwards. And then they were having to wait until a debate on South West Africa at the UN had ended, to make it easier and less embarrassing for nations favourable to South Africa. And then because of heightened tensions in Angola for May Day. Whatever the reason, on the 3rd of May, the cabinet finally approved the plan. The order, 'Execute Reindeer', had been given. D-Day was the 4th of May.

"At 1600 on D minus One we flew 1,300 kilometres over Botswana. We landed after dark and spent the night in a hangar. Few of us slept."

Elanza moved her head in his lap.

"Were you scared?" she asked.

"We were young and invincible. I'd say we were anxious to get it over but not scared. We were the best; no one could hurt us."

At 0400 they started fitting equipment. As well as two days of dry rations they had three water bottles and ten magazines with twenty rounds each, the second from last round a tracer so that they knew when to change. They had grenades that fragmented, grenades that made smoke and grenades that just burnt people. The older soldiers called them Willie Petes – white phosphorous. They straightened the pins on the grenades to make them easier to pull out and then taped over the ring to avoid accidental detonation. Their standard rifle was the R1 but with a folding stock to make it less cumbersome during the drop. The R1, identical to the Belgian FN and known to the British Army as the self-loading rifle, was made under licence in South Africa by Armscor. It was a very powerful assault rifle. Its 7.62-millimetre bullet could go through a brick wall and still kill someone on the other side. Some of them had separate bags containing radios, mortars or medical kit attached by a line that could be dropped after the parachute had opened, dangling below.

Two hours before the drop they boarded, and the aircraft headed north. A complex series of air movements had started that they never witnessed but saw the effects of when they hit the ground: five Buccaneers armed with eight one-thousand-pound bombs, another Buccaneer with seventy-two rockets to give support to them on the ground, Canberra B12 bombers fully loaded with three tons of a special type of anti-personnel bomb, their own transport aircraft, and then the first helicopter movements.

"The first of us to be inside Angola arrived on board the helicopters, establishing an area for extraction and refuelling on isolated and deserted bushland twenty-two kilometres east of Cassinga. Ten men went to protect the site, along with the Mobile Air Operations Team, two hundred-litre drums of aviation fuel, and the Chief of the Army, determined to see it all for himself. More men, more fuel and medical teams joined them. And a single Intelligence officer."

The Air Force also had an aircraft fitted for electronic warfare to jam the Cuban and SWAPO radio transmissions, and a spotter aircraft. They hoped that electronic jamming might delay the arrival of Cuban reinforcements from a camp fifteen kilometres to the south of Cassinga. The Air Force wasn't keen on risking its valuable fighters as the Cubans had MIGs in the area, but the last-minute intelligence on the new tented camp area persuaded them that they had to use the fighters for ground attack.

The bombers arrived late. Two minutes. Not that it mattered much to the people on the ground.

"It was 0802, the morning muster parade. Almost the whole camp gathered on the parade square. Four thousand people having their usual morning meeting – who went to work in which field, who to make shelters, who to accommodate the flow of refugees. We deliberately timed our attack for that occasion. It was part of our plan. Senior commanders were on parade; almost everyone was in the same location at the same time."

The four Canberra bombers came in at five hundred feet, textbook RAF and NATO practice. They'd trained to the same standard. Each aircraft carried three hundred bomblets. They only had one use; they were the most effective anti-personnel bombs ever made. Each ten-kilogram finless bomb was a round, black, rubberised container about the size of a football, filled with explosive and steel balls. They hit the ground, primed themselves and bounced back into the air, detonating at thirty feet above the target. They called them Alpha bombs. The effect of 1,200 of them, unexpectedly, in a parade ground of four thousand people was to sow havoc. People were literally shredded to pieces, indiscriminately. Four Buccaneers with thirty-two one-thousand-pound bombs followed, precision bombers. There seemed little point in being precise after the Alpha bombs. One of the jets attacked the new camp using thirty-millimetre-high explosive fragmentation shells against canvas tents.

"The combined effect upon Cassinga was catastrophic, like poking an ant's nest with a stick. Smoke, flames, dust, bodies, fleeing people, confusion and terror. People alive in the ruined buildings were unsure where to step, the floors covered in blood."

Elanza gripped his leg.

"Angel, that's terrible. So indiscriminate."

"It was war, Elanza. It happens in every war. That's what we told ourselves afterwards anyway."

"And you believe that now, Angel?"

Angel shrugged.

"I was just a soldier, Elanza, doing what I was told."

"I don't believe you. I think it shocked you. I hope it shocked you."

Angel said nothing.

"What happened then?" she asked.

Angel felt tired, as he had then. With eyes closed and limp hands he told her everything: of children ripped by cannon fire while sheltering in canvas tents, of corpses littering a trench, of a baby girl alive and unhurt under a grisly pile of bodies, of his own Intelligence officer chopping off a man's arm and pushing a flailing prisoner from the helicopter.

Elanza rubbed the back of her hand over her eyes.

"And the women and children? You shot them?"

Angel couldn't lie to her.

"Some of them, Elanza."

"That is so sad, Angel," Elanza said, her face wet. He wiped her cheek with his sleeve.

"But the baby girl. You saved her, Angel."

"Maybe. Who knows."

"No, Angel. You saved her. I know."

Angel held her tightly.

"The Intelligence officer. Bastard," Elanza hissed. "Who was it? You should have reported him to someone."

Her anger surprised him.

"You know him, Angel," Elanza said. "It was the instructor who killed the tattooist. The one who fractured a man's skull with a rock. You told me about him when we met. You know his name."

"Yes, Elanza, I know his name."

Her fingernails dug into his arm.

"He chopped that man's arm off. He pushed another man to his death from the helicopter," she hesitated, spitting out the words. "You know his name."

"His name, Elanza, was Nels."

Elanza bent forward, wilting, her head in both hands. Angel held her tightly.

"Finish it, Angel," she said quietly. "Tell it all."

"The next day we flew back to Bloemfontein. After a day to write reports and hand back equipment we were demobilised and sent home. Two days after the raid we were back at home for the weekend and then at work on Monday morning. In the middle of a lecture I looked at my hands, the dirt of Cassinga still engrained in them, the blood from children in the pile outside Dimo's house still under my fingernails."

"What happened to Dimo?" Elanza asked.

"He got away. There were two hours after the initial air attack and before we'd recovered from the bad drop and could encircle the town. Plenty of time. We came away with nothing. Not Dimo, not Greenwell, no prisoners. Just a few documents so we could prove to the world that what we had done was justified. In the end the whole thing could have been done by the Air Force. They could have bombed it flat and we might have stayed at work. The result would have been the same. They called it 'a jewel of military craftsmanship'. It was a game, a stupid game of pride to show ourselves how strong we were. The generals wanted to demonstrate their worth and the Minister of Defence wanted the power and the glory."

"Who was that?"

"The Minister of Defence? He's now our Prime Minister. Botha."

"Did we do those things? Was it all for nothing?"

Angel didn't answer for a while.

"No one is sure how many we killed. We had three dead, one probably drowned when he dropped into the river, a dozen injured, some seriously, but none of them died. Six more had minor injuries from the actual drop itself. The closest estimate is that 624 Africans died, of whom 167 were women and 298 teenagers and children. A further 611 were wounded, but some may have crawled into the bush and were never found. Maybe 150 Cubans died, mostly in the air strikes on the armoured column of reinforcements. They've never admitted the number."

He moved and sat upright.

"They gave us R1s; 7.62 millimetre. You can shoot it through the wall of a house and it'll kill. Trouble is, when you do that you can't see who you're killing."

He breathed deeply.

"The worst thing were those damn Alpha bombs."

Both Elanza and Angel were crying. He'd never talked to anyone about it.

"I saw plenty of women and children. Some of them civilians, a lot of them in uniform," he said. "You can put a twelve-year-old boy in camouflage. You can give him a gun he can hardly carry. Did he have any choice? Does that make him a soldier? Is it right to kill him, to shred his small body with fragments of hot metal?"

Elanza held him tightly. He'd taken her on the journey with him, to a past he hadn't wanted to revisit. He'd shared with her things he hadn't shared with anyone else. He loved her and she would always love him back, no matter what.

"Angel, are you a spy?" Elanza asked.

It was a difficult question to answer. He worked for the National Intelligence Service, but in his experience espionage involved writing reports for others to read as Lombard and Roux were both keen on his department delivering intelligence reports daily. Angel was an analyst with language skills, and eighty per cent of the information he analysed came from open sources available to everyone. The remaining twenty per cent of the jigsaw puzzle came from covert sources, spies. Angel's job meant turning all of this information into intelligence, and he didn't need to know who had come by the information he had to analyse, or how they had come by it. He just needed to know that it had come from a reliable source.

He'd met some agent handlers in the department, but operational personnel usually had a job outside of NIS that they did openly as a disguise, sometimes for many years or their entire working lives, a 'living cover'. And they looked like regular people; in fact, the more ordinary the better. If you thought of the person who would be least likely to be a spy, then he or she would be the best one for the job. Their wives, or husbands, and children usually had no idea. Good spies went to their graves without anyone ever knowing.

Real spies lived with the threat of exposure. Their handlers sat with sweaty palms in cafés waiting for an agent who might do what he'd promised or might not, but the agent had most to lose. Agents didn't know, when they said goodbye to their kids when they left for school, if they would be home in the evening to see them, or never seen again by anyone. Real spies' marriages broke down thanks to the hundreds of small lies that concealed unexplained absences and whispered phone calls. It often came as a surprise to themselves that they could lie so easily and so convincingly to their loved ones.

"I'm a translator and I write reports. Ralph's gone. I'm still looking. I have some resources."

TWENTY-ONE

Nels sauntered along University Way, the Kenyan sun hot on the side of his face. He was in no hurry. He'd eaten breakfast at the Norfolk and it sat heavily in his stomach, slowing him. It was Nairobi's historic and most expensive hotel but Nels hadn't cared about the cost. He would include it in his bill to Snyman so ultimately the bitch Elanza was paying. The buffet, an excellent grill of gazelle, giraffe and zebra, cooked on coals, skewered on Maasai swords and served on cast-iron plates, had been excellent. He needed some time to digest and sat for a while in Jevanjee Gardens, wasting time, watching Africans with suspicion.

Nels could smell River Road to his left before he got there. He crossed over Moi Avenue at the end of Biashara Street to the Khoja Mosque, loudly decorated *matutu* taxis stopping and honking at him, the drivers maniacal and drugged. He stopped and scoffed at comical firemen in plumed hats on parade at an ecclesiastical looking fire station, a radio mast like a church tower on one corner. He glanced at his watch and found he was still a little early. He had planned on ten o'clock, when the bar should be quiet. Few people needed a mid-morning hooker.

The building was painted green at the bottom and pink on top. A large plastic palm tree hung above the entrance and a sign, hand painted, advertised 'Night Club House'. Mr Business was counting money when Nels entered. He looked up from three piles of soiled notes, the filthy paper his grimy reward from a dirty trade. He recognised the large white man and smiled.

"Ah, my friend. Welcome back."

Nels scanned the barroom. The large man with the facial burn was missing an ear, a gnarled stub of white cartilage and dried brown blood attracting flies to the side of his face which he didn't bother to swat away. Another man sat on the couch next to a girl in tall shoes. He had a head wound and an arm roughly plastered with bolts sticking through linked by a metal bridge. Nels peered into the back of the room. There was no one standing against the wall. It was as quiet as he'd hoped. Just the four of them, and now himself.

Mr Business was cheerful.

"Good to see you," he said, moving to stand in front of his money. "How are you?"

"Well, I guess I'm better than your two friends."

Nels looked at the four of them, wondering about weapons. He worried about the girl. The large man was stupid enough to believe he didn't need anything, that he could crush with his hands, his fingers like old wrenches in a tool set. The other man had plaster on his right arm. Nels knew from firearms training that only ten per cent are truly left-handed. He imagined the man could swing a club but it

334

would be unwieldly and weak. Mr Business could possibly be a shooter, but there was something guttural and classically street-gang-like about his ratty features that suggested a traditionalist, a knife man. He couldn't decide on the woman and it troubled him.

Nels pointed to the two men.

"Did the boy do this to them?"

Mr Business put his hands in his front trouser pockets.

A knife man, thought Nels. *I knew it.*

"No, not the boy. You didn't tell us that someone would be watching his back. I would have charged more money for that."

Nels didn't understand. He couldn't think of anyone who might have an interest in protecting Ralph.

"A white man?" he asked. "Like me?"

"A black guy," said Mr Business uneasily. "Strong. Very strong. With short hair."

Nels smiled and out of the corner of his eye watched the man with his arm in plaster stand and casually put his hand on the back of the couch.

And you have the club, he thought, pleased at his own perception.

"So, I guess the boy got away, then."

Mr Business didn't speak and twitched his nose.

"Which way?" asked Nels.

"When he came out of the airport he got on a bus."

"Out of the airport? You didn't get him before?"

"No. He went in and then came out again and got on a bus."

"A bus to where?"

"I don't know."

"Really?"

"Another three hundred might help me remember."

Nels stared at him and deliberately spoke as he would to a child.

"It will be easier for you if you tell me now."

Nels wondered about the big man, concerned he was sidling behind him. Nels looked around, still smiling, flexing his legs, loosening his wrists. He loved this moment, the time before action, the adrenaline building.

"Okay. He got away. Never mind. I'll just take my money and I'll be off."

Nels wasn't smiling anymore. He was standing on a springboard ready to jump, tense but confident.

"What money?" Mr Business asked, edging forward, his hands still in his pockets.

"The money I gave you. You failed to do the job. I want it back."

Nels waited. He was ready now. Nels knew he had to stay on his feet. He had to keep moving and not get put on the floor and stamped on, at least until the odds against him had been reduced.

"Plus interest," he added.

The big man came first. Nels was ready for the sucker punch. Perhaps the big man would imagine that Nels wasn't aware what was happening.

He looked at the man's ear, weeping blood, and knew what he should do. He drove towards the big man with both elbows forward to dig in his chest and forearms up to snap his collarbones, forcing his way into a Muay Thai clinch with the man's head held tightly between Nels' arms, pulling the man down and forward into his chest.

Nels held him, his hands linked behind the man's head and his forearm grinding painfully against the damaged ear, controlling the man with his head held down and his posture bent, neutralising the man's short punches and using his own knees on the man's head and chest.

The man in plaster was coming now, a short hardwood cudgel in his left hand. Nels locked the clinch and used leverage, gravity and the big man's own bodyweight to turn him. He moved the big man between himself and the guy in plaster, who was reaching with the cudgel over the back of the big man, trying to reach Nels' head but unable to get to him over his buddy's back and tripping over the big man's feet.

Nels started knocking the big man backwards when he wanted to move him, always keeping the big man between himself and his other opponent. The big man would then push back towards Nels, making it easier to turn him, changing the clinch from a defensive move into an attacking one.

Nels started alternating heel kicks to the stomach and knee cap of the man in plaster, with continuing knees to the head and face of the big man in the clinch, constantly moving as in a dance. The big man's short useless punches were slowing. Nels could feel the effort draining out of him and intensified his own knee action, making good contact to the man's jaw, knowing it was just a matter of time before he scored a knock-out blow.

It came sooner than he expected, a lucky strike to the side of the man's head made him collapse in a dead weight. Nels supported him for a while then dropped him to the ground. Nels quickly stood side-on to the man with the cudgel and used his forward leg to kick his shin, keeping some distance between them. Nels stretched forward underneath the man's left side, twisting and pinning the arm with the cudgel against Nels' shoulder as he reached behind the man's head with his other arm, pushing him away and down and in complete control. The man screamed and let go of the cudgel. Nels grabbed his right arm by the metal bridge between the bolts protruding from the plaster cast. He held it like a handle and swung the man's already broken bones against the wall. He fell with a whimper and lay still. Nels quickly went to the big man on the floor and kicked him repeatedly in the face with the flat of his foot and his heel. Two down.

When he turned around Mr Business was very close. Nels had been wrong about the knife. Instead he had a spike for stabbing, matt black, the handle round and ridged like a rifle's fore-stock for better grip, the spike triangular in cross-section and sharpened to a point. The spike and handle were one piece of painted steel, the whole thing not more than twelve inches in length. Mr Business held it firmly, the spike pointing up at forty-five degrees and level with Nels' chest.

Nels had watched real knife fights. An attack with a knife was savage and brutal and scary, the blade seldom used to cut or slash but in a frenzied repeated stabbing action. Mr Business obviously had worthwhile experience and had chosen his weapon with some thought.

Nels' rule of thumb was to get close to a gun and keep distance from a knife. Nels didn't have the luxury of choice on this occasion, the spike now inches from a point underneath his sternum. His barroom discussions about knife attacks always ended with a simple question: trap or strike? Some said trap the hand holding the knife, others said to forget the weapon and strike the man. Nels had further refined his preferred course of action. It depended on distance. If the knife was close, trap the hand, if further away strike the man. In Nels' extensive studies of the subject one other thing had emerged. Energy and rage can be crippling.

Nels stared at Mr Business with eyes wide and screamed at him, forcing blood into his red face, his veins pulsing. He punched the hand holding the spike then grabbed it and pulled it against his own body, trapping it, then attacked hard and fast Mr Business's head with punches, using only the points of his knuckles. Trap and strike, trap and strike.

Mr Business was wiry and strong for his size, twisting his spike hand to free it and reaching for Nels' throat with the other. It turned into a frantic furious wrestle, both men screaming and spitting.

Nels tried pushing him then quickly stepped back, pulling him forward by the hand holding the spike. Mr Business stumbled slightly. It was enough. Nels quickly let go of the hand, stepped backwards and flicked his left foot powerfully into the man's groin. Mr Business fell on to both knees, still holding the spike.

Nels talked to him like a friend, as though he wanted to help.

"Tell me now," he said gently. "Where did he go?"

"The aerodrome."

"What?" said Nels cheerily. "Are you playing a little game with me?"

Mr Business vomited and choked.

"He came out of the airport where the big planes are and got on a bus. Then he got off and walked towards the aerodrome where the little planes go," he sighed. "Wilson Aerodrome."

"Oh, okay. I've got it now."

Nels took a step backwards and with the opposite foot kicked him hard under the chin. His head twisted away and he lay down, beaten, the spike rolling on the bare concrete floor.

Nels stood and looked around, exhaling in short gasps, looking for the woman. She'd gone. He turned towards the bar and picked up all the money, stuffing the three piles of notes that Mr Business had been counting into his pocket.

"For services rendered," he said to himself. "Pest control."

He pulled a chair against the wall next to an exposed joist for the floor above and dragged Mr Business to it, hanging him ceremoniously by the thick gold chain around his neck.

When he'd finished, the woman was standing in front of him. Nels looked at her curiously, a little impressed. She was quite pretty, with Afro-Indian hair that had been straightened then curled into ringlets at her shoulders. Long clear plastic earrings hung halfway down her neck. She had a very short black and white dress in a close zebra stripe pattern that hung off one shoulder and clung to her body. The *panga* that she held raised in two hands was broad and blunt on the backside, the blade sharpened on the inside. It looked more like a machete than a cutlass, with a sturdy black plastic hand grip, Nels imagined good for cutting fruit from a tree or felling sugar cane. She was unsteady on high heels that bent her feet grotesquely at the toes.

Nels put both his hands up, moving them about to distract her, looking in her eyes not at the weapon, talking loudly and quickly. She took a half step backwards. It was what Nels had been waiting for. Perfect range. He did a wide outside kick at her fingers, like a crescent kick but aimed and with some follow through. The *panga* clattered to the floor. Before she could move he punched her hard in the throat, her larynx compressing with the force of the blow. She bent at the waist, both hands clutching her neck, and rolled onto her side as if asleep.

Nels turned to the door and checked the time. Midday. He wondered what was for lunch at the Norfolk.

*

Roux found Angel retired hurt, nursing wounds in his subterranean office at the Comitia.

"Christ. What happened to you?"

Angel wasn't sure what to tell him. In Nairobi he'd staggered to the screeching man holding the side of his face and held him by the good ear. He'd talked Swahili. Asked him why? Who? The man could give no name. A man, square with a fat neck, had given them money. Angel had drawn a figure in the dust and pointed to his arm. The man nodded. When Angel had looked around, Ralph had disappeared.

"I believe Nels recruited some local hitmen. You can get them in the nightclubs on the River Road. He probably gave them a hundred dollars each to get Ralph. They took their job seriously. I had to intervene, and when it was over Ralph had gone."

Roux nodded. "It wouldn't have been too difficult for Nels' hitmen to find Ralph in Nairobi."

"No. They would have found him the same way I would have: asked around. There aren't too many places a young budget traveller would stay. I mean, he wouldn't be in the Norfolk."

"That was my fault."

Angel shrugged.

"Can we do anything about Cornelius Nels?" he asked.

Roux and Lombard were fighting to make sure the Service became the leading intelligence provider, but Military Intelligence also had the ear of the Prime Minister.

Lombard knew that intelligence was power and that it could be manipulated to provide the Prime Minister with whatever view the proponent wanted to encourage. The Defence Force had the view that all South Africa's problems were due to communist influence and that revolutionary armies supported by the Soviets should be controlled in the buffer zones of the border countries. The military also had a huge home-grown defence industry, Armscor, to protect and promote. Sometimes it was necessary to exaggerate the threats to justify the development of Armscor's exceedingly costly defence systems. The National Intelligence Service's view was that the problem with African National Congress sponsored terrorism had always been an internal one and would only be resolved by a political solution, not a military one. A hard-fought agreement made in Simon's Town to thrash out which agency provided what intelligence had been annulled by the head of Military Intelligence before the ink had dried. Lombard maintained influence with Botha only through the quality, reliability and impartiality of his Service's intelligence analysis, thanks to people like Angel. Highlighting the illegalities of a Military Intelligence operative was not going to encourage harmony and cooperation between the two departments, and now was not the time for the National Intelligence Service to be the cause of a return to the turf wars with the Defence Force that had preceded the Simon's Town agreement. Nels would have to wait.

"No. There's a political dimension."

Angel scoffed.

"Isn't there always?"

"So, what's he like?"

"Ralph?"

Roux nodded.

"I like him. He's a bit like I was at his age, but not so good-looking."

He touched the side of his face, put two fingers on a dressing taped above his eye.

"In what ways is he like you?"

"Well, like me, he's modest."

"Ha ha. Funny."

"He's a little naive, but not stupid. Laid-back, but not slow. You feel that he's always thinking, there's always stuff going on in his head."

Angel thought of his own childhood in England, the wet yellow stone of the school building, the way boys did well at exams or in sport without any visible effort having been made, without any preparation. At school you were expected to do well but ideally without trying too hard.

"Perhaps it's the education system over there."

"Anything else?"

Angel remembered the trip through Uganda, police all around but Ralph staying calm, monitoring their progress past the hydro-electric plant on the Nile crossing at Jinja.

"He's observant of what's around him – physical things and places."

Like the rocket engine test facility at Rooi-Els and the missile site at Overberg? Roux wondered.

Angel thought about their conversation and Ralph's parting comments.

"He's empathetic about people. Including me."

Roux looked at the maps covering the wall, now of the whole of Africa.

"It sounds like he'd make a good spy."

Angel smiled.

"Is he going to be okay?" asked Roux.

"Well, he hasn't much money. He told me he had fifty dollars but I think he lied. I'd say he had some hidden away. At a guess he may have a couple of hundred still. He's been living and travelling cheaply until now."

"That's not going to last long. He's over halfway but still has a long way to go," said Roux.

He wondered if he should mention Lombard's concern about the photographs of Rooi-Els and Overberg, the worry that Ralph may have been working for a British agent called Zac, the truthful status of South Africa's nuclear programme. Of all the secrets he'd kept during his career this one troubled him the most. It was a secret he wanted to throw away, as though he had hold of something that burnt his flesh.

"The police stole his camera, the bag and all his film," he said.

"Which police?"

"The South African Police. Our police."

"Why?"

"It was before he met Elanza, while he worked at The Diplomat hotel in Joburg. They thought he might be involved with people from the club in the basement. They were hoping he'd have some gay porn."

"Ralph's not gay," said Angel.

"If you get the opportunity, slip him some money without his knowledge, just so that South Africa has reimbursed him, so to speak."

Angel laughed.

"I thought South Africa would be giving him lots of money."

Roux shrugged.

"Who knows? That's in the future. It sounds like he needs a little advance right now."

"Why are we helping him?"

"South Africa is not helping him. I personally still think he's just a lost kid wandering around. I told the boss that at the beginning."

Roux looked at the maps.

"Any ideas?" Roux asked him.

"I went to the airline check-in to ask if they remembered Ralph and knew of his plans. They have a small station at Nairobi, just two girls and an English manager. The girl who'd been working at the time was off-duty and the manager didn't want to talk to me. *Piel kop*."

Roux laughed.

"My first assumption is that he'll go north overland, try to get all the way to Cairo and then across Europe. That's what I'd do."

"What if he flies back to Johannesburg from Nairobi and uses his original ticket?" Roux asked.

"I checked with Zelda at SAA to see if he'd done that. Now it's too late. The flight he had a ticket for has already gone and he won't have enough money to buy another one."

"What about going to Mombasa and then taking a sea route through Suez?"

"He knows nothing about the sea or working on a ship. I don't think that option would even cross his mind. Even if he thought of it I'm not sure that it would be viable. Not many captains would take on crew at a port like Mombasa."

Angel moved to the map on the wall.

"I don't think he'll go back into Uganda so his most likely route is out through the top of Kenya, here, to the west of Lake Turkana and then follow the Nile through Sudan and Egypt."

"Who are you going to ask to help?"

Angel thought about their options, about who he could ask.

His first thought was the British, a small but highly professional service with an incomparable network of agents in North Africa. They set the standard for espionage. There were some problems though between the South Africans and the British. Angel's agency had a stormy relationship with the British due to South Africa misusing diplomatic cover in the 1970s. Their relations with them had been slowly improving but the British focused on providing espionage training to newly independent African states who were developing their own intelligence services. In the process they could recruit the best students to work for them. When these freshly minted intelligence agents went home and found themselves in positions close to the heads of new states, they could report back to their friends in London. The British were very keen to find out more about South Africa's nuclear ambitions and Angel, London born, would have been an obvious target for them to develop as a source deep within the South African security apparatus. Angel felt sure that if he contacted them his own counter-intelligence team, the *Heining*, would quickly be all over him.

In the past the United States had been very active within South Africa, aware of the economic opportunities for investment and, contrary to outward appearances, maintained financial and cultural links with the apartheid government. A tip-off from an American agent had led to Nelson Mandela's arrest. Everyone knew, however, that the African National Congress had historically maintained close friendships with countries such as Libya, and various Islamic revolutionary and fundamentalist Middle Eastern states, and that these were unstable sponsors of terrorism. The Americans, like the British, were now keen to make sure that the ANC should never get access to South African nuclear weapons and missile technology. Angel's personal view was that the Americans had an arrogant and decadent way of living, and no matter how much cash they threw around they didn't make especially good spies, or spy masters, in the gritty places of Africa. The Germans struggled in Africa but the German BND had helped train the old South African Bureau for State Security. In return for information about ANC members being trained by the Stasi in East Germany, NIS helped them where they could.

NIS had, however, established sometimes very complex liaison channels with other intelligence services in Africa, usually by placing agents operating under cover of private business concerns. Crucial to the success of such liaisons was building strong interpersonal relationships, often over bottles of good Cape wine. NIS concentrated on 'the big five': Nigeria, Kenya, Uganda, Zambia... and Egypt.

The Egyptian General Intelligence Directorate, more commonly known as the Mukhabarat, had some notable achievements, mostly directed at Israel. In 1970 it crippled an Israeli oil rig in transit from Canada to Sinai with explosives while right under the noses of Mossad and the CIA, and prior to the Yom Kippur war in 1973 the Egyptians concealed massive plans to invade Israeli-occupied Sinai by calculating the trajectories and timings of American spy satellites so that it could move military units into position without them being observed.

"If my assumption is right he's probably already out of Kenya."

He put his finger on the map. South Africa's NIS had very little contact with the Sudanese, whose interests were domestic, the internal problems between the Muslim north and Christian south of their own country, and the Arab world. To the Sudanese the Republic of South Africa seemed a long way away.

"There's not much we can do in Sudan. It's too volatile. I think I'll call Alim in Cairo."

"I agree. Do it now."

Angel picked up the phone and turned on a desk speaker so that Roux could listen in.

"*Sabah il kheer, Alim. Kayfa halak.*"

"I'm fine thanks, Angel, and your Arabic is rusty."

"And how is the export–import business?"

"We are very busy, Angel. The El-Nasr Company never rests. How can I help, my friend?"

Roux didn't speak Arabic. Agents like Angel Rots would be the future of the Intelligence community. Apartheid was unsustainable; everyone knew that even if they didn't care to admit it. There would come a day when the majority would rule the country, and rule the Intelligence Service. When that time came Roux stood ready as a South African patriot to put the country first and to participate in a smooth transition, reaching out to those who many regarded as an enemy. He would need Angel Rots to contribute to the building of a new intelligence institution, one that served all the people in the country. Angel was more important to the future of South Africa than he might currently imagine.

Roux walked to the wall and looked at the map. He tried to follow the course of the Nile in southern Sudan with his finger, but it was difficult to trace.

Angel joined him at the map.

"What is this town here in Sudan at the bottom of the river?" he asked.

"Juba."

"Looks like the only thing around there."

"It is."

"Know anything about the place?"

"It's a regional administrative centre. About eighty thousand people. A big UN presence, aid workers tripping over each other doing good. Wet from April to October."

"Access?"

"By air."

"No land access?"

"Nothing at all to the east from Ethiopia; to the south there's a road from Uganda but it's in an atrocious condition and heavily mined by Amin; a road to the west eventually meets a railhead after about a thousand-kilometre detour; and to the north is the river. Juba is the end of the line for river barges coming south down the Nile from Khartoum."

"Or the start of a river barge going north," Roux corrected him.

"Exactly. Other than Sudan Airways the river is the only way out of there."

Roux scratched the side of his face.

"You need to go there."

"What?"

"I think you should go to Juba and look around."

"Why, Nick? Why is this so important?"

"We've been through this, Angel. We want to know what happens to the money."

Angel threw his hands in the air.

"I don't get it. The money is a hundred and thirty million dollars. So what? What is our GDP? Eighty billion? Government expenditure must be twelve, fifteen billion. Ralph's money is just a rounding error."

Roux looked at him.

"Okay. Let's look at it another way," Roux said. "How

about I'm your boss, that's the job, and I want you to go? Will that do it?"

Angel was shocked by his anger.

"I've always had high hopes for you, Angel, but sometimes you should just shut up and do what you're told."

Roux waved a finger at him.

"You need to be grateful for the opportunities this country has given you."

He took a breath and exhaled forcefully.

"You still have an identity not associated with South Africa and a cover story outside of the Service?"

Angel nodded.

"Use them. Go to Juba. Find the boy. Understood?"

Roux turned back to the map on the wall and put a white shaking finger on southern Sudan.

"This is just water everywhere," Roux said.

Roux had just had an idea. He'd have to run it by Lombard. It was brilliantly simple but solved all their problems. He turned to Angel.

"Look, I'm sorry I lost my temper. And I'm sorry about Nels. I shouldn't have told him about Nairobi."

"We had no idea he might plan to kill Ralph. And we've no real proof he was involved."

"I should have guessed though. There's a lot of money at stake."

Roux still had his finger on the map.

"Is that all wetlands?"

"In the wet season it's a swamp covering the same area as England. The name for it is derived from an Arabic word for a barrier or obstruction, something impenetrable."

"Really? What's that?"

"It's called the Sudd."

NORTH AFRICA

5TH MAY TO 24TH JUNE, 1982

TWENTY-TWO

Juba was a river port, the White Nile's southern terminus in Sudan. The town was a dusty compound, a mixture of traditional circular huts, conical roofs like ice-cream cones thatched in papyrus, and square mud-walled buildings draped in tarpaulin sheets. Wide open gutters full of waste ran around a market area with traders under faded beach umbrellas selling peanuts amid shops roughly built of unfaced concrete block, some proudly displaying an inadequate stock of worn hand tools and black water tanks. A group of boys pushed weary thin cattle with long horns, thick at the head but tapering to fine points that nearly touched where they met above the cow's head. The cattle raised a red cloud of clay dust as they walked past the Juba Hospital. They stopped and snorted through bulbous bristly black nostrils outside a doorway as a nurse in starched whites swept bloody water from inside onto the street.

An aid worker, professional and business-like with sensibly styled hair, had given Ralph a lift from the airport.

In another setting she might have managed photocopier sales representatives, or been an enthusiastic team builder in human resources. In Juba she had become an expert in local bovine.

"Eighty per cent of the population is employed in agriculture in Sudan and ten per cent are nomadic. They look after fifty million farm animals. Eighteen million cattle. Most are a breed called Baggara. They are with the Arabs in the north. Down here the cows are Nilotic."

A man, deeply scarred, pushed the cattle past the hospital door and then leant on a long stick, staring at Ralph from underneath three straight parallel lines ridged across his forehead.

"What's wrong with that man's face?"

"It's scarification. They do it with a red-hot knife when they're teenagers. Boys and girls. The main thing is that they must not cry."

"Why?"

"It's a sign of coming of age. For boys it shows that they are brave enough to fight and ready to die in battle; for girls that they are ready for the pain of childbirth."

There were people by the side of the road so tall that Ralph briefly wondered if he might be hallucinating in his fever.

"Each tribe has a different pattern of scarification. The tall one, he's Dinka. I'm not sure which clan though. There are twenty-six. He's probably Malual, not Rek. They are the largest."

Her expertise wasn't restricted to domestic farm animals.

"Nuer, however, have lots of little dots all over the face, arms and legs. Where are you staying?"

She spoke quickly, and her conversation jumped like a child.

"I thought the Hotel Africa."

"It's popular," she held a finger up to him in warning, "but don't eat there. Have you registered?"

"Registered what?"

"Registered with the police."

"No. Do I need to? I just got in."

"I'll take you. You have to register with the police in Malakia."

Malakia was a few kilometres out of Juba town, a traditional village with another marketplace where the actual life of Juba took place. It was full of Dinka.

"You can stay on the floor of the police station at Malakia," she told him. "But the dawn bugle call is a real pain."

Ralph preferred the sound of the popular Hotel Africa.

"You know, you should visit Gilo. It's an old British hill station from colonial days up in the Imatong Mountains. It's high. Really cool. No mosquito or tetse fly. Are you okay?"

Ralph rested his head against the door pillar.

"I felt terrible last night."

"Flu-like? Fever, sweating, shaking chills? Headache and feeling tired?"

"All of that."

"Probably malaria."

"Great."

"You have to time the interval between bouts to find out which type. If the fever and chills recur every forty-eight hours it's *plasmodium ovale*. If it's every seventy-two hours it's *malariae*."

There seemed little that she didn't know.

"When would I have got it?"

"If it's *ovale* probably about two weeks ago."

Ralph remembered a fitful night fighting mosquitoes while sleeping in the waiting room of a customs post on the border between Burundi and Rwanda. That must have been about two weeks previously.

"You want lunch? You should eat. We'll get *fool*."

Ralph didn't want to eat *fool*; he felt one.

"You know, bean stew. I know where to go."

Greeks had long been in Juba as merchants, and now apparently as restaurateurs. She took him to one.

"The town has become busier since Chevron found oil downriver at their Unity Field near Bentiu. They're taking twelve thousand barrels a day but I heard it'll last twenty-five years."

They found the only spare table for lunch.

"The question is where to put the refinery. The government insisted on Kosti rather than somewhere local, but now they have to make a 550-kilometre pipeline and the estimate for that is a billion dollars."

She had done a master's in international something at Columbia University and then worked for the UN in Rome. Other jobs for organisations beginning with U had followed in Haiti and Liberia, not so good for shoe shopping but with 'real people' at last. The life of a humanitarian aid worker was clearly one of compromises, and although she said it herself the World Women's Rights Commission had been lucky to have her. She had been tempted by an offer to join the staff of the High-Level Panel on System-wide Coherence with the World Food Programme at a Rome-based agency.

Ralph was curious and enjoying the acronyms.

"With the WFP at an RBA?"

"Exactly."

"And now?"

"I'm a programme officer with the WWRC."

"For what?"

"Safe access to firewood."

Ralph looked at the *fool*.

"What does a programme officer for safe access to firewood do?"

"Desk and field research. Analyse data and define findings. Skills building."

"In firewood?"

"It's challenging."

Ralph struggled to concentrate, his head pounding.

"What does the WWRC do?"

"Provide sexual and reproductive healthcare, protect women from gender-based violence, encourage economic and social empowerment."

"Wow."

She looked at him, nodding her head.

"Quite a job, huh?"

"Absolutely," said Ralph.

"It's all about raising domestic investments through multi-sectoral initiatives and shared value partnerships."

"Wow. Firewood."

"I know. But it's so important. And I'm careful I don't project my own needs and solutions onto their society and culture by saying anything unacceptable."

"Like, 'it's only firewood'."

Had she been wearing a skirt she would have sat up straight and smoothed it with two hands.

"You don't know anything about the aid industry, do you?"

Ralph looked at her blankly.

"You British started it all by having public collections for famine in China and India. The first ever NGOs were British, against slavery and for women's suffrage."

Ralph looked around the restaurant. There were over a hundred languages in Sudan, although Arabic was the official primary one. Nationally, only ten per cent spoke Dinka, but that rose to forty per cent in the south. Around him, in the Greek restaurant, Ralph only heard loud United Nations English.

"Look, aid is given by individuals and private organisations, but mostly by governments."

Ralph wondered if it had been the subject of her thesis.

"Governments provide Official Development Assistance. But it's not for free. Governments do it to reward or strengthen an ally, or to give diplomatic approval. It can provide infrastructure to enable resource extraction."

"Like oil?"

"Like oil. Or assistance can be given to gain commercial access for their nation's industries."

"Like Chevron?"

She looked around her at the tables on a hard dirt floor, the ever-present flies. She used to have such lovely working lunches in Rome. But fieldwork was vital, and so useful to have on your résumé when applying for those executive postings back in New York.

"Like Chevron. Sometimes government ODA is humanitarian," she conceded. "Government aid is about eighty per cent of the total. The rest is from Non-Government Organisations and development charities, or is faith-based aid. Altogether it adds up to tens of billions of dollars and it won't be long before it's a hundred billion."

Ralph did the sums. Non-government aid was a huge industry, a corporation with a turnover of twenty billion, probably employing thousands of people.

"Wow. Is WWRC an NGO?"

She shook her head.

"We are a TANGO, a Technical Assistance NGO."

"In firewood."

They both said it at the same time, and laughed.

"Listen, let me take you to the Hotel Africa. I have time. There's an Innovative Finance for INGOs meeting at three that I can't miss."

When she left him looking for the hotel reception, weak with nausea, he wasn't sure if Virginia had been her name or where she came from. He thought both.

*

Snyman had called asking for an update. Nels had waited for him at the bottom of the escalator to Hillbrow Squash Centre on Pretoria Street since six thirty in the morning, trying to wake up. Nels knew of Hillbrow's vibrant nightlife and open-all-hours culture, the Piccadilly Circus or Times Square of Johannesburg, but only Snyman the crazy Jew would exercise at that time of day.

"Are you always up so early?" Nels asked him. "Nothing warm and soft to tempt you at home in the morning?"

"Come on. I need breakfast."

He took him to Hatikvah on Catherine Avenue, Hillbrow's famous Jewish deli, and ordered *shakshouka*. Nels picked without enthusiasm at poached eggs in a spicy runny tomato sauce.

"What do you know, Nels? What happened?"

"The little bastard got away."

"Great," Snyman said sarcastically. "Where did he go?"

Nels had gone to Wilson Aerodrome before leaving Nairobi and found that all the scheduled flights were domestic, small aircraft serving a maze of dirt strip runways within Kenya. Aid agency planes went international but there were hundreds of them, making thousands of flights.

"He may have gone north to Sudan. Some ground handlers remembered a white boy hanging around but no one saw who he flew out with."

"Sudan? Why didn't you follow him?"

"I couldn't go there," said Nels. "You couldn't either. Not using our passports. They hate South Africans."

"You said he had some help?"

Nels gave up with the food. He wondered why Jews couldn't eat meat and dairy together, and fish for breakfast just felt wrong.

"Yes. A black guy."

"Now who would send a black guy to look after him?"

Nels had been wondering too.

"Elanza?" he asked.

"Don't be stupid. She can't pay for anything without my consent."

Snyman looked at him accusingly.

"Who have you talked to about this?"

Nels felt uncomfortable.

"No one."

"No one? Who told you to go to Nairobi?"

"A guy I know."

"Who?"

"He works for the government."

"Doing what?"

Nels looked away.

"Intelligence."

Snyman dropped an egg, splattering red sauce on his trousers. He scowled at Nels angrily as he cleaned himself with a napkin.

"I don't believe it. You asked the National Intelligence Service for help?"

"They are the only people who could help find someone outside of South Africa."

Snyman brushed his hair back with two hands. It still didn't make any sense to him.

"Why would NIS be interested in him?"

"Perhaps they think Elanza's money is really South African money." Nels paused. "Or the PM does."

"The PM?" Snyman shouted. "What the *fok* did you tell them?"

Snyman looked around at the other people in the restaurant. He knew most of them. The Jewish community was tight-knit, a white tribe tolerated but not revered, and it stuck together. He thought he would make a rare visit to the Great Synagogue on Smit Street after breakfast. He suddenly felt inclined to pray.

*

Ralph's room in the Hotel Africa was a dormitory of about a dozen beds. There was no one else there. The Nile River Transport Corporation steamer service to Kosti departed fortnightly and the boat had left five days previously taking everyone staying at the Hotel Africa, and a lot of the staff, with it. He had nine days to wait before the next one.

Ralph spread his map on the bed. Sudan looked huge, the largest country in Africa. If placed over Western Europe it would have covered from England to the toe of Italy and from Portugal to Switzerland, with the same number of people as the Benelux. It was the same length as from Houston Texas to the top of North Dakota close to the

Canadian border, the whole length of the US but with the population of California.

Sudan on his map had been split into two colours: the top half brown and the bottom half green.

The northern brown half was dry and Arabic, Sunni Muslim. The Nubian Desert from the Egyptian border stretched to the capital Khartoum, supporting little life other than in the Gezira between the White and Blue Niles, and the country stayed dry as far as Kosti. Rain hardly ever fell in these areas and when it did it created raging torrents in the dry river courses of the *wadis* that cut communications for months.

The southern green half was wet and African, superficially at least Christian. The impenetrable swamps of the Sudd and the flood plains of the Nile eventually gave way to rainforest in Zaire and Uganda. It was the home of the Nilotic African peoples that continued beyond the Great Lakes.

Virginia had lectured him on Sudanese political history, as she would have done to a class at Columbia. As usual, the physical geography had determined the politics. Arab Islamic armies had made no inroads south beyond Kosti until the fourteenth century. The Sudd had stopped them. The Egyptians finally invaded southern Sudan in the nineteenth century, desperate to ensure a constant supply of conscripts for the Egyptian Army, and employed General Gordon to push the boundary of Sudan ever further south.

Into this land of opposite extremes came Gaafar Nimeiry, an Egyptian Army colonel born in Cairo and son of an Egyptian politician, who in 1969 led a coup and became chairman of a revolutionary command council before becoming President. Somehow he'd outmanoeuvred his domestic rivals while actively encouraging economic and military assistance from abroad. He had governed one of Africa's most divided countries for half of its independent life.

The south, however, remained problematic. There was a historic hostility from the Nilotic peoples to the Arabs, who were identified with the slave trade and oppression in the south. Egyptian state involvement in the slave trade had continued until the late 1800s, the last vestiges of slavery persisting in southern Sudan until after World War One.

Ralph found his location and put his finger on the map – Juba. He was at the bottom of the green half. The country turned from green to brown nearly a thousand kilometres due north at his next port of call, the river town of Kosti, the destination of the Nile River Transport Corporation steamer that he planned to take in over a week's time.

There were few other travel options. There was simply nothing but scrub to the east through Eastern Equatoria, and no way to loop around the Sudd by entering Ethiopia, itself completely closed to foreigners other than if transiting through the capital Addis Ababa by air. To the west a railway ran from Wau to Khartoum, with a slow train prone to inexplicable delays and breakdowns. There were two roads from Juba to the town of Wau and its railhead, the shorter of the two which went through Rumbek impassable except in the driest conditions. The longer route had little traffic, with rumours of people waiting a month for a lift in the mail truck. It wound eight hundred kilometres through Maridi, Yambio and Tambura, nearly a month's walking through the Nile and Congo basin. Ralph wasn't sure he felt up to it. To the north an unpaved road roughly followed the river but was always closed nine months of the year through flooding. Which left the Nile River Transport Corporation steamer to Kosti. There was nothing Ralph could do but wait; there were no choices to be made, and he had no influence on any outcome. For the first time since leaving Johannesburg Ralph relaxed. The burden of decision-making had temporarily been taken away, and as soon as he realised it fatigue flooded over him. He felt tired with a persistent dull ache in his abdomen that had started in the aeroplane the night before. It would be good to rest. He lay on his bed, alone in the room in the middle of the afternoon, and slept immediately.

*

It was night and he'd been dreaming. A strangely coloured grey and white dog with blue eyes had been running up a field away from him. A woman was smiling and then laughing. She always laughed and he loved her for it. He ran after the dog, jumping leafy green plants, both racing away from water raining down from a machine like a huge cotton reel on its side. Water cascaded everywhere, all around him and the dog, and the woman stood watching and laughing.

Ralph felt terrible, the bed wet with his sweat. He had pain in his joints, at the knees and elbows. He felt sick and his stomach ache felt worse. He should go to the toilet.

Ralph staggered to the bathroom outside in the darkness. It was better not to turn on the lights and attract mosquitoes and flies. In the dark he could only hear and didn't have to see the seething mess in the pit below the hole he had to crouch over.

He crawled back across the hotel to his room and stumbled onto his bed weak and shaking, confused by his fever. It should leave him and return after forty-eight or seventy-two hours. It had started a day ago, on the ground in Loki, but Jim and Quebec Jean and the aeroplane called Betsy already felt as though they had happened in a previous life. He'd know this time tomorrow, or the day after, what type of malaria he had.

Ralph never found out. He slept, unconscious, for three days.

When he awoke the dormitory was empty, and for a moment he hadn't known where he was or how long he'd been asleep. He felt weak but not feverish, his mouth dry. He wanted to ask someone what day it was. He suddenly felt anxious that he may have missed the steamer, but he was still alone and there was no one to tell him. He needed water but was reluctant to make another trip to the toilet. In the end he dragged himself to a broken tap and in a mirror above noticed that the whites of his eyes had gone yellow. He knew what it meant. Not malaria. By confirmation his toilet runs became more and more remarkable as his stools experimented with half the spectrum but finally settled on the colour of grey clay. Not to be outdone, his urine changed from dark orange to brown. Now aware that he needed some help he left his rucksack laying claim to his bed and walked hesitantly into town, his vision ahead just a foggy tunnel.

*

The Sisters of The Sacred Heart of the Virgin Mary had been in Sudan since the 1950s, the first four postulants receiving habit from the Bishop of Equatoria in 1952. Sister Kathleen was appointed the first superior general, as well as the novice mistress, and two years later all the novices were professed and the congregation established. The Holy See in Rome approved the young institute the following year. Sister

Kathleen and her three assistants had been in Juba ever since, responding to the needs of the poor, the neglected, and those who had not heard the Good News of Salvation. They were a Catholic institution with a local congregation that was constantly on the move, but they fought hard to evangelise and educate children in their own school, and in time began other activities like social work and nursing to expand the congregation.

Getting bums on pews wasn't easy. The Nilotic peoples had their own indigenous religions in which cattle played a significant role in rituals. They were indifferent to Christianity, which the north had at one time vowed to destroy. When people in Juba did embrace the Church rather than the mosque, and the English language rather than Arabic, it was more a symbol of resistance to the Muslim government than piety.

But as Sister Kathleen liked to remind them: 'The children are the hope of every nation', and education needed to be given the highest priority. Children, with free minds and enthusiastic hearts, would eventually fill the congregation. It was an inspired strategy, and the sisters' work was helped by southern Sudan having a third of the nation's population while the government in the north provided the same area with only a sixth of the nation's primary schools. All the sisters of The Sacred Heart had to do was keep them alive – not easy when half the children under fifteen were malnourished and in the south there was only one doctor for every eighty-three thousand people – and then teach them.

It had been Sister Barbara who had seen him first. She had been fetching the liturgical calendar to decide the Daily Gospel and happened to glance outside. A boy, looking at the church, had noticed her and raised his hand. She was about to turn away when he rocked forward and fell to the ground. He lay there, immobile, his hand still outstretched. She called for Sister Kathleen.

*

Ralph found himself in a narrow bed in a small room with no window. A white sheet had been tucked in so tightly around him that he found himself unable to move and to his surprise he found that he was naked. He looked around the room. There was little in it: a metal chair against the wall with his clothes neatly folded; a bookcase with religious texts sandwiched between guidebooks and medical brochures; a table with a jug of water covered with a dainty white napkin. He had no idea if he was in a hospital or a prison – it could have been either. He thought he should call out but when he tried his voice, like the rest of him, was feeble.

A noise at the door made him try and turn his head but it was too painful to move, with flashes of bright light and cracks like twigs snapping. When he opened his eyes, four nuns in white tunics formed a semicircle around the foot of the bed.

A friendly motherly lady smiled at him. She had a devotional scapular around her neck with an image on it which she held tightly to her chest in case it fell in the glass she was holding.

Ralph put a hand to his own chest. The wallet usually held on a bootlace around his neck was missing.

"Drink this."

"What is it?"

"Drink it. It will help you rest."

Ralph drank the cloudy liquid and lay his head on a pillow.

"My name is Sister Kathleen."

"How did I get here?"

She nodded to the nun next to her.

"Sister Barbara found you."

Ralph remembered nothing.

"I'm sorry. I've been sick."

"Well, the good news is you aren't going to die. Is he, Sister?"

"Not yet," said Sister Barbara.

Barbara didn't seem very happy but cheered when she spoke to him.

"You have hepatitis."

Ralph groaned.

Sister Kathleen held her hands in front of her as though about to pray.

"Now, don't make a fuss. There are five types, but you will have hep A, I'm sure. You would have got it from dirty water."

Barbara glowered at him in a Scottish way.

"Unless it's the hep B, which you would have got from dirty women."

Ralph groaned some more.

"Don't worry. Your hepatitis is going to be acute not chronic."

"What does that mean?"

"Well, it won't last more than six months," she said cheerfully.

Ralph wanted to howl.

"Most people around here have been infected. This is an area of the world with poor sanitation."

Ralph closed his eyes.

"I've noticed."

"You wouldn't have got it here," scowled Barbara. "Unless you've been here for two to six weeks. The average incubation period is twenty-eight days."

Ralph thought where he might have been four weeks ago. Probably walking through northern Zambia from the Tanzam railway to the bottom of Lake Tanganyika, just as his iodine supply had run out. Five days through remote villages, filling his bottle with unsterilised water from communal standpipes, eating fruit from local markets. Plenty of opportunities for faecal–oral transmission.

"There's no cure. You just have to rest."

Barbara waved a finger in his face.

"And no alcohol."

Kathleen agreed with her.

"Yes. No alcohol and no paracetamol. Too harsh on the liver."

She took the glass away.

"This will help. You'll sleep again now."

"Thank you, Sister."

She straightened up.

"Don't thank us. Christ fed the hungry, healed the sick, enlightened the ignorant and consoled the afflicted."

She wasn't talking to Ralph.

"Don't forget our episcopal motto, Sisters."

A very slight nun answered her.

"So that they could have life."

"Thank you, Sister Brenda."

She leaned toward Ralph to check if he was still awake.

"Our charism, our special gift from the Holy Spirit, is evangelisation. What do I mean by that?"

Ralph didn't know the answer and didn't care.

"We make Christ known and keep him present among the most needy."

Ralph watched Sister Barbara search his clothes. His wallet had been stained with sweat from lying against his

369

chest. It was fragile, the leather crumbling at the edges. She held it in two fingers like something toxic.

"Ours is not an enclosed order. We have few rules. You may have noticed, for example, that we don't always wear a wimple. And we take only simple vows."

Ralph wanted to ask about a wimple but was unable to talk. His eyes felt leaden and his head heavy.

Sister Kathleen looked at him and nodded to Sister Barbara.

"Ours is a journey of faith and hope. Sister Barbara, give the wallet to Sister Hilary."

Barbara reluctantly passed it to the other nun. Hilary opened it and removed a fifty-dollar note.

Barbara snatched the wallet back and peered inside.

"Is that all?"

She went close to the bed.

"Is that all you've got?"

Ralph struggled to speak.

"Give me my money," he croaked and collapsed.

Sister Kathleen rested her hand on his head.

"Sometimes our institution isn't able to meet all the requests asked of us. Our disciples are few and our resources are limited. This money will be a great asset to our congregation. The little children are our priority. We educate to liberate from ignorance, poverty and low self-image, to bring them into the light of God and knowledge. The Lord thanks you for your donation."

"But it's not enough," Sister Barbara hissed.

Ralph tried to sit up.

"Rest. We'll look after you, and then when you feel able you can find us some more money."

She addressed her congregation.

"Sisters. This is an opportunity to reaffirm ourselves and our resolutions, to focus with a single mind on our calling and mission."

Kathleen held out her hand.

"And Sister Hilary… I'll look after the cash."

TWENTY-THREE

·

Angel looked at the Nile from the aeroplane window as it approached Juba's airport. Between Juba and Kosti the river was called the Southern Reach but known locally by different names. Here at Juba it was the *Bahr al Jabal*, the Mountain River, but at the northern end of the Sudd swamp at Lake No, some way before Kosti, it was joined from the west by a river that drained a basin larger in area than France, *Bahr al Ghazal*, the Gazelle River. From that point, way beyond Angel's sight, the river became *Al Bahr al Abyad*, the White Nile. It wasn't simply the Nile until joining the Blue Nile at the confluence north of Khartoum.

Angel planned to focus his attention on the river and anticipated finding Ralph, or proving that he'd been and gone, quite quickly. He didn't want to be in Sudan, his thoughts continually drifting to Elanza. He'd stay at the best hotel in town and 'the firm' could pay. Perhaps there would be a phone in the room and he could call her. South Africa could pay for that too.

Sudan Airways threw him to the ground with determination, an arrival rather than a landing, but Angel felt relieved to be out of the sky. He'd flown through Kenya on two different tickets and had bought the one for the final leg to Juba in Nairobi airport, keen to disguise his place of origin. He travelled on his own British passport, the South African stamps, like the Israeli ones, always on pieces of paper he could later remove. Immigration hated doing it but a quiet word with a supervisor, along with his NIS identification, was usually sufficient to persuade them.

A smiling and polite officer in the terminal at Juba had welcomed him to Sudan without questioning his reason for travel. Angel was vaguely disappointed. He'd been 'getting into' his cover story all the way from Johannesburg, like a method actor. He'd spoken only English, chatting over the meal to a family from York returning to London after a safari, telling them excitedly of his life as an academic librarian at the School of Oriental and African Studies on Russell Square, the thrilling trips he often made to teach aid workers how to correctly catalogue field reports before submitting them to the UN.

"Thank you for coming, Mr Rock", was all the immigration officer had said, and Angel believed that he meant it.

The airport, inside the terminal and out, had been empty. The only other aircraft had been a vintage Dakota, identical to the ones he'd jumped from in the Army, with its engine cowls open, two men standing on a table looking inside and occasionally plucking out fragments like entrails from the dissection of a large farm animal.

Angel was determined not to waste time. He would complete what he needed to do immediately, spend the night comfortably, and leave on the following day's flight. With luck he would be back with Elanza in a little over forty-eight hours from leaving her. He wondered what local handicrafts they sold. He should take her something. Outside the terminal he paid fifty *piastres* for a car and driver and asked with difficulty for the steamer office, talking English to match his cover story but listening to fast-paced Arabic on the car radio with delight.

At the far end of town, Angel's silent driver pointed with a dirty finger to an abandoned office. A brochure in English told Angel what he needed to know. The Nile River 'steamer' run by the River Transport Corporation wasn't a steamer at all, just a collection of half a dozen old barges roped together and pushed by a paddle boat. It was state owned to make sure there would be no competition, guaranteeing its continuing inefficiency. It left both Juba and Kosti terminals on a fortnightly schedule, the timetable complicated by the fact that the upstream journey to Juba could take anything between nine and twelve days depending on the current it had to push the barges against, whereas the downstream trip to Kosti running with the water was always a reliable eight days. The steamer left Juba at dawn on alternate Fridays but people boarded at will and staked a claim to deck space the evening before.

Angel checked the date. It was 13th May, Thursday. The steamer left either the following day or in eight days' time. He asked his driver the date that the last ferry had left Juba. The man nodded and smiled, answering repeatedly in accented Arabic to Angel's English questioning, "*Alssabie*," the seventh. Angel knew now that the next steamer would be Friday, 21st May.

Angel thought back to his previous trip to Nairobi. Ralph had left down Aerodrome Road in the direction of Wilson airport followed by Nels' hitmen. That must have been 4th May. He would have been in Juba at least by 5th May, a Wednesday. The conclusion was obvious. Ralph had caught the steamer on 7th May, nearly a week ago. He had already gone.

*

Ralph lay in bed at Juba's Church of The Sacred Heart waiting for the singing to begin. The sisters checked him regularly but didn't say very much. They watched his condition for signs of improvement so he feigned sleep. That part at least wasn't difficult. Sister Barbara would peer around the door and scowl at the bed, while Sister Kathleen would stand for some time looking at the back of his head trying to determine his net worth. Only the mild Sister Brenda, who brought him chicken soup and sat on the edge of the bed gently spoon-feeding him, her hand at the back of his head, would talk to him. From her he learnt their routine.

They woke at five in the morning to prepare for Morning Prayer, followed by an hour of reflection in their own chambers. At half past seven they took Mass, beginning every day with Jesus Christ in the forefront of their minds. At nine they began their daily work, teaching the children of their congregation, until Sext at midday. The house became busy thereafter in between None, Vespers and Compline, until they finished their day as it began, thinking of Christ. Ralph planned his escape.

On the third day he rose again. It was early morning and he heard the nuns singing prayers in Latin. He put on clothes cleaned by Sisters Brenda and Hilary, threw his empty stained and rotten wallet onto the bed, and quietly slipped out of the house into the town. It had been easy. Much easier than digging a tunnel or building a glider, other options that, in his delirium, he had at times seriously considered.

At the river, down from the Hotel Africa, the steamer had docked, the barges tied to the bank. Piles of fifty-gallon oil drums, old sacks and bales of thatching reeds, moved from one barge to another in an apparently uncoordinated but cheerful ballet. On the river, people crowded into narrow dugout canoes around the barges, while on the far bank thousands of egrets sat watching from the bushes. In the river, crocodile rested on floating papyrus rafts half in and half out of the water.

Ralph had been advised to prepare for an unhurried cruise. The straight-line distance between Juba and Kosti measured 932 kilometres but the river meandered and dodged huge floating rafts of papyrus reeds for 1,436 sticky kilometres. For those who got on board at Juba the steamer made frequent stops at settlements along the way, but there was nothing to buy until Malakal at the far end of the swamp. People took their own food and something to cook it on outside the little camps they constructed on the deck of the barge from old pallets and plastic sheets. It was a long slow trip, made interesting only by the wildlife and remote tribal villages along the way.

Two men had arrived in the dormitory of the Hotel Africa and, respecting his undisturbed rucksack, had separated to either end of the room. They looked at Ralph with concern and kept their distance. He now looked completely yellow.

Surprisingly, while struggling with his rucksack, both had graciously helped him on to the steamer. One had a beard and had once been very fat, carrying loose skin in folds like a rare and valuable oriental dog. Ralph guessed he might be an oil worker as he planned to get off the boat at Adok, two and a half days downstream, close to Chevron's field at Bentiu. As he carried Ralph's rucksack he had proudly and wordlessly shown him a letter in English, a company logo at the head, detailing his joining instructions. Ralph never found out where he came from or understood a single word he said.

The other, a lean Japanese student, supported Ralph around the shoulder. Together they found a space near the front of a barge and pitched camp. Ralph sat watching them as they disappeared ashore, relieved to see them return laden with metal poles and large closely woven nylon bags. With no common language between the three of them they mimed and grunted to each other like cavemen as they made a home for three.

The bearded man went ashore again, returning with pasta and tins of sardines and a low collapsible camping chair without legs that reclined almost to a bed. Together they lifted him and tenderly placed him in the chair which they positioned in the shade of the tent they had constructed, looking forward and to the side so that Ralph could see the river ahead and the reeds that defined its edge. The two of them toasted their achievement with *aragi*, a whisky distilled from cassava.

Ralph remembered Sister Barbara's threatening words about alcohol and declined. He expected at any moment her hand would land on his shoulder, that the four nuns were presently scouring the town and the steamer dock, hunting him down. He pulled a large wide-brimmed safari hat, loaned by the bearded man, further forward to conceal his face.

*

Angel had asked his driver to take him to the market. It had been a difficult conversation. In the end, forsaking his cover story, he'd used Arabic but the Arabic the driver spoke sounded unlike anything Angel had heard before.

He browsed happily for a gift for Elanza, his work done, unable to decide between a crocheted rug or hand-embroidered linens. In the end he found a Toposa tribeswoman, her body covered in parallel lines of welts, and bargained without commitment for some bead work and two hanging calabash baskets.

To the driver he said simply, "Hotel," without knowing where he'd end up. It had been back towards the airport, within walking distance, handy for his flight home.

The Juba Hotel was a relic from a different age when Imperial flying boats had landed on the calm waters of the Nile and ladies in dresses that covered the ankle had drunk tea while men in pith helmets enjoyed whisky and sodas in The Long Bar before the flight continued the following day to Mwanza on Lake Victoria. The years had not been kind to the Juba Hotel but The Long Bar had survived, and two white men sat huddled over a bottle of Scotch that had been nowhere near Scotland.

Angel went to the bar and smiled at a man in a tight white turban.

"Gin and tonic, please," he asked in English. It felt the right thing to ask for in The Long Bar.

"No tonic, sir," he replied.

"Never mind."

"No gin, sir."

"Okay. I'll have what those gentlemen are drinking." Angel tilted his head in the direction of the two men.

The barman smiled a wide smile and touched his forehead.

"Whiky, sir."

He put a dark brown liquid in a glass bottle with no label on the bar top. Angel had thought in terms of a glass, not the whole bottle.

"I'm sorry?"

"Whiky," he repeated.

Angel examined the bottle warily.

"Ah. You mean whisky. Thank you."

"It'll kill you," said one of the two men. Angel hadn't seen which one. He'd spoken in English, but softly and sleepily as though already drunk.

"Are you British?" he asked.

"Yes, that's right. London."

"Lundun," the man said, mimicking Angel's Cockney accent. "I'm British too. Well, sort of. Northern Ireland. Like British but better."

Angel nodded to him.

"And Jean here, he's a Canuck, from Canuckland."

Angel laughed.

"I see."

The man took a long pull from the brown bottle.

"So, what brings you to this shithole from Old Lundun Town?"

"Oh, work," said Angel. He didn't elaborate, keen to change the subject. "Were you two working on the Dak's port engine this morning?"

Both men looked up from the table at him with interest.

"I saw you on the apron working from a trestle when I came in."

"What do you know about a Dak?" the Irishman asked accusingly.

"Only what I learnt from riding in one, before they pushed me out."

The Irishman laughed until he spluttered and coughed.

Canuk Jean stood from the table.

"Come and join Jim and me for a drink," he said, then quietly while nodding at Jim; "Leave the bottle. We've had enough already."

Jim's forehead rested on the table. He looked up as Angel sat beside him and looked at him quizzically.

"We fly the Dak," Jean said.

"Except Jean's bust it," Jim said. "Been stuck here over a week trying to fix it."

Jean looked away. Angel felt that it sounded like an argument Jean was familiar with and wanted to avoid.

"Valve seats burnt right out. Too lean, you see. Got too hot. Reduced power take-offs. Ha."

"So, were you in the Army?" Jean asked Angel quickly.

"Yes."

"Which war?" asked Jim. "The big one?"

"No. How about you? Were you in the RAF?"

"Never. Spent the whole war a civilian," said Jim.

"Which war?" Angel asked him.

"The big one."

Jean leaned forward.

"You were talking about that the other night in Loki. When you talked to the boy about Phillips."

"That's what I learnt to fly in. A Phillips aircraft. Shorts had a hangar at Long Kesh making wings for Stirling Bombers, and Phillips & Powis were assembling Messengers for VIP transport. It was easy to get to learn to fly there if you were keen and helped out."

Jean looked at Angel and winked.

"So, what did you do in the war, Dad?" he asked mischievously.

"Not much."

"But you would have been the right age, I guess. Born in '22?"

Jim had drunk a long way down the whisky bottle, his head rolling forward then springing back as he spoke.

"I worked at Shorts, begged for rides to learn to fly, ended up delivering all sorts of things for the ATA. They'd take anyone with two arms. In fact, they took people with one arm."

Angel looked around the room. The barman had his chin in one hand listening to them.

"What's the ATA?" he asked.

"Air Transport Auxiliary. Old men, battered pilots, women, kids like me – all of us ferrying aircraft from factories to the squadrons. The pilots came from all over the world. Quite a few Yanks, bless 'em. It was a civilian organisation based at White Waltham, sort of attached to BOAC. Which is how I ended up with the airline flying Mosquitoes."

Jean laughed.

"BOAC had Mosquitoes?"

Jim drank. He wiped a dribble with the palm of his hand.

"Leuchars to Stockholm. Every night. Sweden remained neutral; we had to be civilians in civilian aircraft. Our Mossies had Golf registrations and a Speedbird on the tail."

"Why?"

Jim was getting confused. There were two people with him but he found it difficult to hold his eyes open and didn't see who'd spoken.

"Why what?"

"Why Mosquitoes? Why Sweden?"

"We needed something fast to outrun the Germans. They called it the 'Ball Bearing Run'. Load of rubbish. We did that a few times but it wasn't that important. The Americans didn't need Swedish ball bearings so why would we? We carried cash and gold on the way out. Don't know where it went."

He looked at the bottle.

"Russia probably. And to bribe the Swedes not to supply Hitler. And we brought home downed pilots who'd made it to Sweden through Denmark."

Jim's eyes closed.

"And VIPs. We lined out the bomb bay with felt for them, put a seat in it with a little reading light and a thermos. One of our pilots brought back a Danish nuclear physicist. Stupid man didn't put his oxygen mask on. He only lived because the pilot worried about him and did the whole trip at ten thousand feet."

Jim was back at Leuchars in Scotland. The de Havilland Mosquito, the 'Wooden Wonder', the fear of being caught by enemy aircraft in the long dark nights.

"I didn't like the Swedes. They were very clever though. They stayed neutral and made money. Hitler needed fifteen million tons of iron ore a year during the war. He bought eleven million tons of it from Sweden. The Swedes sold Hitler the iron ore that the Nazis needed to make bombs and tanks and guns and warships. It was just business, the commerce of free trade, and sixty million dead people didn't need to appear as a liability on any balance sheet."

Jean couldn't disguise his curiosity. He'd always respected Jim for his flying at least.

"What was the Mossie like to fly?"

"Quick. Two thumping great Merlin engines but in an airframe made of a sandwich of balsa wood and Canadian birch. Twenty per cent lighter than Betsy but with getting on for fifty per cent more power. Now *that* was a tail dragger."

Angel wished he hadn't joined them. Something troubled him that he couldn't identify.

"I'll tell you what Göring said about the Mosquito. He said the British could afford aluminium better than Germany and yet they knocked together a beautiful wooden aeroplane that any piano factory could make. They have geniuses he said."

Jim smiled to himself.

"Of course, Germany had geniuses too but they thought in straight lines. What's always set us apart is that British geniuses think back to front and inside out while drinking cold tea upside down."

Jean laughed.

"I stayed with BOAC after the war. Came to Africa with them. Flew Avro Yorks through Nairobi on the Cairo to Durban route until '48, then for years after that with only freight. They were just Lancasters really. Unpressurised."

Jim took a final swig from the bottle.

"And then I trained BOAC pilots in tropical flying techniques."

"Where was that?"

"Soroti in Uganda."

Jim said nothing for a long time. Angel thought he was nearly asleep, his breathing quiet and steady.

"Lettice was there, an ATA girl from White Waltham. Brilliant pilot. BOAC was happy to use her through the war but afterwards they dumped her. 'Not the done thing, old chap. Can't have a woman driving the aeroplane. What would the customers think?' She was Australian. Told them where to go. Threatened to make all sorts of fuss, so they sent her to Soroti out of the way."

Angel stirred in his seat and Jim opened his eyes and talked to him.

"Lettice had a friend in the war called Diana Ramsey, known to all as Wamsey because she couldn't pronounce her Rs. Wamsey force-landed a Hawker Tempest, a brutal thing to fly. The throttle had stuck wide open so she shut it down but landed at a hell of a speed. Went across a field into a wood. Clean through every tree. Wings came off but the fuselage stayed in one piece. When people got to her she didn't have a scratch. She was sitting on top of the cockpit canopy and wouldn't come down. She was scared of the cows milling around."

Jim laughed and shook the empty bottle.

"Women are wonderful things. Complicated, wonderful things. I love one but she's less than half my age."

Jean wasn't sure who he was talking about. He didn't know any women who would go for an old drunk like Jim.

"I'm old enough to be her father."

Angel slipped away to bed quietly, mouthing 'thank you' to Jean Canuck. He lay in bed troubled, thinking of the pilots, sure there was something he'd missed. Eventually he slept but awoke before the dawn unsure of himself. It was something Jean had said. Angel sat up, suddenly alert. Jean had said two unconnected words in a sentence. He'd said 'the boy' and 'Phillips' but without linking one word to the other. The boy and Phillips. The boy Ralph Phillips.

Angel jumped out of bed. It all made sense. Ralph had flown with them over a week ago. More importantly, he now remembered the barman saying whiky instead of whisky and he suddenly realised that the accent of his driver had been so unusual that he'd misunderstood his Arabic. Angel thought he'd said *alssabie*, the seventh. He'd actually said *alrrabie*, the fourteenth. The steamer office had been deserted because the entire staff had all been down at the river, tending to the arriving steamer, preparing for its departure the next day. Ralph hadn't left on 7th May. There had been no ferry that week. It was a fortnightly service. The steamer left today, 14th May, at dawn. Ralph must still be here.

Angel ran to the door. It was still dark outside. Sunrise here would be around 6.30am. He glanced at his watch. 5.10am. Plenty of time. He looked for his shoes.

"Shit," he said.

His watch was on Johannesburg time. He hadn't changed it. Local time was an hour ahead. It was 6.10am. He estimated he was five kilometres from the river, the wrong side of town. 5K. Under twenty minutes. Angel bolted through the door.

He sprinted south, dogs barking outside a hospital on his right, heart pounding until he reached a sleeping gas station. He stayed on the road rather than run through side streets in the dark, his feet echoing and chest heaving.

At the twin square towers of a cathedral Angel slowed and took his bearings. The river was to his left but he was too far north with no direct route to the steamer dock. He ran south still but now off the main road that curved away from the river, down dirt paths between block houses with flat roofs, heading past a truck park toward the old mosque.

He could see the river now, hear the noise of the port area. He turned left heading east and tripped, staggering and falling into a row of parked motorcycles. He had to be very close. Shaking himself free he sprinted to the port.

Dawn was just breaking over the Nile, the slow flat water reflecting orange. He leant gasping against a pile of logs. He was too late. The old barges had slipped from the bank, the paddlewheel steamer already churning water off the dock.

*

With some relief Ralph felt the barge slip lines and move over flat water in a pink and grey dawn, the white egrets still at roost. The barge moved silently, pushed from behind by the old paddlewheel steamer that had never been powered by steam. The river was ill-defined and slow-moving. From its source at Lake Victoria to Juba the river dropped six hundred metres, but from Juba to Khartoum, over twice the distance, it dropped only seventy-five, slowing almost to stagnation in the Sudd. Over the river and small lakes Ralph watched floating plant life that had formed into huge islands of matted vegetation up to thirty kilometres long. At times he couldn't see the river at all, pernicious hyacinth spreading over the water surface, choking the channels and impeding traffic until the barge forged a path with its blunt bow. Over the hyacinth and the rafts of floating papyrus were grasslands flooded by the river so that it was impossible for Ralph to tell where the water ended and the land began. This flat flood plain the size of Belgium was not the edge of the river, as rain-flooded grasses appeared and disappeared overnight. At the very edge, often far away, Ralph strained to see the wooded grasslands cultivated by Dinka, Nuer and Shilluk.

Entranced, he waved to small fishing communities of two or three thatched homes, completely isolated from the world, perched on dry ground. They took very little fish. It had been estimated that the Sudd part of the Nile could support a catch of seventy-five thousand tons of fish and still be self-sustaining. Only about 11,500 tons were taken, not a fifth of its potential. A valuable export industry lay untapped. A little was dried and sent to the Congo where it was in big demand, but most of that caught was consumed locally.

Ralph's new Japanese friend was called Hisao. He tried to redress the imbalance. Hisao was an expert fisherman, hauling catch over the side of the barge that had locals sighing with admiration. Species identification was his only handicap. He would offer strange looking river-dwelling creatures, some not even resembling fish, to his audience, and if they took them to eat so would he. Mudfish, and at night huge air-breathing vundu catfish powerful enough to pull a fisherman to the bottom, were turned back or their bloody gills used for bait, as were knifefish, deadly to touch and with the shock of an electric eel. Tigerfish, a vicious predator with fierce razor-like teeth, were eaten even though the meaty flesh was bony and slightly oily. Nile tilapia, introduced to eat mosquito larvae and snails and hopefully control malaria and bilharzia, thrived in the brackish waters of the Sudd and were a delicacy. Disappointingly, Nile perch evaded Hisao. It was no reflection of his extraordinary ability but only because they lived in deep-water lakes and not in the shallows of the Southern Reach.

Humming to himself over a little charcoal fire, Hisao would cook his catch, carefully select the whitest meat, and with his fingertips gently feed Ralph fish so fresh that the flesh squeaked against his teeth when he ate it.

For hours they would sit at the entrance to their home, unable to talk to each other, pointing out crocodile, hippo and painted hunting dogs. The quantity of wildlife astonished them. It came as no surprise when, in exaggerated mime after reading aloud a Japanese guidebook, Hisao explained to him that there were more antelope in the Sudd than in the Serengeti.

Together, over tilapia dinners, they marvelled at cranes and pelicans fishing, black and white sacred ibis wading, and prehistoric looking shoe-billed storks with heads like a whale. Ralph thought Hisao showed him that there were four hundred species of bird in the Sudd, although numbers that large were difficult to communicate on two hands.

Ralph had taken a book about Sudan from the nuns at the convent. He consoled himself with believing it wasn't theft. He'd paid fifty dollars for it. From it he read of ever-present threats to the Sudd and that it might not always remain as unspoiled. Construction had started on one of the largest irrigation projects ever attempted in Africa, a plan to divert the Nile around the Sudd by digging a canal to channel the water away from the flood plain. Over fifty-five per cent of the water entering the Sudd evaporated. It was estimated that when complete the Jonglei Canal carrying Nile water away from the Sudd would increase the quantity of water downstream in Egypt by five to seven per cent and provide irrigation water for an additional eight thousand square kilometres of farm land. The Jonglei was to run from Bor in a straight line due north to the confluence of the Sobat River with the Nile near Malakal, a huge German excavation rig named Sarah already at work. The benefits would be solely for Egypt and the north of Sudan. The environmental destruction of a unique natural habitat for herds of buffalo, elephant and hippo, and the detrimental social impact on the activities of the south Sudanese indigenous tribes that depended on the Sudd for cattle rearing, were completely overlooked. To understand Sudanese politics one had to be either a prophet or a fool.

An old proverb said that when Allah created Sudan he laughed. Another said that he cried. Allah alone knew. His influence, however, became more and more obvious when the White Nile widened after Lake No, the Sudd now behind them, and they approached Kosti and the bottom of the brown half of Sudan on Ralph's map. At dawn on the seventh day out of Juba, in the river town of Melut 140 kilometres north of Malakal, Ralph saw his first mosque. The muezzin made *adhan*, the long, ornamented repetitions of his voice summoning Muslims for mandatory worship. Ralph was at the end of Africa. It was the start of Arabia.

*

From Kosti, Ralph wanted to walk but he soon felt lonely and wished he'd caught the train with Hisao. The road had crossed the Nile and, after a two-hour slow walk from the bridge, the road and railway paralleled each other. For a further seven kilometres they ran just forty metres apart, reminding him of what he should have done. The railway then ran in a dead straight line from Rabak to Sennar with few stations. Four train halts had been placed with precision exactly twenty-five kilometres apart. Ralph wondered if it had been built by the British, the distance the same as that between market towns in Dorset.

The road to Sennar went through a moonscape, the temperature away from the river making Ralph weak and stumble. Near to the first halt a crowded train went past and Ralph saw somebody standing on the roof, waving, shouting his name. Ralph watched the train disappear. Sadly he limped along, struggling. Through a haze he saw a thin man sitting by the road, waiting for him. Hisao walked towards him, lifted his rucksack without saying anything and walked alongside him wordlessly, slowly, at his pace. Ralph wanted to cry.

It stayed hot and dry, dust storms, a prelude to rain, reducing visibility and forcing them to shelter from the sun and wind at a sandy town called Jebel Moya, three-quarters of the way to Sennar. While bed-bound and bored at the convent in Juba, Ralph had listlessly read a pamphlet, a data sheet on a new drug by Wellcome that told of the company's historical involvement in Sudan. In the late Neolithic period from 500 to 100 BC, Jebel Moya had been a mortuary complex for pastoral peoples, a combined cemetery and settlement that had been excavated before World War One by Sir Henry Wellcome. He'd dug up 2,800 graves. Ralph watched craftsmen in mud-walled buildings making ornamental beads to adorn the dead, just as they had two thousand years before.

They saw few women. In the south of Sudan, away from Islamic practices, women were subordinate to men but enjoyed much greater freedom than in the north. Female circumcision was not practised in the south and a cult called Zar, that conducted ceremonies to pacify evil spirits and cleanse women of afflictions, did not exist. Women had greater freedom of movement, were consulted on public affairs and played an important role in the mediation of disputes. In the north, girls remained in the household, segregated from festivities, eating separately and after the men.

Hisao, apprehensive at sleeping among the dead, was keen to leave Jebel Moya in the morning, leading Ralph by the hand through the village to the railway platform. Ralph pulled him stubbornly to the road. They would walk.

At Sennar they met the Blue Nile, except that it was brown and turbid. Their walking rate had slowed, the breaks more frequent and longer. In Wad Madani a local thought they were making a dangerous journey and that Ralph should have a lucky amulet. He demonstrated how powerful it was by holding a scorpion. Ralph bought it while Hisao arranged a ride in a lorry to Khartoum.

*

It was the first week of June, the hottest time of the year in Khartoum, with average temperatures well over forty centigrade and the *harmattan*, a hot dry desert wind from the north. Ralph felt tired and needed to sleep at night so he chose to stay at the Hotel Royal. It was seventy *piastres* a night, twenty *piastres* more than the youth hostel, but there were fans in the bedrooms.

He looked thin after Juba and the Nile and ate frequently at the police canteen on El Mahdi Avenue, usually as much as he could eat bowls of meat and lentils for about twenty cents. It was costing just a dollar a day for food and accommodation.

Khartoum had at one time been a focal point in the trade of African slaves to Arab countries. Now there was an aspirational monument to national unity and a large open-air market just south of the Great Mosque, Souq Al Arabi, a large area devoted to gold, a historic trade. The Egyptians had retreated south into northern Sudan when their ancient empire had passed its zenith and was threatened by a succession of Hittites, Assyrians and Romans. Nubia became the source of much of Egypt's gold, an estimated forty tons a year.

Ralph went to the British Embassy, a formidable building in a square by a park looking at, and deliberately overpowering, the Republican Palace. Taking the advice of the man called Rots, he received a call from his parents on a telephone that said 'Unsecure Line', a nice lady from Cheltenham sitting demurely in the room with him throughout, Ralph unsure if it was to stop him saying something he shouldn't or in case he stole the phone.

A familiar voice came through six thousand kilometres of wire.

"Ralph?"

"Hello, Dad."

Afterwards he wished he hadn't called. It was the second of June, the start of the loveliest month in Dorset, his mother's birthday, weather for drinking in the garden of a village pub, The Plough at Manston or The Two Brewers, daylight until after nine at night. Mum would pick vegetables from the garden for lunch to go with lamb, small potatoes with tender skins and crispy beans, and sit under a tree reading until teatime. He wanted to be there.

Ralph looked in the door of the last bastion of the British Empire, The Sudan Club. He could hear the chink of snooker balls and smell the pink gin. An immaculate doorman looked at him and shook his head.

In the souk he bought a turban, a wide strip of lightweight white cotton about ten metres long, not knowing what to do with it. The stallholder spent fifteen minutes teaching him how to wear it until, exasperated, he gave up and prayed, Ralph hoped for him.

He headed to the Egyptian Embassy on Gamma'a Avenue for a visa but dawdled, delayed and distracted by the zoo opposite, baffled why anyone would confine hippo while so many lived so close, just down the Nile a short way. In Khartoum Africa already felt very distant.

TWENTY-FOUR

The lunchtime crowd had spilled out of The Northumberland Arms onto central London's Gower Street, drawn from the beery gloom of the public bar into the early June sunshine like bees.

Jumbo Cameron sat inside at a small table pulling apart a beer mat, thinking of work. October and November the previous year had been busy with four explosions in London at barracks and burger bars. Since then things had quietened down, until yesterday.

"Penny for 'em," said Zac.

"Bloody Palestinians," mumbled Jumbo into his glass.

Zac had heard all about it. The Israeli ambassador had just been shot on Park Lane outside of The Dorchester hotel by Abu Nadal, a militant group splintered from the PLO.

Jumbo threw shredded remnants of cardboard into an ashtray.

"I would like to know how Israeli civil servants can afford to eat in The Grill at The Dorchester anyway. Costs a bomb."

Jumbo knocked his pint back in three wide gulps.

"Another, sir?"

"Thank you, Zac."

Zac stood up to join the throng three deep at the bar.

"Oh yes, can you remember a Ralph Phillips?" he asked.

"Vaguely."

Zac knew that meant Jumbo remembered perfectly. He always did. He hid the embarrassment of owning a brilliant brain, efficient as a well-organised filing cabinet, behind the mannerisms of an inept Great War general.

"He was a walk-in," Zac said, elbowed out of the way by a baying broker in a black suit.

"Where?"

"Khartoum. He walked in and asked to use the phone. Cheeky bugger."

Walk-ins were aspiring defectors or 'offers of service', often with grand proposals or earth-shattering secrets, who appeared out of the blue at the front desk of foreign embassies. There was a protocol for dealing with them, usually disbelief and suspicion followed by polite refusal. If they were serious they'd come back.

Jumbo smiled.

"What did he do? Call his mum?"

"Exactly that." Zac thought of the boy he'd met in South Africa, quiet and serious, reserved yet good-humoured. "Odd fellow."

"The best ones are," said Jumbo.

Zac agreed.

"Yes, I was thinking. We should meet him, see what he's like, see if he'd be of any use."

Jumbo was thinking only of Israel and the conversation he was scheduled to have that afternoon with a youthful and precocious minister from the Home Office.

"If you like, Zac."

"He's done well, sir. Easy to lose your way out there, easy to say the wrong thing, look the wrong guy in the eye and end up with a meat cleaver in your skull. Nobody would know, nobody to help."

"He's not back yet."

"True, true. Many a slip."

"You want to recruit him?" Jumbo asked.

Jumbo's own recruitment had been just as unconventional. An invitation during his final year in '72 from a history professor at Durham to meet a friend in London, an interview for a job that had never been explained where it seemed they'd talked only of the Rolling Stones, an instruction by mail, 'DO NOT REDIRECT FOR ADDRESSEE ONLY' in large red print on the envelope, telling him to report to what looked like a tanning salon in Twickenham. It had been a while before someone quietly informed him that his employer was called the Security Service. Then he'd gone to school. At a remote dairy farm in Yorkshire they'd taught him to measure the dimensions of buildings using his thumb on an outstretched arm, and to take clandestine notes inside his trouser pocket. It had looked like he was playing with himself. He'd expected something clever inside a special watch but they'd given him two inches of a soft pencil and pieces of card cut from a box of tea bags.

"If he gets home we'll make an assessment; how's that, Zac?"

Jumbo started destroying another beer mat.

"Actually, you've reminded me of something."

Zac turned from the bar.

"I thought there might be a small error in a report you wrote, let me see, yes, it was dated 31st January."

It didn't surprise Zac in the least that Jumbo had been quietly cogitating the fine detail of a report written more than four months previously.

"You said that it would take fifteen minutes to drive from the city centre to The Circle."

Zac guessed Jumbo was being purposefully ambiguous in public. He couldn't remember how long the drive from Pretoria had been.

"Yes, that sounds right."

"You were correct. It's only twenty kilometres from the Union Buildings," said Jumbo. "I measured it the other day."

Zac tried to recall South Africa. He'd driven out of Pretoria toward The Circle and then Pelindaba, before meeting Angel at a farm further down the road and climbing Shelter Rock. Zac smiled. Sheltering Rock. Appropriate. He got it now.

"In the north-western part of the country we are referring to, there is an area larger than Germany but with practically nobody in it."

"I see," said Zac, confused.

"If you had all that empty space why would you locate a site like The Circle so close to the seat of government?"

Zac was catching up, as always Jumbo ahead of him. The significance of where South Africa had built and stored its nuclear weapons hadn't occurred to him. At the time the focus had been on how they might deliver them.

"Wouldn't you put the nasty things in the middle of nowhere in case something went wrong?"

Zac had lost his place at the bar.

"Where do they store them in the US?" Jumbo asked.

"Montana, Wyoming, the Dakotas. The big square ones in the middle. They try and keep them at least a hundred miles from a major city."

"Exactly. With that in mind, Zac, don't you think The Circle is in rather an odd place?"

"Perhaps The Circle has to be close to Pelindaba," Zac whispered.

"They aren't here."

Jumbo was right. In the UK, the original uranium enrichment plant, equivalent to Pelindaba, had been at Capenhurst in Cheshire, while Aldermaston and Burghfield, similar to The Circle, were in leafy Berkshire, two hundred miles away.

"And the last time I looked, Tennessee was a long way from Texas."

Jumbo was referring to Oak Ridge, the US Atomic City in the Appalachians that supplied fissile material, and the sixteen-hour drive west down I-40 to the Pantex weapon assembly facility in the desert near Amarillo.

Jumbo looked at his watch.

"Zac, forget that pint. Get me one next time. Sailing Club Tuesday evening?"

Zac's mind was elsewhere. South Africa building The Circle twenty kilometres from the Union Buildings was like the UK storing its nuclear weapons at Heathrow or in Dagenham. It didn't make sense.

"Right."

"I've got to go. See you back at the office."

It was a Friday afternoon. Jumbo didn't expect to see Zac until Monday morning.

"Yes, sir. I'm right behind you."

As always, thought Zac.

*

The train from Khartoum ran north along the Nile. At al-Mogran, the confluence of the White Nile that Ralph had followed from Uganda with the Blue Nile from Ethiopia, the water was surprisingly placid, where Ralph had expected turbulent cascades.

From there to Wadi Halfa it crossed the Nubia, numbered stations the only civilisation in a hot sandy desert. At station number six, train bogies lay abandoned in the sand. Ralph rode with others on the roof of the train, his turban pulled across his face. It was hard not to feel like Lawrence.

From the station at Wadi Halfa it was a one-kilometre walk over the brow of a hill to the Aswan Ferry terminal. A boat left after midday two times a week for the two-day trip to the High Dam. Ralph had been warned that it was important to take your own food and drink, the water on board taken straight from Lake Nasser. Bilharzia, a parasitic disease causing abdominal pain, diarrhoea, and blood in stools and urine, became a major concern. In terms of economic impact it was second only to malaria and endemic in Egypt due to the dam and irrigation projects along the Nile, common in farmers, fishermen and children who played in the water. The intermediary host was a freshwater snail, and Ralph worried about going in the water let alone drinking it, bilharzia the last thing he needed after hepatitis. *Fool* and hot sweet tea were available, however, and included in the 'Deck Class' price of less than three Egyptian pounds – about five dollars. Cabins were available and generally free of the rats that otherwise ran over you as you slept. Ralph risked the rodents and arrived early to claim some deck space before it became too crowded.

Alim called Angel from a noisy coffee house in the street below his Cairo office.

"Who is this guy?" Alim shouted.

"He's just a boy. What do you know?"

"Not a lot, Angel. He caught the ferry to Aswan and has disappeared."

Angel smiled.

"Yes, he's good at that. We need to find him. He may be in some danger."

"When I hear something I'll go myself and hunt for your Englishman," Alim reassured him.

Angel put the phone down, disappointed but then cheered. It may be a good thing Ralph had disappeared. If Alim wasn't able to find him in Egypt then no one could.

*

The Aswan ferry broiled into Egypt. At one time Nubians lived where now there was only the water of Lake Nasser, the construction of the Aswan High Dam destroying Nubia as it was inundated by the Nile trapped in the valley. Fifty thousand Nubians were resettled north of Aswan and provided with land, new homes and financial support. They hated it. The government had built cement block houses, different from their traditional homes and less comfortable. Family groups had been separated and historic rivalries ignored. Many Nubians rented their land to other farmers and moved to the cities, the family bonds broken. A handful returned to Nubia. Ralph looked enthralled at the farming villages they'd established on the shores of the new Lake Nasser – traditional homes, brightly coloured with sand floors and not all rooms having a roof. There was no need. It never rained.

Aswan town was some way from the ferry port. A train went from the quay into town and taxi drivers touted bossily for business. A muleteer offered Ralph a ride on a very thin donkey for a dollar but he declined, walking over the High Dam to the west side of the Nile and then, after ten kilometres through dusty wasteland, crossed back to Aswan town on the top of the Low Dam.

Ralph favoured the river rather than the town centre and continued north to a ferry terminal on the east bank at the outskirts of Nagaa Ash Shalabab. It had been a twenty-five-kilometre walk and taken him ten hours. He was in pain, weak and unfit, his feet bleeding in worn boots.

Beyond the tourist river cruisers small traditional sailing boats moored themselves securely to a dock, working commercially as they had for millennia. An unnamed felucca carrying stone, low in the water, lay on the outside of a raft of similar lateen-sailed boats. Ralph negotiated his passage. It would cost him five dollars, including food.

They sailed by day, Mahmoud the helmsman steering with his foot on the tiller. At night they would camp on the shore close to a fire of sycamore fig. Aswan in June reached forty centigrade by day but only ten at night, and it felt very cold. Huddled by the fire they coached him in Arabic. Ralph wasn't sure how much use it would be. They taught him first most of the parts of a woman's body and then progressed to how to say 'I love you'. Ralph concluded that people were the same all over the world.

It took three slow days to reach Luxor, their speed entirely dependent on the current, a strong Etesian wind blowing towards them from the north making sailing impossible.

They arrived in the dark, slipping under the illuminated Temple, the Southern Sanctuary, with the current behind them, and docked for the night on the Ancient Quay.

It was to be the last part of the trip that Ralph would make on water. From Luxor he walked north again, along the east bank of the Nile through farmland.

*

The construction of the Aswan High Dam had made Lake Nasser the largest artificial lake ever created and had turned the Nile into a huge and predictable irrigation ditch. In simple terms, it had put farmers in control of how much water went to which crop and at what time. Like farming everywhere, there were still problems; in Egypt they were a decreasing fertility of the soil, the weather, and very small farms.

Before the High Dam was built the land had been fertile due to the river flooding, then depositing silt and nutrients as it receded. Now, the life-giving silt became trapped by the dam and remained in Lake Nasser. Downstream, with reduced deposition, the water table rose and the soil became saline. The river now brought regulated water flow and life, but it made the ground salty and crops suffered and died.

And then there was the wind. A wind called the *khamsin* blew from the desert in April for days on end, a 140-kilometre-an-hour sandblaster, shredding plants and produce. There was nothing that could be done. Along with the sand that the *khamsin* carried, the hot desert air could cause a twenty centigrade temperature rise in just two hours. Plants that weren't ripped to pieces shrivelled in the heat.

The farms were small, their size limited to fifty *feddan*, about twenty hectares. Nobody could own more land than that, although people tried to find ways around it. It was a good socialist model but it did nothing for efficiency and economies of scale.

Despite these problems medium-sized landowners, those with six to ten *feddan*, could show a profit, something a grower in Europe could never hope to do with only three or four hectares. Most landowners, however, were peasant smallholders with less than five *feddan*, too small an area for profitable agriculture even in Egypt. These farmers worked for larger landowners as well, or found seasonal work in towns.

How any of them survived was a mystery to Ralph. As he walked he looked at the crops being grown. There was no grass. The water buffalo, milked instead of cows, had to eat something. There was no grazing but there was clover and corn, presumably for animal feed. They grew beans and lentil, wheat and barley, sugarcane and onions. All of them rotating around and around on little patches of land. Around and around.

And then Ralph stopped, unable to move. Like an epiphany he knew the answer and it seemed both simple and a miracle of nature and ingenuity. The alluvial soils were still very fertile, despite the rising water table, and the *khamsin* only blew in April, and then not all month long. The rest of the year there were near optimum growing conditions. That helped, but wasn't the reason Egypt didn't starve.

The secret was double, or even triple, cropping. On each piece of land two or three crops a year could be grown. The fertile soils, freely available water and good growing conditions lasted all year round. There was no winter. Suddenly a farmer's ten hectares became twenty or even thirty hectares of crops cultivated. Although Egypt had the lowest cultivatable area per capita of anywhere in the world, double and triple cropping meant it could survive and its people could be fed. Since the 1960s the average food consumption had increased by a thousand calories a person a day, and the amount of protein eaten had increased by nearly thirty per cent, both to levels similar to those in developed countries.

And not only were Egyptians clever, they were kind. Ralph would arrive in a village, changed into his long trousers and a button-down shirt, and look for an elder male. Most villages seemed to be split into quarters, with four clans. Each clan had a house to entertain visitors, and Ralph never went in the houses where they slept with their wife, or wives, and unmarried daughters. If Ralph saw the women at all they would be veiled. The family was usually extended, the father's single and married sons, and their wives and children, all living in houses in the quarter. Young deferred to old, women deferred to men, and the father controlled all of their possessions and income.

Their most deeply held values, honour dignity and security, came from being part of a family as well as from God. They practised a simple, honourable and benign form of Islam, family and kinship the most important things in life.

The clans often vied with each other for power and influence in the village. Ralph learnt that he could use this to his advantage. Providing food and shelter to a foreigner showed to the other clan elders how knowledgeable he and his sons were of the world outside and of international affairs. They would boast of it in the following days.

A son, if not the father, would always speak a little English, and both were proud when given the opportunity.

"I am the eldest son," Ralph would tell them, but never that he was the only son. "My father is a merchant. A trader."

"And he has land?" they would enquire.

"A little."

A very few feddan, thought Ralph, *but enough for Dad and Mum to grow a few early potatoes in springtime, to pick runner beans through summer and cabbages and leeks in winter.*

Ralph's social standing and position in his own village was then instantly understandable to them. He was the eldest son of a merchant who wasn't landless.

"*Ahlan wa sahlan.*"

"Welcome," the son would translate.

Ralph had learnt from Mahmoud the *felucca* captain to say greetings that sounded *Masri*, Egyptian colloquial Arabic, not the official *Fusha*.

"*Fursa sa'ida,*" he would reply, "*Ismee Mark. Ana min England.*"

When invited inside to eat he would remove his shoes and compliment the son on the house. He waited to be told where to sit, ate with his right hand only and showed his appreciation by giving the compliment of eating seconds. At the end of the meal he would offer money three times until the father would joke, '*U'af! Itassal bil bulees!*'. It was his final word, but Ralph would say '*Shukran gazelan*' and leave a few dollars tucked under his plate anyway.

He did it nine times walking the east bank of the Nile, nearly three hundred kilometres from the tourist sights of Luxor towards the university town of Asyut through Qena and Sohag. He would have been happy to continue for the rest of his life, wandering the countryside, watching with interest the farmers at their work, eating and sleeping in a different village every night with honest, kind Egyptians.

*

Alim had driven from Cairo at half past four, in the cool of the dawn. The previous afternoon a report had been delivered to his desk in a hot office. His company imported air conditioners and he wondered why they didn't have one of their own. He had read the note slowly, the paper already damp from someone else's sweat.

"On the road to Asyut?" he asked no one in particular.

In the evening he'd had a long phone interview with a very nervous rural police lieutenant on his curious report of a wandering Englishman. Then he'd called Angel.

From Asyut, Alim had followed the river south through Al Mutiah, Baqur and Abu Tij. At nine o'clock, thirty-five kilometres from Asyut, he found Ralph hobbling up the road towards him, just outside a town called Sidfa. He drove past without slowing, stopped out of sight and turned around.

Alim offered him a lift. He was heading that way, he said, back to Cairo to his employer, the El-Nasr Export & Import Company, exporting batteries, tyres, industrial equipment, building materials and foods. In reality they exported anything they liked and imported mostly information. It was only a cover organisation after all, a front for the Mukhabarat, the Egyptian General Intelligence Directorate.

Ralph had a pain in his toe that made him limp. He'd started late in the day and, because of it, he accepted the lift. Alim soon convinced him that he'd made the right decision by saying that he had been walking, appropriately, in the month of *Shaban*, when, of old, people scattered and dispersed to find water. Ramadan, literally the month of 'burning heat', was due to start in a few days. It was the 21st of June 1982, *Hijri* year 1402, and from the 23rd people would fast in daylight hours. They became grumpy until they were used to it and would be less likely to help Ralph with food and accommodation.

As they drove Alim talked about farming. Egypt was a desert, ninety-seven per cent of the land area uninhabitable, but the Nile valley and the Delta were the most extensive oasis on earth and home to ninety-nine per cent of the population and all of their food production. Alim had been in the area buying vegetables. It is a noble thing, he said, to grow food, to feed people. Ralph thought about his future.

"So, where have you been?" Alim asked.

"In Egypt?"

"Yes. Did you come from Sudan?"

"Correct. On the Lake Nasser steamer from Wadi Halfa to Aswan."

"And then?"

"I walked over the High Dam and crossed back to Aswan to catch a *felucca*."

"Did anyone stop you crossing the dam?"

"No. I just walked across."

It was a military area. Alim would remember that for later.

"What boat did you take?" he asked.

"Just some locals in an old sailboat. Except we didn't sail anywhere, just drifted down the river."

"What fun," and then innocently, "What was it called?"

"I don't think it had a name. It had a number on it but it was all in Arabic."

"Of course. Who was the captain?"

"Mahmoud."

Mahmoud was about the fourth most common given name in Egypt.

"Is that it?"

Ralph shrugged.

"Nice chap."

"So, how far did you go on your little sail?" Alim asked cheerfully.

"To Luxor. Right under the Temple. We stayed the last night on board tied to the dock and I left at dawn the next day."

"When was that?"

"Nine or ten days ago, I think. Yes, the 12th of June."

"And you've been walking since then?"

"It's been really interesting. All the farming, it's quite amazing."

Ralph had joined fields in open country four kilometres out of Luxor and followed a canal close to the river. He'd stayed off the Cairo road as much as possible, preferring minor roads and tracks through rectangles of crops and small villages. It had been hot but easy walking on flat land, like Holland on a summer day. Navigation had been easy – just keep the big river on the left. He'd walked as he had in the Cape, starting early to cover as much as he could by lunchtime and then resting before ambling for a few hours in the late afternoon while looking for a convenient place for the night. In this manner he could do thirty kilometres a day. If he'd been stronger he could have done much more. The easy flat going had helped enormously, as had his turban. He wasn't sure he wore it in the correct fashion as it covered most of his head, face and the top half of his body, but despite its weight it kept him cool and made him less conspicuous. By his best reckoning it had been two months since his initial infection with hepatitis and he still felt weak. The flat terrain and his turban helped, as had his rest in Juba and on the Nile River steamer under the care of Hisao. He realised he would have been too ill to walk from Kosti towards Khartoum without the help of his Japanese friend. Hisao had flown from Khartoum, to where Ralph never knew. They hadn't spoken a word to each other. He knew nothing about him other than his first name and the island he came from, Hokkaido, cool, green and wet, its climate, area, population and economic activity very similar to Ireland. He missed him.

"I can't remember all the place names," said Ralph.

"Have a try."

"I remember the first night was at a place called Jarajus and the second day I had to do a four-kilometre diversion around an industrial complex at Qus. Then I went straight through Al Ashraf something and stopped just before Qena. That would have been the second night. I think the next stop was a Nagaa place, but there were lots of those. Nagaa Samrah I think. And then through Dishna, and I spent a night near a bridge that crossed over to another Nagaa on the west bank, just around the bend where the river started going north again."

"Nagaa Hammadi?"

"Might have been. Day five was interesting as I was still on the eastern side and after ten kilometres the desert came very close to the river. For about six kilometres there were dry sandy hills right to the water."

"The Jabal al Tarif."

"Was it? Soon after there was some sort of barrier across the river controlling the flow of water."

"It's a barrage. An old one."

"Yes, that's right. I remember the street lights on the road running over it looked like old gas lamps from a Parisian side street. The next two days were big walks. That's when my toe started hurting. And then early in the morning, it must have been the eighth day, I crossed the river at Sohag."

It was the biggest town he'd seen so far and the route led away from the river slightly, through a patchwork of fields, every one lush with growth. He'd walked then on the west side, keeping the big river on his right.

"I finished up in Tahta for the night and then when I left I was stopped by a policeman on a bicycle. There was a bit of a delay until his boss came. He was all right, good English, but I think I only did twenty-five kilometres yesterday through getting held up by him and my toe hurting me a little."

"What's wrong with your toe?"

"I'm not sure. I can't see anything wrong but it's painful. I'm a bit lame."

"And last night you stayed in this place Sidfa?"

"Yes. I felt worn out this morning for some reason and didn't get going until nearly nine o'clock."

Ralph turned to him.

"Do you know, I'm glad you stopped. I'd just about had enough."

"Quite a walk. Take lots of photographs?"

"No. I don't have a camera."

"What? Not even a small one?"

"No. My camera was stolen ages ago."

Alim felt relieved. He believed him. He had no idea why the boy might be important to Angel but his own conscience was clear. He could help South Africa without any guilt of not having served his own country first.

"Did you have any problems with the police?"

"Here? Not really. I was questioned yesterday morning but there weren't any problems. Tahta was the first town I'd stayed in. I think that was the hitch. The rest had been small villages off the main roads."

"What happened?"

"Nothing. I said *'Ana mis faahim Arabi'* and we stood smiling at each other until the policeman's lieutenant came. Then I explained in English that I was interested in studying agriculture and that there was much to learn from Egypt in the science of irrigation and double cropping, and he smiled and gave me my passport back and said *'Hazz sa'eed'*. At least he didn't accuse me of spying."

Alim smiled. It had scared the rural police half to death having GID on the phone threatening to come down and talk to them. He would see that the lieutenant was promoted.

As they got closer to Cairo Ralph noticed more horticulture, a wide array of fruits and vegetables, especially tomatoes and melons, but soon there was no space for farming, Cairo teeming with people.

"It's very busy."

"Cairo has attracted millions of migrants from the countryside, to come to school for education, or to work as unskilled labourers. Twenty per cent of all Egyptians now live in Cairo."

Ralph looked around. Wooden, cardboard and metal huts had been constructed on every flat roof of every apartment building.

"Where do they all live?"

Alim shrugged.

"Who knows? These rooftop shacks – there are two hundred thousand of them. We have half a million people living in the city's cemeteries, in the mausoleums of the dead."

"Who makes sure everything works?"

"You mean sewerage and public transport? It doesn't."

"Somebody must be in control."

410

"The city is in quarters: the Greek Quarter, Coptic Quarter or the Silversmiths Quarter, segregated on religious or occupational lines. They are self-governing."

Alim laughed.

"They have to be."

TWENTY-FIVE

Angel spent the afternoon with Elanza.

"Angel, I'm tired. Sleep with me."

Nervously he lay beside her, both fully clothed. He felt as though he was cheating her and contemplated telling her he was half African, ID code zero seven, 'other Coloured'.

She put her hand on his head.

"You've got really wiry hair."

"It's hereditary. On my mother's side."

"Your mother in London?"

"I've only got the one."

He changed the subject.

"Ralph's in Cairo."

"Cairo? What's he been doing?"

"Walking up the Nile. Talking to farmers."

She held his arm.

"Save him for me, Angel. Get him home. So he can be with his father."

Angel wanted to tell her that that was why he stayed in South Africa, why he was there at all, to find his father.

"I'm going to be with mine again soon," she said.

"Don't be silly."

"Don't give up on them, Angel."

Maybe she knew.

*

Snyman sat with both hands flat on his office desk, staring blankly at the wall. A framed cutting from a colourful society magazine showed him next to a glamourous woman at a Sun City investment company freebie, an international actress who had been paid to attend, against her anti-apartheid principles but she took the money anyway, stared back at him, blankly. He picked up the phone and looked at a different picture with fondness for times past – a photograph of Danelle smiling on an Indian Ocean beach.

"He's in Cairo," he said.

Nels sounded puzzled.

"How do you know?"

"I spoke to his parents. He called them from Khartoum. Told them his plans."

Some Intelligence Service, he thought. *No wonder the country is in the shit.*

"He'll be staying at the Golden Hotel and flying Egypt Air to Athens."

"How am I going to get into Egypt?" Nels asked.

"What do you mean?"

"It's like Sudan. They don't accept our passports."

Snyman thought about the arrangement he'd made with Nels. Now he had to do something to earn his twenty per cent.

"Be creative. Stay away from the airport. Fly to Greece and come back on a boat to Alexandria."

Nels wasn't sure where that was.

"But you have to do it yourself this time. Finish it."

"It'll be my pleasure," said Nels.

Snyman had little doubt that he was telling the truth.

*

Angel's hair was still short but his beard had grown through the itchy stage. He had been to a bazaar and bought a *djellaba*, a loose-fitting light cotton robe, open at the neck without a collar and with long wide sleeves, wider in Egypt than in Arabia. It had a baggy hood that came to a point at the back, useful protection from sun and sand, or to carry the groceries. It was for labourers, dark brown, which he had been told signified among Berbers that he was unmarried. The vendor had winked as he told him. Alim told him that in Cairo he must wear Arab dress. He hoped his Arabic would be as convincing as his disguise.

"Your boy has been sick," Alim said. "His eyes are still yellow. And he's picked up a jigger."

Alim had taken Ralph to the Golden Hotel when he'd asked to go there, a cheap dormitory room, just down the road from his office on Talaat Harb.

"It's run by old Mr Fez, as he likes to call himself. He's the life and soul, playing up the Egyptian stereotype for the tourists. But he'll watch him for me. He'll lock up Ralph's gear to keep it safe, and George the moneychanger is giving a respectable black-market exchange rate for the dollar. He works for me. They'll call me when he moves."

"I'm not sure that he'll have any gear worth keeping safe," said Angel.

*

Khan el-Khalili on the 22nd of June, the day before the start of Ramadan, was quiet. Alim had told Angel to go there.

"Ralph's gone to the bazaar," he'd said, "and Angel, remember, a dog with a bone in his mouth can't bite."

It was an Egyptian metaphor that took Angel some time to translate. Alim helped him.

"The boy is the bone everyone is concentrating on. No one will be expecting you."

Khan el-Khalili was one of the world's great shopping experiences, a Middle Eastern souk forming a labyrinthine collection of skinny alleyways established as a shopping district in AD 1400 that still rang with the clang of metalworkers and silversmiths. The main streets had long ago given themselves over completely to the tourist trade, selling cheap papyrus pictures and plastic pyramids. Off the main drag in the surrounding alleyways were tiny stores and cluttered workshops, some of the best places to pick up traditional Egyptian products. Here was everything from antiques and metal lampshades to locally woven textiles. Cairo's most famous coffee shop, Fishawis, sold syrupy Arabic coffee and sweet tea to tourists and local merchants alike at a rapid-fire pace. For shoppers, the main souk road was Shari Gohar el-Qait. The gold and silver workshops congregated mostly just to the north, while the spice market section was to the south.

In one corner of the bazaar the Neo-Gothic bulk of the Sayyidna el-Husein Mosque, built in 1792 to honour the Prophet Muhammad's grandson, cast a shadow on the tea stands and fortune tellers. Nels waited for Ralph to walk up El-Badestane, a pedestrian route through the middle of the souk.

Angel followed both of them out of an area specialising in copper and brass ornaments, while Ralph sauntered unaware past Bedouin clothing, carpets and antiques.

Nels caught up with Ralph at the junction of Nahasin Road as he took a left at the gold area, running roughly south now towards the Sheikh Mutakhar Mosque. Halfway down the alleyway Ralph stopped. Coppersmiths occupied one side of the square and craftsmen the other. The whole area was quiet, the pre-Ramadan rush over. Tomorrow a lot of bazaar traders would be closed and many had already shut up shop.

Nels kept some distance and fiddled with something in his pocket. Ralph stood at a crossroad, deliberating which way he should go. Nels waited, and then Angel caught a glimpse through the market of Nels with his right hand in a jacket pocket striding determinedly towards Ralph. Angel thought he'd misjudged Nels. He would be too late.

At the last moment, just as Nels was behind him, Ralph turned left again on Shari Gohar el-Qait, the smell of cosmetics, essences and perfumes from vendors opposite the Ashraf Barsbay Mosque disguising the smell of sweat and urine.

Ralph slipped off the main road into a densely packed area of haberdashery that led to a food area. There were no people about. Angel dodged quickly through stalls selling fruit juices and Egyptian pancakes and stepped out in front of Nels, blocking his path. They were alone.

Angel had briefly seen Nels when he'd visited Elanza at home in Hyde Park but this was his first good look at him since the helicopter ride out of Cassinga. He hadn't aged well. The once powerful body was still large but the muscle that at one time had filled his neck and shoulders had been replaced by fat from too many *braai*s and too many beers. There was a blotchiness to his face, on his cheeks and forehead, from too much sun, or too much rum. He was unmistakably the Parabat instructor who had beaten him, he was the Intelligence officer at Cassinga, but years of bitterness and cruelty since then had shrunk him to a man older than his years. Angel remembered the dead, the massacre of women and children in a small town in Angola, the smile on Nels' face as he'd pushed a man from the helicopter to fall grasping at the air.

Angel said his name, quietly.

"Nels."

Nels stopped. There was no fear, just curiosity. He didn't freeze, no intention of flight. He was going to fight.

"Who are you? How do you know me?" asked Nels.

Angel's hood was up, his face in shadow.

"Scientia Munit," said Angel.

They were the words on the old Bureau of State Security crest: 'Knowledge Protects'.

Angel had never been very good at set-piece fighting, two opponents facing each other as if in a boxing ring. It was always so predictable, like sex. You do this to me, and I do that to you. What was he supposed to do? Swing a right and block a left, two three, like a dance move? Run at him? Kick his shin or groin? Or something gymnastic aimed at his head? Angel never knew. Whatever he did the outcome would be the same. It would always end with him locked close with his opponent, like wrestling, never standing apart making precise textbook kicks and punches.

At one time he'd been forced against his will to be the guinea pig on an innovative Israeli self-defence course, a bruising month in which bald, rabid instructors had advocated threat evaluation followed by pre-emptive strikes of speedy violence before running away. Angel had later summed it up to fascinated but uneasy colleagues as: stay focused, hit first, be furious, and then fuck off. It became known to all from then on as 'The Four F course' and reduced on Nick Roux's order to a less dispiriting and damaging week in duration.

Angel walked at a fast pace towards Nels and wrapped both arms around him as though giving him a hug but with his lower body twisted to protect his groin from Nels' knee. Under normal circumstances Nels would have been pushed backwards against a wall, or over onto his back. Nels, however, had been walking towards him at a similar pace and their momentums cancelled each other out. They stood stationary, pushing each other, locked at the head and neck like two prop forwards in a scrum. Angel waited for an arm to free itself from his back, to come up in between them as a punch to the stomach or face. Would it be left or right?

Nels chose left, which surprised Angel but helped him, as he could catch Nels' fist in his own more powerful right hand and drop to his knees, pulling Nels down on one side, trying to twist him. Nels leant back as he was pulled down, to stop from falling forward onto his face, and they ended up both kneeling, still facing each other, holding hands.

Nels' free hand came forward and clutched Angel's throat low down, just above the clavicle. He felt Nels squeeze, pinching. Vulnerable points exist all over the body but most of them are from the collarbone up. In the small area of the neck they are the spinal cord, the windpipe, and the carotid arteries taking oxygenated blood to the neck, head and brain. Nels' hand was roughly below the fourth vertebra, below the point where the common carotid artery split into two branches, trapping both carotid arteries against the trachea.

Angel tried to beat Nels' arm downwards with his free hand, to break his grip, and then, failing, tried to beat it upwards. Nels kept squeezing.

Angel, feeling lightheaded, leant backwards, bending at the knees and rolling to one side. Nels' grasp on Angel's throat was broken but now Angel lay on the ground, Nels above him. With two hands Nels held the hood over Angel's head and slammed it against the floor. Angel felt the skin split above his eye. He knew that most fights were over very quickly. In only five or six movements, without a single kick or punch having been made, it felt like it was over for Angel. He dragged himself away and tried to stand.

Nels was quicker, and barged him, shoulder down, pushing him over a shop counter. It was a butcher's shop, closed early because of Ramadan. Angel fell in a heap on the other side. When he pushed himself up, only his head and shoulders above the counter, Nels was leaning over the table, a gun from his jacket pocket pointed at Angel's head.

It was steel grey at the front and brownish at the back, with a black rubber sleeve over the grip. Angel had heard about them but never seen one.

The British Welrod 'Assassin's Pistol', a bizarre and unusual handgun, its noise muffled by baffles as in a car exhaust, had been designed during World War Two for use by irregular forces and resistance groups. It was a cylindrical, thirty-centimetre-long tube with a simple, reliable and, most importantly, quiet bolt action. The grip was also the magazine. It held, for optimal performance, only five rounds, and it could be removed for easy concealment. With the grip taken off, the integrated barrel and noise suppressor could pass for anything. It looked like a bicycle pump. It was extremely quiet, little louder than the noise level of normal conversation.

The end of the silencer was hollowed so that it could be placed tight against someone's body, a man in a crowd or a boy in a souk, and fired virtually noiselessly. In those circumstances the noise was best described as a snap of the fingers followed by a match striking. Officially it was still a secret weapon, mostly for fear that, due to its simplicity of design, it could be easily reverse-engineered by any terrorist with access to a good farm workshop. Although designed in 1943 it was still available for use in 1982 by British Special Forces, and others.

Nels was breathing hard, his right hand shaking. The bolt of the Welrod was operated by twisting a knurled nut on the end of the barrel to unlock it and pulling a plunger backwards. It wasn't cocked until the plunger was pushed back in and the end twisted back to its original position. Although with practice it could be done quite quickly, the Welrod had never been designed to be anything other than a single-shot weapon. It was supposed to be used at point-blank range, quietly assassinating with just one shot fired. Nels was unfamiliar with the weapon. He needed to look for the nut to locate it, and the gun twisted away from its aim on Angel's head.

Angel, still focused on the gun, felt around underneath the shop counter for anything he could use as a weapon. His fingers touched something flat with a handle. It was a butcher's cleaver, a large rectangular hatchet for hacking through bone.

The cleaver wasn't sharp. It didn't need to be. Angel brought it up and down quickly, with a lot of energy. Nels' arm, chopped clean through at the elbow, fell onto the counter top, the Welrod still held tightly in his fleshy fingers. Nels, just like the African at Cassinga, looked around and sat down carefully.

*

Egypt Air's desk at Cairo airport had no customers and Angel had a clear view of Ralph trying to buy a ticket. It was obvious there was some problem.

"Athens. Sixty-five dollars," said the ticket agent.

He sat behind a desk, fat and sweaty with a big moustache. Ramadan had just started and Angel imagined he would be feeling hungry and uninterested.

Ralph took a small plastic bag from his pocket. He had a little over fifteen dollars. He was fifty short, exactly the amount taken by the Sisters of The Sacred Heart in Juba.

Angel saw a cleaning trolley, unattended outside of the washrooms, a grey overall coat over the handle. He put his hand in his pocket and pulled out his own brown leather wallet. He quickly sanitised it but left all the cash, 150 dollars, and debated leaving a note. *For the camera, with love from the South African Police.*

Angel had always wondered why his government had become involved with Ralph, convinced that there had to be more of a reason than Ralph's inheritance from the sale of Blackie Swart's farm. He hoped that whatever the reason he and Ralph had made a difference, that it was a small something that may momentarily weaken his adopted country but would ultimately strengthen South Africa and bring injustice to an end, peacefully.

Ralph didn't see the man approach. It was just a cleaner, talking Arabic, who handed the ticket agent a wallet.

Wordlessly the ticket agent took out some money and held out his hand for Ralph's fifteen dollars. He handwrote a ticket and handed it to him with the wallet. Inside was a hundred-dollar bill. Ralph looked around for the cleaner. He'd gone.

Angel watched him board at the gate.

"Go to your father," he said and walked away.

*

Roux found Angel clearing out his basement office at the National Intelligence Service. Angel would be sad to leave it. He had enjoyed the solitude.

"What about Koos Snyman?" Angel asked.

"Leave him to me," said Roux.

"And Nels?" asked Roux. "What happened to him?"

In the bazaar Angel had taken a rope, used for tying the feet of carcasses before hanging them on a hook for sale at the butcher's shop. He'd pulled it tight around the pulsing stump of Nels' arm and twisted it with a steel for sharpening knives, telling Nels to hold the improvised tourniquet with his other hand or he would pass out from loss of blood. He'd lowered his hood and looked at him, talked to him in Afrikaans, Nels' own language.

'Your people could be great,' he'd told him. 'Afrikaners are determined, courageous, resourceful and innovative. But you've grown arrogant, like a hide to protect yourselves, and in your arrogance you've forgotten that you are just men, such as I, and not Gods.'

He'd left him, taking the Welrod after peeling the gun from the lifeless fingers of a severed arm with a tattoo that looked like an upside-down jellyfish.

"He'll turn up," Angel told him.

"South Africans like Nels always turn up," said Roux. "I saw Lombard about a new assignment for you." Lombard had approved his idea of what they should do with Angel, and even 'The Grim Reaper', head of the *Heining*, was onboard. "I think he's forgotten all about the money from Elanza Swart's inheritance leaving the country. It's the season for Southern Rights apparently. It's all he can talk about. He's wishing he was at his beach house at Hermanus watching the whales in Walker Bay, or out shooting a springbok somewhere in the Karoo, anywhere but the office."

"A new assignment? Not my old post?" asked Angel.

"No. A promotion for a new job. An important one. They call it Project Hobo."

Angel thought of Elanza.

"Based here or in the field?"

"Here, office based in Pretoria. Domestic travel only. Some liaison with the Israelis. Better come upstairs," said Roux. "Do some real work."

*

Koos Snyman thought of his wife. He'd been drinking, a bottle of good Scotch half empty. Danelle had been a trophy, beautiful. He smiled, remembering when she used to call him Kosie. Not for a long time now. He took another drink. She would be all right. It wouldn't take her long to find a new host, like a parasite.

He heard the two cars turn up. Not police anyhow. That was good. Danelle would be upset if the neighbours started talking. They didn't need 'Police' written on the side for Snyman to know that they had come for him.

*

Angel found that Elanza's illness had progressed.

"I have diarrhoea constantly. And I've got funny ulcers in my mouth."

She imitated the doctor.

"Lesions on the hard pallet and gums."

She opened her mouth for him to see.

"Please move in," she asked.

He would have liked to stay, to take care of her, but he hardly looked like domestic staff and they'd never give him a pass to live in Hyde Park.

"Ralph said he wanted to join the British Army," he said, desperate to cheer her. "I dissuaded him. He's going to be a farmer instead."

Elanza smiled.

"Father would have liked that. Watch over him, Angel. Like you watch over me."

"They've arrested Koos Snyman," he said.

"My father trusted him," said Elanza.

"Fathers aren't always right."

"It's all about our fathers, Angel. Ralph doing this crazy, pointless walk through Africa only to prove to his father that he's a grown-up. And me. Since Father died I've been looking for ways to forget, thinking to kill myself, and I've finally succeeded. And you, Angel. You needn't be here at all. You've seen things men shouldn't see just to be here to find your father. Do you think they know how powerful their influence has been?"

Angel sat beside her, their shoulders touching.

"They want me to go to an AIDS conference in Durban. Make a speech. I'm not sure I feel up for it."

He held her hand.

"Let me feel you," she said.

He took her hand and nervously guided it to his face. She touched him. Felt his lips, his nose. She turned her head to hide the tears in her eyes but didn't remove her hand, stroking his face.

"Dear Angel."

He wanted to tell her that he was half Swazi and that he understood. Swaziland had the highest rate of HIV in the world – twenty-six per cent of adults.

And she was right. He had come back to South Africa all those years ago to find his father. He'd put up with abuse during his national service to be allowed to stay in the country, saw horrors at Cassinga, all for his father.

Angel loved her and wanted to tell her but he'd left it too late – Elanza had fallen asleep.

SOUTHERN ENGLAND

28TH JUNE, 1982

TWENTY-SIX

R alph had flown to Athens in an Egypt Air 737 and seen the pyramids at Giza as the aeroplane banked after take-off and turned north. He'd never had a chance to see them from the ground and somehow didn't think he'd ever be back. It had taken an hour forty in the air and Africa was far behind.

In Athens he'd rented a twenty-dollar room, ten times what he'd paid in Egypt at the Golden Hotel, and spent an hour in a hot shower. He'd met two nurses from Sydney and with a new confidence that surprised him invited them to join him for dinner. It'd been that easy. He'd eaten two five-dollar lasagne dinners one after the other while they got drunk on ouzo and watched him.

At dusk the next evening he'd boarded a sixty-hour non-stop bus through Europe to London. It had cost him fifty of Angel's dollars. He'd survived the trip on tinned tuna, crackers, and stale water from the toilet cubicle at the back.

A ticket from London Waterloo railway station to Gillingham, Dorset, had just about cleared him out. If lucky he might have enough money for a cup of tea on the train.

Ralph picked up a pay phone and asked for a reverse-charge call.

A woman asked primly, "Will you accept the charge for a call?"

A tired voice sighed and answered, "Yes, I will."

"Hi, Dad."

"Hello, my son. Happy birthday."

It was the twenty-eighth of June. He would be home for his nineteenth.

*

The conductor read the stations over a crackling tannoy. Ralph sighed and relaxed into the seat, comforted by the familiar litany, relieved to finally hear the long-awaited recital that signalled the way home: Woking, Basingstoke, Andover, Salisbury, Tisbury, Gillingham. The train would continue on through fields of black and white cows, but Ralph rarely travelled further west. Gillingham had always been his stop, the end of the line.

With a hundred miles to go Ralph thought for the first time of his future. He had nothing planned, just a small English country town, grey-green in the winter and golden-green in the summer but always green. The trip now nearly over he wondered why he'd come back. When he'd left, thinking only of the adventure ahead, he'd said goodbye to a high-school sweetheart and at the time it had been a wrench that felt like something inside would snap. He couldn't remember the last time he'd thought of her, not since Elanza.

Two men ran along the platform toward the departing train as it made to leave London. They nimbly sidestepped a platform guard who, frustrated at having failed to stop them, puffed with bluster into a burnished whistle. The train whined like a wounded animal and then hesitated as if in pain and limped to an unexpected stop. The two men boarded, late and sweating, and looked around for a seat. The younger stocky man, solid like a second-row rugby player, had short cropped hair, almost bald, and a closely shaven face that shone. He must have recently been in the sun with more hair and a beard, distinct stripes between brown and white skin making him look like a thickset tabby cat. The other looked unusually round and pink.

The round man squeezed in beside Ralph before asking, "Is this taken?"

The other man slumped across two seats opposite. He opened a broad paper and hid behind it so that Ralph could only see his hands, freshly scrubbed but with engrained blackness on the sides of his index fingers and at the tips where his nails had been trimmed.

"Been somewhere nice?"

The newspaper hadn't moved and Ralph glanced around, unsure if the man intended talking to him.

"I'm sorry?"

A face appeared above the headlines.

"You've got a good tan. Been on holiday?"

"Not really. Just travelling."

"Ah."

Ralph hadn't been on holiday for years. Holidays required camping in the rain in Snowdonia and climbing wet Welsh mountains, or burning on a hot Spanish beach and swimming with coloured Mediterranean fish. Travelling had been different, like a task that had to be completed. Ralph realised, with regret, that he'd travelled blindly in a series of jumps. He'd focused too hard on the next destination along the way rather than slowly savouring the locations around him. He remembered people more than places, those who had helped.

"Where?"

"Hmm?"

"Where have you been travelling?"

"Africa."

"Africa? What, all of it?"

"Not all of it. Cape Town to Cairo."

He put down his paper and looked at Ralph intently. The round man slightly tilted his flushed and glowing head, only pretending to read his book, listening carefully.

"How?" the stripy man asked.

The same questions, thought Ralph, always the same questions. No one ever asked about 'separate development' in South Africa, or the effects of tribalism in Uganda, or the disparate economies of northern and southern Sudan. People wanted to know how he did it, how far, how long it took, where he slept, what he ate, how much it cost.

"How did you do it?"

"I walked."

Ralph looked out of the window, ignoring the men, fascinated by the orderly little fields of England after the large untamed spaces of Africa. He felt uneasy, as though the two men needed to form a judgement of him, that he was being evaluated by strangers as in an interview. His apprehension was increased by the stripy man who, clear of the camouflage of his newspaper, appeared a little too friendly and relaxed, as if they had known each other for some time.

Ralph went to the bathroom as the train approached a station, hopeful that the two men would have left when he returned, and glared at himself in the mirror. His hair, longer than it had ever been, fell in blond curls over his shoulders. His face looked thin and brown but his beard was still ginger fluff rather than black stubble. He was faintly angry. It didn't look like he'd grown up at all.

The two men looked at other passengers as they boarded at Basingstoke, laying claim to the space around them and Ralph's empty seat.

"What do you think?" Zac asked.

Jumbo Cameron puffed out his cheeks.

"I'm not sure," he said. "He's very," he searched for the word, "opinionated."

"He'll grow out of it."

Jumbo shifted his weight in the seat.

"He's a loner," he said.

"That's good, isn't it?"

Jumbo seemed unsure.

"Write your report. We'll see if he pops up somewhere."

Zac looked around and noticed Ralph walking back down the carriage. He nodded to Jumbo, who with plump pink fingers pushed two small black canisters, round like short pieces of plastic tube, into the pocket of Ralph's jacket.

*

On the train the round pink man and the stripy man looked at Ralph curiously.

"Tell us, how did you do it?"

"I told you. I walked."

Ralph prepared himself for the next questions: how far, how long, where he slept, what he ate, how much.

"You walked through Africa? How far is it?"

Ralph turned his head from the view outside the window to look at the stripy man.

"In a straight line it's exactly 4,500 miles but the route I took was nearly double that."

The round pink man had put his book down.

"You walked all the way?" he asked.

Always the same questions. People had no idea of the geography.

"No. I walked a quarter of it."

"How long did it take?"

"I left Cape Town on the 1st of January and got back here this morning. All told it's been six months. I walked for a hundred days, but not consecutively."

The stripy man sat on his newspaper so that the little table between them wasn't cluttered.

"And the rest of it? In a bus or something?" he asked.

"A lot of it was on boats. There's a big lake in the middle of Africa that would stretch from Southampton to the top of Scotland, and the River Nile is navigable for almost half the length of the continent. I walked a quarter, and nearly another quarter of the total distance was on water."

"What about the other half?"

"I got rides in pickup trucks, lorries, quite a lot on the railway. I got a ride in an old plane for a little way."

"Where did you sleep?" the round pink man asked. "Hotels?"

"Not really. I only spent thirty-nine dollars on accommodation. It would have been more but I did a runner from a bed and breakfast in Kenya without paying. Most of the time I slept by the road somewhere."

"Thirty-nine dollars a night?" the stripy man asked. It seemed reasonable. Twenty-two or twenty-three pounds.

"Thirty-nine dollars in six months."

His brow furrowed and he looked away.

"You slept by the road? Were you camping? It sounds very dangerous," the round pink man said.

Ralph hadn't thought about it.

"I don't know if it was dangerous. I didn't have any problems. Oh, I was arrested for spying in Uganda."

The stripy man looked out of the window.

"What happened? Were you formally charged?"

"No. There was a vehicle crash close by and I sort of got away."

"You sort of got away."

Ralph didn't say anything. He wasn't sure if he believed him.

"Did you get tummy troubles?"

The round pink man thought it was a natural question to ask. He always fell ill while on holiday abroad. All that foreign food.

"I think I had malaria and hepatitis at the same time. You know, the type of hep you get from dirty water."

Ralph thought that needed clarifying.

"I'm still getting over it. I could scare you to death with some traveller's toilet tales. And I think I've got a jigger in my toe."

"What's a jigger?"

"It's a tiny flea that lives in the sand and burrows under your skin. It sits there chomping away getting fatter and fatter. All you can see to start with is a little black dot which is its bum. It lives inside you, growing ten times its original

435

size from feeding off your blood, and throwing eggs out of its bum back onto the ground. Hurts like hell."

Both laughed.

"I bet your mum and dad were worried. It sounds dangerous to me. You must have had an angel watching over you."

"Why did you do it?" the stripy man asked.

That, thought Ralph, was the question. He looked out of the window at southern England in June, so green that he wanted to hum *Jerusalem*.

"The truth is I didn't mean to. I spent some time in Joburg working in a bar and then I made a bit of money acting in a TV commercial. I wanted to see the 'real' Africa so I walked to Victoria Falls. Then I just kept heading north. I thought I could join my flight home in Nairobi but the airline wouldn't let me on. So I had to come all the way. Overland."

Ralph looked at the stripy man and wondered if they'd met before.

"Maybe I was just trying to prove something."

"Prove something?" he asked. "To who?"

"Myself."

The stripy man smiled.

"How much money did you have?"

"I left Johannesburg with 450 dollars but some nuns in Sudan stole fifty from me. I still had a bit left when I got to Cairo. I think the trip through Africa cost 385 dollars."

"How much is that?" the round pink man asked.

The other answered him.

"Two hundred and twenty-five pounds."

"How old are you?" he asked.

"I'm nineteen today."

"Oh, happy birthday," the round pink man said cheerfully.

The stripy man had a smile on his face.

"So, you were eighteen, alone, and you walked two thousand miles, travelled nearly eight thousand miles all the way through Africa, kept going even though you were carrying a few interesting tropical diseases, dodged arrest for spying and escaped from thieving nuns, and lived for six months, all on just over two hundred quid."

"Yes. I suppose I did."

All three of them, surprised, looked out of the window at the green and pleasant land and at a cathedral spire towering above a river valley.

Jumbo talked to Zac, ignoring Ralph as though something had been finalised, as if he'd seen enough.

"Have you seen the cathedral?" he asked. "Quite magnificent. Four hundred and four feet tall but built on a swampy bog. Bishop Poore took the credit, but of course Elias did all the work."

The two men left together silently at the City of Salisbury and stood on the platform looking at Ralph through the carriage window until they both walked over a pedestrian bridge and stood on the platform opposite. Ralph craned his neck when the train pulled away. They hadn't left the station to visit the cathedral. He could see them standing to wait for the next London-bound. It would take Zac straight back to where he'd just come from, back to Waterloo and the glass office block on Westminster Bridge Road with a petrol station at its base, London's worst-kept secret, and Jumbo Cameron to his busy desk six stops up the Northern Line at the top of Gower Street.

*

Just before Gillingham railway bridge, as the train slowed to a stop, Ralph saw a bedsheet draped over some bushes in view of the track. There was a message handwritten on it, 'Welcome Home', his aunt and two young cousins waving vigorously above it.

An old man waited on the platform. His hair hung in grey strands over a bald head, and a paunch above his belt pushed the bottom buttons of his shirt open. Ralph felt that the man had aged rapidly, as if on an exponential curve, but his face still had that way of crinkling up when he smiled, just as Ralph remembered it.

"Hello, Dad."

"Hello, my son."

The old man stood looking at Ralph, unsure what to say.

"Your mother has been frantic since your call. Where've you been?"

He'd meant since Ralph had called from London that morning, but the same question applied to the time since he'd left for Cape Town more than six months previously.

"Come on. Let's go. I'll tell you both all about it."

On a bench outside the station a girl moved so that the sun fell on her face and hair. A large brown dog lifted its head from her knee.

Ralph and his father noticed her at the same time.

"I'll take this to the car," he said and lifted Ralph's light rucksack with one hand.

Ralph, the girl and the dog looked at each other and all three of them smiled. Wordlessly she held his arm. Ralph put his hand in his jacket pocket. He pulled out two black plastic pots and looked at them, puzzled by how they'd got there. They were a little over 35mm long with grey snap-on lids and letters written on the top with a thick blue marker. On one the letters R-E, on the other a solitary letter O.

SOUTH AFRICA AND ENGLAND

2003

TWENTY-SEVEN

Elanza, her pneumonia unimproved, looked fine and papery, as if made of tissue. She had chest pain and difficulty breathing, and no matter what Angel did he seemed unable to stop her severe wasting. He didn't need to be continually told the seriousness of her condition but her doctor called him at work regularly with vaguely disguised warnings, conditioning him for that day when there wouldn't be any need for disguise. Angel tried to ignore the pessimistic reports, remembering other dreadful times that they had struggled through, and encouraged her to keep on fighting, proud of her but aware that ultimately it was an unwinnable battle. It hadn't been easy for either of them, Elanza often angry with herself and the world.

At one time, maybe fifteen years ago, he'd gone to see her and immediately felt sorry for her. She'd been sweating, scratching wounds on her torso, hopping from one foot to another because the lesions were on the soles of her feet.

"Shall I tell you how all this started? It's good to know, right? To study your enemy."

Angel had said nothing.

"I've been asking about it. The pathophysiology is very complex. It's the HIV that gets you. AIDS just finishes you off. The HIV virus enters the body. In my case a shared needle. His blood straight into my blood. Bam. Job done. It replicates rapidly. That's stage one, the so-called 'acute' stage. It destroys something called CD4+T cells which are a component of the immune system. Three to four weeks after infection it's usual to get flu-like symptoms. It often goes undiagnosed. Mine did. I just thought I'd bought some bad drugs. 'Opportunistic' infections can start at this very early stage, like the CMV that led to my blindness."

"Elanza, please."

She'd held up her hand to silence him.

"Then there's a latent period when not much happens. Good old CD8+T cells are activated and they kill HIV-infected cells, allowing CD4+T cells to recover. That's why not much is going on for three years and you can live a normal life drugging and whoring. At the end of stage two, though, you get weight loss, enlarged lymph nodes and… and…"

She had become angrier, Angel unable to comfort her.

"And then the big one. Fifty per cent of people die within ten years, so let me see. Oh yes. Any day soon."

He had taken her hand and passed her a towel as she'd started coughing.

"In the end you get AIDS because HIV has killed all the CD4+T cells. When a blood test for p24 antigen levels shows that you are HIV-positive, and you get a CD4+T cell count of less than two hundred, you are officially AIDS ridden. Your Human Immunodeficiency Virus has opened the door to a 'defining' illness, like my old friend cytomegalovirus, and you have Acquired an Immune Deficiency Syndrome. I take comfort in the big words. Makes you feel you've got your money's worth."

She had gone to the sink then, nauseous.

"I couldn't tell you which one of the many men I slept with had herpes, by the way. He wasn't wearing a sign. I'll never know who made me blind."

She had started crying. Crying had always been the most difficult for Angel, more difficult than anger.

"Or Kaposi's sarcoma. That's another herpes bastard. Gives you these skin cancers."

She had held up her foot to show him.

"Violet plaques."

He had gone to her as she held the sink, waiting for her to vomit.

"Eventually they'll break down and start 'fungating'. Which will be something to look forward to anyway. Terminal diseases are so... interesting."

She had exhausted herself and stopped talking. Angel, as always, had felt helpless.

"I'm sorry, Angel. I'm taking a new thing. An 'antiretroviral'. It's called AZT. I don't sleep. I don't eat. Makes me want to throw up. Good job I'm rich, though. This stuff is so expensive."

She had taken a huge pill.

"The heart grinds rotten things," Angel had said.

She'd shouted at him again: "Shut up with all the African shit! Talk like a white man."

Angel had remained silent and let her talk.

"How can they bomb a shopping centre? Hyde Park. Right here. Three injured."

She'd changed the conversation without realising.

"It's that Mandela's fault. They should lock him up."

"He is," Angel had reminded her.

"It'll go back to the bush, you know, with them in charge. Thankfully I'm dying. They'll be murdering us in our beds anyway."

Angel had always found it gruelling when Elanza was irritable and mulish, and questioned how he could love this side of her, until, as always, he excused her obstinate headstrong manners, knowing them to be a symptom of her wretched cheerless condition.

Angel had helped her to a chair. He thought it then that she'd told him about the will.

"Talking of death," she had said, "I've changed my will. Not by much. I'm leaving some to medical research. There's still a lot of money despite my having wasted it. And Koos Snyman's best efforts, of course. Extraordinary, but it appears that the rest of the world is still functioning financially, even if South Africa isn't. I'm told I'm worth a hundred and sixty million dollars. And you are the executor. You know what that means."

Angel had been too drained to interrogate her about it.

And then there had been the time, Angel thought eight years ago, when Elanza had picked up her first pneumonia. She'd been using a new spray medication which she inhaled in a noisy squirt from an aerosol. It'd made her cough.

"Don't worry. It's only PCP," she'd laughed.

The lesions had at that time been on the side and tip of her nose – purple blotches the size of a penny.

"And I'm on combination therapy now," she'd explained. "More tablets. Stops resistance. The old AZT wasn't doing the job. This one pill has got two, or more, ingredients. I

444

don't remember. If I'm a good girl and take them every day I might get a few more years."

She had chuckled but, as always, had ended up in a coughing fit.

Angel had tried to cheer her up.

"Ralph is a farmer, south of Lisbon. He speaks pretty good Portuguese apparently. And he's started a rugby club. Thirty-something-year-old expats who should know better and some Portuguese soccer players. They played a game against a visiting Royal Navy submarine."

Angel realised now that he'd been proud of him.

"Those sailors must have been underwater so long, like turning out cattle from a *kraal*. Of course, Ralph's team lost. Ralph had never been a rugby player really. He broke two ribs. Old men pretending they're still young."

Elanza had held his hand.

*

Angel spoon-fed the broth a cleaning lady at the office had made for him to take to her. He held her head carefully, like a child, her hair thin on her scalp.

"I have some news about Ralph," he told her.

She smiled and opened her mouth obediently.

"He's in Cambridgeshire."

"Where is that?"

"In England, in the middle somewhere."

"What's he doing there?" she asked, soup dribbling down her chin. Angel wiped it away tenderly.

"He's travelling all over the world buying fresh produce, vegetables."

"Vegetables?"

"He's running a business, probably not very well. He's lost a ton of money trading Argentinian sweetcorn."

Angel laughed and Elanza smiled. After twenty-one years she knew very little about Angel's job. He talked randomly of a promotion, of a new boss, of the office moving out of Pretoria's central business district to Arcadia. She knew it was government work, that he was well thought of, that his translation and report writing sometimes took him around the country and occasionally abroad. He would return from these foreign trips tired and silent. He would politely dismiss the maid and the gardener for the weekend and quietly cook and clean for her, scold her for forgetting a medication and for smoking, sit her warmly in the sun while he swam countless lengths in the pool, and then read stories to her all evening, stories of Africa. For a while she wondered if he had another woman, or whether she should encourage him to get one, but she would forget to talk to him about it and then blame herself for being selfish and fearful of losing him.

"How do you know this?"

Angel couldn't tell her. In 1985 NIS had opened Rietvlei, based on heathland around a dam south of Pretoria, as a world class National Intelligence Academy. At the new 'Farm', a programme called Owl Sight had been developed, with cooperation from the Italian state security machine SISMI. Roux considered the Italian Secret Service very underrated and excellent in the field of technology, particularly the interception of satellite communications worldwide.

"A little bird," Angel said. "I keep an eye on him."

Angel put down the soup bowl and tidied her up.

"I've enjoyed following what he's been up to," she said. "It's been a small reason to keep going."

Angel understood. They'd both lived vicariously through the triumphs and tragedies of this only vaguely remembered person doing things unfamiliar to them in an environment far different to their own. Watching Ralph's life had been like watching a soap opera. He'd become a novella they could pick up and put down at will, his normal ordinary life simple and comforting, an escape from their own problems. They had analysed his loves and commiserated with his losses, toasted his successes and debated his mistakes, all without him having any idea that he'd become an important part of their lives, that he had brought and kept them together.

They sat quietly for a long time, holding hands, content that there was no need to talk.

*

In the Arcadia building, near to the embassies and hotels of historic Pretoria, Deputy Director Angel Rots stretched and looked around his office, the new headquarters one of many changes. Gabriël Lombard had left before the first free elections to help create a fully democratic constitution for South Africa. Nick Roux had taken over his job but recently retired. Angel now worked for the second black African director general of the new South African Secret Service, the first one quickly fired by the President for fabricating intelligence reports. The director general had always been a political appointment, and Angel did the real work – both knew it, both accepted it.

Angel missed Nick Roux. He remembered the day when he'd finally realised that South Africa would change. He'd been standing with Roux at Waterkloof Air Base, nervous of boarding a noisy old executive jet to fly to Ysterplaat for a prison visit near Paarl. Roux had astonished him. For three years, a senior minister, a member of the State Security Council, had been meeting the nation's highest profile prisoner, a convicted violent communist saboteur, taking him home for his wife to cook him dinner and reporting back only to the President. Even Roux had known nothing about it. Roux had given Angel a parcel to carry, a suit of clothes for Prisoner 46664. Angel knew who'd been the 466th prisoner at Robben Island in 1964 and had thought, *This is it; this is the end of it.*

Angel's phone rang and it cheered him.

"Hello, Nick, this is a nice surprise. How's retirement?"

Roux had found it hard adjusting to having perpetual leisure time.

"Dull. I went through some old things and I sent you a video tape. Are you able to watch it now?"

"Now?"

"Please, Angel."

Angel watched a court setting, a feed from a monitor taken seven years previously at the Truth and Reconciliation Commission, an attempt in restorative justice at the end of apartheid. A man stood to attention while being questioned by judges, a subtitle on the screen stating 'Human Rights Abuses – Bisho'. Angel remembered it well – a massacre by the security forces against a demonstration in a town in the Ciskei.

"Are you watching?"

"Yes. Who is he?"

"Called himself Peter Farnham. He worked for the Civil Cooperation Bureau in '88 in charge of Intelligence. Left the SADF in 1991 and joined the Ciskei Defence Force."

"Bisho," said Angel.

"Bisho. Then he became a senior staff officer in the new South African Army, when he wasn't at a Truth and Reconciliation Commission Human Rights Violation Tribunal. Unbelievable."

"Why do you want me to see this, Nick?"

"Look at him. He did God knows what evil but thought that if he called the black guys 'sir' often enough it would all be forgotten."

The man on the monitor turned to make a point to one of the judges. His right arm had been cleanly amputated at the elbow.

"There's something else, Angel. I had a call from Elanza's doctor. He failed to get you on the phone at work and was redirected to me. Someone at the office doesn't know that I'm not your boss anymore. I'm pleased to see that the bureaucracy hasn't improved. Angel, I have some sad news."

Angel listened to his old boss and mentor, his friend Nick Roux.

*

The new director general came from King William's Town in the Eastern Cape, and in the DG's palatial office Angel spoke Xhosa.

"I need some time off, sir."

The director didn't answer him.

"Brief me on Asher Karni."

"He's a dual national, South African and Israeli. 'Businessman'. We're sure he's been supplying nuclear technology to Pakistan. We need to raid his home near Cape Town. Sea Point, I believe."

"No time off, Angel," the DG said. "There's this Pakistan connection and an al-Qaeda threat. You are my Arabist. I'm under pressure from above. She who must be obeyed."

The director reported to the Minister of Intelligence Services, her parents ANC activist friends of the President from the time of exile in Lusaka. It put additional pressure on the DG.

"Now is not the time."

Angel had expected his response.

"There's a funeral in Johannesburg. And I need to go to England."

"Where in England?"

"London, then possibly somewhere called Eli or Elee. I don't know how to say it."

"Is your English still all right, Angel?" the DG asked him.

"Sir. If you talk to a man in a language he understands, that goes to his head. If you talk to him in his own language, that goes to his heart. Mandela."

The director paused and looked at him.

"Yes, Angel. I remember."

Angel stood at the door when the DG called to him.

"Oh, Angel."

"Yes, sir."

"The minister wants to give your old mentor an award."

"Nick Roux?"

"She's recommending that Mr Roux should get an Intelligence Lifetime Award from the President himself."

"He deserves it," said Angel.

*

450

In Arcadia, Angel picked up the phone.

"Hello, Jumbo."

"Angel, my dear fellow. *Unjani?*"

"*Ngikhona*, Jumbo."

TWENTY-EIGHT

Angel found the door by the sound that certain Englishmen make, a sort of shy whinny. Other than that the London Ship Club would have been impossible to find. A very small sign by the entry bell gave it away, but only to those that knew the club burgee.

Joshua 'Jumbo' Cameron had been vague with directions when he'd called Angel at his office in Pretoria.

"The LSC. It's a sailing club. In the City, by the river. Cruisers for the most part. We tried some racing but there were too many arguments. Upset the bar staff."

He had insisted they met on a Tuesday, club night, full of bores like him and noisy so that no one would hear them talk. They'd been friends since boarding school, had shared pointless early morning runs through foggy cold town streets, elm leaves rustling under their feet. It came as a surprise to both that they'd ended up as opposite numbers in similar organisations, although through very different ways.

Jumbo lowered himself carefully into a deep leather chair, his drooping jowls rattling like halyards against a mast, and ordered a beer.

"Difficult to get a decent pint anywhere in London," he moaned.

"Not even The Northumberland Arms?" Angel asked him.

"I wish."

Jumbo's department had moved office nine years previously to the old Imperial Chemical Industries headquarters at Thames House. He missed Bloomsbury.

"The old Northumberland Arms on Gower Street used to pull such a good pint at lunchtime. Not that anyone drinks at lunchtime anymore."

Jumbo missed that too.

"The new place is handy for the club though."

"And convenient for the south side of the river," Angel said.

Jumbo's 'business partners' had moved at the same time from Century House in Lambeth, to be closer to the river near Vauxhall Bridge.

"Yes, that too," agreed Jumbo. "By the way, how is Nick Roux?"

"Bored."

"A very clever man. Send him my sincere best wishes for a peaceful retirement."

It surprised Angel that Jumbo thought so highly of his old boss. Angel and Jumbo were the same age but Jumbo had been in the Security Service for thirty years. Angel wondered if he had thoughts of his own retirement.

Jumbo had been a member of the London Ship Club for just as long and had seated Angel for dinner in between an old woman who smelt of cats on his left and a tall man in an inky dark suit on his right; Angel wondered if he worked as an undertaker.

Jumbo spoke of the people either side of Angel as though they weren't there. He didn't introduce them.

"These two? There are just two types of people in the world, Angel. Those you'd want to be in a life raft with and those you wouldn't."

Jumbo didn't clarify to which group they belonged.

The wine waiter came around and Angel said, "*Obrigado*."

"So, Angel, lots of languages still? I speak some French. Not very well. Seems to depend on whether I'm buying or selling. If I'm buying they understand me perfectly. If selling they haven't got a clue. Odd."

The waiter from Evora poured.

"Ah. A Côtes du Rhône. Not sure which côte."

Jumbo drank deeply and thoughtfully. Angel imagined he needed to think about the wine.

"You need a lawyer, Angel. Club's full of them. You're sitting next to one. Known him for years. Wouldn't trust him with toffees." He leant forward. "He's the sort of man who would try and trick a new boy with the port." Jumbo reminded himself of the wine. "Lovely to see you, dear boy. Can you tell me why you are here? Woman problems? Women?"

Angel looked at the two people beside him: the tall thin pallid lawyer and the malodorous old woman. He assumed they were both members of the sailing club but couldn't imagine either of them being tossed around on a small yacht.

"Don't worry, Angel. All safe here. He's deaf and she's stupid. They both think I'm with MI5."

Jumbo laughed.

"You know why we still call it that, Angel?"

Angel shook his head.

"Because if we were known by our real name people would have to call us the SS." Jumbo curled himself into a round ball with laughter, unable to speak. "Can you imagine? The UK's internal spying organisation. The SS. I ask you, who thought that up? Not that I work for them."

Angel couldn't hide his surprise.

"You work for SIS now?"

"No, not really. Sort of in between the two."

He's a hybrid, thought Angel, *probably always has been; running a department with no name.*

"Intelligence-gathering is not that clear-cut, as you well know, Angel."

Angel did know – from years of service in departments with ever-changing acronyms. He knew that the Security Service in the UK concentrated on domestic threats and the Secret Intelligence Service provided foreign intelligence. He knew the problem here, as at home in South Africa, was that many domestic threats originated overseas and demanded foreign intelligence.

"The lines get blurred, you see," said Jumbo.

"And WMD?" Angel asked.

"A good example, Angel. In fact, for a long while that was my particular pigeon. It's the responsibility of the Security Service to control the proliferation of Weapons of Mass Destruction, most of which is by rogue foreign states and outside of the UK. Blurred lines again."

"Rogue foreign states like South Africa?"

"We thought so at one time."

Angel passed him a blue file.

"Ah, lovely," said Jumbo. "You're going to give me a blow job."

Angel knew the joke. In the old Service between the wars decoded messages had been circulated in blue-jacketed files known as Blue Jobs or BJs. They hadn't anticipated today's more physically intimate interpretation.

Not for the first time Angel wondered about the British. He had been born in London, sent to school in Dorset and could have easily followed a path like Jumbo's. He respected them but he'd never understood them. They had a way of being flippant with serious matters and yet intensely serious about trivia.

Jumbo glanced inside the blue jacket.

"Ah yes. Mr Phillips. I wondered when he'd crop up."

Jumbo drank some wine and turned to look at the bar.

"Zac's over there, look. Say hello."

Angel nodded to a large and bald man who raised a dimpled mug in salute.

"He tells everyone he's a management consultant. Brilliant. People don't have any idea what he does but no one ever asks." Jumbo concentrated on his wine glass. "An accidental encounter started it all," he said. "I think it may have been January '82, the year some idiot vice-commodore organised a freezing cold winter rally to Yarmouth that nearly killed off half the members."

Angel had always assumed that Jumbo had sent Zac to South Africa in a mad rush, not a thought about his cover, to tickle things up a bit and see if anything crawled out of the woodwork. He probably shouldn't have sent him but there had been, as Angel knew, an interesting development.

"Zac had drawn a big blank until luckily bumping into a teenage English backpacker, Ralph Phillips. Together they got as high as kites on a beach and out came a tale of where Ralph had been and what he'd seen," Jumbo explained. "Zac couldn't believe his luck. Until then he'd thought he would be coming home empty-handed, tail between his legs."

Jumbo waved an empty bottle in the direction of the waiter.

"In December 1981 Ralph flew to Johannesburg, nearly twenty-two years ago. Would you like me to tell all?" Jumbo asked. "I felt like the son of Nun."

*

Jumbo Cameron beamed cordially at other diners around the restaurant of the London Ship Club but Angel knew he wasn't acknowledging old sailors, only anxious of the whereabouts of his new Portuguese friend, the wine waiter from Evora.

"Zac and I met Ralph on a train to Dorset," said Jumbo, relieved when bottles appeared at their end of the table. "His name went on a report, no further action, and Ralph gets on with his life. Less than a year later the name flagged up. For some reason that I never understood he wanted to be a soldier and he'd gotten into trouble."

Ralph had joined the British Army. Other boys from his school forged ahead with service careers but Ralph stumbled. He found this difficult to reconcile because he loved it. He loved the daily physicality, absorbing new skills like a military sponge, the variety of training challenges. The problem turned out to be most of the other soldiers. He found them often inflexible and became frustrated by their sometimes lethargic thought processes and sluggish responses to situational changes. It wasn't a one-way street. Other soldiers had a problem with him. Ralph would read instead of drink with them at a club in town on a Saturday night and then go alone to a village pub on a Sunday morning with the newspapers. In a hundred tiny ways there were unassailable breaches between them. They would turn to him to answer questions on navigation or radio procedure but exclude him from a quick kick-around on the football pitch and then not invite him to that boozer with girls known to be easy pickups. Ralph blamed himself. He had recoiled like his self-loading rifle from the chummy group camaraderie essential in army life.

"That was a big mistake," said Angel.

Jumbo scratched his head.

"When? Oh, yes. February '83. A frosty night navigation exercise."

It had come to a head at Sennybridge, a thirty-seven-thousand-acre Ministry of Defence training area with a straight access road called Church Hill to the top of the Brecon Beacons, cut like a staircase in the Welsh hillside by an ambitious Royal Engineer.

"He left his squad and found his own way home because an officer wouldn't listen to him and continued leading them all, cold and tired, the wrong way. The Army was very impressed from what I remember. He broke some sort of record. Got back six hours before the rest of them. But not very 'Army', if you know what I mean. You have to sympathise with them. They can't have soldiers just doing their own thing and leaving their platoon to muddle through in the dark."

To Ralph, as tired as the rest of them, the way home had seemed obvious. Even in the blackness the dogleg shape that looked even blacker could only be the forestry plantation that led to a valley and a track by a meandering stream to the waiting Bedfords. The officer preferred his soldiers to follow, quietly. Ralph had slipped away, alone.

"So, he left. Services No Longer Required. Conduct Exemplary. He told them to take the eight-figure number starting two four six five that they'd given him and put it somewhere alimentary. Never been a great team player though, has he? That didn't matter to me. I collared him just as he handed in his kit, minus one kitbag canvas green and one beret size seven with cap badge, and suggested he might like to see a mate of mine in London. My 'mate' sent him to a security firm, guards for art galleries and night watchmen for City offices, that sort of thing. Where was it? Diamond Street?"

Jumbo scrutinised his glass to remember. Of course, Emerald Street. They had an unmarked glass door opposite the Emerald Street nick. You got buzzed in, then went upstairs for the regular office, with a pretty girl on reception, people pushing bits of paper around and a tall rangy Rupert, ex 'vulgar-fraction' Lancer, always on the phone haughtily selling static guards for exhibitions at the Tate Modern and the Royal Academy. And Ralph could tell Ian and Innes, the old grammar school mates he lodged with in Lewisham, that he worked 'In security, in the control room'. Working long shifts to explain his absences from the pub. Working days and nights to explain his nocturnal movements. But he wasn't a security guard controller. He didn't go upstairs and chat with 'the Sandra' or 'the Dawn' when she wasn't answering the phone. He went downstairs through an airlock, with heavy doors and a monitor in the middle, to where the real action took place, to the Trainer.

"The renowned Trainer. Didn't he have a surname like a Christian name? Allen? Tom?" Jumbo asked the old woman, who beamed with pleasure at his attention.

"Peter. John Peter. That's right, the retired six foot seven Welsh Guards warrant officer, with a scary scarred face cratered from some childhood pox, a Queen's Gallantry

Medal, and a dapper line in brown shoes and brown hats to go with his pinstripe in town."

Jumbo started eating.

"I remember the Trainer particularly liked it when he came back with the complete airline meal on the little tray it's served on."

It had been one of those silly tasks like getting a footballer's signature or your photo with a topless model, tasks that can reveal so much. Of special note to the Trainer was how well he'd taught him to lie. Ralph convincingly told him that he'd gently persuaded a plump and understanding stewardess to give him the meal tray and that he'd then ravenously eaten it all on the Tube home. The Trainer remembered being very impressed by how well Ralph did it. He wanted to believe him. Alas it became clear to him that Ralph had helped himself to a used one from a rubbish skip at the airport. The coffee stains in the little plastic cup had given him away. It ended up as a small black mark to an otherwise faultless performance.

"You did use untrained people," said Angel.

Jumbo just smiled. It had been a project developed initially by some free-thinking high flyers at the Home Office for cheap but valuable domestic surveillance. Sometimes the recruits were military, but from any rank and with diverse periods of service and from any branch. Equally they could come from the Civil Service, or from one of the professions. The Church had provided notable recruits, including a young vicar from Tyne and Wear, a keen amateur boxer, who had beaten up two youths he'd found trying to steal the church silver. Fleet Street had provided an investigative journalist sacked by his paper before he discovered too much about his editor's dodgy business dealings and cocaine-fuelled wife-swapping parties with a Chief of Police. Occasionally they came from people destined for nationally important British companies, or strategically important British industries. The recruits were given some one-to-one basic tradecraft, which it had never been expected they would need, but it gave an opportunity to evaluate if they were interested and whether they were interesting. The Service called them 'meerkats'.

"You had a network of eyes and ears," said Angel. "Like the SS," he joked.

"Very funny, Angel. Our meerkats were nothing sinister, not a secret society or 'messengers of terror'. All we asked was that they occasionally stuck their head up, had a look around and warned us if there was anything nasty."

*

Jumbo ate until he'd cleared his plate. Angel picked aside soft cabbage from hard chicken, the food reminding him of school.

"Fast-forward three or four years and Ralph is at an agricultural school in Shropshire."

"Harper Adams," Angel interrupted.

Jumbo couldn't disguise his surprise.

"You heard?"

Angel drank some wine, quietly.

"Did that information come from Rietvlei?" Jumbo asked. "I'd like to talk about that sometime."

Angel wished he hadn't said anything. He felt sure Jumbo would want him to trade some information in return for the help being provided.

"We had some interests around Shropshire at that time,"

Jumbo said. "Threats to RAF training bases at Shawbury and Cosford, Army barracks at Tern Hill and Copthorne, and a concern that Harper Adams might be hiding a nest of student vipers. I sent Zac to ask for Ralph's help."

The dessert made a brief appearance. Angel declined and watched Jumbo eat something shockingly pink that wobbled in his spoon as if alive and intent on escape. Jumbo talked of Zac in-between slippery crimson mouthfuls.

"Zac went as a driver for a rugby team, a match between Harper Adams and Stafford Police, I believe, and chatted him up in the canteen after the game. He wasn't that keen; in fact, Zac had to remind him in no uncertain terms of his obligations. He fitted perfectly, you see."

Ralph, bless his cotton socks, had become a bit of a politician and elected to be President of the Students Union. Roy Grimsay, the Principal, had always been an old friend of Jumbo's organisation. Ralph just had to keep alert in case someone had witnessed a punch-up with a short-haired bloke, or anything unusual. Vehicles making unexplainable rendezvous in unexpected places, gossip, drugs, money, college kids with the type of girls that real students wouldn't be able to afford. And weapons, especially weapons. Jumbo worried most about the terrorist threat. If Ralph heard anything he'd just go and see Roy. No one would suspect the SU president for going to see the Principal. He had hundreds of reasons to need to talk to him.

"Did he deliver?" asked Angel.

"It turned out to be tremendously successful. I recall one notable triumph. We were very pleased."

"Anything since?" Angel asked.

"Not much then until Ralph ended up farming in Portugal and Zac received a call because he'd tipped off customs about a suspected load of drugs coming to England in a lorry load of his potatoes. A false alarm – the driver had been smuggling a few crates of wine."

"And now he's at this place in Cambridgeshire, Fresh Grown Produce Ltd, near Ely, buying and selling vegetables, travelling the world."

"So I believe," said Jumbo. "Haven't had a lot to do with him lately."

Angel had always known when Jumbo lied.

"Whatever I can do though, Angel, I'm happy to. If you feel you have something that needs putting on a legal footing, this inheritance, I can certainly recommend someone."

Angel rubbed tired eyes with finger and thumb.

"Joshua."

"Yes," said Jumbo.

"Joshua was the son of Nun. In the Bible, Joshua sent two men to spy on Jericho."

Jumbo was impressed.

"Very good, Angel. Well done."

"You did too," said Angel. "You sent Zac, and Ralph."

The man on Angel's right asked him to pass the port.

"Ha. Told you so," roared Jumbo.

He picked up the decanter and slammed it down on Angel's left in front of the old woman.

"I imagine it will get around to you eventually," he shouted at the smiling cadaverous lawyer.

Jumbo and 'the undertaker' were the very best of friends.

*

The funeral took place in Brixton Cemetery, and Roux had made the arrangements for eleven o'clock. It seemed a suitable time of day to remember the dead.

463

Few people were there other than the priest, Angel and Roux to see Elanza buried next to her father. Angel read the headstone and laid a wreath of king protea, South Africa's national flower. A black car, blacked-out windows, with security and driver in the front, waited patiently beside them.

"Who's in the car?" Angel asked.

"The Professor, and an old friend of Blackie Swart's," said Roux.

Angel stared at it.

"I'm executor of her will," he told Roux. "There's the small matter of the money. She's split it into three equal parts. I'm told her estate is worth over two hundred and fifty million dollars."

"Who inherits?" asked Roux.

"A range of medical charities gets a third. An AIDS charity based in Brighton England, called AVERT, working globally but with a big project in the Eastern Cape. Another one called mothers2mothers that reaches out specifically to Africa. An important research centre in Melbourne Australia called the Burnet Institute. A host of smaller ones, all based here in South Africa. All seem," he searched for the word, "appropriate. She didn't tell me what they were before she died but I don't believe there's been any coercion. I think all of them could be said to directly benefit South Africa. And Ralph obviously. He gets a third."

"And?"

"Me," said Angel. "I get a third as well."

"I'm curious," said Roux. "Shouldn't she have given more to you? It seems a little unfair. Elanza hadn't seen Ralph for ages and it was you who cared for her for twenty-one years."

"She was very emotional at the end. And stubborn. I think it was a sort of thank-you gift for Ralph. Without him, Elanza and I would never have met."

Roux looked around at the flowers.

"You'll have to give it up, Angel. I'm sorry. You fell into this through the course of your work as a government official. It was government money in the first place that bought Blackie's farm. You'll have to give it back to the state. Lord knows they need it."

The black car started its engine.

"We'll have to let Ralph keep his third, if she genuinely wished that to be. How much is that? Eighty-three million dollars? Continue to keep an eye on him, just to make sure that South African money isn't being used against South Africa in any way."

"I doubt that. I think he's likely to spend it all on a boat."

Angel looked toward the black car.

"I guess Mr Botha's investment wasn't so bad, then. The government will get two-thirds of the money back at least, in one form or another."

Angel did a calculation in his head.

"That's 166 million dollars for the sixty-four million dollars that the state spent on Blackie's farm back in 1974. Twenty-nine years ago. About three and a half per cent per annum. Not a brilliant rate of return but better than losing the lot."

"It's not the government he expected to benefit though. I'm sorry, Angel. About the money," said Roux.

"I didn't want it anyway."

"Angel, there's something I want to tell you. It's about Ralph."

Angel tried to look through the windows of the car at the people inside.

"We weren't interested in the boy. Blackie's money, his inheritance, was irrelevant."

"Why did you have me follow him through Africa?"

"At the time we were worried he may have accidentally taken photographs of our missile facilities in the Cape, photographs that would have been damaging if they'd fallen into the hands of other intelligence agencies."

Roux put his hands in his pockets and straightened his back.

"In the end his photographs showed nothing."

"What was it all about, then?"

"It was all about you, Angel."

Roux poked him in the chest.

"Counter Intelligence caught you talking to a man we knew as Zac, a man we suspected of being a British agent."

Angel hung his head.

"The *Heining*."

Roux put his hand on Angel's shoulder.

"I remember being so angry with you, Angel, so disappointed."

Angel looked at the grave.

"We had you follow the boy, just to get you out of the way. I needed some time to decide what to do with you. I even had a thug from Military Intelligence lined up to take you out if I'd given him the word."

"Nels," said Angel.

Roux nodded.

"But I had no idea that you two had a history and that Nels would welcome the opportunity to settle old scores."

Roux looked at Angel's face, dark and hard as though chiselled from a shiny rock.

"And then I had an idea. I felt let down by you, used. I would use you."

"You kept me in play?"

"Correct, until the very end of apartheid. I used you to

466

help me convince the British that we had the bomb. I gave you a job on the edge of Project Hobo where we could trickle out phoney details of the programme for you to pass on to Jumbo."

Angel suddenly realised the significance.

"We bluffed it all?" he asked.

"Yes, Angel, we made it all up. When international inspectors were finally allowed access in '94 they found nothing, because there had been nothing."

Angel felt guilty.

"The effort that must have been involved. I never meant to jeopardise all that. I wanted to prevent a disaster."

"You helped, Angel. We wouldn't have been taken half as seriously if Jumbo had told everyone it was all a hoax. The British and Americans wouldn't have put nearly as much pressure on the ANC and the new President to control their members who wanted to slaughter all of the whites as soon as they had power."

Roux held his arm.

"Our deception saved a lot of lives. The UK and the US believed we had nuclear weapons and negotiated harder with the new black government to ensure that there was no bloodshed."

Jumbo had been right, Roux the cleverest of men. He deserved the medal.

"I'm sorry, Nick."

"Don't be. Don't feel bad either. Jumbo wasn't stupid, even though he came over as an oaf. He knew we didn't have the bomb."

"What? He knew?"

"I used you, Angel, to make Jumbo think we had the bomb; he knew all along that we didn't, so he used you as well, to make me think he believed we did."

"He played me back?"

"That's right."

"Why?"

"The same reason as me. To prevent bloodshed. It happened to be in everyone's interests for us to have the deterrent, to have control."

Angel looked at his feet, trying to collate new data but labouring like a computer low on memory.

"Did Jumbo lie to his own government?" he asked. "Did he not tell them?"

"I doubt he lied. He just didn't share his suspicions. There was plenty of evidence to say we did have a bomb. You had given it to him."

"I don't understand. Why didn't he tell them?" Angel asked.

Roux looked at the black car.

"The UK is South Africa's most important trading partner," he said, "but that's unimportant compared to their Foreign Direct Investment in this country. UK businesses have hundreds of billions of dollars invested in South Africa. Big name PLCs, like Anglo American, Vodacom, Holiday Inn, BP, Unilever, all have a UK parent and are listed in London, all with UK institutional shareholders. The potential financial loss from an economic collapse due to an unruly transition was enormous."

"You mean if South Africa had gone like Zimbabwe at Independence?"

"That was the British fear. So, they said, 'Look, ANC, the Boers have the bomb. You'll get power and we'll help, but be mindful of their concerns. Keep them happy and do it peacefully, because if you push them into a corner and they drop a few bombs there won't be anything for your new black government to govern'."

Angel understood.

468

"And we, the British, will lose a lot of money," he said.

Roux felt old and tired. He was starting to think he would enjoy his retirement.

"The philosophy of politics is about managing economics; everything else is bullshit so that you keep your job."

Angel, confused, remembered the documents he'd come across mistakenly filed in his cabinet that he'd smuggled to Jumbo, the photographs he'd occasionally found lying about and sent to the British.

"How did he know we didn't have the bomb?"

Roux made ready to leave, turning wearily from the grave.

"Have you seen Oak Ridge in Tennessee?" he asked.

"The US facility?"

"In the end there was nothing you could have given Jumbo that would have convinced him. We had the uranium, but to enrich it? To produce 235, to make fissile material? No way. The Americans needed one building a mile long for gaseous diffusion. It took twenty-five thousand people just to build it, the biggest building in the world, thirty-seven acres under one roof, part of a 4,500-acre laboratory site. We couldn't have hidden a facility like Oak Ridge, done something even a fraction of the scale, without everyone knowing. We didn't have it, and Jumbo knew it."

"We had Pelindaba." Angel couldn't believe what Roux had said. "We had a vortex separation process – they're small units; we didn't need the same area as Oak Ridge."

"Ah yes, Pelindaba. Our nuclear research and uranium enrichment centre out at Harties Dam. You know it well, Angel, from your weekend rambles in the countryside."

Roux shook his head.

"The Pelsakon cascade was a very inefficient process, Angel. The uranium was going around and around in that thing for two hundred days before it reached weapons grade. We didn't produce anything at all for two years because the Teflon filters blocked. There were always production problems. One time, all the small holes in the jet nozzles filled with solid uranium due to some impurity. In addition to all that, the energy consumption proved to be enormous, we couldn't remove the waste heat, and the level of enrichment and quantity produced remained low. Lots of production records to prove otherwise. All fake. We wildly exaggerated the amount of HEU they actually produced."

"But we still have it," said Angel. "When they dismantled the bombs the uranium-235 was removed and cast into ingots. It's under guard in the old silver vault at Pelindaba."

Roux raised an eyebrow.

"Really?"

"Yes. The Americans want us to give it up but the government won't do it. It's ours; we made it."

"Have you seen it, Angel, a half-ton lump sitting there in the vault? A sinister pile, glowing in the dark maybe?" Roux asked.

Angel looked at him quizzically.

"It doesn't exist, Angel. Our new government is playing the same game that we did. It's a bargaining tool. You don't need to have a bomb to get what you want – just demonstrate the ability to make one and the means to deliver it. Ask North Korea."

Roux looked at Angel and felt sorry for having deceived him but relieved that they'd remained friends throughout, pleased that his conviction in Angel hadn't been misplaced. Angel had made a significant contribution to his country. At the end of apartheid Angel had been something of a hero to those in the new Intelligence Service who knew of his betrayal, those to whom Roux had helpfully told of Angel's leaking of nuclear secrets to the British to guarantee a peaceful transition. His career had prospered under a black African government. He was Deputy Director of Foreign Intelligence in the South African Secret Service, Roux's old position when he'd recruited Angel twenty-three years previously.

Roux shook Angel's hand and then walked past the car nodding his head. The black car followed him out, slowly.

Angel went back to the grave and looked at the headstones. He thought of a Swazi saying: 'Ayilahle boNkhosi'. It literally meant 'Throw it away, people'. People said it when someone had lost a friend. Life went on. He picked up the wreath of protea flowers.

*

Angel, stiff and hungry, had missed lunch. It had been 180 kilometres from Pretoria and he'd been sitting for two hours in the back of a government car driven by a young white chauffeur from the office, the wreath of protea beside him. He would have enjoyed going by train but they hadn't improved.

Angel had no idea that Treilea would be such a huge town, forty thousand inhabitants, Safoil a massive industrial complex. Huge cooling towers burped steam and noise amid a maze of pipes. A free-standing chimney, high as the Eiffel Tower, stood over conveyor belts a kilometre long, bringing coal from neighbouring mines. It had become the world's largest petrochemical complex, the biggest built at one time on a single site, on Blackie Swart's farm.

Angel looked for Roodhuis, Blackie's old farmhouse, to lay his wreath where Elanza had grown up. He walked aimlessly around town until, in desperation, he laid it at the end of a street – Swart Street.

It looked toward the guts of the Safoil plant. Angel picked up the wreath again and went back to the car. He couldn't leave Elanza looking at that.

At the highway the driver stopped.

"Back to Pretoria, sir? The office?"

To the east the N17 led to Swaziland. Angel had seen the road signs. He thought it probably 220 kilometres from Treilea to Mbabane. Two and a half hours. He'd travelled through by train in 1969, nearly thirty-five years previously, and had never been back.

He thought of the office, the threats.

The People Against Gangsters and Drugs had attacked Planet Hollywood, a restaurant in Cape Town's Waterfront tourist area, in 1998, but since then their activities, and those of the Muslims Against Global Oppression, another Islamic-orientated vigilante group, had tailed off. The threat from imported Islamic extremists remained high, and countering radicalised small cells attracted to al-Qaeda, who could move freely along South Africa's long and porous border, became a daunting task. It wasn't his job anyway. NIA not SASS had that responsibility. Domestic Intelligence, not foreign.

There existed, however, a much closer cooperation within the intelligence services, less infighting, fewer power struggles. That proved to be Gabriël Lombard's greatest legacy from 1980 when he started NIS and Roux had recruited Angel. Today, no one, neither NIA nor SASS, wanted South Africa to become a haven for foreign terrorists. Information directly from Angel's department had led to the arrest in Cape Town in 1999 of Khalfan Khamis Mohamed after bombings in Kenya and Tanzania. Angel had been working recently with the US to pick up within South Africa Saud Memon, a Pakistani with al-Qaeda connections. They had operations planned, work to do. He could be back at the office before five o'clock and get three or four hours' work done.

Angel sighed.

"Arcadia, please. Back to the office."

Angel thought grimly of the work ahead but then cheered. He'd go out to Hartbeespoort Dam at the weekend, stay over at a lodge on Harties and get some exercise, take a long hike in the rocky ridges of the Magaliesberg. He knew a safe place to leave Elanza's wreath, somewhere with a wide view south, a view over the clean grasslands of the highveld. He'd go to Shelter Rock.

THE BRITISH VIRGIN ISLANDS

2017

EPILOGUE

The yacht *Pacific Wave*, wide in the beam but powerfully rigged, effortlessly pushed aside sixty tons of blue water. On her stern the name had been softly highlighted with a white shadow, along with the home port – London. She was five thousand sea miles from home, enjoying tropical water.

Ralph, his face tanned under a wide hat, sat with two fingers on the wheel. The yacht sailed herself, the wind forty degrees off the port bow, the main and runner on hard, a turn or two on the big genoa just to keep her balanced.

Through a gap in the reef past Mosquito Island the North Sound opened wide, the water sheltered on all sides and almost completely flat off the yacht club dock at the east end of the bay. Ralph came alongside the long YCCS pontoon and threw lines.

A dark-haired girl climbed up the companionway steps wearing a bikini and sarong, a phone in her beach bag beeping as though someone had summoned her. They stepped off together and walked through gardens to a bar and a pool looking over Eustatia and Necker Islands.

The barmaid lived locally, in the Valley on Virgin Gorda.

"Hey, guys."

"Hi, Ginny."

The Yacht Club Costa Smeralda remained quiet outside of regattas. Curious boaters would often dinghy past, unsure if they could visit. Ginny's only customer looked to be an old man sitting at the bar. He had very short greying hair and a clean-shaven face, mid-sixties but still powerful. Ralph thought he might be a retired US Marine or a fit New York stockbroker. In his experience they were either one or the other. A look passed between him and the girl, but then everyone looked at her twice.

"I'll grab some loungers by the pool. Get me a drink," she said.

Ralph smiled at Ginny.

"Two glasses of Minuty and a big bottle of Pelegrino, please, Ginny."

At the bar the man sat looking at his glass.

"Nice yacht," he said.

Ralph couldn't place the accent. He'd become very good at it. He could now surprise Canadians by saying which city they came from. But he had been wrong about the old man. Not military or a stockbroker. And not New York, not the US – much further east.

"Yeah, she's okay. Got used to her now," said Ralph.

"Yours?"

"Well, technically she's owned by a company."

"Ah, for tax reasons."

"No. Nothing to do with tax. She's owned by a British

company, not a British Virgin Islands one. It's to limit the liability."

The man seemed to understand.

"In case someone goes overboard?"

"In case I poison someone with a dodgy burger."

They both laughed.

"You charter, then?"

"When we can. Not enough."

"Mmmm… I get it," said the old man. "Americans?"

"Yep, mostly. Boston or Austin. Don't know why."

"Works out okay?"

"Oh yes. Love 'em. Shouldn't be allowed to use the radio, though. They all sound like they're a moon shot talking to Houston. Brits are just as bad. Some of them have voices that have sparked revolutions."

"Like mine?"

Ralph had embarrassed himself. Of course. Excellent accented English.

"You sail around here?" he asked.

"Mostly. Pick up in St Thomas and do a tour up to Virgin Gorda and back. Usually a week's trip. We're quiet in the summer. Our guests are usually in Maine or Rhode Island on their own boats then."

"What, from Memorial Day to Labour Day?"

"That's right. Funny that back home we'd say summer lasted from Chelsea Flower Show until Cowes Week."

The man smiled.

"Any pirates?"

"Loads. They all run chandleries."

Ginny brought Ralph his drinks.

"There you go, man," she said.

"Thanks, Ginny."

"Local?" the man asked.

Ralph had become used to the questioning. For the past fourteen years he'd been watching the world go by at a sedate eight knots, and he felt he'd mentally slowed down to that pace. Nothing bothered him very much.

"Sort of. Been here a while now."

Fourteen years. Ever since a London lawyer interrupted you during a typically difficult day at work and surprised you with a letter from a dead woman in Johannesburg and a big cheque. Sign here please, Mr Phillips, and have a lovely life. I hope you kept the letter.

"Learnt a lot, I guess?"

"For sure. There's loads that I know now that I wish I'd known then," agreed Ralph.

"Such as?"

"Umm, naked Twister."

The man laughed and muscles quivered in his neck.

"You?" asked Ralph. "Where are you from?"

"All over." The man smiled. "It's complicated."

"Passing through?"

"Yes. Just passing through."

"Need a yacht? No. Not this time, right?"

"No. Not this time. It sounds fun, though. I met a bloke at the airport in Antigua. Hell of a delay. What's that airline called?"

"Leave island any time."

"Yeah. That must be it. He worked in London. Had a vacation here on a boat. He loved it. Zac someone."

"Sadly not with us. I don't know anyone called Zac."

Good for you. You still lie very well. Didn't answer too quickly. No fumbling or looking away. Well done. You've had years of practice, of course. Must have come in useful for work, with all

480

that foreign travel. What did you do? Oh yes. A vegetable trader. Excellent. Perfectly understandable justification for moving freely around the countryside. Brilliant 'living cover'. Follow the sun to find the sweetest corn in Morocco, Senegal or Israel. Maybe somewhere cooler for cheaper broccoli. Where would that be? China? Chile? Ukraine? Take a few photos of irrigation booms, harvest rigs, cold stores, factories. Take a few more while looking at Egyptian potatoes, not that you ever bought potatoes as the job had been done to death, but the fields were enticingly close to those interesting tunnel entrances at a huge construction site in the middle of nowhere. Take a sneaky picture of those Italian-speaking businessmen with the silent pouting hookers, a tango of memory stick swapping taking place with an impatient sweating waiter in that fancy Buenos Aires restaurant while you sit the other side of the room discussing garlic prices. And some more of the guardhouse and security to that Turkish co-located 'civil' and military airport, the one with no name, that you took through the window of the hire car on a drive-by while you distracted the farmer who talked anxiously of his pesticide application records, the airport that he knew nothing about even though his leek fields went up to the shiny razor-wire fence glinting in the Anatolian sunshine. You'd take pictures of anything they asked you for. Anything Zac needed.

Ralph paid for his drinks from an old brown leather wallet. The man saw it and smiled.

"Good luck with the boat." He looked at the girl on the lounger. "And everything else."

Ralph walked away but then turned and went back to the bar, still holding the drinks.

"I'm sorry. Have we met before?" Ralph asked.

"No, I don't believe so."

Ralph fumbled glasses and a bottle held by the neck onto the bar top.

"My name's Ralph." He pointed toward the dock. "And the boat is called *Pacific Wave*. Just in case you change your mind."

"Okay. I'll remember."

"And your name?"

The man got up to leave.

"Mr Rock."

"Rock," Ralph repeated.

Halfway back to the lounger Ralph looked back, Angel Rock already walking down a path towards the sea.

"Who were you talking to?" the girl asked.

"Some bloke. Talking about the boat."

They could see the boat from where they sat by the pool. Four people in a dinghy were taking pictures of her. She had that effect. It had been the reason he'd bought her. If she looked right, she'd go right.

"Did he come from the US?"

"No, England. A big lawyer, I should think, here to open some offshore accounts. Or empty them. But there may have been something else in his voice as well," he said.

The girl opened a tablet and started to read. Ralph looked over the pool to the bay. Kite surfers were flying in a billionaires' playground.

"Have you got a thing on that to translate?"

"Sure," she said. "What language?"

Ralph wondered. He'd never forgotten the man in Uganda with surprising and unmistakably accented English. What do they speak in Swaziland? Swazi? English? His name had sounded more German. Rots. Danish? Dutch?

"English to Afrikaans."

She hesitated.

"What word?"

"Rock."

She tapped away and then laughed.

"Funny. It's similar but you would never guess it."

"I think I could."

He looked at her and then out over the bay.

She put the tablet down and stared at him before felinely stretching in the sun on the lounger.

"I'm hot. Take me back to the boat."

Ralph looked at her curiously.

*

Angel walked from the bar to a helipad at a nearby hotel. A canary yellow Robinson rocked while waiting for him, chirping, its rotors already turning. He climbed in and put on headphones.

"All done, Mr Rots?" asked the pilot.

Angel had debated coming, but in the end had decided that Ralph was an essential part of his memory of Elanza. Ralph wasn't important to him personally, or to the Intelligence Service. He'd been a topic of conversation with Elanza, a relaxing diversion to their own problems in the way one might ask, 'I wonder what old so-and-so is up to these days?'. Angel's job, and his access to the Owl Sight communication interception technology at Rietvlei, had made it easy for him, almost as a leisure pursuit, to follow Ralph as he stumbled through his life. Continuing to keep a curious trivial eye on him helped to remind Angel of the woman he'd loved.

"Yes. Everything done."

The helicopter took off over a beautiful bay of blue water and small islands with perfect beaches. Angel looked out of the window.

"Magnificent."

"Angels' view," said the pilot.

Angel looked at him.

"What?"

"What the angels must see. Retiring soon, I hear."

"Yep, just tidying up some loose ends while I can."

"When did you join the Service, sir?"

"At the beginning. 1980."

"At NIS? With Professor Lombard and Nick Roux?"

"Yes."

"You'll have seen some changes in thirty-seven years."

Angel thought of what he'd just left at home. A fourteen-year-old boy shot in Soweto by a foreign national that had led to xenophobic violence against foreign shop owners. The Nkandla report showing that President Zuma had stolen millions of tax dollars for his new home. Leaked documents. The spy cables. Senior politicians in nuclear talks with Iranian officials.

"Same shit. Different colour," said Angel.

"Think you'll be coming back to the BVI?"

Angel looked down at the exquisite Oil Nut Bay, natural beauty unspoiled by development.

"If needed," he said. "I've eyes on the ground. If needed I'll get a call."

*

Ralph and the girl walked back down the pontoon. As she stepped on board, a helicopter passed overhead and she glanced up.

Before the hill cut off his view, Angel saw her. It appeared to him that they looked straight at each other, but quickly the helicopter lifted over Gorda Peak and the girl, Ralph and *Pacific Wave* were gone, replaced by the blue of the channel leading from the BVI towards St John.

ACKNOWLEDGEMENTS

Many encouraged me, probably without realising, and it was always unexpected. I would especially like to thank: Katie & Will, and Kathleen M-B; Viv & Nicola and Simon & Carol from Milton-on-Stour schooldays; Ian, Mark B and Dr Katherine from SGS/SHS; Heather in South Africa; Will B, David in Cumbria, Andy & Gina, and Julian (especially Julian) from Harper Adams; PK and Vera in Portugal; Tim, Toley, Calum, Hamish, Ros, Caru and Ellie, all from G's; Dogga; John & Lyndon from the sailing club; Len in the Virgin Islands; structural editors Philippa and Parul; Helene for persisting with an early draft; the captains and crews of British Airways Gatwick based 'triple seven' fleet who talked aeroplanes and entertained in St Lucia; Bob in Grenada; Sabina for allowing me to stay at The Stone House, Marigot Bay and quietly finish everything off; Fern and Sophie at Troubador Publishing; and Lynn for putting up with it all every day.

EASTER FARM

BY MP MILES

*E*aster Farm is a romantic thriller set in Portugal in 1996 with characters taken from *Shelter Rock*, the story of a boy's journey through Africa.

Apartheid has ended, and Angel Rots is progressing his professional career by fighting corruption in arms procurement - in this case mothballed Israeli jets sold as new to the highest bidder in a deal brokered by his nemesis the one-armed Nels.

Ralph Philips, now farming in Portugal and falling in love, comes to Angel's attention after tipping off customs about a suspected drugs haul. With smuggling gangs threatening Ralph's vegetable growing business, and his new girl, Angel once more must personally intervene to protect the English boy.

On the plains of the Alentejo, Angel's professional and personal worlds spectacularly collide.